ZI

THE TREASURE

The TREASURE

THE CIRCLE of DESTINY 2

A NOVEL

by Jim & Terri Kraus

TYNDALE HOUSE PUBLISHERS, INC. | WHEATON, ILLINOIS

Visit Tyndale's exciting Web site at www.tyndale.com

Copyright © 2000 by Jim and Terri Kraus. All rights reserved.

Cover illustration copyright © 2000 by Alan Cracknell. All rights reserved.

Designed by Justin Ahrens

This novel is a work of fiction. Names, characters, places, and incidents are either the product of the authors' imagination or are used fictitiously. Any resemblance to actual events, locales, organizations, or persons, living or dead, is entirely coincidental and beyond the intent of either the authors or publisher.

Library of Congress Cataloging-in-Publication Data

Kraus, Jim.
    The treasure : a novel / by Jim & Terri Kraus.
      p. cm. — (The circle of destiny ; 2)
    ISBN 0-8423-1836-4 (sc)
    1. Family-owned business enterprises—Fiction. 2. Young men—Fiction.   I. Kraus, Terri, 1953- II. Title.
PS3561.R2876 T74 2000
813 .54—dc21   00-037786

Printed in the United States of America

06   05   04   03   02   01   00
7   6   5   4   3   2   1

CENTRAL ARKANSAS LIBRARY SYSTEM
LITTLE ROCK PUBLIC LIBRARY
100 ROCK STREET
LITTLE ROCK, ARKANSAS 72201

*New York City
April 1841*

The sun lay an hour beyond the eastern horizon. Night's last glistening black embraced the city, save for the glowing hiss of the gas lamps, which lay interspersed between the birch and linden trees lining the elegant street. A carriage-for-hire, pulled by two sturdy dappled bays, slowed, then stopped. The driver snagged the reins, jumped to the cobblestone street, and scrabbled at the door handle.

"Sir . . . ," he called into the carriage, "this is the address you gave me. We're here."

The young man in the carriage snorted awake and rubbed his hands across his face. He ran his tongue over his lips, wetting them, then sat upright.

After a long moment, he stepped out and stretched. Reaching into the watch pocket of his velvet vest, he took out a twenty-dollar gold piece and flipped the coin to the driver.

"Keep the change. And remember your promise. No one hears what went on in your carriage tonight. You gave me your word as both a professional and as a man, correct?"

Gage Davis's handsome smile lit up the darkened street. He had done nothing ungentlemanly but enjoyed pretending he had.

The driver grinned broadly in reply, tapped his forefinger to the bill of his leather hat, and clamored back up to his seat.

Gage yawned as he climbed the cool gray marble steps to the family mansion. He did not ring but simply twisted the heavy brass door handle. One of the massive doors creaked open.

A brace of crystal lamps lit the vast entry hall. Edgar Hethold, Gage's nearly omnipresent valet, stood in that pool of light, hands folded, eyes averted.

"Morning, sir," he whispered loudly. "Shall I bring coffee? Breakfast?"

"Ah . . . as always . . . my faithful Edgar. Did the carriage wake you?"

Edgar barely moved his lips to sound out "No." His gaunt face did not hint at any emotion. Gage did not expect otherwise.

"Yes . . . some coffee perhaps," he said. "A biscuit or two. Whatever is on hand."

Edgar nodded, then spoke softly. "Your mail, sir, is on your desk in the library."

Gage tossed his fancy greatcoat on an uncomfortable, ornately carved French chair in the corner and added his brocade coat in a heap on top of it. He undid his gold cuff links and removed his mother-of-pearl collar stud. Kicking off his shoes, he padded to his leather-topped mahogany desk. There a lamp glowed dimly; he turned up the wick.

A tall stack of correspondence awaited. He stood as he shuffled through a dozen unopened letters. Most were marked with the bold handwriting of business. Those would remain unopened until lunch, at the earliest.

About midstack, he stopped at the dainty lines from a feminine hand. He lifted the letter to his face and inhaled. A scent of roses filled the room as he broke open the delicate pink wax seal and scanned the contents, smiling slightly. Finished, he placed the letter on a corner of the desk and returned to the stack. Another letter bore feminine handwriting; he looked at the return address and tossed it aside unopened.

At the bottom of the stack was a letter postmarked Cambridge, Massachusetts. He knew what it contained. He sliced it open with a pearl-handled silver knife.

"So . . . as I expected. Harvard wants this old boy, too."

Gage grinned and put the letter away in a drawer of the desk. Then he sat down, tilted back in his chair, lifted his stockinged feet to the desktop, and sighed, staring out the large paned window overlooking the formal gardens. His grin slowly evaporated, replaced by vague, wistful yearning that only the dawn would see.

CENTRAL ARKANSAS LIBRARY SYSTEM
PERRY COUNTY BRANCH
PERRYVILLE, ARKANSAS

CHAPTER ONE

Boston, Massachusetts
September 1842

The distance between New York City and Harvard University was but three hours by rail, yet a gaping chasm separated the two worlds.

Gage Davis sat back on the plush seat and closed his eyes to the dusk.

He was never quite certain which world he preferred. Midway between the two cities, there would be a lurch—an actual physical lurch—both to his body as well as to his heart and thoughts.

He would leave one world and enter another.

The cushioned, velvety quiet of his father's private railcar muted most sensations, but to Gage, the dividing line was so abrupt as to always be noticed.

The railcar rocked with an elegant, crystal-rattling shudder. Gage's eyes snapped open. Steel girders clicked past outside the window of the railcar at full speed—twenty miles per hour. Through the metal framework, Gage looked down and saw the muddy reflection of the moon on the Connecticut River. Just to the north of the bridge lay the city of Hartford.

"Halfway," whispered Gage. "We crossed the bridge at Hartford, and we're halfway . . . and in half the time of a stagecoach."

He listened for a moment to the clack and clatter of the wheels and rails.

And how is it that I feel? How should I feel? he asked himself.

His heart was no longer in the orbit and pull of New York City–his hometown. Only days prior, Gage had told his father that New York had become a city fouled with hustling financiers and tycoon-to-be-hopefuls.

Perhaps it is just that I am beginning to see it as it always was, he thought as the train rocked along heading north.

Now alone and in the dark, he slipped toward the subtle pull of Boston, Cambridge, and the intimate whirl of Harvard University.

Behind its private and ivy-covered walls is a place where truth and beauty have meaning and worth, he thought. *Harvard proves that not everything comes with a price tag attached.*

He wiped his face with his hand and chuckled to himself.

But then again, I have found that the currency of old New York works very well behind its ivied walls.

There was a faint rustling from behind. He spoke without turning. "Edgar, what are you doing hushing about in the dark like that?"

A full dozen seconds passed before the hollow-cheeked Edgar, standing in the deep shadows of the sleeping chamber, spoke. The voice was the rich rumbling baritone of a man not given to many words. "Sir, I am packing your proper dress whites and collars."

"Edgar, I shall miss you so this year," Gage said with a sigh. "As a freshman, you were my salvation. Now that I am a sophomore, I will have no one to remind me of the somber and dignified nature of most social events."

Davis waited another twelve seconds.

"My good sir, you do not need a valet to instruct you on the way of the world. Long ago did the pupil outdistance the teacher."

Gage hid his pleasure. He would not laugh or smile, for he knew that Edgar seldom, if ever, spoke with the expectation of either. Edgar had been with him the first year at Harvard. His expanse of rooms at Mrs. Parsons's home was indeed more than sufficient for a man and six valets and servants, if he so desired.

But Gage realized that few, if any, students came to the university with a manservant. Some fellows, mostly from America's most prominent and wealthy families, hired day help, to be sure, but a full-time, live-in valet was something quite far removed from the norm.

During the first year of Gage's studies at Harvard, Edgar had provided a full range of services. He had made Gage's life as a student easier. No need to worry about clean and appropriate attire. No need to worry about meals after hours. No need to worry about the proper gifts and notes that a wealthy young man must send.

Edgar had taken care of all those pesky details.

But Gage Davis watched the eyes of others who called on him, as Edgar edged away into the shadows. Seldom did friends or acquaintances mention his manservant, but if they did, their words displayed a hush of envy . . . or a knot of anger.

This year will be different, Gage told himself. *It is high time that I learn to be a gentleman student without the aid of faithful Edgar.*

Though he never mentioned it, Gage realized that Edgar had been both hurt and ultimately relieved by Gage's decision. A valet found reward in serving a captain of industry, a wealthy socialite—but a young boy, just barely into college—well, that was another matter altogether. This year Edgar would return to the family manse in New York City. His skills at organizing would come in handy to Gage's father.

My father . . . will find Edgar helpful, Gage mused. *He truly will.*

The words of the elder Davis still echoed in Gage's thoughts. Their parting this year had not been peaceful. The veins in his father's neck had pulsed as he stormed about his private study.

"I see no reason that you continue with this foolish waste of time!" Arthur Davis had fumed. A full thirty-five years older than Gage, the man was a close duplicate—except shorter and grayer, with a thickness about his middle. He had the same sharp, dark eyes that could penetrate with a glance, the same elegant nose and clean chin that women found so patrician and often irresistible.

"You're the smartest young man I know. You have a keen sense of everything to do with business. That sense can't be taught or learned. It is a gift. It is simply in your blood. Just as the hunt and hunger for wealth and treasure is in your blood."

The younger Gage remained silent, sprawled over a dainty chair covered with nearly a thousand dollars of imported hand-painted silk. He hoped his sullen expression would communicate his feelings without having to give them voice.

"Stay with me this year," his father said, his words now pleading. "I need what you have . . . I need your instincts. The business needs it."

Gage remained resolute. He shook his head.

"Not this year, Father. I spent all summer doing your bidding. And most successfully, as you well know. Now it is time for me. Regardless of the passion of your entreaties, I am returning to Harvard."

His father waved both his hands, dismissing his son's words. That simple gesture made his father appear like a dockworker trying to talk over the din of a shipyard. At that instant, Gage was most aware that the docks of sweating and foul stevedores was a milieu from which the Davis family was only a few decades removed.

"You are wasting your time there, Son," Gage's father insisted harshly. "You will have lost a sterling opportunity by being absent from the city. Don't you want to be a wealthy man in your own right? Don't you want to retire before you reach your third decade? Isn't that your dream? You will regret this decision someday."

Yet at that odd moment, Gage quietly wondered just whose dream he was pursuing.

This evening, he shrugged and refused to let that thought linger.

When Edgar withdrew, like a ghost, into the dressing chamber, Gage was left alone. He reached into the satchel at his feet and withdrew an exquisite, butter-colored, leather-bound journal. He ran his thumb over the gilt letters on the cover that were his monogram, then opened the book and spread the pages out on his lap.

Withdrawing a pencil from his breast pocket, Gage could not help snickering. Each time his father saw him use a pencil rather than the more refined and cultured pen and ink, he would grimace.

"Gage! How many times must I tell you! A pencil is for people who work with their hands, not for people like you."

Gage would ignore his father and delicately touch lead to paper. He never let on that these pencils had been imported from France and that each handcrafted piece cost more than most day laborers earned in a week.

He began to write, his words beginning to blacken the page. The journal was peppered with odd snippets of verse, drawings of people and places, paragraphs of description, clever bits and phrases that Gage found amusing or interesting.

No one had seen these pages, not even Edgar. The drawings and poetry that Gage placed in the journal were so unlike his public persona that he felt obliged to keep them hidden.

He could imagine what his father would say.

"Poetry? What are you thinking? It is clearly a waste of time for a captain of industry. A complete waste. Makes a man weak and sensitive. You must be strong to survive."

Gage bent closer to the page, and with a few careful strokes and a thatch of shading, he drew a delicate rendition of the window and his own reflection in the glass.

He leaned back and turned the drawing to the light. *Quite the likeness, I must admit.* He saw his father as well in the drawing.

In Gage's simple self-portrait there was the family's noble profile. Gage drew a shock of dark hair, poised to drape across his forehead. He penciled in the lips full, but not quite sensuous, and then the eyes that were clearly the most dominant feature of the Davis men.

Gage's eyes were a dark, somber, penetrating gray. Gage used their piercing color to stab at business competitors as cleanly and precisely as a collector stabs a lifeless, but beautiful, butterfly.

The eyes could also pierce a young woman's heart, but with much different results.

He began to write.

FROM THE JOURNAL OF GAGE DAVIS

I have promised myself that I will remember all that I find important this term. So much of what I had hoped to retain, I have lost–lost over the summer as I tumbled back into the world of finance. But this year shall be different. When my soul fills or my spirit soars, I have promised myself that a record will be kept–if for no other reason than to remind myself that I have indeed journeyed into the world of knowledge and beauty and felt at home within its cultured environs.

I must admit that not even a single remnant from so many sterling evenings of clever conversation can be found in my memory. So many clever ripostes and clever stories are gone forever.

Yet I must recap, however briefly, the past year as a student and some of my freshman experiences.

During that first month as a new student, I admit to a great deal of apprehension–mostly concerning the course of study and the great difficulty that so many said are part and parcel of a Harvard education. The first round of tests and examinations passed and I admit, without boasting, that I scored very high. The lowest grade I received was a 90 out of a test of 100. All the rest were higher–some even at 100.

It was not that I studied harder than others–quite the contrary. I studied much less than some of the fellows in my class. I must be thankful for my native and inborn intelligence. It appears that I am simply facile with words and figures.

My father's assessment of my abilities is accurate.

And because of my awareness of my abilities, the rest of the year, I seldom opened a book or spent more than a minute or two in study. Other fellows, working on a particular paper, would write and then revise and write again. I, on the other hand, would simply write once and would always receive very high marks.

That left more time to enjoy other activities at Harvard. And there were many.

One of my favorite haunts is a quite ordinary establishment–the Destiny Café. The entire place could stand a thorough cleaning and painting, and its furnishings are a jumble of styles, most of which are a day or two removed from the rubbish heap. Yet the food and spirits are good, the companionship outstanding. I have whiled away many an afternoon and evening in pleasant conversation and laughter.

And it is only three blocks from my residence. With Edgar's assistance, 619 Follen Street is quite the haven. Other fellows in my class live in such squalor and rank environments. And they all seem to revel in their debasement. I find no charm in soiled socks and trousers and old, unwashed dishes being strewn about a room.

Even though their residences lack cleanliness and order, there have been get-togethers that could be described as epic. One lasted an entire weekend, and certain participants passed out where they stood, regained awareness after a few hours, then continued with their merriment. I enjoy the spectacle, though I am not one to ever overindulge. It is more amusing to watch their merriment than it is to attempt to duplicate it.

'Tis a pity that some of these young fellows, from fine and well-known families, can sink to such degradation so easily. Perhaps they act differently elsewhere.

Yet I admit that the reputation of the wild, uninhibited nature of Harvard is quite well deserved.

During the year, I returned three times to New York City, other than at Christmas and Easter, that is. Each was at Father's behest. I know that I am too young for the responsibilities he thrusts on me. Walton should be his choice to mentor, but I see that Walton has not the stomach for the art of the deal nor the finesse needed for the business of the development.

I am not sure why I am skilled at these endeavors either, save to say I am. Others who attend these meetings, men three times my age, often remark at the conclusion of our discussions that they have seldom been in such a charged environment.

I see my father beam when they relate such words. Yet, I am not ready to join him. And, after all, Walton is the son who will follow Father at the helm of the family business, not me.

I have gone on too long. I will close now. But these words may someday be important. If the story of my life ever requires a retelling, then these pages shall be an invaluable aid for those doing the writing.

And then again, they may be the words of a fool, ringed with sound and fury, signifying little.

Time will indeed tell.

With that Gage closed the book, slipped the pencil back into his pocket, and closed his eyes, letting the gentle rocking of the rails lull him into a light sleep.

<hr>

The train arrived in Boston several hours past midnight. Gage slept until the first hint of dawn lit the crowded rail depot. He rose, washed quickly, then met the foreman of the company of teamsters hired to move his belongings.

Gage left Edgar standing on the steps of the private railcar. If he had not known better, Gage would have sworn that Edgar's voice cracked as he issued a last somber good-bye.

"Take good care of Father," Gage called out. "His memory is not as sharp as it once was. It will be up to you to keep him on course."

Edgar nodded and called back, his deep voice going reedy, "You may count on me, sir."

It appeared that Edgar had to restrain his arm from rising in a farewell wave. Such displays were done by common folk, not proper manservants.

Gage insisted on personally accompanying his trunks and cases as they were unloaded from the train and loaded on the swaybacked cartage wagon. This particular team of stevedores did not look trustworthy in the least. Gage had heard tales of expensive items suddenly listed as missing when possessions were moved.

It was not as if the loss would strain his finances, but replacing cuff links or shirts or other possessions would be such a bother. Boston, while a thriving city in its own right, was no New York City.

There are men's furnishings and then there are men's furnishings.

I would prefer not to make a trip to a tailor simply to replace a lost collar stay, he thought.

And Gage found it amusing to ride in the back of the livery wagon, feeling the early morning autumn sunshine on his face. It had been the rare summer day when Gage had managed to spend time in the open air.

Enjoying the breeze and the warmth, he leaned back against a room-sized wardrobe and drew his knees up. He shaded his eyes from the glare, ignoring the curious stares from people on the street. All five of the teamsters sat up at the front of the wagon, beefy shoulder to beefy shoulder.

The wagon bounced and rattled through posh Beacon Hill. Gage made no attempt to hide as some of the city's more prosperous citizens took a morning stroll. He thought he recognized a face or two. If the Bostonians out for their morning constitutional saw Gage, piled on top of a pyramid of trunks and cartons, they most likely dismissed him as simply a well-dressed baggage boy.

Cambridge, Massachusetts

From the sidewalk Gage saw a flicker of movement out of the corner of his eye. There was something—or someone—moving along the outside third-floor stairway of 619 Follen Street. He focused on the street below, then called out to a particularly clumsy teamster, "Careful there, my good man! That wardrobe is not your average barrel of pickles that might be casually tossed about."

The form on the third floor seemed to hesitate, then took a step forward.

That crafty Mrs. Parsons. I should have guessed. She has gone and rented that room.

Last spring, the day that Gage had packed up and headed back to New York City, Mrs. Parsons, his landlady, had sidled up to him. "Mr. Davis," she had shouted, as she always did, "I will assume that I will see you again the first week of September?"

Gage had nodded.

"You have my bank draft for the summer months?" he had spoken loudly towards what he hoped was her good ear.

She had wizened her eyes, thought for a moment, then also nodded. She turned and pointed to the top floor of the house.

"Up there . . . that door at the end of the third-floor balcony. The empty storage room. Do you intend on making use of it next year?"

He had shaken his head no and thought, *Why would I need a stuffy room under the roof that has no ventilation? I have more than enough storage.*

"Then you have no need of it? Good."

Before she left, she yelled out, "Farewell for the summer then, Mr. Davis."

And now, the summer gone and students returning, Gage watched as the new boarder occupying the tiny, hot, cramped room made his way down the steps. Gage knew in an instant that he was a new student at the university. No one in town would have been foolish enough, or poor enough, to have rented that wretched room.

As the newcomer drew closer the sun lit up his profile.

Land sakes, Gage thought to himself as the young man stepped into the afternoon light, *that is a handsome lad—if I understand only a fraction of what the gentle lady folk find handsome in a man. I dare say that young man will torment a few hearts while at Harvard.*

Gage gave his "wonderful-to-meet-you" smile, introduced himself, and grabbed the young man's hand in a bold, engaging handshake. He imagined for a moment that the new boarder thought to retreat in terror from his bold greeting.

"Joshua Quittner," the newcomer finally replied, "from Ohio. Shawnee."

He may be handsome as the devil is clever, thought Gage, *but if I looked, I would wager I could find corn tassels and wheat straw in his pockets.*

To Gage, Joshua looked lost and confused. *Maybe,* Gage thought, *I should take pity on the poor bumpkin. After all, we are roommates of a sort.*

It was nearing the supper hour, so Gage invited the young man from Ohio to join him at the Destiny Café. The Destiny was situated conveniently between Mrs. Parsons's and the campus of Harvard.

"The place is one of my favorite haunts," Gage said, winking. "The food is edible, the servers most comely, and no one minds if you linger and spend an hour or two in conversation."

Gage tried not to smile as Joshua followed at his heels, much like a lost puppy will follow anyone who offers a kind word or two. Gage stopped inside the door of the restaurant and took a long look around the café. Hordes of students lounged about, talking and producing a clattering hum.

"I see they haven't bothered to sweep the place out since last semester," Gage said.

He watched as Joshua actually looked at the floor and almost began peering under the tables.

"It's not that bad, my friend," Gage said, laughing. "There's a table over there. I dislike eating standing up, don't you?"

Joshua nodded as if he were not sure he could recall ever having eaten standing up.

"When it fills at lunch, tables become a rare commodity. And the real horror of this place is that regardless of how many thousands of dollars I offer, the owner refuses to permanently reserve my favorite table."

Joshua nearly stumbled. "Thousands? You offered him thousands? And he refused?"

Gage pulled out a chair and brushed a handful of crumbs from the table with his handkerchief.

"Joshua, you must forgive me. It's my wretched attempt at humor again. I didn't offer him money. The owner . . . that sour-looking gentleman by the door . . . has a strict first-come policy. I never thought to bribe him to get a table."

A table behind them erupted in loud laughter.

"But now that the idea has been presented, I just may investigate the possibility this year."

Joshua looked as if his thoughts were reeling.

"I can tell you're hungry. Melinda will be here in a breath. She'll fill you in on what delicacies they are offering this evening."

In no more than a minute, a huge selection of food was piled up in front of Joshua. Gage grabbed his ale and sandwich and stood up.

"You must excuse me for a moment," he explained. "It has been months since I have seen a few of these faces. Do forgive me as I visit. I know it's a dreadful vice. But it is what one does at the Destiny."

Just then a voice rang out over the rackety noise.

"Gage! Over here! Gage!"

It was a woman's voice, and Gage immediately turned and made his way towards it. There was a hint of anger in the greeting.

"So how have you been, Gage?"

"Busy. Very busy. Spent the summer in New York with Father, working on his behalf. I told you that his affairs would be most time consuming. Investigating investments, negotiating the odd contract. Things of that nature. Boring business matters, actually."

The young woman, Miss Emily Brockhurst of Cambridge, did not appear to listen. A young woman with obvious charms, she cooly adjusted her sleeves, blinked her eyes, then began to speak in a cool, even tone. With each word, the chill increased.

"So I recall at the end of the spring semester . . . a few months ago, wasn't it? I heard you promise to write to me. A gentleman's promise. A promise that a young woman considers to be binding. And because of that promise, do you know what I did every day? I would go to the post office and ask the postmaster for my letter from New York City. The one that a gentleman friend said would be sent general delivery so as to not inflame my father."

Gage winced as if he knew what were coming. He had met Emily near the end of the last semester at a tea held at the University Club. Within less than an hour that day, she had placed her hand on his forearm and whispered that they should find a quieter place to converse. He had smiled and nodded.

And now those memories came back in a tangled rush.

"The postmaster and I have become quite familiar. Asking every day for a letter that has yet to arrive, I am sure he thinks I am on my way to becoming an addled spinster . . . thinking that a gentleman who promised to write . . . would actually write to a pathetic creature like myself."

The young woman leaned closer. Gage was certain that the lull in conversation in the Destiny was caused by the young woman's performance, now becoming almost shrill. Yet from the corner of his eye, he could see that Joshua was launching into two apple dumplings without paying the slightest attention to what was happening around him. Joshua didn't even seem to notice the serving girl, Melinda, who hovered at his table. *He is ignoring both her and this episode as well. How noble,* thought Gage, *or else he was truly famished.*

Emily paused, her eyes and lips looking as if she had just bitten into a sour grape. "And you know what the charming man at the post office suggested the last time I ventured there without receiving so much as a note from my imaginary gentleman?"

Gage knew he possessed no answer that would deflect her anger.

She tightened her eyes and placed a steely hand around Gage's wrist. "He's a bachelor, you know. An old, withered man, at least four decades old. He suggested that if I do not hear from my gentleman friend in New York . . . well, perhaps, *he* could begin corresponding with me. At least then I would suffer no further disappointments."

Gage closed his eyes. He was immensely grateful that it was not raining—for if this woman carried an umbrella with her, he was certain she would have applied it at that point to his head.

" 'No further disappointments'—that is what he said, Gage."

He did not raise his eyes for a second. He knew, without considering the reasons, that he should act the contrite suitor, beleaguered with remorse. *Can I look as contrite as the world's most humble penitent? And just how does a penitent look?*

He found her eyes with his and stared at her. At the end of his silent stare, he felt her hand relax on his wrist and saw her eyes flicker downward for a breath or two, then soften when they found his gaze again. *She has forgiven me already,* he told himself, *but will want me to suffer a little longer.*

"Miss Brockhurst, I may live to be threescore and ten and endure every harsh punishment known to the devil and to man, yet I am certain I shall never feel more pain and guilt than I do at this very moment. How can a wretch like myself hope to ever deserve the friendship . . . or even a nodding acquaintance with you? I am such a horrid person. You are right to divorce me now from your life. I have no value or standing as a gentleman."

He halted, stared hard again at the young woman, then lowered his face to gaze at the floor. "You must leave and never see me again. I am not worth the light that it takes to illuminate my form. You must never look upon me again."

Have I gone too far? he thought, hiding his grin.

Miss Brockhurst blinked several times. The hand that had grabbed hard at Gage's wrist opened, and her palm ever so slowly moved down the back of his hand and slipped under his open fingers.

"I am a reprobate. I am the vilest and the lowest manner of a gentleman. Ha! I should vow never to use the word *gentleman* and my own self in the same breath—for as long as I draw breath. I am such a worthless fellow to have twisted your pure and sweet affections as I have. You must never see me again."

"Gage . . . No . . . Don't say that. Please, you mustn't blame yourself." She lifted his chin and offered him a soft, comforting smile. "I was angry . . . but I understand. You were busy with your father's business. I have no right to insist that you correspond with a silly thing like me."

He waited to reply.

"No . . . ," he went on. "I am a wretch and do not deserve your friendship."

She squeezed his hand, then traced a line down his cheek with her finger.

"No, sweet Gage, it is I who must apologize. I have been too demanding. You have worked and slaved all summer, and I have done little save complain that you did not write. It is I who should ask for forgiveness. Truly, I should be begging you to keep me as a friend."

Gage waited again, knowing most likely everyone at nearby tables was listening to this melodrama. He had no choice save to continue with his lines and trust they would not seem rehearsed or overused and familiar. He looked up and blinked as if to fit the appearance of a tear.

"Perhaps then our sins have cancelled each other's out. Perhaps we can continue on as we were and make no mention of this dreadful summer again. Can we do that, Miss Brockhurst . . . I mean Miss Emily?"

He thought he saw the glistening of a tear in her eye.

"We shall most certainly do just that, Gage. We shall never speak of this again. That would be most gentlemanly of you."

He took her hand in his. She hesitated only a moment, then embraced Gage in great welcome. As he held her, Gage saw two friends of his, Albert Towes and Benjamin Gorton, who had been seated at the table behind them. Each of their faces glowed with a great sheen of surprise and admiration. Albert shook his head in disbelief and then, very deliberately, mimed an enthusiastic round of applause. Benjamin joined in the mute applause.

Without giving voice to the words, Albert mouthed, *How did you do that?*

FROM THE JOURNAL OF GAGE DAVIS

Such a homecoming.

I was scarce at the Destiny for a moment when Emily—whom I thought was a sweet, naïve child—soundly attacked me for not holding my promise of writing to her over the summer.

Gads. If every woman to whom I have promised to write berates me in the same manner, I shall be tied up through the winter, explaining and apologizing.

I cannot blame the poor girl. Her father, an assistant provost at Harvard, is such an acerbic man. My letters would have been a balm to her during the long summer.

I have resolved to take my promises more seriously this year. I desire no more such episodes as this evening.

It appears that my young housemate—Joshua Quittner—most likely my age or a year or two my senior—is a most likeable chap. He seems every bit awestruck by everything that goes on here. We strolled through the campus before returning to Follen Street. I pointed out some of the buildings and classrooms that he would need to know when classes begin.

He was profuse in his thanks. Perhaps he imagined all the students here to be uppity and aloof. I will endeavor to show him that is not the case.

And what struck me most odd is that he is enrolled at the seminary—training to be a pastor. I have seen my share of pastors, and he shares not one wit of similarity with them. He is indeed quite handsome—my original evaluation was validated by Melinda's long, lingering stares in his direction. He is quick to laugh, and that is most unlike every pastor I have met.

Though a bona fide member of this university, he nonetheless remains a country bumpkin. His clothes, I am afraid, have never been in style in any corner of civilization. Perhaps they are well suited for field or farm work but not for the study of God, I am sure.

As I write this, I realize that by making use of my cast-off clothing, one could build a substantial wardrobe. He and I are of similar stature—perhaps he could make use of the clothing I left here from last fall. I will make the offer to him on the morrow.

I inquired as to his rationale for seeking to become a man of the cloth. His voice lowered, his demeanor changed, and he became most serious. He said that God deserved our full service and that he would be privileged to offer his life for his creator. He offered these words with such weight and drama that I felt moved. As he spoke of his dream, I felt cheated that I had no such comparable noble goal.

But then again, I need no dream, for I will be rich within a year of leaving this place. That much I know. It is my gift.

And as we neared Follen Street, the young country boy asked when he might expect the rest of the fellows in the house to arrive. I refused to laugh or make light, but I explained that other than his room and Mrs. Parsons's rooms on the first floor, the house was rented by myself.

The look on the lad's face was priceless. It was as if I struck him with a bag of gold and let the gold dust float about him.

I told him of our family's curse—that we make money, and lots of it.

To get him home after that admission, I nearly had to take him by the hand and lead him there directly.

And as I am readied for bed this night, I must admit that I am truly looking forward to this year. The addition of Mr. Joshua Quittner will add a curious, albeit pious, element into my world.

⚜

It was a wet Friday evening at the end of the first week of classes. Gage sat alone at the Destiny. It was odd that so few customers had taken refuge there that night—often it was the busiest evening of the week. Besides Gage, there were only four other patrons. He recognized a few of them from last year, but they seemed engrossed in a serious, private conversation.

Melinda made her way from the kitchen. "Alone? Gage Davis alone on Friday evening?"

He had been lost in thought and could offer no witty remark in reply. In the past, he and Melinda had bantered in a most familiar manner—so very contrary to the rules of server and customer.

But that is the way of the Destiny, Gage told himself. *And I do enjoy her company, though in no other place would such an association be tolerated.*

As he struggled to find a clever word, a roll of thunder crashed from the north.

"Well . . . it's the rain that is keeping them all away," she said. "There could be no other reason for Harvard's most eligible and charming man to be seated at a table by himself."

"Melinda," he replied, laughing, "I am glad to see that working alongside all these clever Harvard fellows has finally improved your skill at observation. Of course that's the reason. The rain has kept my friends from my side—there could be no other explanation."

Melinda took a chair, pulled it to his table, placed her arms in an inverted V, and rested her chin in her hands.

She is a winsome woman, Gage thought. *It is a pity that she languishes in a place such as this.*

"So tell me, Mr. Davis, how has your first week of studies gone? Have you kept up with all your pressing academic—and social— demands? I understand that you no longer have Edgar, the faithful valet, with you."

"News travels quickly here, does it not?"

"Cambridge is a small town, Mr. Davis. And there are those who have read much into Edgar's absence."

"Such as what?"

Melinda leaned forward, looked about, then whispered, "That you have lost a fortune over the summer and were forced to do without. That you had to forsake all your luxuries. That Edgar was the first to go."

Gage laughed heartily.

"It is so curious how rumors start. Who told you that?"

Melinda stiffened. "That would be betraying a confidence now, wouldn't it?"

"Melinda," he cautioned, "I have ways of finding out."

"Unless they involve large sums of bribery money, Mr. Davis, I will not be swayed," she said, grinning.

He reached into his pocket for a handful of loose coins. "It is all I have," he said. "Will it buy what I need?"

She laughed and waved her hand at him. "Mr. Davis, you slight me. Such a paltry amount. I would expect a bigger handful." She playfully pushed his outstretched hand away.

"And Melinda, you promised to call me Gage and not Mr. Davis."

She smiled and nodded. "So tell me, Gage, how has the first week gone? How are you and your housemate getting on?"

"So you did notice him when he came in. I thought as much."

"How could I not notice him?" she said, resting against her chair. "Such eyes . . . such a face. Like a peach waiting to be picked."

"A peach? To describe a handsome fellow like that?"

Melinda offered a most curious half-smile in reply, her eyes closed, as if lost in her recollection.

Gage knew in a moment what lay behind her expression. "Remember, Melinda, he's a minister in training. Lead us not into temptation and all that."

She held up her hands. "I know. I know. It's just that he combines a sweet innocent look with something darker and more alluring. It's an odd but most beguiling combination. And being a pastor makes the temptation all the greater now, doesn't it? What do you know about him?"

Gage filled her in on what he had learned of Joshua. It was not much. Joshua did seem to spend most of his waking moments either at class or deep in study.

Gage moved on to a more welcome topic—himself. "And my classes have gone well . . . at least to a degree. I have a poetry class in which the professor has no idea of what a poem means but is most proficient at knowing how the verses are constructed and the number of beats in every line. The author's meaning and passion are secondary to the style in which it has been written. And then there is the study of business science in which the professor has, I swear, never left the confines of this institution. I do not think he has bought a new item of attire for a decade. How then can he know how business moves? It is beyond me. That man would be eaten alive if he tried to conduct his brand of business in New York. The rich and powerful would have his head. Yet I dutifully take notes and repeat back what nonsense I have been given."

He took a long swallow of ale.

"That's what New York can do to a man. It will make him tough and competitive. Not like what you find here in Cambridge. Give me a New York man and I will show you a fighter. That's New York, all right."

Melinda watched his eyes as he spoke. When he finished, she

hesitated before asking, "Gage . . . is it true what they say about New York City?"

"What do they say about it?"

"That it's grand and bursting with music and lights and gaiety. And handsome men."

"Who says that? And why do you ask such a curious question? Boston is a smart city, and it's just across the river."

Melinda traced a line with her finger on the table. "It's filled with men from . . . from Boston. I guess I don't like Boston men. And to be honest, I haven't been to Boston in five years. Never seem to have the time—or the money, I guess."

Gage wanted to take her hand but knew that action would be suggesting something he could not deliver. "New York is a fine city, Melinda, but not that much different from Boston. Just bigger."

She gazed at him. Her words were clear and deliberate: "It must be wonderful to be young and rich and bursting with promise."

Not knowing how to reply, Gage remained quiet.

From the kitchen, someone called out her name.

"It must be quite wonderful," she repeated as she stood and slipped away from the table.

Gage watched her as she left. A clap of thunder rattled Cambridge, followed by a piercing shard of lightning. Rain began to splatter against the window.

It is quite wonderful . . . isn't it?

❦

Two full weeks of classes transpired and Gage had but only once crossed paths with his new housemate, Joshua. Gage believed that every one of Joshua's classes was early, the first hour of instruction, for he heard footsteps creak down the stairs well before dawn. If Gage's class began at 10:00 A.M., he would rouse himself perhaps fifteen minutes before the hour. He would then dash about trying to bathe, shave, dress, and eat in those scant minutes. More mornings than not, Gage would find himself sprinting down the steps and

Follen Street, still knotting his tie, as the tower bell sounded out the hour.

A few minutes late for class proves no loss, he reasoned, *for most of those initial minutes are simply taken up in social niceties and chitchat.*

Even though it was a Saturday, Gage found himself wide awake as the dawn broke upon his window. He spun about in his bed, smoothing out sheets and pillows, but no arrangement or position offered him comfort or rest.

He sighed, ran his hand through his hair, and slipped out of bed.

The beginning of autumn was indeed a most glorious time in Cambridge. The foliage burned and blazed in a hundred colors, and the sharp hint of the coming winter lent the air a clarity and crispness that it lacked in summer.

Gage slipped on a set of comfortable boots and a thickly knitted Irish woolen sweater. He paused at his door and took a great breath of air. The city remained quiet. A horse and carriage sounded faint in the distance. A gentle hush of wind rattled the leaves, but the sounds were muted and soft, as if painted in watercolors.

It does feel good to be up early . . . perhaps this is why Joshua rises so early.

He strolled down Follen Street, his only companion a dog who bounded out from between two homes, sniffing and woofing. The shaggy yellow dog snuffled once at Gage's leg, then ran in circles about him with the joyous excitement that only a dog could muster.

Gage whistled and the dog leapt about. His companion stayed with him until Harvard Commons came into view. All it took was an errant and brave squirrel racing in the opposite direction, and in a yellow flash, Gage was alone again. He watched as the dog disappeared, crackling through a tall hedge of privets down the block.

A moment later, Gage stood before Steinmann's Bakery. The window was covered with a fog created by the warmth of loaves and rolls piled high in wooden boxes. The scent of freshly baked bread was lush and dense—almost viscous enough to cut. Gage entered that swirl of scents, his stomach growling.

"Well," Gage called out, more than a bit surprised, "now I see where it is you go every dawn as you clump down the steps."

Joshua turned to face him, holding two fist-sized rolls in his hand. He had yet to shave, and his pillow had set his blond hair in spiky tufts. He attempted to speak, but his rounded cheeks gave him away.

"It's all right," Gage said. "Just let me purchase a few tidbits and I'll join you."

He peered about at the offerings. "How do you stand working here?" he asked the stocky woman behind the counter. "If it were me, all the profits would be consumed before day's end." She smiled and handed him a trio of sweet, knotted buns, packed with nuts and sugar.

"Come join me," Gage said. "There is a place down the street that offers Cambridge's best coffee—although no doubt you have found that as well."

Joshua appeared most sheepish. "I have. I study until I simply pass out from fatigue, and then I arise and am famished. I am hungrier here, and I do no manual labor. Working from dawn till dusk on the farm never produced this level of hunger."

Within minutes, their breakfast rolls had been eaten. Their first cup of coffee, drunk Boston-style with lots of cream, became two, and then three.

Being Saturday, the town seemed to be slower coming to life. Only a few people were out walking, and merely a handful of carriages and delivery wagons had passed along the street. The sun had just cleared the trees on the east side of Harvard Commons, and the windows in the administration building winked with gold.

"It is pretty here," Joshua said. "I thought I would find nothing attractive about the sights in a town such as this. But it does have its own charm."

Gage nodded. "Cambridge is quite pretty. And I would say that a lot of city dwellers might think there is no beauty in a landscape in which no buildings and roads exist."

"Truly?"

"I know my mother, for one, gets nervous even traveling up the Hudson Valley to Hasting-on-Hudson. She claims the single roadway is designed to make her anxious since it limits her choices."

"Truly?"

"Joshua, there are those who think that behind every tree lurks an Indian or a bear. My mother is one of those people."

"But there are no bears in Ohio—at least none that I have seen."

"Doesn't matter," Gage replied. "She would fear that someone imported the beasts into the woods simply to scare her."

Joshua laughed.

"It is true," Gage said. "Living your entire life within the confines of a city like New York will do that."

"And you don't think that?"

"Of course not," Gage replied. "I know there are no bears nearby who are waiting to maul me—imported or not. I'm not frightened of the unintentional beast. It's the intentional ones that frighten me."

Joshua laughed again.

"So what are you frightened of, Joshua? Not bears, I take it."

"Only in bear country, wherever that is," he replied.

He waited a long moment before he continued.

"When I came here . . . to Harvard, that is . . . a lot of people back home said I would be scared stiff by the big city. And some said that I would be frightened by the classes and the demands."

"And you're not?"

"Well, I am concerned. It seems to me as if every other student has gone to a preparatory school and learned much more than I ever did. That doesn't frighten me—it just makes me want to work harder. I'm not frightened, but challenged."

Joshua gazed at Gage, then said cautiously, "Gage, what are you afraid of?"

A curious look of self-awareness showed on Gage's face as he answered: "Nothing."

A moment passed.

"And everything."

Joshua did not speak and Gage continued. "I know I am a most fortunate fellow. Our family has acquired a great deal of money. And sometimes, in the back of my mind, I am most fearful that it will all disappear in a puff of smoke somehow. I know that's foolish of me, considering that my father has placed the family wealth in a dozen different banks and invested in many different companies. One fails, and the rest will stay sound. So that little fear makes no sense–but even so, it is there."

Gage could not look at Joshua directly, and for a moment, wondered about his sanity. Why share such an odd and most personal thought with an almost stranger? But he continued. "Even if half of the family's resources were lost, we would be able to live as we do now. And losing half is unthinkable."

"If you did lose it all . . . what would happen then?"

Gage shook his head. "Well . . . that just can't happen, so it makes no sense to dwell on it."

Joshua took another sip of coffee. It had gone lukewarm. "I know why I'm not afraid," he said confidently.

"Why?" Gage asked.

"Because whatever I do and wherever I go, I know that God is there with me. What can occur to me that God does not know of? There is nothing that he is surprised by. And if I am his follower, then I shall be protected always."

"And you sincerely believe that?" Gage asked.

"Of course I do. Don't you believe in God?"

Surprised by the question, Gage sputtered, "Of course I do. What fool does not believe in a Supreme Being and a creator of the universe? Only a simpleton would say there is no God."

"But it's more than just that, Gage. Belief is more personal. One does not simply say there is a God and be done with it. Man needs a relationship with God, not simply an acknowledgment."

Gage slid back from the table. He did not know why he had suddenly become uncomfortable. He stood up. "Well, this has been interesting. But I do have several appointments to keep and I must return home to dress."

Both men knew it was a lie.

"Gage . . . I did not mean to infer anything. . . ." Joshua appeared almost sheepish.

Gage offered his broad smile in return. "I know. I know. You believe your way, and I will believe my way. That's the American way, right?"

Joshua stood and put his hand on Gage's shoulder. "There is only one way, Gage. If you should ever find yourself truly frightened, God will be there. He alone will provide the answer. You need to call on him."

"And I am glad that God will be there when I need him. If I am frightened, I will do so. I promise."

Joshua knew the conversation was over and nodded as if in agreement.

The two walked back to 619 Follen Street without speaking another word.

CHAPTER TWO

November 1842

Gage reluctantly opened his eyes. He yawned loudly, then stretched awake. From the yard below came the sounds of a rhythmic chopping.

Joshua must be tending the woodpile again, he thought as he combed his hair with his hand. *I must talk to the boy—let him know that Saturdays are days of rest around here. When there are no classes, there should be no work.*

During the first months back at Harvard, Gage fell into his established rhythms. Within the first week, he identified which professor took attendance, and which did not. Those who did not and who offered an early morning class seldom had the benefit of Gage's attendance. Again he found the material and studies to be simple. He had a quick and complete memory, and a one-time hearing of a term or an explanation was always sufficient. Without any true effort on Gage's part, he would once again be listed as a dean's scholar this term. Most of his fellow students offered their good-natured dislike to his easy path to scholarship.

He spent a great deal of time at the Destiny, as did many Harvard students.

"It is here that the future deals to affect America will be forged," Gage told his faculty advisor. "I am meeting with future owners of railroads and factories. Why should I limit my studies to a dry classroom lecture?"

And his advisor, though he was reluctant to admit it, agreed.

Without Edgar helping from the wings, Gage was a shade less precise and less polished, even occasionally wearing his shoes twice between shinings.

Gage enjoyed the pace of college. He relished the ability to sleep until noon if desired—and he often did following a late-night discussion or a more spirited gathering.

Yet this morning he knew he did not have that luxury.

Within the hour he had washed, shaved, dressed, and stepped out into the crisp fall air. He wore his blue brocade jacket, said to be the rage on the Continent this fall. *I wonder if they tell the French folk that a certain style is all the rage in America?*

He stopped for a strong coffee and a thick slice of warm bread. He scanned the headlines of the early edition of the Boston paper while he ate.

It was past nine as he gulped the last of his coffee and hurried across campus to a quiet, well-tended neighborhood. At his mother's insistence, he had offered to accompany the daughter of an old family acquaintance to a financial meeting of a sort. He could easily have refused the request but did not. If he missed this appointment, small ripples of social consternation would have formed. Personally, he cared little about such rules and obligations, but he would keep his promise to his mother.

"Even though they have suffered financial reversals as of late, their name still carries a great deal of import in the proper Philadelphia circles," Gage's mother had said, "and it is proper and kind to help those who are less fortunate than us." Her words had chilled to condescending as she concluded her lecture to him a few weeks prior.

So this morning he hurried, adjusting his tie as he walked under the graceful oaks and lindens that lined one of Cambridge's more proper neighborhoods.

Gage extracted his pocketwatch from his coat and snapped open its thick gold cover. *Only half past. I'll be there with time to spare. Hannah will have no reason to be nervous.*

While attending Harvard, Morgan Hannah Collins had taken up residence with shirttail relatives in town, a respectable and well-situated family, their two daughters now grown and married. Linked with Hannah's own family in a most tenuous fashion, they provided her with the appearance of propriety and correctness. A single woman from a good home, living away from her parents, was obliged to keep proper appearances. This living arrangement provided that necessary moral and social protection.

Hannah's given name, Morgan, was after a solemn, extremely dour, and very wealthy grandmother. But Hannah did not resemble her in appearance, sensibilities, or resources. Though Hannah's moral reputation was safe from accusation, her choices in life were not. Much to her parents' chagrin, Hannah was of the first women in her family to seek out higher learning. In fact, she was one of the first women anywhere to think that a university experience was even necessary, let alone desirable.

"Hannah, you'll just muddle up your thoughts if you attend Harvard," Gage had teased her when she first spoke of her intentions several summers prior at a charity function both families had attended. "And no man desires a woman whose thoughts are constantly in a swirl—that is, unless she is rich, beautiful, and willing."

He smiled as he said those words, but Hannah bore no signs of amusement. "Honestly, Gage," she had replied, "I know that you speak only in jest, but my first response is to pummel you soundly."

The young woman from the proper Philadelphia family not only shocked her friends and family by insisting on attending a university, but she added insult to that injury by announcing that she was hoping to take up the study of medicine—anatomy and body parts and scalpels included.

"Why, that sort of liberal thinking is simply shameful," Gage's mother had said, sniffing. "She is totally disrespectful to her parents."

But Gage enjoyed the feisty young woman. Besides being bright and articulate, she was quite pretty, nearing beautiful. Her musical, enthusiastic laugh sparkled in her eyes and tilted her head back just so. That natural and free-flowing sense of joy and fun-loving demeanor transformed her from an attractive woman to a stunning beauty.

Yet Hannah's beauty not withstanding, her life was not serene and carefree. The specter of a fortune lost hovered about her. Darker secrets lay underfoot, as if they were a draft on a chilled December night. Her father had squandered much of the family fortune in a series of highly speculative business deals, all in vainglorious efforts to outdo his own tyrannical father. Others gossiped that a woman was involved, a scarlet woman from New Jersey, and that his inopportune chase of wealth was done to impress her. Even more sordid episodes were voiced in whispers. Once one of the wealthiest men in Philadelphia, Collins's losses and their causes had become some of the town's most shocking and poorly held secrets.

Gage's mother, Isabelle Worth Davis, knew the gory details of the story, as did most of her friends—all from New York's most select and wealthy families. While this group of women seldom spoke more than a hushed word or two about the tragedy, Gage knew they secretly reveled in watching the powerful tumble. Sending Gage to help Hannah was a great way to discover even more sordid details.

But not from me, Gage thought as he walked up to the door. *You will not learn them from me.*

Hannah, who was waiting at the door, greeted him with a familiar burst of radiant enthusiasm. As the two of them made their way to the carriage station on the east side of the campus, Hannah took his arm.

"Shall I get rough with your uncle if he refuses to loosen the purse strings of your trust fund?" Gage asked.

Hannah responded with a gale of her infectious laughter, her head tilted back in glee. Gage loved its musical lilt. He saw her face in profile, outlined by the warm fall sunlight. As she laughed, Gage's heart stirred.

She is a most beautiful woman, he thought to himself as they walked. *I must admit that she possesses a goodly amount of charm. And I admit that I am not immune to her appeal.*

Hannah squeezed his arm. "Don't make my uncle the target of your harsh business manners," she said, her words still tinged with laughter. "If you do, he will collapse as a house of cards and be drafted away on the wind."

"But you need an increase in your funds," Gage said, growing more serious. "To study at Harvard, even while staying with relatives, is not an altruistic activity. If you worry about purchasing books and pens and clothing and the like . . . how can one study under that pressure?"

Hannah nodded. "But Uncle Winthrop is looking out for my best interests," she replied. "He wants me to have sufficient funds remaining at the end of the year and at the end of my studies."

Gage snorted. "A bank account does you no good if you have been tossed out of school for not paying tuition."

He paused and stole a long glance at Hannah. "Hannah, I will not be too harsh with him. Just enough to bend him a little."

Hannah giggled. "You could simply say *boo!* That would bend him double."

They both chuckled as they neared the corner of Ellis and Fountain Street. At the end of the block, Gage spotted a familiar form. Joshua Quittner stood at the far corner, brushing wood chips and leaves from his clothes and hair. Gage hailed his new friend.

Joshua had stopped moving. Even from a distance it was apparent that Joshua's eyes had widened. Gage stole a quick look at Hannah.

He knew why.

And for a moment, the two men shared the exact same emotion.

It was the first of many such shared moments.

❧

"Is he always so taciturn?" whispered Hannah as they turned the corner.

"Joshua? Taciturn? I do not think I would use that word to describe him."

"I would admit that he is handsome, but I do not think he said a word, other than a grunt or two in agreement. At first I thought he was a mute and that you were playing one of your horrible tricks on me."

Gage feigned surprise. "Me? Horrible tricks? My reputation has been maligned. I demand that you retract that libelous statement."

Hannah giggled as she pushed his arm away from her own. "Libelous? Gage, even describing your tricks as horrible is a charitable exercise."

He stopped and turned to her. "How can you say that?"

Her lips puckered wryly. "Do you recall the time last year when you convinced your entire business class to answer the professor in made-up gibberish? Wasn't the poor man near tears when you finally relented and admitted it was a jest and that he had not awakened in some strange dream?"

"It was never proven that I was the mastermind," Gage shot back.

"And what of the time every chair in the lecture hall was turned to face backwards, then nailed to the floor in that manner? It took the custodian nearly a full day to right the room."

"Again . . . only rumors link me to that event."

It appeared that Hannah could not keep from grinning. "Gage, you're a sweet boy and a dear friend, but I would not put it beyond you to acquire a mute friend just for this type of situation."

Finally Gage relented, dropped his air of mock persecution, and laughed. "Dear Hannah, I make jest with pompous people who need a bit of levity in their grim and sober lives. Someone with a laugh as quick and as melodious as yours need not worry."

She took his arm, and they began to walk again.

After a moment, she said, "So he's not mute, then?"

Gage waited a moment for dramatic effect, then replied, "Oh no, he is a mute, and I am certain your insensitivity hurt him to the quick."

But he could not hold the pretense for long and erupted into laughter. Hannah shoved him off the sidewalk and began to run towards the carriage stand.

⁕⁂⁎

Gage disliked Hannah's uncle the instant the two shook hands. Gage wanted to pull his hand away and wipe it on his jacket, so limp and lifeless was the man's proffered grip.

In a room at the Boston Athletic Club that smelled of bourbon, tobacco, and money, the three positioned themselves around a highly polished table. It was clear Winthrop Collins was looking for the head of the table, a choice made most difficult because of its round shape. And it was also clear that Winthrop, a nervous little man who eyed Gage with a withering stare, distrusted his attendance.

"My dear niece, Hannah," he said, his words methodical and devoid of life, "I see no need to involve others in this most personal discussion of finances."

Hannah waved a hand at her uncle. "Don't be silly, Uncle Winthrop. Gage is an old friend of the family. You know his father, I'm certain. In fact, his dear mother insisted that he come with me today. He has agreed to squander a pleasant Saturday afternoon helping me make sense of this stack of dusty papers and all sorts of confusing numbers."

Gage fought the urge to laugh as he watched Hannah actually flutter her eyelids at her uncle, who looked as if he had just swallowed a lemon whole.

"I see no need for such . . ."

Hannah cut his sentence off half-spoken. "Gage will help me understand this silliness of trusts and spending limits and the like. It will actually do you a favor—not having to explain everything twice and thrice, most likely."

Winthrop Collins sighed so deeply that it appeared he might deflate and collapse into an empty suit of clothes. "Very well, Hannah. I should not be surprised by anything concerning your proclivities and activities."

Gage watched as Hannah feigned a wide-eyed expression. "Whatever do you mean, Uncle Winthrop?"

Winthrop offered a weak stare in return, hoping that his niece was indeed offering a naïve question and not making his frustrations a matter of jest.

Gage marveled that Hannah held that innocent look until her uncle muttered some dark words to himself, then reached into his valise.

"Shall we proceed?" Winthrop took out a paper, detailed with long vertical rows of intricate figures and notes. "Let's begin our review of the last several years of activity on your grandmother's trust account. We shall begin with its founding at your birth and review each year's deposit and accrued interest."

As her uncle bent to the paper and began to drone, Hannah rolled her eyes at Gage in an expression that summed up her distaste over dry figures and reports.

So comical was her expression that Gage snorted to suppress a laugh. Hannah let her eyes return to normal as Winthrop jerked upright.

"A question of a fiduciary nature, Hannah?"

Gage watched as she held fast to her childlike expression of befuddlement. Winthrop waited a second, then again began a long recitation of numbers and interest amounts, compounded on a yearly basis. He spoke for nearly an hour, and by the time he neared the finish, the stack of papers in front of him had grown to a depth of several inches.

Despite the numbing evenness of Winthrop's presentation, Gage listened intently. He made no notes, scribbled no figures, but anyone watching him could detect fierceness in his attention, as if he were a hunter silently readying for the kill.

When Winthrop paused, Gage leaned forward and cleared his throat. He spoke in a quiet, rumbling voice edged with just the tiniest sliver of calculated menace. "When has the interest been credited to the account?"

"Excuse me?" Winthrop replied.

"The interest on the trust. When are the funds posted to the original funds?"

Winthrop, perturbed at being interrupted again, narrowed his eyes. "They are not added to the general account. They are deposited to a secondary, interest-only account. That occurs after the meeting of the bank managers and the trust executor."

Gage licked his lips. It was an involuntary gesture. "But then the beneficiary's accounts are diminished, since it appears that a full six months of interest is lost owing to the time elapsed in securing the approval of the bank's manager and trust executor. Hannah's trust has lost the time value of that money for that entire period."

It took the shocked Winthrop several seconds to reply. When he did, his words were near venomous. "And your point, Mr. Davis? After all, this procedure has been in place for as long as the trust has existed, which is as long as you have been alive, I might add."

Gage was not cowed in the least, having practiced with his father in situations a hundred times more critical, more tension filled, with far more funds at stake.

"Perhaps so, but the bank has been using the trust fund's reserve of accrued interest payments for one half of the time it has been on deposit—all the while without offering any compensation to the trust holder, our innocent and unknowing Miss Collins."

It was apparent that Hannah did not follow Gage's logic, but it was also apparent that Winthrop did. His expression turned more sour than before.

"And again I must ask, what is your point, Mr. Davis?"

Gage stared back, keeping his face blank and in complete control. He enjoyed the hunt even more than the capture and kill.

"My point is, Miss Collins is owed money by the bank. Not having pen and paper to check my calculations, I must estimate that the trust fund is owed at least $5,760 of lost interest."

The number startled Hannah, and Winthrop nearly collapsed in his chair.

"Of course I may be off a few dollars. But I do not think I am. An accountant must be brought in to review my conclusions."

Uncle Winthrop drummed his fingers on the table.

Gage continued, "And this overlooked money needs to be repaid within a fortnight. I am sure Miss Collins does not want to become embroiled in a long, aggravating dispute with the bank. After all, her education is her chief concern, would you not agree? And rectifying problematic bookkeeping practices would detract from her studies. Don't you concur?"

Winthrop sputtered in indignation as he shuffled the papers. After a few moments, he had snugged the records back into a tidy stack. He then spread his palms flat against the table.

"I see how such things . . . as an inquiry into this matter . . . would be a great distraction to my niece. It is difficult enough for a woman to master such higher learning. Let us not make it harder." Winthrop then looked as if he had swallowed a second whole lemon. "I-I will see to it that her trust is credited for the oversight."

Waiting the appropriate amount of time for a reply, Gage smiled. "Well then, that is just grand, is it not?"

He stood, walked to Hannah, and helped her out of her chair.

"Then our business is concluded. Shall we seek lunch here, or perhaps there is some other establishment that might be better suited?"

Gage knew that Hannah, because she was a woman, would not be allowed in the club's restaurant. The club had been a men-only retreat since its founding more than a hundred years prior. Gage realized that no one's money or influence would likely change that bylaw.

To Gage's surprise, Winthrop actually appeared to understand. He gathered the papers, slid them into his case, and locked it with a great flourish.

"Yes, there is a very nice restaurant just around the corner. Saturday meals at this club are notoriously ill prepared. I think they actually allow the chef to work a five-day week."

Gage nodded. "What is the world coming to, Mr. Collins, with such lax and forgiving employers?"

FROM THE JOURNAL OF GAGE DAVIS

Such an interesting day.

Hannah and I set off to do battle with her uncle, the weasel-like Winthrop Collins. Why is it that some men engender immediate feelings of ill will? I am not a man who allows emotions to interfere with business matters. But his demeanor, and as I found out, his appalling lack of concern over proper banking and accounting practices, made the conclusion of the day all the more satisfactory.

Hannah now has enough additional resources at her disposal not to have to worry about petty problems like tuition and wardrobe and books. The amount was more than five thousand dollars. While it is not a princely sum, compared to what my father would make in a year, for her needs it should prove sufficient.

After lunch and our good-byes to her now despondent Uncle Winthrop, Hannah and I strolled through Beacon Hill and peeked in a number of the more stylish haberdasheries and millinery shops. We had a most marvelous time trying on some of the newer fashions. I was sorely tempted to purchase an exquisite topcoat made entirely from buttery-colored, buffed deerskin. But I did not. The price was dear. Not that it mattered to me. I found the sum to be quite acceptable, but Hannah heard the figure and nearly blanched in response.

"That much for a single coat? I could outfit myself for a year for that amount."

I pretended to be disinterested in the coat after her words. There was a huge gulf between what I found acceptable and what Hannah found acceptable. The difference was jarring. And I had no reason to prick again at her family's loss of stature and privilege.

I did, however, ask if the tailor would write his address on one of my calling cards. Perhaps I will drop him a note commissioning such a jacket. It would be superb for chilly autumn afternoons such as this. The jacket truly gives the wearer the image of being a rugged—albeit well-groomed—frontiersman. I think our cultured young ladies back in Cambridge would find it most exotic, perhaps even beguiling.

I simply will not wear it in Hannah's presence.

I asked Hannah if she thought the coat made me look adventuresome and attractive. As her answer, she rolled her eyes in a most revealing manner.

That gesture alone told me all that I needed to know, but she kept talking. She laughed and said I am too filled with myself. She claimed that I am nearly beyond human assistance.

I know she was jesting . . . wasn't she?

After such a pleasant day, we found ourselves back at the Destiny—going from the ridiculous to the sublime—or is that the other way around?

As I expected, Joshua was there, as excited as a new puppy to see us. He did not admit it, nor would I force him to admit it, but I am sure he was waiting for us at that empty table for almost an hour.

Hannah does make that sort of impact on men.

And Joshua, even though he is on his way to be a man of God, is not free from those desires. That much is apparent.

I am sure that he would have waited days, not just hours, had she requested it.

I shall have to sit down with the lad and instruct him (gently, of course and with soft censure) on the gentlemanly art of squiring a lady. He must not be allowed to make a fool of himself. After all, he is living at my address.

At this moment, he is much too eager. That image of a puppy, leaping on its master for a shred of attention, is quite accurate.

But back to the matter at hand—a description of our evening at the Destiny. Besides myself, Hannah, and Joshua, there was Jamison Pike. He is also a Harvard student—studying journalism. He also writes for the *Crimson Review*. He possesses an incredible talent with words, matched with a terrifyingly fierce, and almost beautiful, cynicism.

I believe that the chemistry of that evening was most unique and that fact has begun to bond this serendipitous group as friends. We are all so different in most every way, yet the night was magical and memorable. So much laughter. So much to share.

Nearing the end of the evening, all had departed the Destiny save the four of us and the poor scullery help in the kitchen. We sat in the dusty, gold-colored dimness, and our words flowed freely. We began to talk about the future—both the future of our own lives and the future of the country.

Such discussions never occur at home. Both my parents, but more specifically my mother, assume that my future is all but a certainty: I will follow my father and brother in business.

Joshua voiced his goals—serve God, lead a church—just like his father and grandfather. Hannah told me later that she thought his words sounded practiced and rehearsed—as if he were merely reciting someone else's thoughts. I thought her critique was overly harsh. The words may have sounded practiced, since I am sure Joshua has repeated them many times over the course of the last few years. Just because a man knows his destiny as a certainty does not make his goal any less noble.

I envy Joshua. He knows where he is going and desires to achieve it with all his heart.

I, on the other hand, am usually very certain of where I am going. But at times a tiny speck of doubt enters my thoughts and refuses to budge. I dismiss it, but that small whisper lingers long. Yet when Hannah asked me, I repeated my father's dream—to be rich, to follow my father and brother, to lead New York society. Someone needs to be wealthy and powerful. Why should it not be me?

I admitted to them that I had a fondness for the better things in life, if not the best altogether—like crisp linen sheets, boats, and the opera.

Quiet followed my speech, then Jamison spoke.

"I am not one to criticize you, Gage, but to me, having a goal of becoming wealthy is like walking on a path with no destination. How do you know when you have arrived at the end?"

I suppose that is true; it is difficult to know how much wealth is enough. Yet I will have the pleasure of having life's best with me as I travel that path towards a destination that does not exist. I may never discover an end to the path, but I am certain the accoutrements and luxuries along the way will make up for any lack of a clear finishing line.

Jamison mouthed the most anarchistic sentiments. He must have been listening to the odd folks at the Brook Farm, founded and flourishing only a few miles from where we sat. I have heard that the residents have banded together, holding possessions in common, and live as one extended family, sharing what they have. That might not be a bad idea if all the folks were as productive as the next. I know better than that. Some would work hard, and the others would prosper from their labors.

And if people like myself do not take charge of industry and expansion in this country, then who will? America needs people like my father—people willing to build and develop. People with vision and courage.

Well . . . I do sound like my father. I spoke to him about this Brook Farm community during my last visit home, and he turned red as a radish in response. He flustered and fumed. "It's the most insane idea I ever heard. Those people ought to be arrested for this foolishness. And they're college people too—professors among them. That's why your time at Harvard is such foolishness!"

I let him rumble on till he ran out of steam. Though I do not agree with all he says, his stance does have merit.

Jamison's destiny? To no one's surprise, he wished to write and travel and experience great adventures. I only hope that life does not disillusion his dream. He is a cynic, for sure, but even a cynic must have faith that an adventure is worth living and telling others about it. Otherwise it has no value. I told him that travel and experience is but sound and fury, signifying nothing, if it does not change one's life.

Hannah's response? She claimed again that she wants to be a physician—especially to poor, unfortunate children. But she is a woman, and the last time I checked, women do not become doctors. Can you imagine if a man entered the doctor's office and saw a member of the fairer sex there in a white coat? Why, even the most adventuresome would flee in embarrassment. I admit that I would be extremely squeamish to have a woman see me the way my doctor sees me. The very thought puts me in a pucker.

Yet, even though I think it a foolish and quixotic dream, her audacity is most commendable. If I can, I will assist her in this dream. Had I not had a secret yearning for the woman, I would simply laugh and let her encounter the cruel reality of the world.

Wouldn't the expression on some stodgy professor's face be payment enough for what assistance I could offer? There would be our prim and proper Hannah with a scalpel in hand, slicing into human flesh.

Enticing—is it not? Perhaps I can begin to make discreet inquires even now. Certain wheels must be put in motion and grease applied to others.

I will, of course, never mention any of this to Hannah. There are some altruistic acts that need to be kept secret.

And she mentioned Oberlin as a possible college at which to obtain a medical degree. Oberlin—in Ohio of all places! That's where our noble farm boy Joshua is from. How civilized can that state be?

But I do have an acquaintance who has family in that area. I am sure they will know whom to talk with . . . and how much it will cost.

I know that Oberlin actively encourages women as students, and the college was actually audacious enough to admit a Negro boy as a student. If any college would be liberal enough to teach Hannah how to be a doctor, it might be Oberlin after all. And this Negro boy had been admitted only a few years after that ruckus in Virginia over slavery. My mother heard from a number of the "best people" living in Richmond that every day was marked with fear and consternation, seeing as how that Turner fellow murdered more than fifty honest white people. Such a tragedy.

Perhaps they do things differently down South. There was even talk of South Carolina succeeding from the Union. I was too young to recall much, but my father worried over his shipping interests along the coast—and continues to be worried today due to the talk that still goes on.

But allow me to return to that evening at the Destiny.

Even though Hannah has such a goal, she did jest at her parents' view of her mission at Harvard. And that is to find a weak-willed, yet very rich, suitor. I have seen such men at the corners of Hannah's life—and this scenario may just prove to be the truth.

Even though she laughed as she spoke, I heard a glint of truth in her words. I watched Joshua as she mentioned this, and while I am not an expert in such matters, I would guess that part of his heart was already breaking. I am sure he thinks that her goal is too calculating and cold for our sweet Hannah.

And all this after having known her for less than a day.

If she does indeed find her rich suitor, Hannah will need to reconcile her dreams with what society requires. All in all, I do not think such an outcome is too disagreeable–to either Hannah or an intended mate.

To be honest–and I will vow here and now to always be honest on these pages–I have not been unaffected by Hannah's charms. I watched her as she spoke. Could I be the suitor she seeks? True, up till this moment, we have never discussed such things or even hinted at it. I am rich and will be richer soon. That is part of her quest, is it not?

This may be something to consider: Hannah could very well be part of my future.

And as for my financial future, Jamison and the rest of his liberal friends may scoff at my goal of becoming wealthy–but such a goal does provide many benefits. Jamison–and Hannah–will soon discover how useful wealth is, and how hard life is without it.

And now it is nearing dawn. I must conclude. Even though tomorrow is Sunday and I sleep later than normal, my stamina does have a limit.

CHAPTER THREE

Cambridge, Massachusetts
February 1843

As Gage stepped out on the balcony of the house at
619 Follen Street, the wood creaked and groaned as if in protest.
The cold air bit at his face and hands. He squinted across the snow
to the edge of the property. The sun, weak and pale, barely remained
visible over the line of trees to the west.

How do I get into these predicaments? I should be ashamed of myself.

He hesitated only a second, shaking his head to clear those
thoughts, and charged up the steps.

I sure hope dear old Joshua will be my ticket out today.

Gage knocked on Joshua's door. Since the walls were so thin,
Gage could hear a rustle of papers, then the sound of feet padding
across the floor.

Upon spotting Joshua, Gage poured out his story in a chilled torrent.

Never a bounder on purpose, Gage had badly miscalculated this
day. Months earlier he had agreed to attend a recital with Hannah,
followed by dinner at the Harvard Club.

*Because I keenly feel an attraction to Hannah, I owe it to myself to play
out the hand,* he had reasoned.

But he had not figured on his chance meeting with a certain lady–
a most captivating Nora Wilkes–at the Destiny just the day prior.

And now that same Nora Wilkes was seated in his parlor, enjoying a flaky scone and offering no hints as to her promptness at leave-
taking. And Gage was in no hurry to see her leave. In fact, he had
insisted that she stay and join him for tea.

"Gage, how could you . . . ," Joshua began to scold.

"Please, Joshua, no lectures right now. I know I deserve one, and I
know what you'd say. I've heard it before," Gage replied, his breath
visible in the cold air. "You can save it for me until tomorrow when
I'll repent and promise to do better. You may even present me with
a lecture on morals and turpitude and all the rest–and I promise to
pay attention. But please, Joshua, you hold my only way out for this
imbroglio. You must agree to help."

Joshua held his scolding expression a moment longer.

"The recital tickets await you at King's Chapel. A reservation for
8:00 P.M. is in my name at the Harvard Club. You alone, of all my
friends here in this liberal town, are the only man I can trust with
this assignment. Be charming, but promise not to take advantage of
our sweet, innocent Hannah."

Gage did not wait for his answer, for he saw Joshua's eyes widen
as he withdrew a fat handful of bills from his pocket and thrust them
into Joshua's reluctant palm. He knew that Joshua would relish this
opportunity to be close to Hannah and that he would not attempt
anything untoward.

"You are a prince, Joshua, a true prince. I trust you, above all others, to be the man you say you are. You'll treat her with Christian
decency. Ready my sermon for the morrow. I am sure that I will
need it."

⌥⌥⌥

Gage drew Joshua's door shut and took a deep breath.

One problem settled.

He paused for a second, combing wildly at his hair, smoothing the
lapels of his velvet jacket, and tugging at his sleeves. Downstairs he

hesitated at his doorway, catching a glimpse of Nora, unaware of his stare. Seated before the fire, she raised a delicate cup to her lips. But in comparison to her mouth, the fragile china looked almost harsh and awkward. The power and the clarity of this sight tightened Gage's chest. He had never felt such a thudding response to a woman.

It is not that I am so disconcerted by beauty, he told himself, *for I have been with beautiful women before. But she has something else indeed—a most delicate beauty surrounded by the most powerful presence that I have ever encountered. When such graceful elegance is combined with such strength—that is cause for any man to lose his bearings.*

Nora Wilkes, of the Portland Wilkeses (politics and shipping) was a student at the Boston Conservatory of Music. She resided in Cambridge, at the far eastern boundary of the town, at the home of her aunt and uncle of the Boston Wilkeses (politics and manufacturing). She seldom, if ever, ventured into Cambridge proper. The conservatory was across the river in Boston, and a woman of Nora's breeding would never have patronized the Destiny Café, save for a splintered axle on her hired carriage.

As the wheel snapped from its hub, the carriage driver cursed and swore loudly, then apologized profusely to his rider. He stomped off in search of assistance, leaving Miss Wilkes in a cold and drafty carriage. She glanced out the frosted window, saw the warm, inviting glow of the Destiny, and despite the fact that she was companionless, slipped out of the carriage and entered the restaurant.

She said later, as she spoke to Gage, that she was most surprised no one seemed the slightest bit upset or concerned that a single female had entered the establishment unescorted.

"As if it were a normal, everyday occurrence," she related.

Gage entered the Destiny only a moment after Miss Wilkes. Again, destiny was at work at the Destiny. Gage had left his rooms in a hurry that morning, having overslept, and had forgotten to carry his gloves with him. The Destiny was midway between campus and 619 Follen Street, so he had slipped in the café to warm himself and perhaps partake of a coffee.

In the open area by the front door of the Destiny, he had come upon the young woman. Wrapped in a deep green winter coat, she was seemingly unsure of what to do and where to go.

Gage stopped and turned to face her. It was the first time that his breath came short.

"Pardon me, miss. Are you in need of assistance?" he asked, attempting to keep his eyes from widening.

It was a sudden flash of beauty, he would recall later, *that all but caused me to stumble into muteness.*

The young woman smiled at him, her dark eyes clear and piercing, her white skin reddened by the cold, her dark hair tumbling down at her cheeks and throat. Gage claimed that her stunning features would have given pain to the old masters—for they could not have captured her essence and beauty on any canvas, no matter their skill level.

When she responded, her voice was lower than he had expected. "I was, until this moment."

"Might I escort you to a table?" Gage stammered.

He helped remove her heavy coat, watching every fluid movement of her arms, then guided her into a chair at a deserted table. Then sat across from her.

When he remained silent, staring, she waited, a demure smile on her lips.

Gage actually tried to start three sentences, but as he began to mouth the first words, he realized they all sounded foolish to him. So he stopped, regrouped his thoughts, then tried again.

The fourth time he was somewhat successful.

"That is your carriage down the street? The hired carriage, I mean. The one that is empty. I mean the one that has a broken . . . I mean . . . the one with the wheel that is . . . the one."

He mentally slapped at his own face, trying to regain composure. The usual Davis sureness and social aplomb had vanished.

The young woman turned and gazed down the street in the direction Gage had motioned. "Yes," she replied. "That is my carriage. Or was, I guess. The driver went off for assistance, and rather than slowly freeze to death, I thought I should take refuge in a warm place."

Gage scrambled to fashion a reply.

"Well, then . . . the Destiny is warm, at any rate. I mean, it is warmer than outside . . . and the outside is not warm at all. . . ."

A hint of panic began to creep into his voice, so he allowed a thin slice of silence to remain at the table.

The young woman cocked her head sideways and offered amiably, "I'm Nora . . . Nora Wilkes." She extended her hand.

As Gage reached toward her extended hand, he told himself, *Gage! Get hold of yourself. You sound and appear as the world's biggest innocent suddenly overcome with naïveté.* He finally replied, "And I'm Gage. . . ."

For a single second, he felt as if he could not recall his surname. But it came, and with that, a semblance of normalcy returned to his thoughts. "Gage Davis . . . of the New York Davises. And I have never been happier that one can no longer trust the craftsmanship of the American workman."

"Excuse me?"

"If the workman had done his job correctly, your wheel would not have broken, and you would not have ventured out into the cold. You would have had no reason to visit this less-than-savory establishment. And if that were fact, then I would never have had the honor of meeting you this day."

"You are a gentleman . . . Mr. Davis," she said, delicate brow uplifted.

He basked in her assessment.

She leaned closer to him. His heart beat faster.

"Are you an honest man?" she asked, her voice not much louder than a whisper.

"I . . . I am told that. Yes. I am an honest man."

"Then what you said—that this place is . . . unsavory? That is true?" Her eyes sparkled as she spoke, as if she took some pleasure in that discovery. "I have never been in an unsavory place before.

A civilized, proper woman like myself . . . why, I am not sure how
to act. You will offer me advice, will you not?"

She began to laugh softly. Gage would later recall that the sound
caused the very air to appear golden and shimmering.

"I will. But you are doing well enough on your own," he said. "It
is as if you had been born to the place."

She laughed louder and placed her gloved hand over his.

He felt her touch to the very core of his bones.

***

And now that same woman was in his parlor.

He entered the room, almost as if he were an intruder.

"Is the tea acceptable? Is it brewed correctly?"

She nodded.

"Again, I must apologize for having to run out like that. It is a rude
host who abandons his guest."

Nora's laughter tickled the air. "Gage, there is no need for elaborate apologies. You were not gone long."

She tilted her head a degree and caught Gage's eyes. For that long
moment, he felt as if her eyes had found his innermost being. It was
not unpleasant, he thought, yet somehow similar to what a butterfly
must feel as examined by a collector.

She continued, "I am sure that you spent no unnecessary time to
extract yourself out of whatever commitment you had forgotten."

So great was Gage's surprise at her assessment that it took him a
minute to register his shock.

"Or did you deliberately overbook your social obligations this
afternoon . . . just in case I proved to be a less than captivating
guest?" she asked evenly.

Scrambling, he attempted to formulate a cogent reply. "I . . . I was
not . . . I mean . . ."

She pursed her lips slightly and set her cup down. As she did, the
sleeve of her dress caught on the table edge, riding up her arm nearly
to her elbow. Gage could not help but stare at the finely drawn flesh.

She ignored his obvious staring and allowed a smile to color her words. "Why is it that men think they are so good at hiding the truth when just the opposite occurs? A man's fabrication is like a ship letting a sail out to catch the wind. It is obvious to all save the man who stands at the front of the ship."

Nora proved a most accommodating guest, for she lightly laughed at her own words. "Gage, do not worry. I am not offended. Honestly, I do not know you well enough to be offended."

Gage managed to find his breath but did not find the power of speech just yet.

"I am, however, somewhat concerned about the poor person who was expecting you, and another appeared in your stead. I am assuming that it was an old family friend who could not become too upset over your substitution. Am I right in my estimation? I am told that I am a most intuitive judge of character."

Gage steadied himself to launch a vigorous defense. Nora held up her hand, bidding him to stop. He raised a hand as if to interject, but after only a thought, lowered it.

"I am not truly a bounder. It is just that . . ."

He had readied a fast explanation of family obligations and obedience to his mother, but he discarded the words.

"Miss Wilkes, I have never done such a thing before in my life. I truly have not. You asked if I was an honest man yesterday, and I replied that I was."

He was sure that she did not quite believe him now.

"But after you assented to sharing afternoon tea with me today, any and all previous engagements would simply pale in comparison."

He was sure that Miss Wilkes appreciated being appreciated.

"I had no choice but to cancel. Perhaps it was at the last moment, but both Joshua, the young man upstairs . . ."

"The handsome man I saw bound down the stairs a few minutes ago?" Nora asked.

"Yes, the handsome one," Gage replied. There was a tiny, caustic edge to his words as he once again realized the impact Joshua had on women. "I am certain he viewed this opportunity as a godsend

... and I think the friend of the family will view it in much the same light."

"Truly?" Nora asked.

Gage realized that she wanted to be absolved of any pain that could have resulted in Gage's decision. And it was then that he knew Nora wanted to stay that afternoon, almost as much as Gage wanted her to stay.

"For truth, Miss Wilkes, for truth. What has occurred and what I have transpired to make occur, is best for all parties concerned."

"That is the truth?"

Gage offered his beaten-puppy look, a practiced expression if he were to admit it, and tried to appear as earnest and honest as possible.

As Nora gazed into his eyes, her demeanor softened.

"Then, Mr. Davis . . . I think I would like a second cup of tea. I agree with you. Your choice will no doubt be a good thing for all concerned."

The eighth chime of the tower bell echoed into silence.

Nora spoke, her words dipped in reluctance. "I really must be going. But I have said that prior to the eighth bell, haven't I?"

Gage nodded. He knew that despite how progressive and free a modern woman might be, she still must be concerned with what people might think. And she must be doubly concerned as to her aunt and uncle.

"They are dear, sweet people," she explained, "and they said that they would be home by the tenth hour. If I am not home by that time . . . well, I do not know what they might think—or do. Back in Portland if a single woman is found alone on the streets after eight in the evening she is arrested."

Gage looked startled.

"Now, don't be silly," she added. "I was jesting. I have stayed out until nine, on occasion. But there have never been any constables in my vicinity."

"Shall I call one this evening?" Gage queried softly.

"If you do, I will offer you up for arrest as well." Her words were thick as honey—and as sweet. "And I must be rested for tomorrow," she continued. "My voice needs to be rested as well."

"Your voice?"

"Yes, I have a guest solo at a church in Boston tomorrow."

As Gage helped her with her coat, she turned her head. Her cheek brushed against the knuckles of his hand. His heart leapt in response.

"And which church do you attend, Mr. Davis?"

As he tried to recover from the unexpected and most delicious touch, Gage again stumbled with his words. "I . . . back home . . . back home we are members of the Episcopal Church on Fifth Avenue around the corner from our home."

Nora continued to button her coat.

"But what church do you attend here?"

Gage blinked.

We are not members of any church here. And I do not want to be obligated to two churches. That would not make any sense, he reasoned to himself. Aloud he said, "Well, when I am home, I make a point of attending church as often as business permits. I think that it is important to consider. And we do offer a great deal of support—as befitting our resources, of course," he said.

"But what about Cambridge?" she asked. "There are two Episcopal churches within walking distance of my home."

"Indeed?"

Eyes glinting in astonishment, Nora said, "Surely you can spend an hour on Sunday morning giving back to God?"

After our family has given him more in one week than most men will offer in a lifetime? Gage asked himself with considerable skepticism.

Gage thought for a moment, then nodded. He knew that in life, as well as in business, sometimes one must appear to surrender in order to strengthen one's position.

"Miss Wilkes, you are absolutely correct. I should be attending church more often."

Her expression turned cotton soft.

"I did not intend to scold, Gage. I really didn't. I have no right to do such a thing."

He offered her his arm. He would escort her to the carriage stand on campus.

"No, Nora. You are not scolding. You have offered a sober reminder. I am sure that church . . . any church . . . will provide a great benefit to me."

As long as no one expects me to support two churches, he thought wryly. *And while I am certain that God would not make such a request, I daresay any number of pastors would.*

"And to assure my attendance, you must tell me at which church you will be singing. My spiritual well-being might very well depend on your honest reply."

A most curious look crossed her face—a smile combined with an expression of wonder and thanks. It was as if she had been presented with a big, dramatic opportunity.

In a flash, she squeezed his arm and leaned towards him. She whispered the name of the church in his ear, making sure he heard every word.

Gage knew he would never forget the words—or the feeling of her lips nearly brushing against his flesh.

Gage did not hurry home after seeing Nora to the carriage stand and helping her into a carriage.

He offered no parting intimacies, nor did she appear to expect such an offer. But on his roundabout walk home, he could think of nothing else save his few hours with her.

Her laugh. The gentle pressure of her arm on mine. And her mouth only an inch from my ear.

Nora's image and voice and laugh swirled in his thoughts. When he found himself walking almost aimlessly, he stopped, peered about, then spun on his foot, having gone several blocks in the opposite direction of 619 Follen Street.

He rounded the corner and almost stumbled. There, in front of his residence, was a carriage with two fine bay horses. Their breath was visible in the cold, and shimmering steam rose from their backs.

Gage quickly made his way to the carriage. As he neared, the door swung open. Edgar, as somber as ever, wrapped in a black coat and wearing a black top hat, alighted from the carriage.

"Sir," he said, his voice no louder than a gentle hiss. Yet it enveloped the chilly darkness.

"Edgar," Gage replied, "is everything all right? Is something wrong with Father? Has something happened?"

No expression could be detected on Edgar's face.

"No," he replied. "Everyone is fine. Your father sent me to give you this letter."

Gage quickly accepted it and tore it open.

"Your father desires you to return home for a week. He needs a second at a most critical business engagement."

It was unlike Edgar to supersede the contents of such a letter in this fashion. Gage immediately understood that Edgar had underlined his father's request.

Gage did not answer directly.

"Edgar, come inside for a moment. Warm your hands. And inquire if the driver would like to take a rest inside as well."

Edgar nodded, spoke to the hired hackney driver, then followed Gage to his door, remaining a few steps behind him.

Once inside, Gage turned to Edgar. "Why did he send you? Why not simply a messenger?"

Edgar paused. His white cheeks appeared even whiter with the cold. "He claimed you would ignore any letter sent by messenger."

Gage would have done exactly that.

"And he needs your help. Will you come?"

"Of course I will, Edgar. Just give me time to put some things in my bag."

"Sir," Edgar said, his words bloodless, "that is my responsibility. Perhaps you have a note or two to write, informing those who might notice your absence."

Startled at first, Gage hesitated.

"Yes, thank you, Edgar. You're right. I do have notes to write."

As Edgar edged his way into Gage's dressing room, Gage called out, "Please pack the light blue shirts. They make me look innocent, don't they?"

Gage would have sworn that he saw Edgar fight off a smile.

Dear Joshua,

I want to hear all about your assignation with Hannah. You must promise to remember every detail. I instruct you to keep whatever monies you did not spend.

Even as he wrote the words, he was certain Joshua would do no such thing.

I have been called to assist my father in New York. I will be gone a week, perhaps two. Would it be a great bother if you were to distribute the following notes to my professors?

You are a great friend.

And I do want to hear your sermon on moral turpitude.

(Or do the less-than-admirable thoughts of a young man require repentance as would actions themselves?)

Your friend,

Gage

Gage penned quick letters to only two of his seven current professors.

The other five will not know I am gone, and I will find it an easy matter to catch up on the classes' progress when I return.

In the two letters he did write, he asked for considerations owing to his father's most urgent and unusual request. He was certain that his requests would be granted. His father had promised a huge endowment to the school—under the unspoken condition that his son graduate.

After Gage finished those notes, he took out a page of his personal stationery and sat motionless with pen in hand for nearly five minutes. Then he dipped the pen in its well and began to write.

Miss Nora Wilkes,

I have been in a quandary as to the salutation on this note. I would have offered a more intimate greeting, but that might be my desires showing, rather than reality.

I offer you my deep regret that I will not be able to hear your solo at church. When I arrived home this evening, I found my father's manservant waiting for me, carrying with him an urgent request that I return home immediately. My father is in fine health—so this is nothing of a life or death nature. Yet he has insisted that I be in attendance at several business engagements and meetings he is hosting this week.

How can I refuse after he has given me so much?

I am hoping that I will someday—in the near future—be able to sit and listen to you again.

Perhaps upon my return, we might meet again for tea.

In your debt,

Gage Davis

P.S. I know my honesty has been called into question. If there is one iota of doubt in your mind as to the authenticity of the contents of this, please inquire with Joshua Quittner, the fellow who also lives at 619 Follen Street; he is studying to become a minister of God. Surely his word will be sufficient to verify my words.

G. D.

When he was finished, he turned down the wick of the lantern. The room grew dark. Edgar waited by the door, two large suitcases at his feet.

"All through, sir?"

"All through," Gage said and stepped out into the icy air once again.

New York City lost much of its charm in the winter, thought Gage as he scratched off a thin layer of frost from the carriage windows. His father's polished and ornate carriage bumped its way towards the family manse as the sun rose.

The trees are bare, the air swirls with acrid smoke, everyone is bundled like mummies, and the only benefit I can see—or at least smell—is that the horrific odors have been greatly reduced by the cold.

At times, he wondered why anyone would choose to live in the city.

As the carriage rattled along, Gage watched gaily dressed men and women exiting exclusive dining establishments and social clubs.

The sun is rising, and only now are these folks concluding their evening. Where else but in New York?

Edgar remained silent the entire trip home, resisting every effort Gage made to draw him into conversation.

"Your father needs you, sir. That is all that needs to be said."

Gage bounded up the front steps of his home and threw open the heavy door. As the bang echoed throughout the house, a rustling came from the study at the far end of the hall. The door was cracked, allowing a thin smear of light to wobble into the dark hall.

"Father!" he called as he began to walk towards the room.

He heard no response.

"Father!" he called out louder and pushed the door open.

From the desk glowed a single lantern.

"Why don't you shout louder and wake the entire neighborhood?" an annoyed voice said. "Please, Gage, have some common sense and shut up. One might think you are part rooster from your early crowing."

Gage knew in an instant who was speaking from behind his father's massive desk—his brother, Walton.

"But he sent for me. I thought he would be up . . . waiting for me."

"He is not."

Gage waited impatiently. It was unusual to see Walton in his father's study, and even more unusual to see him awake this early.

"Is he well?"

"Who?" Walton asked abruptly, as if he had more important things on his mind.

"Our father? Is he well? Edgar didn't say much."

"Edgar never does. That man gives me the shivers. Always sidling around in the shadows. I would have fired him long ago if it were up to me."

Gage stood in front of the desk. "And it is not up to you."

"Obviously."

Walton glanced up for a heartbeat, then back to a handful of papers.

"So, is he well?"

"Who?"

Gage stepped closer, his hand clenching into a fist, but said evenly, "Walton, it is early, and I have not slept all night. Please, can we be civil today? Might you abandon these annoying games and simply answer the question directly?"

It was clear from Walton's expression that he found great joy in tormenting his sibling.

"I don't understand your impertinence, little brother. I would have thought that of all the family, Father has kept you constantly apprised of his goings-on. To hear otherwise is a great surprise."

Walton paused again, until Gage was just about to shout at him, then said slowly, "Father is fine . . . for the most part. A spell now and again, but he naps and all is well again."

"And Mother?"

Walton arched his eyebrows.

"Isabelle Davis will bury all of us, you know. Nothing will stop her."

Gage tried to hide his feelings. He hated the practiced, angry tension that seemed to mark their every conversation. Gage tried his best to be pleasant and even tempered. But after every biting comment, he found his own anger harder and harder to hold in check. He hoped that a change in subjects would defuse the situation.

"What meetings are so important that I had to leave Cambridge?"

Walton looked up.

"I am sure I have no idea. Father keeps his own counsel on his business matters. Oh yes, I forgot. He does tell you about them all, doesn't he now?"

Gage winced but held his expression even. He knew what Walton said was true. His father did share more business matters with his younger son, almost to the exclusion of Walton, the rightful heir apparent.

Walton added with a twisting sneer, "I am sure that you two will have it all figured out in no time."

Gage could not hold back. "Perhaps if you were civil to him, then you might be included more often—and I wouldn't have to leave school as a result!"

Walton stood up and threw the papers into the air, almost aiming them at Gage. "It's always you, isn't it, little brother? You are the poor one who has to be inconvenienced. You have to leave Cambridge. You have to miss one of your precious classes. It's always you."

Gage held his hands up in surrender and kept his words calm and even. He knew the words could so easily escalate in tone and volume. He was not ready for a fight this early.

"I simply asked about the meeting. That's all. Just tell me about the meeting."

Walton snorted. "I have no idea, nor do I care to know. But what tidbits Father has tossed out at the dinner table is that a group of New York's finest and faceless bankers and swindlers want to raise money for some odd scheme they claimed will make everyone richer than they are now. However, this group needs cash and someone with a good name. It seems as if our father has both."

"That's it? That's all? Some people are seeking potential investors?"

Walton stood and walked to the door. "That's it, little brother." Before he closed the door behind him, he called out, "I hope you have a good appetite."

"Why is that? Is Mother planning one of her feasts?"

Walton halted just long enough to answer. "No . . . it's Father this time. He killed the fatted calf, don't you know."

Walton allowed a humorless chuckle to escape from his mouth, then he slipped out and clicked the door shut.

Gage closed his eyes for a long time. He rubbed at his temples. He had hoped that things had changed while he was away, but it was apparent they hadn't.

❦

It was more than simple investments, and for that Gage was grateful. To return home simply to shill for money would have been upsetting.

Arthur Davis had stumbled upon an eccentric inventor by the name of George Shirdler. It was pure serendipity—Arthur had missed a coach and standing beside him was a disheveled man, carting about a box of wires, strips of metal, and a series of black cones. Arthur, like his son, would strike up a conversation with anyone, anywhere.

Shirdler was most secretive, but Gage's father, after a dinner and three bottles of expensive French wine, finally began to understand what Shirdler was attempting to develop. Davis had heard of the telegraph, but Shirdler promised his device would soon make that invention obsolete.

That was when Arthur Davis began to get interested.

He could have financed every bit of the research and development without straining the family bank accounts—but there was no glory in using one's own money.

He struck a deal with Shirdler. For 75 percent of the rights to produce this invention, Arthur Davis would find all the money Shirdler would ever need. All Davis asked is that Shirdler approach a small syndicate of investors that Arthur was acquainted with. Shirdler was to drop the name of Arthur Davis as one being interested in the patent.

When they found out that Arthur Davis was about to invest his money in the project, the group would stampede their banks to cover what portion of the funding remained. The senior Davis carried that sort of reputation in investment circles.

That way, this separate group of investors would put up the

THE CIRCLE OF DESTINY

needed funds, Arthur Davis would maintain majority control and never have to spend a dime of his own money.

Gage whistled at the great simplicity of his father's plan–developed through a chance meeting at a coach stop.

What Gage had to do was act as an official go-between–he could be impartial, uninformed, or however else he needed to be to accomplish his father's ends.

And his two weeks in New York were most successful.

Besides this small group of wealthy financiers, twelve other newly rich men were clamoring to join in this investment. If Arthur chose to oversubscribe his needs, he could have done so very easily.

Yet while Arthur Davis was slippery, he was never dishonest. To sell more shares than were actually available would not be a seemly thing for Arthur to do, so that possible action was dismissed.

On the way back to Harvard, Gage had had to make do on a public coach since his father's railcar was unavailable. After being assaulted with odd smells and the occasional squawking chicken, he was tired. Night fell as he hurried back to 619 Follen Street. When he tossed his valise into the room lit only by moonlight, he glimpsed a pale envelope lying on the floor, just by the front door. He bent down, detecting a hint of rose. The letter was subtly dusted with the fragrance.

Gage knew that scent was a good sign.

He scrambled to light a candle and then tore open the envelope. He knew whom it was from.

Dear Gage,
  Of course I believed you.
  But I did ask Mr. Quittner, just to be sure.
  I look forward to your return.
  Please call upon me at your convenience.
  Regards,
  Nora

Gage fell asleep that evening with a smile on his face and woke much the same way eight hours later.

June 1843

The last three and half months of the term flashed by in a heartbeat. At least that is how it seemed to Gage.

Being behind by the two weeks spent in New York doing his father's business, even Gage found himself rushing to catch up with studies and papers and reading. While his grades did not reflect his absence in class, his social life was impacted. He was at the Destiny far fewer times than in the past. Even his close friends remarked that he was becoming the bookworm and recluse that he had always made fun of before. He would smile, nod, and hustle away, often with a stack of books under his arm.

During the free evenings that were open to him, he often found himself in a drafty church or concert hall listening to the beautiful Nora Wilkes. And that singular and most joyous pleasure managed to hasten the end of the last few weeks of his second year at Harvard.

CHAPTER FOUR

Cambridge, Massachusetts
September 1843

If anyone had asked Gage how he spent his summer, he would have pondered a long moment, then responded with a blank look and a shrug. It was not that the summer was uneventful; it was too eventful.

Gage's father had postponed nearly a hundred meetings, conferences, and appointments until his son's classes at Harvard had come to an end for the year. Gage dutifully accompanied his father to every one of those appointments. And Gage knew why it was important to his father.

He could listen to a five-hour-long, mind-numbing dissertation on a particularly arcane point of investment law and policy without losing focus. And at the end of the meeting, when almost everyone else would simply agree just to relieve the boredom, and when others would sign contracts that contained detrimental clauses just to escape, Gage would, like an arrow, find the one point of vulnerability in the argument or plan.

And there he would attack—or defend, depending on his financial position. It was the ability to remain sharp and poised as others wilted and lost interest that often provided Gage with such a definite advantage. His father knew it, and so did his business competitors.

It was rumored that if you were proposing a deal with Arthur Davis, one brought along three contracts. One would contain all manner of almost devious clauses and wording to benefit the other party—rather than Arthur Davis. The second contract would be much less advantageous to the presenter—and offer both parties an equal stake. The third would offer the advantages to Arthur Davis, capitulating on all the standard points of contention. If Gage was absent, the first contract would be offered—and Arthur Davis had been known to sign ill-suited contracts. The second was offered if Gage was in attendance. And the third would be the one actually signed.

Gage smiled when he heard this story. And he thought it was certainly true.

June and July were a whirl of business meetings. Gage and his father left home early and often returned well after midnight. August offered some relief as Gage helped his father prepare for his trip to the Continent in the fall. Gage spent as much time in the New York City Public Library as he did at the offices of the *New York World* newspaper, gathering information. He was searching out new techniques, innovations, and novel inventions that his father might provide funding capital for. Arthur Davis was wealthy for good reason.

During the last week in the city he visited the laboratory of George Shirdler for the second time. Shirdler claimed to be close to refining his major improvement to Sam Morse's telegraph invention. Morse had investors galore, and a patent. Gage's father, as well as scores of investors, were intrigued with the idea of simply tapping at a wire to send messages instantaneously across great distances.

The inventor showed Gage all types of strange and impressive electrical apparatuses. He assured Gage he was but months away from his grand breakthrough.

"It will put that pompous Morse in his place and make his blasted telegraph obsolete," Shirdler insisted as he wiped his stained hands on his already blackened shirt.

⚜

Now that summer was over, Gage was back in the less competitive environs of Harvard.

Gage spent most of his first day back at Harvard in the stuffy, much too warm office of a professor who taught on the theory of applied business techniques.

It was a meeting that was unplanned, and a bit unwelcome.

Gage had left most of his belongings and all his furnishings at 619 Follen Street over the summer. The previous summer he had shipped all his clothing and books and bedding and most of the rest of his possessions back to New York and his parents' home. During those hot months, he had not opened a single box or crate, having more than enough wardrobe and personal items remaining in his rooms to never need to wear the same item twice.

So moving back to Cambridge for his third term was a much simpler matter. A few trunks carried recent book purchases, several more were filled with the latest in fashion, and others held an odd assortment of items he felt he simply must have with him. Rather than a team of stevedores, he made do with hiring two stocky gentlemen and a small, flatbed carriage.

When he arrived at his door, he noticed an envelope wedged in the doorjamb at eye level. "Urgent—for G. Davis" was scrawled across the envelope. In the upper right-hand corner was printed "A. C. Brent."

Gage winced.

The letter was from Professor Ambrose Brent, who had taught Gage during the spring semester in his sophomore year.

"An insufferable bore," Gage stated after his first class, "and a man who is quite out of touch with the reality of money and power."

The letter was quite brief: "G. D. Davis, I must meet with you at the earliest possible moment after you return. It is a matter of the utmost importance. A. C. Brent."

"Is it true? Can messages be sent via copper wire with clarity and speed?"

Ambrose Brent scuttled about his crowded, cluttered office.

Gage bent and subtly dusted the chair before sitting.

"It appears that it is no parlor trick," Gage explained. "Congress has set aside a handsome fund to run wires from the Senate to Baltimore as a test. Why Baltimore has been selected and not New York is a matter of great conjecture back on Wall Street."

Ambrose pitched his head back and offered a quite annoying laugh, akin to the braying of a mule, Gage thought.

"Wall Street—that's rich, Gage, most witty."

Gage rested his folded hands in his lap. *Why did he call me in? To simply ask about the telegraph? He could have read about this in the newspaper—at least as much as I'm willing to tell him.*

Ambrose walked around his desk and shoved a thick pile of papers to the side. A few fluttered down to the floor, mixing in with some earlier arrivals.

"So then, if the government is involved, it must be an honest proposition, right?"

Gage shrugged.

Ambrose looked queasy. "But that's what others tell me."

Gage nodded. He had no intention of telling Ambrose anything.

"Are you looking for additional investors? I have heard that your father has begun an informal, albeit very quiet, campaign to induce others to invest in this wondrous invention."

Gage knew the entire plan was most sensitive, since all the intricacies of the improved apparatus had not yet been finalized. Shirdler insisted that his device would work a hundred times better than Morse's would—and more cheaply. What he needed was time and a few more dollars for research. But the quirky inventor was closemouthed—many jealous competitors were all too eager to steal from him. Gage suddenly felt a stab of worry.

If a second-rate business professor had heard about the news and the most recent developments, what impact would that have upon the entire plan?

Gage attempted to remain nonchalant. "My father investigates many opportunities. I am sure that if he has considered a telegraph system of some sort and finds that the plan has merit, he will make such plans known."

Ambrose whispered, "Surely you can tell me, Gage. You know of my reputation for being discreet."

"There is nothing to tell. I know as much about this telegraph scheme as what I have read in the newspapers. Some say it will come to naught. Others claim it is a fabulous advance. I am sure time will tell."

"But, Gage . . . if it provides an opportunity to invest early . . . I would like to partake. I hear the gossip about these things."

"But that is just what it is—gossip. You, of all people in Cambridge, should be aware that talk, like the money supply, can easily become inflated."

Ambrose eyed his former student with suspicion. "And there is no group seeking out those who would like to purchase shares in the new venture?"

Gage shook his head no.

"Are you sure?"

"Quite sure."

Gage was greatly relieved that the story was based only on rumor and innuendo, both of which were in great oversupply in New York City these past few months.

Ambrose appeared crestfallen.

"You mean it's just talk? And there is no new development?"

"Well, there is the telegraph of course, but as of this moment, it appears to be oversubscribed in comparison to its possible payoff."

"Drats and double drats. I thought for one moment that I could have—for once—been in the right place at the most opportune time."

Gage bided his time, then asked calmly, "Where did you hear such a rumor in the first place?"

Ambrose tilted his head and did not offer a reply.

"Didn't you yourself–in your classes–teach us all that we need to investigate such speculations in person? Didn't you instruct us that if a company is secretive and furtive, then it might very well be hiding some deeper secrets?"

"I did."

"And yet you still gave credence to this unsubstantiation?" Gage asked.

"I had it on impeccable sources," his professor replied.

"Impeccable sources?"

"Indeed. Otherwise I would never have called you into my confidence like this."

Gage was most puzzled. "May I ask, Professor Brent, the source of such rumor? I may be able to understand the nuances of the story if I could know the origin."

"Ah . . . that's where this story takes a most curious turn," Ambrose said in his languid professorial tones. "The source of this rumor, as you put it, was guaranteed to be correct. The person who told me shall remain unnamed but is of the most unassailable character and reputation."

"And he has said what of the origin of the rumor?"

Ambrose leaned in closer. "My source claimed it came straight from the son of Arthur Davis."

Gage sat back in surprise, making no attempt to hide it.

"As I heard it, the story came straight from the financier's son," Ambrose said with finality. "And that would be you, would it not?"

<hr />

Gage left Professor Brent's office in a quandary. He could not have been the source of the rumor. He had spoken to no one. Even his father insisted that the two of them maintain a strict confidence. Too many business arrangements, his father always said, were spoiled by the premature announcement by one side or the other.

And Gage was quite certain that his brother, Walton, knew even less of this development than Professor Brent had known. He simply did not enjoy the world of business, and such a matter would have bored him greatly.

As he walked to the Destiny, Gage resolved to ask his father about the curious report. *Perhaps I will post a letter this afternoon,* he thought as he made his way up the very familiar front steps.

***

A chorus of hellos and greetings met him as he entered. Despite the fact that Gage was well known, and liked by most, he kept his closest ties to a minimum. There was Hannah, of course, and Joshua, his housemate, and Jamison Pike. The rest were but casual acquaintances.

He walked from table to table, greeting those he had not seen for several months with great earnestness. He stopped at a few tables and shook hands, inquiring as to summer activities or the particulars of this family or that. Occasionally his laugh would punctuate the general noise, cutting through the many animated conversations that swept through the restaurant.

For the most part, his actions and expressions were honest and true. Yet a few of his friends, his very close friends, could tell a subtle difference in his words and tone between the moments he was most comfortable and those in which he merely acted the part of friend and confidant.

At last Gage made his way toward where Hannah sat alone at a table near the rear of the room. Pretending not to know her, he extended his hand towards her. "Gage Davis," he said with a muffled laugh. "You must be new here."

"Why, yes," she said, playing along. "It is my first day at Harvard and I am most perplexed by . . . well, by everything."

"A common occurrence," Gage replied, dragging a chair close to hers. "Yet there is one constant that must be maintained here at dear old Harvard."

Hannah fluttered her eyes. "And what might that be?"

"That every woman who attends this august establishment—and as you know, that number has now risen to be in the dozens—all must consent to one matter."

"And what might that be?"

"That every Harvard woman must agree to become enamored with me at least once during their years at Harvard."

"Truly? That is a tradition here at the 'Old Crimson'?"

Gage nodded.

"Then I shall allow that infatuation to occur now . . . ," she said with a laugh. She waited no more than six seconds, then added, "and end now."

Gage chuckled in response and offered a warm, brotherly hug. "And how have you been, my sweet Hannah? Has all gone well in Philadelphia this summer?"

For a moment, her smile disappeared and a look akin to pain flashed in her eyes. But she recovered quickly.

"All is fine, Gage. Mother and Father are fine. Philadelphia has remained as Philadelphia has always been—boring, hot, and fetid in the summer. However, I was not prepared for the surprise my father presented us with this year."

"And the surprise?"

"I'll have you know that the Philadelphia Collinses spent an entire two weeks in Cape May with my great-aunt. While my mother dislikes the salt air and all that, I find the sea particularly invigorating. It did seem to suit my father. He spent hours trying his hand at fishing."

"Fishing? Your father? Seems awfully out of character for him. Was he successful?"

"Not in the least," Hannah replied. "And yet there he was, day after day, dressed in a collar and tie, with his dress trousers rolled up to his knees, casting into the surf. I do not believe he had so much as a single bite."

"Your father . . . his bare knees showing? How shocking."

"Even my mother consented to walk the beach at dusk," Hannah said as Gage showed great surprise, "although she was covered head to foot and carried a wide parasol to ward off the little of the sun that remained."

"Your mother? On the sand? With the angry waters only inches from her feet? And the earth did not shake?"

Hannah giggled. "And I found a way of entering that same water. Do you recall that I bemoaned the fact that as a Collins–of the Philadelphia Collinses–I would never be allowed to touch seawater unless my ship sank in the Atlantic?"

Gage laughed. "Of course I do. You had us all in stitches that day."

Hannah lowered her head. Gage peered at her expression.

"Is my Hannah blushing? I am shocked–and most intrigued." He held a hand under her chin and raised her face. "You *are* blushing! Hannah!"

Playfully, she knocked his hand away. "I am not blushing at all. It is simply warm in here."

Gage leaned forward, lowering his voice. "So tell me what happened. You know I will get it out of you eventually."

"Well," she said, her eyes brightening, "it happened one afternoon when my parents had taken to the boardwalk, and my cousins and I were left to our own devices."

Gage smiled. "Are these cousins from the proper Philadelphia Collinses?"

"Heavens, no. No one from there would have dared think of the idea. This group of cousins come from those 'horrid Pittsburgh Collinses.' Mention that branch of our family and my mother always dismisses them with a short sniff."

It was obvious that Gage was enjoying himself. After months of endless business meetings, Hannah's story was as refreshing as a cooling shower on a hot summer day.

Hannah placed her elbows on the table and related her tale. The Pittsburgh cousins, all female, all of similar ages, along with Hannah, slipped out of the grand house and "borrowed" their aunt's horse and cart. The entire group took the cart to an isolated stretch of beach, miles south of town.

They urged the horse through a thickness of sea grass and up a pitched dune of sand, then tethered him to a scrub pine, twelve or so yards from shore.

"If a horse could look nervous, this one did," Hannah said.

The entire group of cousins then raced, laughing and shouting, to the water's edge. In no time, Hannah related, they removed their shoes and socks and began to dance and run in the ankle-deep surf.

"Suddenly," Hannah said, her eyes sparkling as she recalled the event, "Hazel turned to us and said she was bored with this wading and wanted to 'experience' the ocean—that's how she put it."

"Experience the ocean?"

Hannah nodded, then continued. "Hazel ran back to the cart, removed her long dress, stripped down to her chemise and bloomers, and with a whoop, leapt like a great fish into the ocean."

Gage was transfixed. His grin went from ear to ear. "That is the truth? Really? And then what happened?"

Hannah averted her eyes. "Then we all joined her in the water. It was such a liberating experience—to be carried about by the waves."

"You all were in the water with her?" he asked, nearly incredulous. "In the same manner of dress?"

Hannah nodded.

"But, Hannah . . . you could have been arrested. All of you. I am sure you were violating some law concerning public decency."

"Gage," Hannah chided, "the second layer of a woman's normal dress is just as modest as the first. And besides, we were miles away from the nearest human. Our modesty never came into question. And remember, I am studying to become a physician. The human body holds little mystery to me now."

"But I am wishing I could have been there."

Hannah slapped Gage's shoulder as a sister slaps a teasing brother. And in that instant, Gage regretted his summer. He had no tales of such youthful freedom and abandonment; he only had meetings and endless contract discussions.

Finally, he spoke. "You must never tell Joshua this story," he warned.

"Why not?" she asked.

"The story and its images will drive him into a state of such agitation that he will never recover."

Hannah eyed him suspiciously. "You are jesting now, of course."

"I am not. I am a man of the world, and I will never be able to look at you in the same innocent way I have been accustomed to. Think of the shock it would provide to our naïve and uncorrupt Joshua."

Hannah muddled that over and at last nodded.

Gage then added with a smirk, "It would be best if I told him."

For a moment there was a hint of agreement on Hannah's face—until she realized what he had said. Then she scowled and punched his arm.

"Gage, you are the most wicked man I know," Hannah said, laughing. "And I love you for that."

⁂

"Has Joshua written you over the summer?" Hannah asked Gage later over a cup of tea. They had been together at the Destiny for more than two hours.

"Not once," he replied, "and I did write him two notes."

"I wrote to him as well. And not one word in reply. That is most rude of him."

"He may be far from the post office," Gage said, offering an explanation. "And the postage may be dear for our impoverished Joshua."

"No more dear than to me," Hannah countered. "It is not as if I have a great deal of excess funds."

"But, Hannah," Gage gently countered, "his poor and your poor are two different realities. His poor is not having enough food to eat. Your poor never encounters that reality."

"Well, I suppose I might forgive him. But I will still make him pay for his oversight. I truly did want to hear from him this summer."

Gage wanted to tell Hannah not to toy with Joshua's heart. It was obvious to Gage that after Joshua spent that one evening with Hannah using Gage's funds, Joshua was quite smitten by her. It was so apparent to Gage, although he was unsure if Hannah noticed any of the telltale signs. Gage also knew that Joshua would be no more than a friend to Hannah, and that fact would bring pain to Joshua's tender heart.

But Gage knew such a warning of the heart was not his to give.

"Speaking of letters," Gage said, "I have a most sensitive question–of a personal matter–to ask you."

"Gage? A sensitive question? How can that be?" Hannah asked lightly. "Do not the two terms cancel each other out?"

Gage joined in her merriment for a minute, then he became serious.

"Hannah, I am not joking now. I do have a question."

Hannah softened and placed her hand on his. "I'm sorry, Gage. Please, feel free to ask."

"And you will keep this matter confidential? And never tell anyone?"

"If you ask for secrecy, I will provide it."

Gage reached into the breast pocket of his coat and withdrew a thin envelope. The paper was creased and the writing smudged, as if it had been handled many, many times. He turned the paper over and over while he spoke.

"I met a woman last year."

Hannah raised her eyebrows in surprise, but she did not utter a word. No one in their small circle knew this fact.

"I met her the day before you and Joshua went to that recital."

"Who is she?" Hannah asked. "A student here?"

Gage shook his head. "She studies at the Boston Conservatory of Music."

"And you have been in her company often? No one was aware. When did you have time to court another woman? Wasn't our friendship enough?"

Gage smiled, then looked at the envelope in his hands.

"Well . . . I did not get to see her often. But I am . . . I find myself thinking about her at the most inopportune moments. I wonder what she is doing."

"Did you see her over the summer?"

Gage shook his head again. "She was back home in Portland. I wrote her . . . about business and deals and the like. I wanted to be with her, so I told her of my days."

"Maine?" Hannah asked. "You have found a woman from Maine?

I thought you said anyone from Maine is either a potato farmer or a lobsterman."

"I did," he murmured, "but she is neither . . . to be certain."

"So, Gage, what is your question? Is the query something only another woman might understand?"

He slipped out a single page from the worn envelope. "She wrote this to me. It was the only note I received."

Hannah pursed her lips and tried not to appear pessimistic.

Dear Gage,

Thank you for the letters. I am glad that you are able to help your father in that way. Those meetings sound most interesting, although I must admit to being baffled by all things scientific. I have spent most of my summer helping my mother care for her mother, my grandmother. At times, she can be a most vexing charge.

I have also provided music for several churches in Portland. I trust that you are faithful in attending as you promised me you would be.

I look forward to seeing you this fall. I shall return to my aunt and uncle on 27 September.

With warmest regards,

N.

With great deliberation, Gage folded the letter, slipped it back into the envelope, and then into his breast pocket. He looked past Hannah, as if his eyes sought out an image hundreds of miles away.

"And your question is?" Hannah asked, breaking the silence.

Gage shook his head and focused on Hannah again. "Are these the words of a woman writing to a man she finds interesting?" he said, patting at his chest, "or are they merely polite words and could have been written to anyone—such as a cousin or a passing acquaintance?"

It was clear Hannah saw the yearning in Gage's eyes. "You want to know if she fancies you?" she asked softly.

He nodded.

Gently she placed her hand over his. "I think she does. The letter sounded warm. She signed it 'warmest regards.' That is a good sign.

It would be the type of letter I would have written to someone I might have interest in . . . or slight stirrings for . . . or a certain fondness."

Gage glanced up, his eyes brighter, his smile hopeful. "Truly?"

"Truly," she added, but she looked as if she needed to convince herself of those words.

At past midnight, Gage awakened to a furious tapping at his door. At first he expected to see Edgar, hovering in the dark with ominous news. But it was Joshua, and he now sat before Gage in absolute panic.

Gage turned the lamp up and drew two chairs up to the parlor table.

"Joshua, would you like a drop of port?" he asked, holding his laugh in check.

Joshua was so rattled that he did not offer his usual blustery, almost indignant refusal. He simply said no and then blurted out, in an embarrassed rush, his story of this evening. After Gage had left, Joshua had walked Hannah home from the Destiny. The walk was an unexpected pleasantry, especially after Joshua was thoroughly berated by Hannah for not writing over the summer. And when they parted at her door, Joshua claimed that, though he was not sure who leaned forward first, their lips had met and shared one indescribable kiss.

I wanted to warn her of toying with his heart, Gage scolded himself, *but I was reticent about raising the topic. I should have told her. I should have.*

"So, Gage," Joshua asked, pacing back and forth, "is a kiss such as this . . . I mean . . . does the kiss indicate . . . is this the first step on the road to matrimony? Is she expecting me to become her suitor?"

Gage tried his best not to laugh and failed. He clasped Joshua's shoulder.

"My friend, you are an innocent among wolves here at Harvard."

Joshua appeared puzzled and a bit angry. "I am not an absolute child," he replied. "There have been women in my past . . . women from Ohio."

Gage chose not to argue, knowing that a man with wounded pride hears little and understands less.

"Joshua, I know you are not naïve. But the women here may be a bit more forward than you are accustomed to."

Joshua nodded in agreement. "They are nothing like I am used to."

"Now pay attention. I will tell you all I know." Gage pursed his lips. "This is the sum total of my knowledge." He held up his thumb and forefinger in a circle. "Nothing. Absolutely nothing. Zero. That's how much I know."

Joshua appeared dumbstruck. "But, Gage—you are a man of the world. Here at Harvard . . . I mean, I have heard the rumors and stories. You know, about women. I mean, they all say that you truly know."

Gage shook his head. "Alas, the stories are inflated. My reputation is more bold and smart and savvy than I am in reality. A nice problem to have, since it does mean that women see me as a challenge. But rest assured I am often at a loss to understand the mechanics of a woman's mind and behavior. Now this incident with Hannah—I will admit that I am surprised. I would have never expected her to respond in that way."

"So what do I do?"

Gage shrugged. It was the first time Joshua had ever seen him unsure.

"Relax. No one now expects you to ask for Hannah's hand in marriage—least of all Hannah. A simple kiss is not a precursor to a mandated proposal of marriage."

Gage watched Joshua's eyes. They were not happy.

"You are sure of that?" Joshua asked, looking a little hurt and even more disappointed.

"I am sure. Not every woman does such things, but some do. I am certain Hannah was expressing her emotions *du jour* and was not intending on the kiss signifying a lifelong commitment."

"And of that you are sure?"

Gage breathed out a great sigh. "Well . . . no, I am not. For a moment, I am sure. Then a moment later, I am undecided."

"But surely, Gage, you must be sure of something when it comes to the feminine mind."

"Joshua, if you learn only one thing at Harvard, you must learn that a woman's mind and thoughts and emotions are completely unknown to at least half the people on earth."

"Half?" Joshua asked, confused.

"I meant men—half the world—find it impossible to understand the other half—women. Women are a bafflement to me. Yet I do know Hannah. And I am sure that Hannah expects nothing more from you. Perhaps she saw this as a friendly kiss—a gentle show of affection between friends."

"Has she ever kissed you?" Joshua asked. "You're her friend too."

"A gentleman never kisses and tells, Joshua."

"Gage, please. I am desperate. Tell me. Has she kissed you? Or Jamison?"

Gage narrowed his eyes. "No to both questions. I know she has not kissed me. And Jamison literally would have exploded if she had kissed him."

"Then this is serious? She wants more?"

"Joshua, I truly think not. After all, she intends on becoming a doctor, and that is years away. How could she cloud her future with such an emotional entanglement?"

Now it was Joshua who sighed. "I suppose you're right. It's just that . . ."

"I know," Gage said. "I know how you feel. I truly do."

And I wish I could tell him about Nora, Gage thought, *but I cannot. Not yet.*

CHAPTER FIVE

Cambridge, Massachusetts
November 1843

My dear Father,

I trust this letter will find you well. After speaking to Edgar on my last visit, I must urge you to place more confidence in his ability to schedule and monitor your business arrangements. It is true that he has no official training in business matters, but he can be an invaluable aid to assist you in marshaling out your time.

I will quiz him upon my return at the end of the month–so you had best follow my recommendations.

Harvard has been abuzz these past few months. It is said that the Prince of Belgium is planning on a visit. I am quite certain that few, if any, of my fellow students had any idea of who that might be. But they were charmed with the idea of having royalty visit.

And then there was this chap, William Weeks, who brought a rowboat with him to school. It was not exactly a rowboat–but a long and skinny boat only inches tall. He called it a rowing shell. Gads, does it skim the waters. Within a fortnight, there were a dozen others on the river, including me. It is a wonderful way to spend a few hours on the calm waters of the Back Bay.

Classes go on in a most predictable manner. I enjoy them and glean what I can from the professors' often inane observations. This semester I am attending two classes on the literary classics: Shakespeare, Milton, Chaucer, and the like. With these works, at least there can be no real dissention over what happened when.

I am glad that you and Mother are getting away this season. Christmas in London is said to be delightful. You must look up that new writer Dickens to determine if any of his work might be serialized in the News. I have heard that if his name appears on any British publication's masthead, the publisher sells an extra twenty thousand copies. That would be a great boost to the circulation.

Our delightfully eccentric inventor, Mr. Shirdler, claims to draw ever closer to his expected breakthrough. In his last correspondence with me, which included all manner of drawings and diagrams—none of which made the least bit of sense to me—he made claim that he should be ready within a month, perhaps two. Would it not be most fortuitous if we could best Mr. Morse and the government? Our investment would find itself tripled and more. I hope our investors are not losing patience.

I have found no further evidence on how the rumor of our interest in this new development found its way to Cambridge. I could not imagine any in the original group willing to compromise their financial stake by breaking confidence. I know it was neither you nor I.

I must admit, although I dislike myself completely for even considering this scenario, that I wonder if Walton somehow leaked the news to his friends and it wound up back at Cambridge. After all, my professor did mention the "son of Arthur Davis." But I am certain, due to Walton's complete disregard for all matters to do with business, that it could not have been his words that launched this rumor.

I suspect that nothing will come of this—of any bad consequence, that is.

Mr. Shirdler did suggest that additional funds might be required to finish his work. It was detailed in his letter to me—approaching the length of a missive. There is this fellow in the engineering school whom I trust completely who might be able to review Shirdler's notes to detect any charlatanism.

I have begun to realize afresh how energized and alive I feel in the midst of such dealings and intrigue. Perhaps you have been right all along—and that I am simply born to these tasks. Our successes of this past summer give me the confidence to make such a statement.

We have done quite well, have we not?

While in London, by the way, could you purchase a raincoat for me? There is a tailor in Knightsbridge who claims to produce the finest in coats. I have enclosed my measurements on a separate page.

Please take care on the voyage.

With all my regards,

Your son,

G. D.

He sealed the letter with a drop of wax the color of a winter cardinal, then addressed the envelope and tucked it into his breast pocket.

I shall not trust the vagaries of any postal system with this. There is that messenger outfit on Knowles Street. I am certain that they will guarantee its arrival before my parents set sail.

Humming a jaunty tune, he retrieved his greatcoat from the closet in the hall and set off.

And besides, Nora said she would be at the recital library this afternoon. Knowles Street is but a few steps away.

❧

"Surprised by my presence?" Gage asked as he slid in the chair opposite Nora. He had never been in this section of the library. A quartet of tables was arranged in a large square, almost like an island in the midst of a sea of books. One wall of shelves held flat portfolios tied with black ribbon that contained handwritten scores and orchestrations. At the far wall, on a raised podium, was a lone librarian, his head buried in a ledger. He peered up as Gage tried to silently walk past. He sniffed once, and Gage heard the harsh scratching of a pen on paper.

Nora sat surrounded by books and a volley of composition sheets, all marked with scribbled notes along with musical passages. She offered him a most welcoming smile.

"Yes," she replied in a whisper, setting her pencil down midstanza and twisting a lock of her hair with her finger. Gage recognized it as her one nervous gesture. "No. Well, I mean, I hoped you would come. Didn't I almost invite you when I mentioned that I would be here?"

Gage nodded. "It would have been hard for me not to be here. But not simply because of your obtuse invitation. I truly wanted to see you. You have been back at Cambridge since the end of September, and I have only seen you at recitals or at church services. There has not been a single time when it has simply been you and me."

Nora twisted and untwisted her hair. The dark strands shimmered with hints of red in the afternoon light.

"Well, there was that recital in Newton, wasn't there? We were alone then. At that tea following the cantata."

"Alone?" Gage said in mock surprise. "For perhaps three minutes . . . four at the outside. The remainder of the afternoon we had as an audience the entire deaconess board."

Nora lowered her head and tried to hide the sound of her musical giggling. "But none of them heard very well. And I know this because their piano was dreadfully out of tune. I thought I might actually injure my hearing had I played longer. So I am certain that they did not follow our conversation in completeness."

"You, Nora, recall things differently than they actually were. The piano was fine—at least to my ears. And the dear old ladies clung to us as if we were life rafts in the middle of an Atlantic storm."

From behind them came a harsh warning. "Quiet, please. This is a library and not a saloon."

Gage tightened his mouth so as not to laugh and leaned towards Nora. Her eyes sparkled with merriment.

"And I am certain our librarian friend has much call to enter saloons to determine their level of noise," Gage continued in a conspiratorial tone.

And with that Nora erupted into laughter, holding her hand over her mouth.

Gage watched as her shoulders shook and her black-red hair fell in waves, covering her face.

"Honestly, Miss Wilkes," the librarian called out, this time standing to mark his words, "if you can't control yourself with your guest, then I suggest that you two separate."

Gage, his back to the librarian, whispered, "I didn't realize we were joined." And with amused panic, he began to pat himself, as if checking for connections.

Nora doubled over again, filling the room with the music of her laughter.

The librarian called out a loud and brittle, "Hush."

For a minute, Gage and Nora remained silent. Then Gage patted his heart and twisted his face in surprise. "A connection . . . I knew it."

Nora's entire body shook with laughter this time—all the harder to stop because it had been forbidden.

The librarian slapped the desk. "This is intolerable. I must ask you two to leave immediately. You are disturbing everyone else."

Gage looked around. "He is seeing things. There is no one else here. Perhaps he really does visit saloons."

With that Nora lost her battle against laughter. She turned to the librarian, held her hand up in mute apology, and began to gather up her papers. "I'm sorry," she said, gasping for breath between her laughs. "We'll go. I'm sorry."

Gage helped her with her papers and hurried out under the baleful stare of the librarian.

Once outside in the cold air, Nora turned to Gage and shoved his arm. "You got me thrown out of a library! That has never happened to me before. What will my aunt and uncle say if they find out?"

"Me? I merely said a few words. It was your boisterous and most raucous laughter that did it. A most *bourgeois* exhibition, I must say. And I am quite sure that it will come as no surprise to your aunt and uncle. They have been expecting an outburst like this all along."

As she readied to offer another push, Gage darted down the street. She gave chase, laughing and calling out for him to stop and take his medicine like a man.

He did not stop until they were outside the door of The Astor Rose, a fine restaurant by Cambridge's standards, just south of Harvard's campus. Out of breath, they both stopped, and she fell into his arms for support.

"You run fast for a woman," he said breathlessly. "I thought you might actually catch me."

She shoved him again. "Good wind and endurance. All those voice lessons. And digging up potatoes as a child."

He delighted in holding her, even if it was only done in play.

"I knew you were a potato farmer after all. I knew it."

She stepped away from him and, with her free hand, smoothed at her hair, turning her head in a delicate manner. The sunlight fell on her face, revealing her flushed cheeks and bright eyes. She gazed up at him, offering him a slow, deliberate smile.

A voice echoed in his head, *I can bear this no longer.*

He hesitated only a sliver of a second. Lifting her chin, he bent and kissed her.

She closed her eyes only at the last possible moment. He felt her lips, soft and pliant, tremble as a flower in a breeze. Her arms tightened around him.

She has kissed me in return, his thoughts cried out.

He stepped back. As he stared down at her, her eyes fluttered open. Her cheeks were rosier than before.

"And now you want to get us thrown off a public street? Gage, you are incorrigible."

He looked about them on the street, as if he thought she had actually noticed a constable bearing down on them.

"Incorrigible . . . yes, I admit it. And in addition, I am now famished." He pointed to the doorway in front of them."Shall we stop in here for refreshment?"

Nora suddenly became aware of the restaurant beside them. "And you can afford this? As a college student?"

"Let's just say I can afford to splurge every now and again."

She studied his face and eyes. "Well, then, if you insist. I will consider this to be in payment for your misbehavior today."

If misbehavior gets me time alone with you, then I shall continue my life of crime, he thought happily.

⟡

Nora sat back, satisfaction on her face. The waiter swooped down on her plate and noiselessly carried it away.

"Did you enjoy everything?" Gage asked.

"This was, without a doubt, the finest meal I have ever eaten," Nora said with a long sigh. "Everything was perfect."

"Best meal ever? Really?"

Nora nodded. "My mother is a wonderful woman, but she is not an accomplished cook. Meat and potatoes."

"More potatoes than meat, I imagine," Gage added and smiled. "Potato stew and potato cakes and potato bread and potato wine and the like."

"I knew you were incorrigible," she replied. "I just never realized how deep that character flaw extended."

Gage could not help but smile. The meal had been wonderful. Every taste became all the more vibrant and rich because of his companion. He had been surprised that she agreed to his impromptu and most impulsive invitation.

And what was even a greater surprise was that she did not mention his impulsive kiss again during their entire meal.

She dabbed at her lips with her napkin. "And just how often do you do this?" she asked with a sweep of her hand.

"Do what? Have dinner?"

"No, you silly."

"Every day—at least once."

"Be serious, Gage. I want to know."

"How often do I do what?"

"Dine in such expensive places."

"Not often."

She eyed him as if she did not quite accept that as truth.

"Well, not very often, at any rate."

"And you can afford all this? Without even considering the cost? I am sure this meal will cost you what my father earns in a week."

Gage drew himself up closer to the table and folded his hands. "I have not mentioned much about my financial situation before. I thought it might not be appropriate."

Nora looked surprised. "I am not prying, Gage. I truly am not. I just do not want you to go into debt over me. I am sorry for asking."

The mood of the evening shifted, and Gage felt a chill. Nora appeared as if chastised.

"I did not mean that I thought you were prying, Nora. I just seldom speak about my family's finances."

She did not speak, and he continued. "The cost of this meal is inconsequential to me, Nora. Our family is quite . . . secure. I assist my father in many of his business dealings and am well compensated for it."

When Nora next looked up at him, her eyes caught the light of the candles at their table. She smiled. "Then if you are rich . . . may I order dessert? I have never eaten cherries *flambé* before."

Gage breathed a great sigh of relief. "By all means. Cherries on fire it is."

<hr />

The waiter scooped up the last bit of the sweet cherry mixture out of the silver serving dish and placed it on Nora's plate. Gage waved his share off and asked for coffee instead. She took great delight in finishing the last small spot of dessert.

"So, you are really a wealthy man, then?" she asked softly.

Gage nodded. "I am. I hope that does not disappoint you." He gazed straight into her eyes.

"It doesn't. . . . Really wealthy?"

Gage nodded again. "Wealthy enough."

Nora shook her head. "I would have never guessed it. I mean, you are always very finely attired, but the way you followed me to all those small recitals and bad church cantatas, I never would have imagined a man of wealth and status weathering such dismal performances. You could have your pick of the best of everything. And yet you came to see me."

"Well, when I go to the opera, the contralto seldom chases me down the street afterwards."

"I am sure she would if she knew you better," Nora replied as she reached up and twisted her hair with her finger.

Gage smiled to himself.

"Rich?" she asked again with a sly smile.

He gave another slight nod.

"And you enjoy all of it—secret deals and smoke-filled rooms and endless paperwork? You really find pleasure in it all? I am just so curious, because you do not seem to fit my idea of a business baron."

"Well, I don't smoke and I seldom do paperwork. But there are deals to be sure . . . and contracts and the like. And I do enjoy that part of it. I am very good at it. Everyone would agree."

She waited a moment.

"Everyone?"

"I guess so, Nora. It's not the money that I truly like, but it is the way we all keep count. I know there are those at Harvard who think the real value in the world is truth and beauty and poetry and the like. I enjoy all that—I truly do—but that is not what makes the world go round—or stay in motion. It is not what causes my heart to beat faster."

"It's not?"

"No. Money does that. It's what I know. I am good at making it. It is in my blood. It, above all other things, is what I have faith in."

Nora studied him. He knew she wanted to say something, but she hesitated.

So he continued. "Someone has to be skilled at this. Otherwise, America would not continue expanding. There are incredible opportunities out there in industrial development. There are factories to be built and products to be marketed. And factories will employ lots of willing workers who will use their earnings and purchase all those products. People like me are needed. I have great faith in the future of America, too. Money and America—that's my religion."

He meant his words to be mostly playful and boastful, with just a hint of his more serious ambition. But as he watched Nora's expression, he realized she was hearing the wrong words. Every idea he attempted to describe came out canted and odd. And if he were to backtrack on them now, it would appear he was simply saying the words Nora wanted to hear.

That he could not do. He may be many things, but a calculating opportunist in matters of the heart was not one of them.

"Nora," he said, reaching for her hand, "it is not as if I only dream of money and success. There is more to me as well. I do value the fine arts and culture and the rest. But a man must follow what he is best at. If a man is to deny his strengths, then what sort of life will he lead? I am skilled at business. I admit that. And as a result, I am sure I will become even wealthier than my father. There should be no shame in that."

He found himself marveling at his openness. He had never discussed his dreams and goals with anyone before. His words gave his ambitions the clarity and dimension that they lacked up until this moment.

"America needs people like me, Nora. It does. America is growing and moving. Every day it moves farther and farther west. People like me will build railroads and excavate mines and open stores and erect factories to make the things settlers need. There is a grace and poetry to that as well."

"I'm certain there is, Gage. And I understand what you're saying. I commend you for having such an expansive vision. You're right. America does need people just like you."

But the smile she gave him seemed not as full as usual and perhaps a little forced, Gage thought. "Someone needs to have faith in America," he said firmly, as if trying to convince himself. "And part of that faith is to have faith in money and what it can build and provide. Becoming wealthy is just a by-product—a nice by-product, of course—but it is the only goal in my life."

She placed her hand over his. "Gage, this has been a wonderful dinner. And you have been the most marvelous of hosts. But it is growing late, and I have promised my aunt and uncle that I would return in time for a late supper with them." She laughed. "And just how will I explain the fact that I will not be able to eat a single bite of it? Oh, Gage, you continue to vex me even when you are not at my side."

Gage smiled. The chill he had felt earlier seemed to disappear. He stood, offered her his arm, and escorted her out. "We could run back to your home. That might build an appetite for you? Shall we?"

* ❦ *

His disappointment was obvious and thorough. Gage had hoped Nora might accompany him to New York for a "day of thanks" celebration of God's blessings. And Gage was very thankful for Nora. So he had made tentative arrangements for his mother's spinster sister to act as their official chaperone.

But Nora declined his invitation, offering him the most sincere regrets. "Gage, it sounds like a truly marvelous time, yet my parents are expecting me—as well as my aunt and uncle. I couldn't disappoint them."

Gage claimed that he understood, although he had hoped that a week in New York might be alluring enough to change her mind. It was not.

He remained worried over his expansive monologue over dinner at The Astor Rose. Could his ambitions and dreams of industry and money have caused Nora to reconsider her opinion of him? His worry had proved groundless to date. She remained cordial on their long walk back to her residence that afternoon, and she received him quite warmly the next time he called.

But now, after her saying no to his invitation, he would be alone for an entire week. Other than Walton, and a skeleton staff at the family home, no one would be in attendance that last week of November.

And Gage was not fond of being alone.

He was even less fond of being alone with Walton. His short

vacation from classes appeared so bleak—even Edgar planned to visit his sister in Utica.

But Gage was nothing if not resourceful.

Instead of inviting a single guest, he invited three: Joshua, Hannah, and Jamison, his closest friends on campus, and those most likely to be immune from the effects of his obvious wealth. While they all knew he had resources, none of them knew to just what extent. Although Hannah knew most of his family and was aware of their social position, she had never been to the family home.

But he nevertheless trusted that none of his friends would change their attitude towards him because of the extent of his wealth.

Until you see how a man lives, his father said, you have no clear concept as to his riches.

Gage believed that Joshua would be immune to the distractions of his riches, that Jamison was too cynical to admit to any attraction, and that Hannah would find much of the lure almost familiar, owing to her family's lost wealth.

New York City

After his guests had been shown to their rooms, Gage tossed his coat and hat on his bed and hurried down to the kitchen. It was midafternoon, and he wanted servings of tea and coffee to be readied before they left for the evening.

The trip from Cambridge to New York City and the Davis manse had been pleasant enough but not totally restful. Gage disliked having to battle with the crowds who seemed to multiply during this season. He and his guests traveled on the regular train and purchased seats in the coach section. It was a deliberate choice. Gage had decided not to schedule his father's private car. *That might be too ostentatious,* he had determined to himself.

He felt at ease now, enveloped in the cushioned luxury of his parents' home.

The elegant Greek Revival mansion was the family's main residence and occupied nearly an entire city block. Its impressive columned facade hinted at what one would find inside—enormous rooms of priceless antiques, furnishings, and art from all over the world.

Gage took the steps on the back staircase two at a time. At the bottom he nearly collided with Walton, who appeared to be hulking in the shadows.

"Gage, so nice of you to drop by," Walton said, with a hiss in his tone.

I have been home less than a minute, and it has already begun, Gage thought. "Walton, let's not start this. I have friends here. It would be nice if we could all remain civil in the presence of my guests."

"Friends?"

"Three chums from Harvard. You know one of them. Hannah Collins from Philadelphia."

Walton soured his lips. "A Collins? Why her? And who are the other two?"

Gage ignored his caustic remark. "Jamison Pike and Joshua Quittner."

Walton's eyes closed to slits. "And you invited them for the night?"

"Not the night. The entire week. For the thanksgiving observance. I promised I would show them the sights of New York."

Walton exploded like a wet log tossed on a blazing fire. "A week! How dare you! No one asked if I minded. Now I have three of your 'chums' parading about here all vacation long. The least you could have done was notify me. I was expecting a week of peace and quiet, and now I have to deal with four Harvard ruffians."

"Calm down," Gage replied, more sharply than he wanted to. "None of us are ruffians, by the way. And this is my house too, Walton. The last time I checked with Father, he has not yet signed it over to you. So be civil if you can."

"Easy for you to ask, little brother. You're not the one being imposed upon."

Gage was within an inch of grabbing his older brother by the lapels and pushing him against the wall. "Listen, Walton, you are seldom in attendance at any function here. You're usually locked in your room or slinking about the back stairways like you are now.

And the place is spacious enough. Of what concern are a few guests to you?"

Walton thumped his forefinger on Gage's chest. "Listen! It's all my concern. I'm the firstborn here—not you! And don't you forget it. Your little friends can stay—but keep them out of my way."

And with that he turned and sidled up the steps. At the top he paused and pivoted toward Gage, his face near hidden in the darkness. His words were malevolent, each one absorbing another flicker of light from the hall. "And why did you not invite the enchanting Miss Wilkes? I am sure that with Mother and Father gone you could have had a gay time."

Without thinking, Gage leapt up the steps. "How do you know about her? I never mentioned her name before. Did you intercept a letter? Tell me!"

Walton sniffed and turned away. "There are a great many things I know, little brother, and the how and why are of no concern to you," he said before disappearing.

Gage sat down on the top step and remained there for nearly ten minutes, until his emotions returned to normal.

He does this every time, Gage chided himself, *and every time I let him win by being stupid and replying in kind. Why don't I simply ignore him?*

Gage took a deep breath and began to walk toward the kitchen.

And how did he find out about Nora? I am sure that he saw an envelope addressed to me. But if he stole one of her letters, I will ignore my natural restraint and thrash him soundly—brother or not.

❦

Hannah breezed into the parlor and spun about, holding the folds of her dress as a dancer might. The dress swirled like an umbrella in the rain.

"Am I presentable?" she asked. "Will this dowdy old frock pass New York muster?"

"I am certain that it will, for all eyes will be on me this evening," Gage replied.

"Vanity, thy name is Gage Davis."

"Just being realistic," he said.

"And this bag—is it too large for an evening in the big city?"

Gage eyed it critically. "No—I think it is just fine. Remember, we are not meeting with the cream of high society this evening. It will be a simple, quiet dinner with friends."

Hannah swept into a chair close to the warm hearth. "And where are our two gentleman friends? I have always assumed that it was womenfolk who spent too much time getting prepared for an evening. I think my speedy assembly tonight disproves that old tale."

"You might be right, Hannah, but remember this—you womenfolk have a much more pleasing starting line than men do. It takes a great deal of effort to turn the mug of someone like Joshua into a presentable public offering."

"And now I know that you jest. Joshua would look presentable regardless of his attire or coiffure—even in sackcloth and ashes."

"Hannah," Gage said playfully, "I had thought you of all people would not place a great deal of importance on a man's physical attributes. I thought you would be interested purely in his intellectual abilities."

"Well, pshaw again. I have eyes and I use them," she said, placing her hands on her hips in a defiant gesture. "As I am sure you never do with those of the 'gentler' sex."

Pretending to be shocked, Gage placed his hand on his heart. "Hannah, I am deeply wounded."

"Gage Davis! You are impossible," she said, launching her purse at him.

"True, but that is what makes me so endearing."

Hannah smoothed her skirt and straightened the cuffs on her blouse. The next several moments were quiet save the snap and hiss of the fire. Gage returned to his reading as Hannah stared around at the richness of the room and the exquisite details of decoration.

Finally Gage folded the paper and placed it on the table next to him. "What are you thinking?"

She hesitated before replying. "Does it ever bother you?"

"Does what ever bother me?"

"All this," she said with a sweep of her hand. "Having all this. Living in such luxury."

Surprised by the query, Gage responded, "No. Why would it? It is ours. And we come by it honestly."

Hannah picked a piece of lint from her dress. "It's just that you have so much. This is the most opulent home I have ever been in. Why, the furnishings in this room alone are a hundred times more valuable than . . . than Joshua's entire village in Ohio."

"I think that's an exaggeration. But even if it were true, is that a bother?"

Hannah focused on the fire, avoiding Gage's eyes. "It's just that I think of all the less privileged. I wonder why some have so much and some have so little."

Gage felt his cheeks flush. "And I should feel guilty for being born in a family where perseverance and dedication are valued? My father worked hard for this. I have worked hard as well."

"I remember you telling me something . . . and let me paraphrase it . . . Joshua's hard work and your hard work being two different kinds of work."

Gage stood up in frustration. "And I see you have made a vow of poverty as well."

Now Hannah swiveled toward him, her eyes flashing in anger, her mouth agape.

"I know that what you are wearing is last year's fashion," he continued, "but, I imagine, still hundreds of times more dear than any gown in Shawnee."

Hannah stood as well. "It's not the same thing, and you know it," she stated harshly.

"Oh, really? I daresay it is exactly the same thing. And it's called *hypocrisy* the last time I checked."

"Hypocrisy?"

"Yes, that's what I said. And I'm sorry if it hits close to home."

They glared at each other.

"What about hypocrisy?" Joshua asked as he and Jamison entered the room. "Are you talking about us in our absence?"

Hannah and Gage stared at each other one last time, then turned away.

"They must have been," Jamison said, "for they both are flushed with embarrassment. But fear not, we will not press you to find out which one of us has been so labeled. After all, Joshua knows it is him and there is no sense in shaming the lad further."

Joshua began laughing. "The true hypocrite is the one who never recognizes his own hypocrisy. And we all know who that is, don't we, Jamison?"

Gage held up his hand and whistled. "Enough, enough now. I know that we are nearly famished—and perhaps that has made us all a bit testy. But I must add that all of the blame is on you two gentlemen and the inordinate time you took preparing."

Hannah's icy glare softened, and at last, she offered her friends a smile. "As if the extra time did either of you any good!"

Then she bolted from the room, skirt swishing, heading for the front door and the waiting carriage.

The quartet of Irish sailors took to the stage in an enthusiastic storm. The crowd, packed into a long narrow storefront facing the docks, responded with shouts and calls and whistles. A slight young lad stepped out and held up his hands for quiet. In a nearly opaque accent, he shouted over the remaining din that he and his friends would be performing a few songs from back home.

A tin pennywhistle appeared, then a fiddle and a concertina, and within minutes the young man was dancing and singing, and the room was awash with energetic music.

Gage and Jamison bobbed to the music, and Hannah clapped her hands. Joshua was the only one who resisted at first, but he finally gave in and clapped as best he could with the fast rhythm of the songs.

On the other side of the room, a tightly muscled man rose, his gold earring glinting in the lantern light. On the man's shoulder was the tattoo of an eagle, clutching a ship in its talons. Because of his bulk, he looked incapable of delicate maneuvers. However, he extended his hand to a woman next to him and bowed. In a moment, the two were doing a jig punctuated with shouts and complex steps and jumps as the band played furiously. People around began to clap louder and shout encouragement. When the last note died out, the room exploded in applause and cheerful bellows. The band ignored all the requests for additional songs as they made their way to the bar.

Gage beamed at his friends as the shouting and laughter ebbed to a modest roar. Everyone was smiling. And without saying a word, the three men undid their ties, letting the black silk hang limply around their necks. The four from Harvard were not the only well-dressed patrons at the shipyard establishment. Mingled in the crowd were ten or so other patrons in evening suits and gowns. Even a top hat or two dotted the tables at the rear.

"There is no better place for such joyful music," Gage explained.

"How did you find out about a spot like this?" Jamison asked. "I would never have imagined such an intermingling of classes."

"If one is willing and open, one can find hundreds of such places. That is what makes New York such a rare jewel. Much more liberal than Boston or Cambridge, for certain, in some regards."

No wait staff had yet visited the table and when a serving girl showed up with a platter of food, all but Gage looked surprised. Except for Melinda at the Destiny Café, none had ever seen a female waiter before.

"These are Dublin coddles and these are boxty cakes," he explained. "It's my regular order here. They assumed you would all join me. Will you? It's not fancy food, but it is most filling."

No one had to be persuaded to partake, and before the band returned to the stage, the entire platter was consumed.

"I can order more," Gage offered. "Are any of you still hungry?"

Joshua and Jamison immediately raised their hands in protest, groaning that another bite would cause them all to explode. Hannah simply slumped to the table, cradling her head in her hands.

The quartet had now moved, from the bright jig music, to more plaintive and sad ballads of home and hearth. Melancholy voices raised in song, and a room-sized chorus joined in the haunting refrain.

Gage stretched. Checking his pocketwatch, he said, "It is now 2:30 in the morning. It's time to go, friends. We have a full schedule tomorrow, and I know some of us need more beauty sleep than others. And I shall be a gentleman and resist naming names."

Jamison and Joshua slipped out first, hoping to secure a carriage. Gage warned that they were not plentiful in this stretch of the city. Hannah remained with him as he called the waitress over to settle their accounts.

It was obvious that he did not want to be overheard, but Hannah could not help listening to his words.

"And, Marie, how is the family?" he asked.

"All are fine, Mr. Davis, and I thank you most kindly for asking."

"And the little one—recovered from his bout with the chilblains?"

"Indeed he has. And my mother offers a thousand thanks for your help with the doctor and all."

Gage acknowledged her words with a simple smile. He took two twenty-dollar gold pieces from his pocket and forced them into her hand. It was perhaps five times the value of the meal itself.

"Now you take care. And give the little one a hug for me."

The waitress appeared as if she were about to protest and give the coins back when Gage held up his hands. "I'll hear none of it. You always remember what I like to eat, and you hold an open table for me. I appreciate that. And this is the way I show that appreciation."

And with that, he rose, took Hannah by the hand, and went out into the chilly night air.

❦

A bell in the distance chimed three times. The peals reverberated along the narrow canyons of the streets of lower Manhattan. The sounds were mixed with muffled voices, faint music, and the thudding *clop-clop-clops* of horse-drawn hackneys. The sounds ebbed and swelled down the streets like a slow, indistinct tide.

"It's three o'clock in the morning," Joshua said aloud and in obvious amazement. "I do not think, in my entire life, I have ever been
willfully awake at this hour."

"And this bad influence on your life is Gage's fault," Hannah called
out. "He has kept us all out too late."

Jamison smirked. "And he has held a gun to you to keep you here?
You had no chance to make your escape?"

"None whatsoever. I have been held captive," she replied with a
laugh. "And while I did not see a gun *per se,* I am sure that he had
one. How else could you explain Joshua's wanton behavior?"

Joshua bristled. "I have not done anything wanton. I have
observed others doing wanton things, but that does not make me
wanton."

Jamison clasped his arm around Joshua's shoulder. "And you are
sure of that, my friend. Is that a sound theological principle?"

Gage was at Joshua's other side.

"Do not answer him, Joshua. This is a time of discovery and
exploration—not a time for theological discussions. And besides,
there's our carriage. I do think it is time I got you all home. We have
a busy week ahead, and I don't want to exhaust you on our first
night out."

❧

"So tell me, Joshua," Gage said later in the week as the four friends
jostled through the very well-dressed crowd, "what you think of the
opera. And do not censure your views. I want the truth."

The crowds bumped and flowed about them, jockeying for a
better position near the curb and the line of waiting hackneys.

"Well, I was amazed by the scenery and the decorations of the
stage. Until this evening I could not imagine that a barge on the
Nile could be so faithfully recreated within a building. It was most
impressive."

"But what of the singing?" asked Jamison. "You're the only one
who has never seen such a performance and can provide a true
review."

Joshua looked slightly panicked.

"I will not be offended," Gage promised.

"But how can I insult the performance when the tickets were a gift?" Joshua asked. "That hardly seems proper."

"I assure you, I can take it. Besides, the tickets are just a portion of the family's allotment. Extras are useful for entertaining. They would have gone unused if we had not taken them."

Swallowing, Joshua replied. "At first I thought I was simply not accustomed to the songs or lyrics because I could not make out a single word anyone was singing. Don't laugh, but it was not until the first act was nearly over that I realized they were all singing in a foreign language."

Gage's eyebrows lifted. "Truly?"

Joshua shrugged and held up his hands in surrender. Obviously, he was embarrassed, though he offered a wide smile in his defense. "I suspect I might have known or read about the fact that most operas are done in Italian—or is that German? And yet until tonight, I had never heard an opera in person. And even after tonight, after hearing one, I still have a very scant idea on what the story was about. I know it involved Cleopatra and I have the basic plot points down, but even at the end, I remained puzzled. I could make out a few words because of my training in Latin, but very few. One thing does puzzle me, however. Does everyone in New York speak Italian?"

Jamison and Hannah giggled as Gage slapped his arm around Joshua's shoulder.

"I suspect none of this crowd does. It's just that the story is familiar to most of them. They have seen it a season or two ago. And I will let you in on a secret that is not well kept—the majority of this crowd simply goes to the opera to be seen. The rest of the singing and music is simply an amusing diversion, a pleasant backdrop for their strutting and preening."

Jamison added brightly, "Since I dozed off during the last bit, the performance has met my standards for a cultural event of the highest order."

"And what standard is that?" Hannah asked.

"It was boring enough to put me to sleep in front of a thousand people. If it's culture, it must be boring."

"Well, then," Gage said, "what I have planned next should be the exact opposite of your standards, Jamison. I hope you are all ready for it."

❧

The sun was but a moment from gilding the East River. Of the four, Gage remained the most alert. The other three slumped in various stages of weariness against the leather seats of the hired carriage.

Following the opera, Gage had visited another favorite after-hours establishment—this one with a decidedly Italian atmosphere. Loud music, heaping plates of noodles, and cloves of garlic hanging about the restaurant were in stark, juicy contrast to the refined and rarified atmosphere of the opera.

"Surely you cannot be tired yet? We have just begun."

Joshua simply moaned and closed his eyes. Hannah dismissed Gage with a tired wave of her hand. Jamison shook his head in disbelief.

"You mean this is normal for everyone in New York City? Being awake for both sunset and sunrise?" he asked.

"No," Gage said, chuckling, "and I must admit that even for me, such late hours are not the norm. But there is the occasional meeting that defies the clock. And then there is all the entertaining that accompanies such business."

"My stars," Hannah said, her eyes nearly closed, "and I thought business was an easy affair. Talk a little. Sign a contract or two. If I had to do this more often than once a year, I would be in hospital, for certain."

She nodded in Joshua's direction. His breath was steady, his limbs relaxed.

"Shhh," she whispered. "One of the faithful has given up the ghost."

"Well, we are blocks from home. Let him sleep until then." Gage turned to Jamison. "And you and I had best get cleaned up quickly.

I have taken the liberty of making an appointment this morning with Mr. Ralph Harshon, the editor of the *New York World.* I hope you don't mind, but I think that you should meet him."

Jamison sat up as if jolted by lightning. "What! With Harshon of the *New York World!* But I didn't prepare. I didn't bring any of my work. I can't . . . I mean . . . he's the editor."

Gage smiled. "Yes, I know that. And I took the liberty of sending him past copies of the *Crimson Review.* He knows your work."

"But . . . but Gage . . . why? I was not aware you even knew the man."

"Well, Father does have investments in several newspapers. The *New York World* is the largest of them. That's why you have this appointment."

Jamison ran his hand over his face. "When? I need a shave and a bath and my clothes need a pressing and . . ."

"You have time, Jamison. You have time. There is Edgar, remember? Our appointment is not until 10:00. And that will leave our two innocents plenty of time to recuperate from last night."

By now, Hannah, as well, had fallen asleep, leaning heavily against Joshua, almost as if she were using him as a pillow.

"Relax, friend. We have ample time for breakfast. Ample time indeed."

"So the interview went well?" Gage asked as he and Jamison entered Tubb's, a tavern several doors down from the newspaper offices. The walls were decorated with framed front pages from newspapers around the world.

"Very well, I think. Harshon is a legend in newspaper circles, though he was nothing like his reputation."

"He wasn't drunk and he didn't throw any copyboys out of the window?"

"Exactly. He was a nice fellow. He said he admired my work. It needed polishing, of course, and one writes with a leaner prose for a newspaper. The *Crimson Review* approves of its reporters embellishing and adding gilding to the stories. Harshon doesn't."

101

"Did he offer you a job?"

They sat down at a nearly clean table. Gage swept the remaining crumbs away with his sleeve. Before Jamison could answer, a waiter appeared, and Gage ordered two of the daily specials and a pot of strong coffee.

"No, he didn't exactly do that. I told him that I want to finish my studies at Harvard. He said I could learn all I need to learn by doing it rather than studying it. The pity is that I am sure he is right. He said one learns how to be a reporter and a writer by reporting and writing—not by answering inane questions from a professor who has never written under a deadline."

"But did he offer you a job? I don't want to see you working at the *Times* or the *Globe*."

Jamison took a long sip of his coffee.

"At his insistence, I told him again that nothing would happen until graduation. While I may have my differences with my parents, I do need to honor their wish to see me graduate. He said to come see him as soon as I take off the ridiculous mortarboard cap they will make us all wear that day."

"That's good, as long as you promise me that you'll take him up on his offer."

"That I promise," Jamison said. Then he added, "And I want to thank you for this. I never could have gotten in to see him if it wasn't for your help."

Gage waved off his thanks.

"It was truly a trifling. And as I said, your talent would have been sufficient. I simply made sure you saw the right person first. No sense in wasting your talents by starting as some copyboy."

The two ate their meal without further discussion. The din of conversation grew around them. The staccato noise of reporters and typesetters and runners slipped in and out, all shouting out orders for meals and drinks.

Gage saw that the jangling clamor of the place enlivened and energized Jamison. Without being obvious, he watched every move that everyone made. One could soon spot the senior reporters, dressed in well-tailored suits, and the copyboys, with ink smudges on their shirts and hands, and the typesetters, nearly bathed in lead dust and ink. Snatches of conversation clattered in numerous choruses, as if peppered with the clanking rhythm of the newsroom and printing press.

Gage finally spoke after the lunch rush had passed. "You like this, don't you, Jamison?"

It was several moments until Jamison answered. "I have never felt more alive than today. I am exhausted and almost disoriented from lack of sleep, but I am . . . I am at home here." He lowered his eyes and stared at his hands lying flat on the table. "I know that people call me a cynic. And I suppose that is often accurate. But here all that world-weary, doubting skepticism is gone. This is life. Doing this, being part of all this—it would make everything right." He looked up into Gage's face. "Do you know what I'm trying to say? It's as if everything else is but a faint rehearsal for life. When I can live here and do what these people are doing—that's when I really will understand life," Jamison finished.

"I do know what you're saying. I think I feel the same way about business and industry and negotiation. That's when I am most alive."

Jamison smiled in agreement.

Then Gage said, "Can I ask you a question, Jamison?"

"By all means."

"Have you ever been in love?"

"With a woman?"

Gage slapped his shoulder. "No—with a donkey. Of course with a woman."

Jamison acted as if the slap had bruised him deeply. "I simply didn't expect such a question from you. Based on your reputation on campus as a ladies' man, I would have thought you knew all there is to know of love."

"Well, I can assure you again that reputations are not always to be believed," Gage said.

"To answer your question—I have not. There was a young lady

back home in Pittsburgh whom I escorted to several events. While I was delighted to be with her, I could not construe that to be love."

Neither of them spoke for several moments.

"Have you been in love, Gage? Are you now? Is that why you asked?"

Gage looked away as if he were pondering a confusing question.

"It is this talk of the future and what drives our passions," he replied. "But if I answer this, you must assure me that it will remain a confidence between us."

"You can trust me, Gage. I would have no one to tell and nothing to gain for the telling. . . . So are you in love? Recently I have noticed occasions when it appears that your thoughts are elsewhere."

"I'm not certain," Gage admitted. "There is a woman—Nora Wilkes is her name. I find myself thinking about her more and more often. Like now, for instance. But I do not know if that is love—being preoccupied with someone, that is."

"I don't think it is."

"Then I may not be in love at all."

"Is this Nora attractive?"

Gage's eyes appeared to cloud. "She is the total essence of all things gracious and feminine, I would say."

"Have you kissed her?"

At first Gage jumped, shocked. Then he relaxed, smiled broadly, and replied, "A gentlemen never expounds on such matters."

"And I have my answer," Jamison laughed.

"But just now we spoke of passion. Yours is to write. Mine is to captain some new industry. Those are our passions, are they not?"

"They appear to be."

"But her passion involves music and concerts and recitals. She sings like an angel. I ask myself if I can share that with her—and do it enthusiastically."

"But I have seen you at concerts, Gage. You appear to enjoy them. And I don't think you are that good an actor to fool me."

"And I think I can be," Gage said. "But there is something else. I'm not sure this is the same as a passion."

"And that is?" Jamison asked.

"It appears that Nora is a churchgoer. And I know that she wants me to share that with her as well. I told her that we support the church around our corner—and support it most handsomely, I might add. I believe that pleases God. I attend church when I can and when convenient. Is that not enough? Do I need to get down on my knees and wear sackcloth and ashes? She has said as much at times that the rich men of the world will need to find humility someday."

Jamison rubbed his chin. "Have you asked Joshua about it? He's our resident cleric. He would know the answer."

Gage snorted. "He would want me in church every time the doors open. That would be foolishness to me. Isn't God something you experience on your own? Does one need to enter a building every week to assure him and others that you believe? And does not my becoming wealthy indicate a certain level of God's blessing?"

"I would say so. But I must add this caveat. I know it would not appear to be true, but I grew up in a parsonage. My father is a rector of one of the larger churches in Pittsburgh."

Surprised, Gage replied, "Are you serious? I would have never thought that of you. You appear much too world weary to have such a background."

"I believe I am weary simply because of my background. And I beg you not to tell anyone about this. All too soon they will begin to have unrealistic expectations about my knowledge."

Gage nodded as if he understood.

"But if you ask me, Gage, I would think that you need not share every passion with a woman. There are some things that men appreciate more—like hunting or riding. Women are not expected to participate in those. Then there are the feminine pursuits of cooking and child rearing and things of a domestic nature. A man needs to grab hold of all of life—that is what drives his passion. A woman needs a home and hearth—and that's what drives her."

"So where does that leave Hannah?" Gage asked.

"Our Hannah?" Jamison asked thoughtfully. "I would say she is a social and cultural aberration. Some women simply choose not to listen to the proper version—my version—of reality."

Both men burst out laughing.

"It has been too long a day. We both need to repair ourselves to our rooms for some much-needed rest. I suggest that we do so now, before we fall asleep here at our table. Come, Jamison. Let's go home. Perhaps we can continue our talk this evening."

"Perhaps you might ask Hannah if my ideas are correct?"

Gage looked puzzled. "But why not ask her yourself? After all, they are your theories, not mine."

Jamison leaned in close, as if unwilling to be overheard. "Because I would fear for my personal safety. As I said, our Hannah is that one in a million aberration."

"In other words, she would land a blow upside your head," Gage said.

Jamison grinned and touched his finger to his nose. "Exactly. And I have better use for my head than that."

CHAPTER SIX

New York City
November 1843

Gage stayed on in New York City for two days after
he saw his friends off at the train depot.

"A bit of business to attend to. I'll be back before classes resume."

And when he returned home, on the silver tray in his office lay a
thin letter.

London
October 30, 1843

My dear son 'Gage,

*I assume that this letter will reach you before we return. One never can
be sure with the post. I see now how valuable a telegraph invention will be.
Communication in an instant! Such wonders! Business will be revolution-
ized.*

*Mother has enjoyed herself as she mentioned. She has purchased a ship's
hold worth of royal antiques from the French. That's what the French
claim. Uncomfortable chairs if you ask me, and we have better at home.*

Managed to find the fellow Dickens you told me of. He does seem to have quite the following here–papers splash his name about. Said I was interested in using some of his material. We did not talk specifics, but I think the English are so civil and polite that they don't ask for what they might actually deserve. He mentioned tea, and I'll bring a contract.

We plan on returning home as scheduled. Let Edgar know. He should prepare then a bit. I would like to have a familiar face at the dock.

All the best,

Father

Gage examined the letter, then stared out on the darkened street. He was glad the trip was going well, but his father mentioned nothing of the meetings planned with potential investors and partners. His father's wording seemed odd and out of joint, as if his words simply tumbled out onto the paper.

Perhaps it is simply the pressures of the voyage and strange food, Gage told himself. *I am sure Father is in control of things.*

He rose and placed another log on the fire, warming his hands. But a sudden chill shivered up his spine.

I will insist that Edgar stay close to him–and tell me if there are any changes in his behavior.

Gage walked back to his desk, trying to push the troubling images out of his thoughts.

FROM THE JOURNAL OF GAGE DAVIS
APRIL 1844

It has been months since I added a single word to these pages. I consistently find myself in violation of my own vow to be more prolific.

Perhaps I can catch up on the highlights of the past few months.

Thanksgiving found me in New York and at home. What made the holiday interesting was that I invited my chums from Harvard: Joshua, Jamison, and Hannah.

Such a grand time we had!

I suspect we had to close Joshua's jaw numerous times a day, so great was his amazement at certain sights he visited. One evening as we were coming home at 3:00 A.M., he quipped that in all his life he was never intentionally awake at that hour.

The opera and the galleries and the museums all sent him into a whirl. It is great fun for me to expose the innocent to such treats. I fear that sometimes in my enthusiasm to expose him to the broader world out there I risk jading his soul in the process. So far I think he has eluded the temptations. He still frowns with gusto if anyone nearby orders ale or spends too long gazing at an attractive servant girl. And the night at Downy's on the waterfront—when the crowd began to dance—I thought he would have to leave the building. But to his credit, he did not, and at the end of the evening was clapping in time with the band. I suspect he saw them as uneducated natives from another land and that the jigs and pennywhistle and all were simply a result of their impoverished heathen culture.

But then again, aren't the Irish a Christian race? After all, isn't St. Patrick one of their favorites? True, Catholics and Protestants have some bad blood between them, but I would think in our modern times, those ancient grudges should be settled and forgotten.

It is curious. The fellow whom I thought I had the least in common with—Jamison—is the one I find easiest to be with.

He is not judgmental. It's just that he believes everyone is always wrong—other than himself, that is.

"If I were king, there would be changes made," he says often. Sometimes I think he secretly wants it to be so. He distrusts so joyfully. "Nothing is as it seems," he says. "Those doing good for the poor are simply in it for the adoration," he says. "Those whose goal is the accumulation of money are simply looking for validation. Those involved in culture have simply run out of useful activities." And he heaps the highest scorn on those who live for love.

"Love is nothing but a befuddlement and concealment of man's baser urges," he said one day as we watched a couple walk hand in hand down the street. "If the social controls were lifted, no man would remain with a woman for more than an evening or two."

I do not share his bleak assessment of human drives and desires, but I like his sharpness and his cutting wit.

At times, I think his world-weary cynicism is but an act; then at others, it seems as though his soul is dark and bone tired.

He will, however, make a wonderful reporter and writer. If anyone can see through the masks and costumes that people employ to hide true motives and real reasons, it is Jamison.

I am so glad that he and the fellow at the *New York World* could meet. I am sure a job awaits him upon his departure from Harvard.

And to be honest—I would much rather have Jamison as a friend and working for me, than to imagine him as an enemy writing things about me.

And then there is Hannah . . . our sweet Hannah.

Yes, I am sure that it is true that we have all been enamored with her at one time or another—although none of us save Joshua would admit that. And even he would need a great deal of prodding.

I have no doubt that our Joshua imagines he might have an opportunity to court Hannah. I do not want to see his poor heart shattered, but I know that Hannah could not seriously consider Joshua as a possible suitor. Her family would disown her. I would wager that not even Hannah—a compassionate person such as she is—would consider abandoning her social standing for love and a shack in Ohio.

This is not to be harsh against her. I know I would not do that either.

Despite that, our dear friend is a rarity. She is a woman who speaks her mind without hesitation or fear. During our trip to New York she accused my family of being too rich. Can a person be too rich? I think not. Such is her audacity.

And while she thinks richness is crass and almost ignoble, my wealth did help her during the spring term.

Joshua and I were in my suite of rooms, discussing some theological matter, I am sure. Everything with Joshua often descends—or is that ascends? —to a theological discussion. (To his credit, he seems to like it when I argue from my non-theological background. I am sure that he could squash me like a bug when it comes to biblical matters and knowledge–but he allows me to talk and rationally discuss matters of sin and death and life.)

There was a tap at the door, and Hannah stumbled in. Her face was anguished, as if she had lost a loved one. We were both alarmed and had no idea of how to calm a distraught woman. Despite my reputation, I've seldom dealt with a woman in tears. I am usually out of the room by that time, having broken a heart and departed.

Joshua and I gathered about her. Between gasps and tears, she related her story. As I have mentioned, she maintains an enrollment in the medical college. For the most part, and up till now, it consisted of chemistry and biology and lectures of that nature. But now, the situation has shifted.

Hannah is a student of good standing. She has offered payment for her classes, and Harvard has graciously accepted her check.

However, the stodgy anatomy professor must have been asleep until now, for he suddenly woke and noticed a female in his class. He claimed that up until that very day, he had no idea a woman was attending his lectures. All he saw was a vast assembly of eager faces of men. How could he not have known? Hannah is many things, but shy and retiring are not two of them.

I imagine that the professor simply suffered from an acute case of embarrassment. After all, he would, within the next week, be unveiling a cadaver–a male cadaver–to the class. And there would be two female eyes inspecting that cold flesh.

Society might rock upon its foundation if that were to occur.

The professor, a mouselike man by the name of Schuyler, refused to allow Hannah back in class.

If the school had refused at the outset, perhaps I would have understood. But they did not.

Upon hearing the last of the story, I could stand it no longer. I ran from 619 Follen Street and did not stop until I stood, breathless and sweating, in front of Dean Samuel Gregory's office.

Without an appointment and without invitation, I simply entered and demanded a resolution to the situation.

Dean Gregory blanched when he saw me. He was aware of my

father's anticipated gift to the university upon my graduation. It will not be an inconsequential amount.

I did not get angry, and I did not threaten to urge my father to withdraw the pledge. Such things are done by brutes and thugs. I pride myself on having more finesse than that.

I simply said that my father's pledge would be doubled if Miss Collins completed every undergraduate medical class that Harvard offered. I would have pushed for every class required to become a doctor—but that would be a victory that would need more than just a donation to win.

Gregory actually stuttered. "D-d-double?"

I nodded.

A doubling of the gift would be all but unnoticed by my father.

Gregory thought for only a moment, then picked up a quill and dipped it into an inkwell. Without looking at me, he said softly, "Please ask Miss Collins to return to her classes tomorrow. And if you please, Mr. Davis, there should be no further mention of this incident."

There is a reason the man is a dean of Harvard. Before I left the office, he asked me to sign a letter confirming the doubled amount.

Such is the way of the world.

And Hannah thinks that we are too rich. Without it, she would be back in Philadelphia attending the quilting circle on Tuesday afternoons and sipping weak, lukewarm tea.

I mentioned that I would write about Nora. She does consume much of my thoughts. Yet I find myself so off kilter when trying to determine the level of our relationship.

Because of her schedule and her aunt and uncle's protective nature, she and I have spent no more than twelve evenings together in the last six months.

Some evenings I depart from her side as if I am floating on air. The conversation is filled with laughter, and she leaves me at her doorstep with the lightest, sweetest kiss on my lips.

Some evenings are heavy with an air of contention, and she departs with not so much as a handshake.

Sometimes she is angered over my flippancy with church and all matters religious. And other times, she laughs along with me at some of Joshua's tales of the unintentionally humorous church people and their actions.

She refuses to allow me to escort her to elegant and sophisticated restaurants, insisting that such things are of no importance to her. I have not confirmed this, but I surmise it is because she secretly desires them and does not want her emotions to be confused by my wealth. If that is truly the case, then I respect her all the more—yet she will not explain that to me.

Despite the uncertain nature of our relationship, I know that there is no other woman I would rather spend time with. Even though we are not in a "singular" state, I have seldom escorted other women to any social event. That is most surprising. Last year, I squired a dozen women to all manner of occasions and seldom visited the same young lady more than once a fortnight.

But now, even though there has been the occasional social affair where a young woman is simply expected, most of my evenings are spent alone or with Joshua, Jamison, or Hannah.

Is this the road to love?

Is this the road to marriage?

I am certain that I would have preferred a better map if it were true.

Nora vexes me and intrigues me and fascinates me.

Perhaps those emotions, all jumbled together, produce feelings of love.

FROM THE JOURNAL OF GAGE DAVIS
MAY 24, 1844

Well, today it came to pass. The first telegraph message was sent from the U.S. Supreme Court room in Washington, D.C., to Alfred Vail in Baltimore, Maryland, by Samuel F. B. Morse. "What hath God wrought," was the message that went over the line paid for by the federal government.

Gads, how much tax money is wasted by these foolish politicians.

Cambridge, Massachusetts
June 1844

Melinda spun away from the table, just escaping Gage's outstretched hands.

"Come back here," he cried. "I am leaving today and won't see you for the rest of the summer."

"And I am certain that I will weep every evening into my pillow," Melinda called out as she entered the kitchen. "My heart will never contain the sorrow I feel."

Gage shook his head and laughed. "The help that one encounters today. Disgraceful. Where is a male waiter when you need one?"

"Who's disgraceful?" Jamison said as he pulled up a chair. The Destiny was no more than a third full. Classes had ended a few days prior and all that was left were final examinations. As each test was taken, another group of students packed up and readied to return home.

"And you're heading back to Pittsburgh?" asked Gage. While he considered Jamison one of his closest friends, he knew surprisingly little about his friend's life outside of Cambridge.

"I am being forced to return," Jamison complained. "My father claims that he requires me to return to determine if the education I am receiving is of sufficient quality."

Startled, Gage asked, ""How will he determine that?"

Jamison looked annoyed, then shrugged. "Another set of final examinations, perhaps. An essay or two. Maybe a summer-length dissertation."

"And he is serious?"

"I believe so," Jamison said as he waved to Melinda. "I suspect if things don't meet his standards, he will refuse to continue paying my tuition."

"But I thought tuition was handled by your uncle—you know, Gregory's assistant," Gage said, confused.

"It is. And don't ask," Jamison said. "None of it makes any sense.

I have resigned myself to this fate. As Harvard's premier cynic, I believe that it is deserved somehow."

Melinda brought Gage's order and he took a bite of the cold chicken leg.

"But that can't take all summer. Even finals only last a week."

Jamison looked up. His eyes appeared tired. "I hope to do free-lance work for the *Pittsburgh Dispatch*. You know that odd fellow over in Amsberry Hall–the one with the red beard that looks like a swarm of bees has landed on his chin?"

"He is an odd duck, isn't he?"

"Yes. Well, his uncle is one of the managing editors," Jamison continued, "and he promised to put in a good word. Of course, it all has to be done without my father's knowledge. He's really set against me ever working on a newspaper."

Gage chewed thoughtfully.

"And what are you going to do this summer?" Jamison asked. "Besides make money, that is."

Gage shrugged. "You mean there is something else?"

"Be serious, now."

"I am serious," Gage said. "I like the world of business. Making money is part of it. It makes me feel powerful."

Jamison nodded as if he understood.

Then Gage added, "But even that power has its limits. I need to be home for another reason. I need to be with my father. His last few letters were on the verge of being confusing. Edgar wrote to me without my father's knowledge. He said that on most days, my father is lucid and sharp. But occasionally he seems lost and confused."

Jamison appeared concerned. "What are you going to do?"

"Edgar wrote that there is no reason to worry. On the days when my father seems out of sorts, Edgar simply cancels all meetings."

"What if he gets worse?"

Gage looked up. Dusk hedged at the sky and the air grew heavy with a hint of rain. The Destiny was all but deserted.

"Then it's up to Walton, I suppose. He's the oldest."

"But I thought he didn't like industry and business."

"He doesn't. But he is the oldest."

Both were quiet.

"Then neither of us faces a carefree summer," Jamison said. "I wonder if that is the sign that one is an adult? The first time a summer vacation is not anticipated with wild, childish joy."

Gage winced at the truth and nodded.

A peal of thunder rolled in from the west. Rain began to fall, and a chilled curtain of air elbowed into the Destiny. Both men tensed as a flash of lightning sparked across the darkening sky.

FROM THE JOURNAL OF GAGE DAVIS
JUNE 26, 1844

I attended a wedding today. Not just any wedding, but that of President John Tyler and Miss Julia Gardiner. The affair was at the wonderful Church of the Ascension. Such a parade of politicians and famous folk—all dressed to the nines. As the ceremony began, I played a little game with myself: for the first time in my life I seriously envisioned being the groom at such an event. It was a most unsettling game—yet I took the game a step further and envisioned the bride to be Nora. I admit that the church was warm—but the flush that heated my face was caused not by the lack of cool air in the church, but by the picture of the two of us being married, being joined together as husband and wife, to be committed to each other forever. I do not fully know if I will ever be able to take such a step.

Why aren't these questions in life easier to answer?

If life were just about making money, then I would never worry again.

CHAPTER SEVEN

New York City
July 1844

How could anyone actually like this city in the summer?" Gage complained as he entered the New York Athletic Club. "Everyone sweats like a farm animal, myself included."

His father walked a few steps behind. Gage watched him draw closer. He had noticed, within the last week it seemed, a slight hitch in his father's gait. It was as if a pebble had found permanent residence in his boot. Of course, the senior Davis said it was nothing and dismissed his son's concern with an impatient wave of his hand.

"Summer is supposed to be hot," Arthur Davis said as he wiped a beading of perspiration from his forehead. "Makes one appreciate a cool fall."

"I would appreciate it fine without the heat," Gage replied. "And what is worse is that the city has taken on a fetid air–more pungent than in years past."

"Nonsense," Arthur said grabbing at the marble handrail on the steps. "This is simply the first year in many years that you have been in the city instead of Southampton during July, relaxing with the rest of the family."

During the past two decades of summers, the Davis family had spent July and August comfortably ensconced at their villa on the beach in Southampton. His mother was already currently in residence there and had been since the first days of June.

"Then why are we not with them?"

Arthur laughed. "Son, we are the ones who see to it that the house in Southampton stays in the family. It's not an inexpensive proposition owning multiple dwellings."

They entered the club's dining room. The somber hall was lined with walnut paneling carved to the depth of a man's hand. An illuminating hiss came from a bank of flickering gaslights.

Despite the noon hour, the room was no more than a quarter filled. A scattered flock of white-haired gentlemen turned to look at the Davises as they entered. Most of the members in attendance that day were older businessmen who no doubt now viewed the long commute out to the eastern reaches of Long Island as too turbulent. The elder statesmen of the business world had left their lives at their summer homes to sons and daughters and other legions of relatives.

Arthur nodded to several of the men, then selected a table in the far corner of the room, not that far from the entry door to the kitchen.

That was most unlike his father. Always seeking the center, he was most comfortable in the middle of any situation, most happy to be seated at the head table, or near it.

But now, within the last few months, that had changed.

Gage did not ask why, but he suspected a reason. If one took notice, his father's right hand trembled as it rose from plate to mouth. The movement was slight and sometimes not discernable at all. But food would slip from his fork or spoon on occasion, and Arthur would stare down at the spill with a mixture of disdain and disgust. To appear weak and out of control was an anathema to the elder Davis.

When the trembling occurred now, Gage simply ignored it and chatted on as if nothing were amiss. He did not know what else to do. Yet the weakness in his father's right hand was most troubling as it indicated a deeper medical problem.

To suggest a doctor was simply not an option.

Gage recalled one discussion, several years prior, between his father and mother that quickly escalated into rancorous tones. His mother suggested that her husband visit a neighbor of theirs, a physician of some renown, for an opinion on some insignificant medical matter.

His father responded in an hour-long tirade against the evils of medical charlatans.

Gage was, above all, a realist. If his father would not listen to his wife, why then would he listen to his youngest son? So Gage watched and remained silent, and deeply concerned.

They ordered their meals, and Arthur Davis picked up a copy of the morning financial paper, flapped it open, and began to read. Gage reached into his case and extracted a handful of papers. The top paper was a letter from his father to the owner of a small textile factory in Massachusetts. It would be sent out in the afternoon posting.

But what drew Gage's attention was the signature.

All his life he had watched as his father signed documents and bank checks and letters. It was always done with a great flourish, as if the bold, strong strokes were a fitting coda to those documents. But this letter was different. The signature of Arthur Davis contained scrawled, edgy lines, and appeared almost tentative and hesitant.

It had been signed just yesterday. Gage's father had slipped into a darker mood, and during breakfast, Edgar had notched his eyebrow and tilted his head just so. It was a practiced gesture, one that Gage intuitively understood.

It meant that this day was not a day to decide on weighty business matters. It was a day to remain in the family home and see to the mounds of paperwork and correspondence. Summer brought a lessening of the mail, but it still threatened to overtake their offices.

So he and his father, with Edgar's silent help, had dived into their tasks. By the first darkening of evening, his father had handled only twelve or so letters and solicitations, where as Gage had handled upwards of several dozens.

That reversal of workload was troubling to Gage as well. It was not because he felt overworked by any means; it was because this weakness was not normal for his father.

And as they rose for dinner, Gage nodded to Edgar, who offered the slightest nod in return. Later that night, after his father had retired to his bedchamber, Gage had returned to the office. A few of his father's letters were precise and to the point. However, other communications were so confused and convoluted that they were little more than gibberish. Those letters Gage simply discarded and redrafted more appropriate responses. He signed each of them with his father's exaggerated autograph.

Today, as the two of them waited for lunch to be served, Gage sat in the silence, pretending to be busy, but engaged in a most worrisome inner dialogue.

If such conditions persist, I have no choice except to stay in New York rather than return to Cambridge. After all, what can those professors teach me that I am not already accomplishing here? What value are further studies if my father is in need of my help? To stay in university simply for the social aspect is not warranted. That would not be the action of a loving and loyal son. No . . . I will observe as clinically as possible, with as great dispassion as I can . . . and if I deem my assistance is required, then I shall stay.

His father hurrumped as he read. "Those fools in Congress. Imagine them using the country's money to fund what should be private enterprise. They have no business handing over cash to that fool Morse."

Gage nodded. He had heard the argument a hundred times before and presented it in innumerable meetings. It had legitimacy, but he was already a subscriber to its truth. He did not need convincing.

And with that, Arthur returned to his reading. A stiff waiter, in a starched black serving coat, brought a basket of small, crusty rolls in a polished silver basket. Gage noticed a bit of tarnish on one side of the basket.

Even the standards here are being compromised, Gage thought, annoyed. *What is becoming of pride in workmanship? That never would have happened if Van Buren were still president.*

Gage could not help but smile.

Even my thoughts are becoming like my father's, he thought. He grabbed a roll, broke off a bite, and popped it into his mouth. *For the life of me, I don't know why I said that save mimicry of my father's sensibilities. I don't care a whit about a spot of tarnish. Doesn't affect the taste of these tidbits in the least.*

As he chewed, he watched his father's profile as the older man continued reading.

If my father continues to slip, then I have no alternative. I must stay home and offer what help I can.

He took another bite of his roll.

That is, if I can find a way to coexist with Walton running the business without reverting to fratricide.

FROM THE JOURNAL OF GAGE DAVIS
JULY 29, 1844

Participated in a grand event today—the official start of the New York Yacht Club. A bunch of fellows gathered on the schooner *Gimrack,* just off the Battery. The day was grand as well, with a pleasant breeze and blue skies. The new commodore is John C. Stevens—a close friend of my father. I daresay that helped us win one of the coveted charter memberships. Being wealthy is not a bad thing, I must admit. Nora would love to take a spin on this schooner.

Southampton, New York
August 1844

"So our time together has proved to be most successful, has it not?" Gage's father said as the carriage jostled and tilted. "I suspect before we began this summer, you never would have imagined that we would have a full subscription to Shirdler's invention. A full subscrip-

121

tion with money remaining to fund the first assembly of a citywide test. That is most impressive. Over a thousand investors poised to earn tenfold the amount of their original investment. Perhaps even more. Our efforts have been remarkable. And you have been an invaluable assistance, Gage, simply invaluable."

"It has been most rewarding. With so many gone from the city, I was apprehensive as to what might get accomplished," Gage replied, not wishing to dwell on his father's appreciation.

"All the deadwood leave, and those who are left," Arthur Davis said, "find it easier to make decisions without interruption or unsolicited advice."

Gage smiled.

It was true what he said. Meetings were attended by fewer people, lasted shorter periods of time, yet more of substance was discussed and results were more dramatic. More time to spend yachting. *Perhaps we should work over the summer and take the rest of the year off.*

The senior Davis had insisted that they take the family carriage to Southampton rather than the railcar: "We can make the trip in less than a day, and once we arrive we will have the carriage at our disposal. I dislike standing about at the train station with a stack of luggage waiting for porters and taxis," his father had said.

Gage would have preferred the trip via rail. The ride was infinitely smoother. Upon arrival, Gage always felt a sense of elegance and exclusivity that a carriage could not match. But he would not argue such a minor comfort with his father.

He could not read during the bumpy trip. Weeks' worth of rain had flooded the dirt roads at the end of July, turning them into almost impassable quagmires. Now the August heat baked the ruts and gullies into a washboard of dried mud.

Along the route, some communities cared for the roads, leveling and adding gravel here and there. But for most of the journey, both Davises tightly held to straps and window frames as they bounced along the bad roadways.

Despite the stomach-jolting ride, Gage was happy. Ever since that lunch at the Athletic Club, his father had been the very picture of stamina and good health. Gage had watched as closely as he could without being obvious and saw no hand tremors or loss of concentration or mental confusion. It was as if his father had entered a time of emotional and mental squalls and had sailed out on the other side into bright blue seas.

Gage's vow not to return to Harvard was not forgotten but was not now needed. If his father showed no further deterioration during the remaining weeks of summer, Gage would have no qualms of returning to his friends and his final year at the university.

Gage smiled.

In his breast pocket, he carried the four letters he had received from Nora since last meeting with her in May. Gage had written to her once a week—posting a letter to Portland every Tuesday evening. He knew that it would arrive, if all went well, by Friday afternoon, Saturday at the latest.

Hers were posted in a less routine fashion.

None of them, Gage realized, could be labeled as "intimate," yet he cherished each. The last letter, received only hours before they departed for Southampton, had been read in a great rush. The last two lines struck his heart and sounded there like a bell had been rung: *I so enjoy your letters—they have been the highlight of my summer. I am impatient until I see you again and can properly thank you for bringing me such great cheer and comfort.*

He sat back in the carriage seat and smiled.

I wonder what she might have meant by "properly thank you"? Obviously she can assign no monetary value to my words. She can offer me no stack of recently penned letters as payment. She can offer no home-cooked meals or pies or cakes, since she is not the mistress of her aunt's kitchen. I am sure she does not imply offering a handshake as a thank-you. That does not match the tone of her letter. Then I can only surmise what her thanks are. And hope.

Gage felt a blush come to his cheeks and leaned farther towards the open window, hoping the warm air would diffuse his skin's reddening.

I can only conclude that she means a . . . a kiss for each letter penned?

He did not think it so far-fetched. After all, they had shared kisses on occasions prior.

If it were a kiss per letter, then I am chagrined to have written so few. I could have posted one daily if the payment terms had been known.

"Gage . . . Gage . . . ," his father said, extending his arm and nudging his shoulder. "Have you taken leave of your senses? I have been calling your name for more than a city block."

Gage shook his head and tried to hide his thoughts. He was fairly certain he had not been successful, owing to the amusement on his father's face.

The elder Davis offered a curious, foxlike smile.

"I shall not ask the nature of your daydream, Son, but I do have one word of advice."

Gage's surprise was apparent. His father had never spoken of such things before. In fact, Gage was nearly certain that he had no thoughts on the matter of men and women at all.

"If your dream was caused by a young lady, and of that I have little doubt, since I recognize the signs," his father began, an obviously unexpected slight flush coming to his own cheeks, "then you must be aware that some ladies are less honorable than others."

Gage tilted his head.

"You will be most wealthy someday. Some people from less privileged backgrounds may try and take advantage of that fact. It helps greatly if a man and a woman come from the same class of people. That's important . . . perhaps most important."

For a moment the carriage rocked and tilted, and both were tossed from one side to the other until the driver found a patch of smoother road.

"And also important is that you be a gentleman at all times. Sewing wild oats is fine for others, but not a Davis."

Gage nodded in reply.

"My advice, when the time arrives to settle down, is to make sure that her intentions are as honorable as your own. And you must make certain that she is a woman of good breeding. After all, you are a Davis."

Another jolt tossed them to the other side of the carriage, followed by the driver's loud and colorful cursing.

"I will, Father, I will."

As Gage pondered the words, a fragment of doubt entered his thoughts, like the tiniest of pebbles in a boot.

Gage looked out the window. It was a long time before he smiled again.

❦

Gage spent most of his time in Southampton sitting on the porch, drinking iced tea, and reading. He had just finished *The Pickwick Papers,* an older work by Dickens. He took a short sail or walked the beach at evening, just before dinner, and avoided the sun and salt water as best he could. He realized that some thought bathing in seawater was a healthy, exhilarating experience, but he was not one of those.

The sea contains far too many creatures that would like to snap off a piece of my anatomy for lunch. As they say, discretion is the better part of valor.

It was not that Gage had nothing else to tempt him. Southampton was alive during the summer and simply simmered over with parties and celebrations. Much of New York City's cultural elite summered there. A simple party might include several hundred guests on its list of invitees. A major gathering might yield nearly a thousand wealthy blue bloods. Summer was the season to see and be seen. During August, there would be at least one major soiree every evening.

Walton was in residence at the beach home, but the two siblings rarely saw each other. Walton's involvement in Southampton's complex and Byzantine social activities occupied most of his waking moments. He would take a carriage out in the morning—not to be seen again until dusk. That's when he returned home to change into evening attire.

Gage's parents followed much the same routine, leaving Gage alone with the servants.

And after a most hectic June and July, the quiet respite was a tonic to his thoughts. He read, penned notes to Nora and Hannah and the rest of them, and napped in the heat of the afternoon.

In the evening, there was a lull as the winds shifted from onshore to offshore. The reeds and grasses no longer hissed. Blowing sand no longer stung at ankles or eyes. The sun was far to the west, and no one needed to squint to ensure pain-free vision. This was the time that Gage took to the dunes that lay between the house and the sea. He brought a thick canvas throw and sat upon it, staring off into the haze that hid the evening.

And he lost himself in thought.

Before the light slipped away completely, he would add a few notes to his journal.

FROM THE JOURNAL OF GAGE DAVIS

I wonder if Father is right—about being leery of women. Nora knows we have money. But as of yet, I have no indication that she is seeking that money. Quite the contrary; she is often seeking out the least expensive option when we dine out. She despairs when I insist on a carriage and prefers to walk nearly everywhere. I do draw the line at walking to Boston. Some distances absolutely require a carriage ride.

But I still wonder. Is she playing coy and innocent?

Should I, as my father said, find a woman within our social and financial circles?

I suppose I could try, but every woman I have ever met from this society, save Hannah, has had her nose perched firmly in the air. I do not think I want a wife like that.

And there . . . I have said *wife* when referring to Nora. Is that the ultimate goal of our relationship? Do I want that? And perhaps, more importantly, does she?

Jamison was right. This is, I believe, the first summer I have spent as an adult. It is not carefree as I remember these days having been. Wives, marriage, career, aging parents. I suspect that is the stuff that adulthood is made of.

The last day of August broke blustery and gray, with a biting, almost winter chill to the air. Rain squalled during the morning and sounded against the huge sea-facing windows like bird shot.

It took Gage no more than an hour to pack up his belongings. He had brought little with him and knew that he would not need some of the lightweight suits until his next visit to Southampton.

Servants and maids hustled about the corridors, carrying trunks and cases, draping furniture with thick bolts of white canvas, securing windows, testing the door locks and the like.

Gage watched the storm blow east out to sea from a perch in the second-floor sunroom. The blinds on the west and north were drawn and lashed. Just the expanse of windows facing the water was open. He sipped a cup of coffee.

Clouds scudded along the shore, waves grew white, and the brave gulls looked tempest tossed as they wheeled about in the wind.

"Ah . . . there you are, Gage. Are you ready to depart our sun-drenched paradise?"

Gage chuckled, nodding to his father. "I have but two satchels to bring home and one is filled with books. I guess I did not plan on being part of the social whirl this summer."

"No matter, Son. You have plenty of time for such foolishness later. Besides, the socializing here offers no consequence to business. No one remembers what anyone says. I have yet to see a single contract in hand or a bill of sale at such gatherings."

"If that's true, then why do you and Mother attend these get-togethers?"

His father bellowed. "Free food and drink, and the choicest entertainment anywhere–watching folks desperately attempting to have a grand time. There is no greater fun."

Gage's father peered about and, with a hint of self-consciousness, draped an arm around his son's shoulder for a brief instant.

"I will miss you when you leave for Boston," Arthur Davis said, his words warm with unexpected emotion.

"And I will miss you as well, Father. We have had a jolly good time this summer. I appreciate your allowing me to work with you. I have learned a great deal."

The elder Davis laughed. "Now I know you are flattering me without cause. It is you whom I have learned greatly from. You are the master at the art of business, not me."

"Then I must have had a great teacher," Gage said.

"And Harvard will provide you an education in Latin and long obtuse words. That's the value of your studies. You will not learn how to conduct business any better than you do at this moment—you will simply have the language to describe it with more flair and polish."

Gage was set to protest.

"It is true, Son, and I think you know it. No class or professor can teach you what you already know."

"School is more than that," Gage insisted.

"I know," his father replied. "There are the friends and associations you forge during these years that will be vital in the future."

"But it is even more than that. It is."

Arthur Davis looked out the windows at the rain. From his pocket he pulled out a cigar and, in a most elaborate ceremony, cut the end and lit it. Great puffs of smoke mimicked the clouds and almost obscured his head for a moment.

"This year I am resigned to the fact that I will not have you at my side. But after you are done at Harvard, I want you to return. Do not think that you will be forced to begin your own business and make your own way in the world."

"Of course, Father. If you want me to work with you, I will. I always assumed I would have a permanent role in your affairs."

Arthur did not turn—just puffed on his cigar. Then he said quietly, "No, Gage, I will not have you work for me."

Gage went over the facts he knew well. Walton, as the elder, would inherit the business, and Gage would assume a secondary role. When a corporation worth millions is involved, even the second in command has a mighty responsibility.

"But you said you want me to return."

"I did."

"But if I do, I will work for you, then Walton."

"No."

Stunned by his father's words, Gage feared the worst—that his father had slipped back into a confused mental state. What he was saying made little sense.

"But, Father . . . I don't understand."

Arthur took the cigar from his mouth and pivoted away from the sea and toward Gage. "You will not work for Walton. You will not work for me. I intend on naming you as my successor. In addition, I intend on making changes to my will."

Gage did not respond for a long moment.

"But I am five years younger than Walton."

Arthur Davis bent closer. His eyes sharpened as if he were bidding on a desired factory. "Walton could be twenty years older, Gage, and he would never have more skill at business than exists now in your little toe."

Gage was set to interrupt.

"No, Son. You know I'm correct. I always thought he would follow in my footsteps, but this summer proved otherwise. Before you returned home in June, I asked Walton if he would be my second during my meetings this summer. And you know what he said? He said no. He said that he had too many important parties to attend in Southampton. And during this entire month, he has not yet asked me about anything that transpired this summer in New York. Not one single question."

Arthur turned back to face the angry sea.

"No, Gage, you will be my choice. You will follow me as head of this company. You will inherit the lion's share of my work. You are the most able of my sons. It is not a difference in love, for that is equal. The differences are in abilities, pure and simple."

Gage was set to protest again.

"There is no need to say another word. Nothing will be done until next year after you graduate." Arthur moved toward the door. "You will follow me, Gage."

His father walked out of the room, trailing an arm of smoke behind him. Gage stared after him, his eyes full of shock.

I am to be head of Davis Enterprises. It will be my company. Isn't it odd ... I have always told others that I will follow my father, never once telling them that Walton was in line before me. I thought it made me sound more important. And now, what I have fibbed about all these years will come to pass.

He took a last sip of cold coffee.

And now I do not know whether to despair or to be joyful.

Gage lowered the heavy drapes on the windows. As the gearing creaked and squalled, it shadowed a softer noise of a man slipping out of a second-floor bedroom and retreating down the back stairs.

From the corner of his eye Gage thought he saw movement and a flash of color ... the color of his brother's hair. He spun around and saw no one.

Did Walton hear what Father has said?

Gage ran to the door and found the hall deserted and still.

If he heard—he would be enraged. He would be furious.

Gage listened for several seconds longer and heard nothing.

It must have been my imagination.

He walked back toward the window, tied the cord tight to the stanchion on the far wall, and slowly made his way downstairs.

He did not see his brother, lost in the shadows of the third-floor landing.

———

Because of the storm and rain, it was nearing midnight when Walton finally arrived in New York City. He retreated to his room just long enough to change into dry clothes, then slipped out again.

At first the hackney driver refused to take Walton to his destination.

"Sorry, sir. They say that neighborhood isn't safe after dark. And it is well after dark."

Walton muttered under his breath, then said aloud, "Listen. I need to get there tonight. And this is a for-hire carriage, is it not? You are not as stupid as you look, are you? Just drive. I'll pay you double what you want. Triple if you close your mouth and drive."

The driver paused, as if unsure of how to treat this obnoxious rider.

"Listen, you fool, move this carriage. I'll give you four times the rate," Walton said, his words venomous. "Now get moving."

The driver hardened his eyes at Walton. Then he turned, nicked at the reins, and set off for the docks.

⁕

"So you can accomplish what I'm asking? It is within your abilities?"

Walton sat with hands clasped together on his lap. He hesitated even to touch the tabletop, as if it would be dangerous to his health. A handful of patrons slumped about a scattering of tables. Each exhibited varying degrees of inebriation.

All save the tight little man seated with Walton Davis.

"For a man who don't tell me much, you sure be askin' a lot of questions."

"Listen," Walton hissed. "I am the man with the money. That means I have a right to be answered. And I want to know if my request is something that falls in your . . . line of work."

"It is. I done work like it before. Complicated jobs, if I say so myself. And no one complained about what I done."

"So you are saying that I can have the situation . . . remedied."

"Listen, I can fix anything for a price. I can make people go away . . . forever, if you want."

Walton thought intently. "No. I want nothing that drastic."

"Take care of things once and for all, if you'd be askin' me. Cheaper in the long run."

Walton leaned forward. "That may be—but it would take all the fun out of the experience, now, wouldn't it?"

The man sitting in front of Walton adjusted his black cap. "If you say so."

Walton rose to leave. "I do." He stepped to the door. "I will be in touch, Mr. French. I will be in touch."

FROM THE JOURNAL OF GAGE DAVIS

CAMBRIDGE, WINTER 1844

Father's news to me at the end of summer has changed nothing and everything. Of course there has been no official announcement, nor have I expected one. But if that is the fate assigned to me, then I must ask myself, What am I doing here wasting my time at Harvard when I could be building and buying and developing?

I have grown more impatient with many of my classes. What is taught simply flies in the face of conventional practice. I am tempted to stand and denounce the professors and their outmoded concepts.

But I do not.

Easier for me to let the facts lie, distorted as they may be. The rest of the fellows will find the truth in their own way, I imagine.

And because of my newly acquired nonchalance, I am beginning to greatly enjoy this year.

It was so wonderful to reunite with Hannah, Joshua, and Jamison. For months, I had been judged by what I did and said, and huge sums of money lay in the balance. But with these three friends, I can speak my mind, and they theirs, and no one thinks ill of another if a new idea, out of the norm, is brought up for discussion.

Joshua and Jamison have brought back wonderful stories from their summer.

Joshua has kept all of us laughing as he told tales of his small church back in Shawnee. I am sure that the people there are no different, under the skin, than those here in Cambridge—but then, maybe they are. He told one story of Spider Jeffreys—the richest man in all of Shawnee County. It seems as if this Spider fellow was a bachelor and possessed a huge tract of productive land. He came to town one day, most unexpectedly, in search of a bride, Joshua said. Wearing his Sunday best, which was only steps above tatters, and his hair slicked back with what smelled like lard, the Spider fellow patrolled the streets and spent much of the day in the local tavern, asking nearly everyone if they might know of an unattached young woman he might call on.

The three of us listened and roared. Joshua has a way with a story, that much is certain. We could picture the scene down to the smallest muddy detail.

Jamison actually did get quizzed by his father for more than four hours upon his return. His father had him recite poetry, give descriptions of the classic literary works, cipher pages of numbers and figures. Jamison was amazed. "It was exactly like finals—only this was much less fun."

Finally his father was satisfied at the level and amount of his education and agreed to let his son return. Jamison spent the rest of the summer doing freelance work for several of Pittsburgh's leading newspapers. He had all the luck in the world. He reported on two murders, a prison riot, ten fires, and the trial of a former mayor who was in jail for beating his wife's alleged paramour nearly to death.

Smirking, he told us that he saw nothing that countered his naturally pessimistic view of people and society.

I said, "And what do you expect from Pittsburgh?" which in turn received a jab from our Pittsburgh native.

Hannah did not talk much of her summer. I suspect she stayed home in Philadelphia and did quilting and needlepoint with her mother. I have heard that her father has lost even more of the shattered remains of his fortune. Such a sad case—and doubly harsh for Hannah, who is now viewed by both her mother and father as the last and best hope to return them to their rightful status and fortune.

And then there is Nora.

Yes, indeed, there is Nora.

I am most happy to report that I was correct in my assessment as to her means of repayment for my letters.

And I have berated myself soundly, after payment was received, that I did not send a thousand more letters of one word each. She would still be in my debt today, and I could extract payment over many, many evenings.

She claimed my letters were the highlight of her summer—so chatty and full of grace and good news. Her summer was spent practicing and performing in several venues in the Portland area. She showed me three small newspaper clippings of reviews of those performances. All were quite glowing. Even taking into account that they were offering a review on a native daughter, the critics gave her high praise, indeed.

We have taken up where we had left off. She laughs and makes me feel warm. She holds my hand, and I forget about the problems of Walton and succession and all that. She leans on my shoulder during an evening carriage ride, and I am without a single worry.

I continue to think this might be love.

If it is not, then I am certain I might not recognize the real thing if it did appear.

Yet, despite all the good between us, there is still a divide.

She asks me of religious matters on a regular basis. My answers remain much the same, and yet, while I give much money to churches and attend when I can, it never seems as if that answer provides her any comfort.

"But there is more, Gage. God is more than that."

I nod. I agree with her, hoping she will be assuaged. She is not. I think she wants me to make some sort of bold statement—like our friend Joshua can make.

I want to tell her that I would say anything to make her happy—but I do not wish ever to lie to her. And to say I felt more would be a lie of the first order. I know God is important to those who cannot get by on their own wits—but I have never been that sort of depend-ent person. God offers help to the lame and unfortunate, to be sure—not to privileged folk like myself.

Yes, I did once admit to Joshua a certain level of fear—but that was a mistake. I am sure that emotion was an aberration. If he were to ask me again, I would tell him differently.

Today I have no fears. Ever since my father tapped me to be his successor, I have no time for fear.

And yet, there is Nora.

To lose her would be a tragedy worthy of Shakespeare. And to gain her love might involve being untrue to myself.

Such is the stuff of epic poems and plays.

Joshua stops by often and we talk and discuss weighty issues of

God and love and relationships. He tells me that I am fighting a losing battle—denying my need for God.

I do not see it that way, and we argue and talk late into the night.

How terribly I will miss him when this year is done. He is the type
of person I wish I had had for a brother. But I suspect Joshua would
say God had other plans and gave me Walton instead.

So be it.

And now it is almost winter. I have vowed to record all in this
journal, but it seems as if my time is so limited. Perhaps when the
snow begins to fall, I will spend less of my time in the Destiny and
more time on my studies and my writing.

But I have said that before.

❦

Boston, Massachusetts
November 1844

Nora planned on returning to Portland for the entire month of
December, so Gage tried to make the best of the days they had
remaining. Nora accompanied him to an elegant brunch at the
Peabody Hotel in downtown Boston. Amidst the delicate chiming
of silver to china, the two enjoyed a wondrous array of delicacies.

To Nora, the cost of an exquisite breakfast or lunch was easier to
take than a dinner. Gage could never discern the actual amount that
triggered her decisions, but she had never once refused his invitation
to lunch or breakfast—regardless of the location. By comparison, she
had balked numerous times at dinners, saying that as she ate, she
would be imagining the cost of the entire meal.

Gage smiled as he watched her eat, knowing that the brunch was
more expensive than many of the dinners they had enjoyed. But
knowing that costs were a concern to her did much to allay Gage's
trepidations. If she was careful with his money now, did not that
bode well for the future?

Her aunt and uncle expected her home before dark, so she and
Gage shared a carriage back to Cambridge. As they passed through

Beacon Hill on the way to the bridge, Nora called out, "Look at that sign at the church there."

The sign read, SPECIAL SPEAKER TONIGHT: J. QUITTNER.

"Isn't that your housemate?"

"It is," Gage replied. "The scamp never mentioned he was moonlighting in such a refined neighborhood."

The carriage continued on.

"I wish I had not promised my aunt that I would be home by dark."

Gage took her hand. "You can offer an inventive excuse. You can say that the carriage lost a wheel. I can bribe the driver to run over a curb."

Nora squeezed his hand. "You are such a tempter. And we have already used that same excuse last month, if you recall."

"Oh, that's right," Gage replied, laughing. "I had completely forgotten about that. Did they believe it?"

"Barely."

"But was not the delay worth it?"

A hazy, dreamy look passed over Nora's eyes. "It was."

Then she sat up straight and let Gage's hand drop from hers. "But I promised. And if you invent a reason to not be home on time, I am sure your plans will not include attending church to hear Joshua."

"Well," Gage said sheepishly, "that is true. If I could extend our time today, it would not be for Joshua's sake."

The carriage clattered up to the home of Nora's aunt and uncle.

Their good-byes were brief and perfunctory, for both saw a rustle of curtains in the front window. Gage was sure that at least one set of eyes remained on them.

He helped Nora from the carriage.

"If you have nothing to do this evening, why don't you return to the church and listen to Joshua? You talk of him all the time, but have you ever heard him preach?"

"I have never heard him preach," Gage admitted. "You're right. I should go."

Again the curtain rustled.

"I think you are being summoned, Nora, or your aunt is practicing her flag signaling."

Nora giggled. "They just want to make sure you are a gentleman."

"Ha. They want to make sure you are a lady and do not try to corrupt my innocence."

She gave him a playful shove. "You are most incorrigible. Why not attend church tonight and see if any of it sinks in?"

He watched her as she mounted the steps.

"Perhaps I will . . . but if it does, I daresay you will miss the old Gage Davis."

She smiled and with her back to the door so her aunt—or uncle—was no longer in view, she blew him a kiss and offered him a wide inviting smile. Then she slipped inside and was gone.

When Gage returned to the carriage, the driver asked, "Where to, sir?"

"That church we passed in Beacon Hill . . . do you know it?"

"The Church of the Living God, yes sir, I do."

Gage nodded to himself. "Take me there."

<hr />

Gage hid in the shadows of the back of the church. He was amazed at Joshua's performance. Joshua, so often ill at ease in social situations, was as a man possessed in the pulpit. His words were sharp and clear, his gestures confident and bold, his words thought provoking and well developed.

Gage, who could read the emotions of a crowd, knew that Joshua had the entire audience in the palm of his hand.

It was not that Joshua presented a polished image—on the contrary. Joshua made no apologies concerning his accent or his background—and that made him all the more charming and endearing.

At the end of the message, Gage heard sniffles and the sound of men holding back tears. Such was the power of Joshua's short message.

He waited for nearly an hour until the congregation gathered around Joshua thinned. Then Gage stepped from the shadows and extended his hand to a very surprised Joshua.

"Your words touched me, Joshua. I have never heard such things before. I never realized what a powerful speaker you are. I heard tears and crying. You moved these people."

"And not you? Did not anything I said reach you?"

Gage stiffened slightly. "I'll not have you saving my soul just yet. It does not require saving. You keep working on the lost."

Joshua grew silent and stepped closer. "We are all lost, Gage. All of us. You show more bravery by admitting your weaknesses than you do by offering a brave facade."

Gage stepped back. "It is no facade, Joshua. I am what I am and I do not need God's help with life. There are those that do. And they need you. You do have a gift."

A moment later, Gage smiled. "Just let me know if there is ever anything I can do to help you. Anything."

He placed an arm over Joshua's shoulder.

And that's how I serve God. That is how I am called, Gage thought silently.

CHAPTER EIGHT

New York City
January 1845

FROM THE JOURNAL OF GAGE DAVIS

Christmas is gone.

The festive parties of New Year are but a memory.

The sky grows dark and leaden. Snow, blanketed with a dusting of coal smoke, covers the campus in a gray cocoon. The bleakness of nature matches the bleakness of my heart.

Nora has bid me farewell.

I am at a loss to explain it all. My thoughts have been in confused agitation for the last weeks, and I am not certain I have the ability to describe the events with any accuracy. My heart is pained beyond belief, and yet there is a wellspring of anger that pours from my heart as well.

My faithful friend Joshua has noticed my black moods and inquired, in his pastoral way, as to the cause.

I do not know why, but I lied to him. I told him that the woman in question is "a snobbish and spoiled woman from the town of Stockbridge."

Why?

I have no answer. I simply could not tell him how deeply I was involved with Nora and how much I cared for her and how her leaving has broken my heart. Such an admission would not suit my reputation. I know such lies are not admirable–but I am not always an admirable man.

I explained that this woman had been most attractive and used all her feminine wiles to twist my heart.

I think Joshua knows some of the mechanics of feminine wiles–since he has suffered some at the hands of Hannah. And what she has done to his heart is minor in comparison to what Nora has done to mine.

I am vexed.

We did not see each other during Christmas, but I sent her a beautiful silver pendant. The cost was dear, yet it possessed a quiet, understated elegance. I was certain that she would like it.

And she did. I received an expansive letter of thanks from her, with her promises of repaying me in kindness for my generosity. I was so happy. I was certain that all was well. I looked forward to her "payments."

She planned to return to Cambridge at the end of January. When she did not arrive back in Cambridge, she wrote several letters, first stating that weather, then an illness in her family, then some legal complications prevented her from returning to Cambridge.

I accepted all that. Her studies are not as driven by a schedule as mine are. And she truly does not require another lesson to gain competency in music. Her voice and skill at the piano and violin are extraordinary.

I did not think anything amiss. I truly did not.

And then the letter came. I believe I knew something was amiss upon looking at the address. Instead of her graceful handwriting, the lines were harsh and heavy.

My premonition was justified.

The letter was brief. She stated first that our relationship had been the highlight of her life and that this letter was agonizing to write. She had enjoyed every moment of our togetherness and found her heart growing closer and closer to mine.

But there was an obstacle.

She said that every time we spoke of faith and God, I either became flippant or defensive. (I would say in my defense that neither accusation is true.) She quoted me as saying, "This is how I am and I will go no further." (I do not ever recall using those words in a discussion of God.)

She wrote that if that is the way I believe and feel, then there could be no hope for a life for us in the future.

She wrote, "I can hear what you are about to say—that I cannot be serious—and that I cannot discard our future over such a small matter."

(She is right. I would have said that.)

The last lines of her letter are as follows:

But it is not a small matter to me, Gage. I take my faith in our Creator very seriously. While I have been with you, I pushed those concerns and beliefs to the back of our conversations. But that did not eliminate them. While at home these past few months, I have had time to think and ponder. While I think my heart would love you if I let it, I simply cannot abandon all that I believe.

We are not alike enough to stay together.

You have chosen and I have chosen, and it breaks my heart to know this.

I pray that someday your heart might change. I pray that you will find peace.

I will always remain a friend to you.

I will always hold you close to my heart.

And I sit here in my darkened room, not willing or able to get out of bed. If such is the pain of love, then why do we pursue it with such vigor?

<hr />

Cambridge, Massachusetts
Spring 1845

Most everyone expected the seniors at Harvard, during their last semester on campus, to be distracted. After all, four years of study were coming to a close. No longer would they live in such a protected enclave, no longer would they be surrounded by such close groups of friends and fellow students.

Some professors joked among themselves that it was the senior stare that gave the students away.

Some stared off into a vanishing point in the distance, worried that they now faced the trials and tribulations of the real world. Others hoped they could recall a fraction of what they had spent four years learning. More yet were simply sad and dazed that four years of liberation were ending.

Gage felt none of that because of the pain in his heart over Nora's rejection. He had not been able to write her back and explain. He knew he could offer no alternative interpretation to change her mind.

He could lie about his decision—but lying about the state of your soul was not a simple sin, and that became more ominous the longer he thought on it. So instead of writing Nora in return, he moped about campus.

Trying to appear as if all were normal, Gage laughed too loud, too quickly, and was always at the verge of distraction. He had not stopped in at the Destiny for weeks and weeks. And when he had, he spent only a few minutes, then walked out without even saying farewell.

Joshua whispered to his friends that it was the pain of a failed relationship. Jamison and Hannah were shocked, since they had no idea he had been in a relationship.

"He can be a bit secretive," Joshua admitted. "Even I don't know the woman in question—some wealthy girl from Stockbridge is all he told me."

"Stockbridge?" Hannah asked. "He said Stockbridge was populated with pretenders and fools. I don't believe him for an instant."

"Maybe it is business worries," Jamison suggested.

"Pshaw," Hannah replied. "The Davises have more money than Midas. They could lose 90 percent of it and still have more than the rest of the world."

The three friends were concerned but could not offer any practical response to pull Gage from his slump.

April 1845

Gage's great soul-draining gloom was made even darker and heavier with the sad news that reached Joshua.

Joshua's father had taken ill, and Joshua was being recalled, as it were, to aid the family in this time of crisis. Joshua planned to set off for Shawnee within a day of receiving the sad letter from his mother. He would miss graduation and the opportunity to say good-bye.

Gage knew that good-byes would be difficult, so great was their friendship. As Joshua readied to leave, Gage offered assistance. He helped pack up Joshua's small library. While Joshua was occupied, Gage slipped a packet of currency and a note into a Bible.

This will be my donation to his church. He would never take it if he knew.

And within less than a day, Joshua slipped out of his life.

Gage heard Joshua's footsteps on the stairs in the dawn light. He sat up. He wanted so to run out and give him a last embrace, a last handshake, share one last discussion.

But he also recognized Joshua's reason for leaving at dawn. It was to avoid just such a scene. Joshua could be a powerful speaker standing at a pulpit, but in closer encounter, he found emotions difficult to handle and control.

So Gage swallowed hard and whispered to the darkness, "Farewell, my friend. I will never know such joy in having a friend as I have known with you. May . . . may God bless your path."

For once, Gage did not feel awkward using God's name.

He lay back down and closed his eyes. But he knew sleep would elude him for a long time.

The three remaining friends gathered that afternoon at the Destiny.

"And you knew of this two days ago!" Hannah sputtered. "And you told me nothing! I would have liked to say good-bye in person. Did you think you were the only ones who would be affected by his departure?"

Both Gage and Jamison realized their error. They all despaired over

Joshua's departure. In his quiet, confident way, Joshua had become a pillar of strength to them. He had found his calling and pursued it with a single-mindedness that left the rest of them a bit envious.

"We were wrong," Gage said, his voice low. "We should have told you. But it was hard for Joshua to leave. Saying good-bye to you might have proved impossible."

"What? Why would it be harder for him to say farewell to me?" she asked.

"As if you really don't know," Jamison said.

"No. I truly do not understand why. Tell me."

Gage glanced at Jamison, then shrugged. "Because he was in love with you, that's why."

Hannah looked shocked. "No," she said with some emphasis.

"Yes, indeed," Jamison replied. "It was obvious to everyone. Not that he ever would have acted on it. But he was in love with you."

"Truly? I thought of us as friends–just friends."

Gage laughed. "Your definition of friendship is a good deal different from Joshua's definition of friendship."

Hannah shook her head in disbelief. "Really? In love? Really?"

It was obvious to Gage that Hannah was both dismayed, and in some small sliver of her heart, thrilled.

"Men. I will never understand them, I guess," Hannah said quietly.

Both Gage and Jamison replied in unison, "And the feeling is mutual."

<hr/>

Later that evening, long after Hannah departed, Gage and Jamison remained. The three had spent hours recounting all their mutual memories, vowing that graduation and distance would never disrupt their friendship–and being painfully aware that it would.

"I did not imagine that any of our leaving would be this hurtful," Jamison said.

Gage nodded. "Neither did I. I heard Joshua's footsteps this morning and nearly shed a tear for his departing."

The noise of the Destiny hummed about them–animated conversation, the clatter of plates, calls of the cooks in the kitchen.

"Do you think we will see each other again?"

"I do," said Gage. "I so enjoyed this foursome. I believe we will remain as friends. If you head to New York for work, then the two of us shall remain even closer."

Gage leaned forward until his face was merely inches from Jamison's. "And because of your skills, Jamison, you are the one to tell our stories. I know that the four of us will do great things. Our stories will need a writer—and you are that person."

Jamison winced. He knew others enjoyed his writing abilities, but to hear the words spoken was almost painful.

"I am serious, Jamison. We are the golden sons and daughters of America. We will be the famous men and women of tomorrow. We will have stories worth telling," Gage responded, grinning for the first time in a long time.

Jamison nodded.

Gage's voice became low and serious. "You must remember all that goes on here. Tell our stories."

Jamison replied slowly. "I will remember. I promise."

The clock on the Harvard Commons began to chime.

"And what of you, Gage? What will you be known for?"

Gage did not hesitate. "Why . . . making money, of course."

"You mean making more money than you do now?"

"The amount we have now will be paltry to the fortune I shall amass."

Jamison squinted out into the darkness. "And that's your goal?"

Gage joined him looking into the night. "It is. It is." But his words had a faint hollow sound as if Gage were trying one more time to convince himself.

Cambridge, Massachusetts
June 1845

Gage stood in the empty rooms of 619 Follen Street.

Funny how small and barren they become without furnishings.

His parents and a few other relatives had made the journey to

Harvard for graduation. Hands were shaken, speeches were made, and banquets were held. The last weeks were a hurricane of activities and parties.

In spite of Gage's disdain for some of his courses, he graduated with high honors and proudly wore the wide purple ribbon over his black gown.

By now his friends had departed. He had said his good-byes—loudly—to Mrs. Parsons, who had shed copious tears as he did. Gage tried not to smile as he knew she was pained not only at his leaving but at her loss of rental income.

He took one last walk through the rooms, his steps echoing against the hard plaster walls. He picked up his jacket from the floor where he laid it, dusted it off, and buttoned it. He bent and retrieved his leather journal, tucking it under his arm.

Then, without looking back, he began to walk toward the carriage stand.

New York City
July 1845

The announcement was made on a Wednesday morning, two weeks after Gage returned home.

Arthur Davis gathered his staff in his office. He had specifically asked his wife and Walton to be in attendance. Gage stood a few feet from his father, on his right. His mother and Walton sat off to the corner.

Arthur called out for everyone to be quiet.

"I can be a man of few words, if I choose—although I am sure none of you would testify to that, would you?"

Several of his senior workers allowed themselves to chuckle.

"I have called you all here to announce a change in succession. And a change in this organization. As you know, my younger son, Gage, has just graduated from Harvard—with high honors, I might add."

A few staff members clapped softly. Gage nodded in response.

"And now that he is back in New York, I have come to realize that I need to make changes in Davis Enterprises. As of today . . ."

As Arthur cleared his throat, Gage's heart beat faster. "As of today, I am announcing that Gage has been appointed as my vice president and will be groomed to take over this company when I step down." Arthur let the words sink in for a minute before speaking again. "Which will not be for many years, I might add, so business will continue as usual. There will be no change in the daily operations, except that Gage is to be included in all of our plans and meetings. Is that understood?"

He was answered by a hushed chorus of "Yes, sir."

"Then that is all I have to say. Let's get back to work, shall we?"

Just then Gage saw the responses of his mother and older brother. His mother was motionless, apparently dumbfounded by the announcement. Walton was nearly as still, but his eyes had narrowed in rage, and Gage could tell, even at a distance, that his hands were clenched into tight fists. Gage did not see Walton's nail puncture his own flesh, drawing blood and staining his palm with warm redness. But outwardly, to those who did not know him, Walton seemed calm.

That's when Gage knew, without a doubt, that Walton was not surprised in the least by his father's announcement.

What Gage could not have known was that lying in Walton's breast pocket was a ticket for Portland, Maine.

Portland, Maine
August 1845

Fog swallowed Portland's waterfront in its vast maw. Walton could hear the bellowing of the foghorns, a clang of bells, and the gentle splash of waves, but all became muffled in the thick cottony whiteness.

Walton shivered. "How anyone could make a living in this dampness is beyond me," he muttered as he made his way to a remote pier on the waterfront. "A few days in this fog, and I would be raving mad."

He could smell the tavern before he could see it—ale, tobacco, fish, and the hint of something more fetid. It was an evil scent that Walton could not identify.

Inside, the air was as hazy from tobacco smoke as the fog was outside. Walton coughed, squinted through the haze, and finally noticed his appointment sitting at a booth in the far corner of the room.

"You brung my money, didn't you?"

"And nice to see you again, Mr. French," Walton said with ill-disguised rancor. "Do you think I had forgotten? You mentioned it many times in your last scrawled letter to me."

"No offense, intended. 'Cept I have a lot of expenses. No one said nothin' about me travelin' to Hispaniola. Fares there ain't cheap, you know."

"Listen, I have your money—all you asked for and more."

Mr. French took the money and stuffed it into his tattered and stained peacoat.

"You will have to earn the rest of your money, Mr. French," Walton said, sneering. "You do know whom to see down there, don't you?"

"I'm the one that told you 'bout this in the first place," Mr. French growled. "I be knowin' who I have to see, all right."

"It's just that I am anxious that the information is both protected and authenticated. You can do that, can't you, Mr. French?"

Mr. French adjusted his frayed pea jacket. "I got enough here to grease what wheels need greasin'. Life be cheaper down in the islands than here. I suspect I could have a few dozen people put away for the cost of one in Boston."

Walton smiled. "There is no need for that, Mr. French. At least not yet."

Mr. French nodded. "I know who to get to and who holds the papers. And it be like I say. I am certain on that."

"See to it that it is. I want this information within a month. Can that be done?"

"Gettin' it pose no problem. Travel time depends on if the wind blows right or not. But a month be a fair time." Mr. French turned back to the table. "We meet here or back in New York?"

"Back here, Mr. French. I have some business to tend to in your absence. I will be in this depressing city for at least that long."

Walton grinned as the door slapped shut behind Mr. French.

So our devout Mr. Wilkes, father of our winsome Nora Wilkes, most recently enamored of Gage Davis, is not the man he claims to be. How wondrous these circles within circles are. If I were a religious man, I would claim it God's handiwork, Walton thought exultantly.

But I am not.

If what Mr. French claims to be true actually is, then Mr. Wilkes is in for a grave surprise. How would his church deal with this interesting bit of news—him being a deacon and all? And how would the straightlaced town council react to this news? Would they let him remain as an elected official? How would his faithful and pious wife take the news? Would the town's society matriarchs let her attend even the local dog show after hearing about her husband's activities?

I think not.

Walton carefully folded the letter.

And I get to prove the value of the Good Book. Doesn't it command followers to honor their father and mother? I wonder how far Nora will go in observance of that particular commandment.

He rose to leave.

So my father thinks his laughter is to be the last and loudest? And he thinks Gage will be king? We will see about that, won't we? With the help of our Miss Nora, we'll see about that.

Walton gave a vacant, hollow laugh and stepped out into the cover of whiteness.

CHAPTER NINE

New York City
November 1845

The room pulsed with the clatter of silverware nicking against fine china and too-loud and too-friendly laughter. Gage placed his fork on the table and leaned back.

To his right sat his father, who had spoken very little during the course of the meal. To his left was a Dutchman, wearing a tight, ill-fitting suit with a stain of unknown origin on its too-wide lapel. The Dutchman, Peter Van Glynt, claimed to represent a syndicate of his countrymen with the mission of finding lucrative investments in America. Pausing only briefly as he chewed through his thick portion of roast beef, he had mentioned the names of ten or so top bankers and industrialists as close, personal friends.

Gage smiled and nodded during the meal, trying his best not to reveal his true feelings. *This man knows McCormick as well as I know the queen of England,* Gage thought to himself. *But I'll bet most of the men in this room will believe his stories and offer him credit.*

Before graduation from Harvard, before being named as his father's successor, Gage would have been loath to attend such a luncheon. But now he felt the weight of Davis Enterprises upon his shoulders. Maintaining that image obligated his attendance.

The New York Industrial League held luncheons such as this, Gage surmised, at the drop of a hat and at the merest whiff of money to be made. The Dutchman was actually the guest of honor at today's fete. He had set up offices on lower Broadway and was making a calculated circuit through Manhattan.

The Dutchman knew of this luncheon in advance, Gage thought, *yet he neglected to visit a tailor before this day–or look at his image in a mirror.*

Gage closed his eyes and massaged the flesh at the bridge of his nose with his thumb and forefinger. He felt a headache coming on. If he had his choice, he would have left and spent the afternoon on the family yacht.

But he did not have that luxury. In the scant few months since he had been named as the soon-to-be head of Davis Enterprises, he discovered that his life was slowly being taken from him. Time, a seemingly endless commodity at Harvard, now shrank to precious minutes at the end of a long day. There were few hours in a week that might be called private. His new life was so unlike his previous four years at Harvard. At school, he could sit for hours, either at the Destiny or bakery, reading the morning papers, drinking coffee, watching the parade of citizens on their way to work, sailing, smiling at the faces of frantic students racing to beat the tower bell as it sounded the beginning of class. He could spend endless hours in late-night discussions with friends. He could stroll about the campus, enjoying the sun or moon and the pleasant air.

But no longer.

The novelty of the first breakfast meetings quickly wore off. Yet so many associates and business partners desired his time that he had no choice but to continue the practice. America was in the midst of an industrial boom, and Gage knew that the future was reserved for those who participated fully.

Despite Gage's busy schedule and hectic affairs, a situation pulled him back to the reality and fragility of the human condition.

It was Gage's father.

Over the span of the past several months, he had become painfully aware of his father's declining condition.

There was no single incident Gage could identify as critical, but the sum of them were most troubling. When he had returned to Harvard for his senior year, his father exhibited the essence of health and vigor. Even Edgar, in his private correspondence with Gage, admitted that Arthur Davis appeared as his old, vital self. Through the winter holidays and the early spring, Gage's father remained in complete control. Always capable of handling a dozen tasks simultaneously, he dove into the affairs of his business with skill and enthusiasm.

All that appeared to change on the very day Arthur Davis announced to the world that Gage was his intended successor.

The first hints were minor lapses in memory, or the odd word used at the odd time. Within weeks of that date, the senior Davis began to physically stumble. He began to insist that curbs were cut too high, rugs were too slippery, thresholds too invisible. It was most apparent to those closest to him. Gage knew Edgar worried, in his reserved manner, that he could no longer prevent his employer from suffering embarrassment in public.

During meetings, Gage struggled with the appropriate response. At first, he did nothing. After all, he was but a youngster and it was his father's company. But soon enough, Gage knew that he had to act. At several meetings, he had been forced to intervene, cutting off his father's rambling statements, sometimes in midsentence. The first time he had done this was in August, just prior to their annual trek to Southampton. His father began the day as usual, with a hearty breakfast and cheerful hellos to his staff. Then, during a morning meeting with a trio of railroad men, Arthur had gazed idly about the room, and then, in a less confident voice, began an odd retelling of the first time he had taken a train ride.

Initially Gage imagined that the anecdote might prove to have bearing on their discussion. It did not. After five minutes of disjointed monologue, Gage realized that his father was simply reminiscing, and his story was not focused on any point in particular.

Gage stood up, cleared his throat and, as his father paused for breath, interrupted and returned the discussion to the matter at hand—negotiating favorable freight rates for Davis's iron foundry in western Pennsylvania. His father glared at Gage, fidgeted with his papers, then lowered his eyes to the table, and refused to participate in the remainder of the discussion.

That evening his father had returned to his normal state, confident and full of lighthearted bluster. Gage had not mentioned the episode to his father, and Arthur did not mention it to his son. Yet in that moment, both men knew a significant transition had occurred, with a shifting of power taking place.

To Gage's relief, his father had remained confident and able for days after that first incident.

Amidst the hope, darkness grew. Without warning, a confused look would cloud Arthur's eyes. When Gage saw it, and soon it was unmistakable to him, his heart would ache. During the month of September, Gage had helped his father return to the family mansion over ten times, riding with him in their private carriage, helping him into his bedchamber, calling for Edgar to tend to his needs, then hurrying back to the press of business.

This particular morning, Gage's father awoke with a fine smile and insisted on accompanying his son to the Industrial League's affair. But by the time their carriage arrived at the affair, Arthur began to slip into a puzzled silence. Gage had read the signs. As was normal now, his father grew quiet—answering questions with merely a single word.

As the carriage halted at the curb, Gage evaluated his options. He decided it would be more damaging to leave now than to attend. After all, a group of members had called out greetings to the Davises as they arrived. Gage had no alternative. To turn away would be the cause of greater speculation. He escorted his father inside the Industrial League, taking hold of his arm to steady his wobbly gait. Even though it was obvious that senior Davis was being helped by his son, several people stopped Gage on his way to the table to ask clarifications on business matters, to schedule a meeting, to inquire after his views on one scheme or another.

And now as the league president called for attention, Gage opened his eyes and blinked. The guest of honor took his place at the podium and cleared his throat.

When the Dutchman began to speak, Gage immediately stopped paying attention. He had heard all he needed during lunch. Gage knew that Davis Enterprises had no need of Dutch money.

Gage looked over at his father, who was scanning the room. His eyes full of fear, at last Arthur noticed his son and calmed visibly.

My father does not need to be here, Gage thought. *And I am not that desperate for funds from Holland.*

He leaned over and whispered to his father, took his arm, and led him quietly from the room. Gage left his father at home with Edgar and a day nurse. Gage instructed both Edgar and the newly hired woman never to refer to her true status. She was to be called a maid, not a nurse. Gage wanted no one to think of his father as an invalid.

His father refused to consult a physician, so Gage went in his stead. Not wanting to be the source of rumors, Gage avoided the Davis family physician. He traveled instead to Harvard. With his father's donation to the school yet unmade, the dean was eager to please his former student.

He requested a private audience with the two top professors of the medical college. Neither man could name his father's illness with certainty, but they agreed that it appeared Gage's father had begun to suffer from the "dementia of old age."

"He'll have good days, and he'll have bad days," Dr. Telling stated, "and in a while—a few months, a year—he will stop having good days altogether."

Gage asked, "And you're certain he will have several good months? That's what you're saying, right?"

The other dean, Dr. Johnson, spoke up. "Since we don't have the patient before us, it is hard to say with certainty. And even from the symptoms you described, I daresay none of us could assign a time-table to your father's condition. I have seen older people slip in and out for years and years, and others slip but once into dementia and stay there forever."

"So there is no hope? My father is doomed?"

"By no means," said Dr. Telling. "He might surprise you and stabilize—such as his current condition is."

"But there is no treatment? There is nothing I can do?"

"None that has proved to be successful. There are those who make outlandish claims, but we have yet to see their claims duplicated. You can make him comfortable. You can assign a nurse to watch over him."

"I don't understand. My father is not old. Why would this condition strike him now—just a few years past the prime of his life?"

Dr. Johnson spoke. "Admittedly, this is more usual in the aged. But I have seen cases of both men and women in their sixth decade who lose touch with reality. I'm afraid illness has no respect for age or social condition."

Gage was genuine in his thanks.

"And, gentlemen," he said at the end of their meeting, "I must remind you that you have promised to keep my visit and the reason for it confidential. It will serve no useful purpose if others would know."

Again, their silence was assured by the promise of the money to come.

Edgar closed the door of Arthur's bedchamber behind him and turned to Gage.

"You should rest as well, sir," he said.

"And I have time for rest?"

"Everyone requires rest now and again, sir."

Gage realized he was tired, more tired than he had been in months. "Edgar," he replied, "I will make a deal with you. I will not return to the office this afternoon on one condition."

Edgar waited.

"The condition is that I require something of you."

"Sir? If I may be able, of course."

Gage smiled. "Join me for coffee. There is a coffee shop only a block away. Accompany me there."

"Sir?"

"Please, Edgar. It's a small favor."

Gage saw Edgar's polite, yet very real turmoil. Gage knew such a request was most unexpected: servants were never expected to socialize with their employers. But today, Gage truly felt the need to talk to someone, someone outside a business setting.

"Edgar, it has been months since I sat down with anyone and simply chatted over coffee. It has been since . . . since Harvard. A half of a year is a long time to do without. Please, Edgar."

Edgar finally nodded in a most reserved fashion. "Very well, sir. If I can be of assistance, then I shall accompany you there."

Gage smiled.

"But, sir . . ."

Gage stopped and turned back.

"Would you mind if I had tea? I have never developed a taste for this coffee drink."

Gage laughed softly. "Of course, Edgar. I believe they serve a hearty cup of tea there as well."

Gage took a table in the far corner of the room. Edgar sat stiffly in a chair opposite.

"A strong coffee, a pot of good English tea, and a plate of biscuits and pastries," Gage told the young, attractive serving girl. She smiled widely at the handsome young man and hurried off to the kitchen.

"There is no need to spend money on sweets, sir," Edgar said, visibly shocked by the presence of a woman as a waiter. "I have had my breakfast."

"Then we'll take the remains back. I am sure someone in the house will have an appetite."

"Very well, sir. I am certain you are correct. Food seldom goes to waste."

The serving girl brought their order and hesitated. "Will you desire anything else, sir? Anything at all?"

"No, thank you," Gage said kindly.

She beamed back at him and offered an abbreviated curtsey in reply.

Gage sipped his coffee. *Have I forgotten so soon how to simply sit and relax and talk? Does a man change so quickly? Or have I simply hidden my true self?*

Edgar, who was most always inscrutable, appeared nervous. "Sir," he asked, breaking the silence, "what will become of your father? I imagine you inquired of his condition during your recent trip to Harvard."

"Truly? I told no one of my purpose of the trip."

Edgar blanched. "No sir, no one said a word. I simply surmised the purpose of the trip. I knew for certain that no doctor in New York City would do."

"Nor would they keep their tongues quiet. I imagine it will take a few months before rumors reach New York from Cambridge."

"But did you not ask for confidentiality?"

"I trust no man to keep silent for long when such a delicious secret is placed on their lips. Men will be men, and they will tell someone soon enough. But by then we will come to some conclusions as to his care."

"There is no hope of a cure?"

"None that they knew of," Gage said softly, then added, "I am most afraid of what will become of him, Edgar. He has been so strong. He was always in charge."

The older man looked away. "Indeed, sir. Your father is a most remarkable man. Coming from such humble beginnings and all."

Gage placed his cup on the table. "He has never said much of his youth. It is as if he is ashamed."

Edgar remained silent.

"Do you know more? Did you know him before?"

"I did not. Once, in a most unguarded moment, he mentioned his life on the waterfront. He mentioned that a small stake on a shipping concern brought him enough money to escape the horrors of that life. And in only a few years, he said, he was on Fifth Avenue, as an equal to the city's elite."

"Then you know the same amount of history as I."

With a practiced deliberateness, Edgar sipped from his teacup.

"Edgar, I see no alternative to what I must do in the interim."

"And what might that be, sir?"

"Assume full responsibility of Davis Enterprises. It must be obvious to you, as it is to me, that my father no longer has the ability."

Edgar cleared his throat. "I believe that is the correct path, sir. The company must be looked after in a proper manner."

Gage leaned back and stretched. "And yet it is not truly mine. My father still controls the stock and ownership. Do I force him to sign control over to me while he still maintains some good, rational days?"

"Perhaps. Is such a document required? I should think your solicitor could offer wise counsel."

Gage snorted a laugh. "I would trust them no further than each could be thrown. No Edgar, on this matter I am on my own. And thank you for being honest with me. I value that."

"I have always been honest with you, sir."

The street outside was crowded with people, all seeming in a hurry to get from one place to another.

"And if I take control, do I then set Walton against me forever?"

Edgar's dour expression tightened. "If doing what is right causes some to anger, then so be it. Right is still right, and you must respect your father's wishes over all others."

Gage turned back to the table. "I spoke to my mother of this."

"And her counsel?"

Gage blinked, pain clouding his eyes. "She said Walton had promised her that if he were ever placed in charge of the company, she would never want for anything. He would provide a substantial allowance for her as long as she lived. She told me I must promise her the same. She even mentioned the sum of money she would need on a monthly basis." Gage rubbed his chin as he spoke. "I never had expected either of them to have premeditated what might occur if my father became incapacitated. It sounded so calculated, so devoid of emotion. My mother's main concern was that she be well taken care of. It was as if she had already dismissed my father from her life. I was most taken aback, so much so that I simply nodded in agreement."

A clattering of plates jangled behind them from the kitchen.

"Is that normal, Edgar? Is such a devoid of emotion normal?"

Edgar waited, as if choosing his words carefully. When he spoke, his voice was colored with a sharp edge. "You must know, sir, that when a situation appears to defy logic or reason, that does not make the situation any less real. If a person acts in such a manner—against what a normal person might expect their behavior to be—well, I believe that the correct interpretation of that reality is that a mercenary always shows their true colors at some point. While I wish never to speak ill of anyone—and I will never mention this conversation again—I must admit that your original assessment of both your mother and your elder brother are accurate."

Gage was relieved. Such had always been his feeling, but never once had another person validated that until now. "And that is how you see the situation?" Gage asked in a whisper.

"It is, sir."

Silence returned to the table.

Edgar began to fidget. "Sir, might we change the subject of our conversation? I regret all that I have said. After all, I am but a servant in your house. I am not a confidant or an advisor."

Gage hesitated, then briefly placed his hand over Edgar's and patted it. It might have been the first physical contact ever between them.

"Thank you. You are a true friend—and a loyal servant. I greatly appreciate this."

The plate of biscuits and sweets was almost gone. Gage picked up the last small half of a sweet maple-flavored biscuit that he had cut earlier, popped it into his mouth, and chewed.

"The one thing that I find hard, Edgar, is being pursued."

"Pursued, sir? By whom?"

"By everyone. Bankers, investors, builders, schemers of all types. Everyone wants either my time or my money."

"I'm afraid you must get accustomed to that. Your father appeared to have the gift for discerning which men were fools and charlatans and which were genuine."

Gage sighed. "And that is one skill I will need to learn on my own."

Edgar nodded.

"And it has occurred so quickly. I am less than a year from walking the halls of Harvard, and yet there are so many who seek out my business acumen. There are so many who seek to curry my favor. There are so many outstretched hands and offers and suggestions. I thought it would be years and years until I was cast into such a maelstrom."

"Well, sir, I believe it is because to others, it is obvious that you are not simply in training but are the actual head of Davis Enterprises."

"Edgar, it is a pressure I did not aspire to this soon. I feel drained because of it."

Edgar said cautiously, "Perhaps, sir, if that is the case, you might find a manner in which to refresh your spirits. I have never spoken of this before today, but I might recommend that you consider attending church."

Gage appeared to deflate. "Edgar—not you, too. First it is Joshua, then Nora, and now you."

"Nora, sir? I am acquainted of course with Master Quittner, but I do not know this Nora. Is she a friend from Harvard?"

Gage blushed. He had not mentioned her name to anyone in New York.

"Yes," he replied, a little too quickly, "she was a friend—who urged much the same thing—and often."

"Sir, it is not simply a polite suggestion. A man who can place his faith in the Almighty is a man who is at peace."

Gage rolled his eyes. "Edgar, I am at peace. It is everyone else that is attempting to rob me of it. And now with my father ill, it does seem as if the fates are conspiring against me."

Edgar grew even more melancholy, if that were possible. "Sir, God never conspires against any man. We have free choice, and he allows us to make foolish decisions."

"And my father made a foolish decision? Is that what God would have me believe?"

Edgar's eyes softened. "Sir, I am not a theologian. Perhaps Master Quittner could answer such a riddle. But I know that the only peace in this world is to be found in knowing God."

Gage held his hands up in surrender. "Edgar, I appreciate your words. I appreciate your concern. But what is vexing me now is nothing that a sermon and a few hymns can resolve. Perhaps one day when I have a less hectic schedule, I will take you up on your invitation. I believe that if God is a god of mercy and fairness, he will wait for me, will he not?"

It was obvious to Gage that Edgar desired to speak more but instead simply sat, still and unsmiling, resisting the urge.

The serving girl came once again to their table. "Sir," she said with pleasant urgency while staring at Gage and ignoring Edgar, "are you certain there is nothing more I can offer you? I would be happy to see to any request. Any request at all."

Gage quickly realized she was offering a good deal more than was printed on the menu board. Edgar cleared his throat rather loudly.

"Miss, if either of us ate another bite, we would simply burst. Everything has been grand, and we have stayed much too long," Gage answered.

"No, sir," she protested. "You may stay as long as you wish."

"A very kind offer, miss. And a most tempting offer as well."

A faint blush lit her cheeks.

Gage fished out a five-dollar coin from his vest pocket and placed it in her hand. "That should take care of things, miss."

She stared down, then slipped the coin in her pocket. The actual tab was less than a quarter of that amount.

"And you are sure that I can offer you nothing else?"

Gage smiled in reply and nodded.

As they walked home, Gage admitted, "There are some pursuers who are more pleasant than others."

Edgar almost smiled. "Sir, I am certain you know that particular sort of pursuit would have occurred even if you had been a poor man. You are not without your charms."

Gage said wryly, "If all the supplicants were as obvious as our server today . . . or as wonderfully constructed and pleasing to the eye. And Edgar—you may take my word on it that they are not. And so much the pity."

Edgar replied, "It appears that gone is the day when all waiters were men. And that is the pity."

Later that evening, after the upstairs chambermaid removed the dinner tray from his father's room, Gage stood outside that door. He carried in his hand a short letter that he had written. He had drafted the letter as soon as he and Edgar returned home. It was brief and concise. No one would be lost in its verbiage, and no clever attorney could find fault in so few clauses. The document was four sentences long. It did one simple thing: assigned all power to manage Davis Enterprises to Gage Lowell Davis II.

He tapped lightly at his father's door.

His father answered with a less-than-robust "Come in."

Gage blinked hard and entered the dim room, pen in hand.

CHAPTER TEN

New York City
December 1845

Hispaniola?" Gage said. "Why in the world do you need to go to Hispaniola?"

Walton did not answer directly. He folded his arms across his chest and leaned back from the table.

Only Walton and Gage sat alone at the massive dining room table. Their father had fallen asleep at the end of the afternoon and would probably sleep through till morning. It had not been a good day for him. Their mother had been absent all day. She was a member of the elite planning committee for the governor's annual Christmas Ball, now only two weeks away. She had been gone much of November, lost in a swirl of meetings and pre-party gatherings.

If Walton had his choice, Gage was sure they would be seated at opposite ends of the table. The distance then between them would be so great that shouting would have been the only method of communication.

But Gage viewed that as extreme, and the two brothers, when they actually dined in house, sat opposite each other on the long sides of the table. While still a distance, they did not need to resort to shouting at each other to communicate.

Not that either of them talked much during meals.

Walton's ill temper was nothing new. He was noted for his brooding, and his harsh silence had simply intensified the day Gage graduated from Harvard. Ever since Arthur Davis had announced his intentions that Gage succeed him, Walton had simmered. And when Gage announced to his family and Davis Enterprises' employees that his father had signed control over his vast empire to his youngest son, Walton had shown no discernable anger. He shrugged as if he expected the announcement, then slipped out of the room, telling no one of his destination, but fooling no one with his feigned nonchalance.

In the month since the announcement, Walton had been absent from home more often than in attendance.

"And so, will you eventually tell me, or will I need to guess?" Gage said.

Walton rolled his eyes with a most practiced panache. "I don't think I really need to tell you anything about this, little brother," he replied, taking hold of his full wine glass, "but being the holiday season and all—I will demonstrate my good nature by being civil."

Gage did not respond as he was sure his brother expected him to. He simply waited.

"Hispaniola is an island in the Caribbean Sea," Walton began.

Gage interrupted. "I know where it is located. Its port is a regular stop for our ships in transit."

"Of course you know. How foolish of me to think otherwise. You have such a keen grasp of everything. You must forgive my oversight."

Walton's favorite after-dinner activity was to goad his brother. Yet this evening, Gage refused to reply to this gambit.

"As I said, Hispaniola is an island in the Caribbean. An abundance of sugar cane."

"Indeed? And is the sugar market strong?" Gage asked, knowing full well that the sugar market had been in a two-year decline.

Walton turned his head as if insulted his brother would test his knowledge so obviously. "Of course not," Walton replied. "Do not think I am so stupid as to not know you study these markets all the time, little brother. I may have been cut out of the family business. I may have been usurped from my rightful position. I may have been conspired against—but none of that makes me stupid."

Gage closed his eyes. "I meant to imply nothing. And we have been over this ground too often in the past month. It is over. Father has decided."

Walton snorted. "You are stuck defending that empty facade, aren't you? We both know the old goat has lost any shred of rational thought."

"He has not. He has good days and bad days," Gage answered, annoyed.

Sneering, Walton picked up his wine glass and drained it. He glared at Gage, then looked away, holding his glass in the air, summoning a servant for a refill.

"You are right, little brother," he said. "This ground has been plowed far too many times this season. And I know what has been planted and what will sprout in the future." He watched the maid fill his glass. Before she turned away, he had drained half of it. He snapped his fingers to call her back. "But that is of no matter now. I see I have little recourse, save to confuse the old man even further and thrust other, more pernicious documents under his trembling pen. But I will not stoop that low."

Gage was set to rise and defend his actions once again. He knew that even on his worst days, his father would never sign a shred of paper presented to him by Walton. Even so, he reasoned, Walton was being served well. If the company's value rose, Walton's share in the value rose as well. Both Gage and Walton would be recipients of assets in the event of their father's death.

"Yes, it is of no matter now, little brother. You have made Mother happy with your assurances of proper support."

"I did not do it simply to make Mother happy. It was the proper thing to do—ensure her comfort," Gage replied.

"And I am now resigned to face my future with a greatly diminished role. And I have come to terms with that. Yet I do wish to make a positive contribution to Davis Enterprises."

"And you will do that in Hispaniola?" Gage asked evenly.

"I will," Walton said. His voice had lost its rancorous tone. "Where there is sugar and molasses, there is rum. And while the unrefined drink is not my favorite, it offers an earthy charm to many."

"Rum?" Gage asked.

"Rum, indeed," Walton answered with a civility that was quite uncommon for him. "I have heard that a certain distillery owner there is nearly bankrupt. Enjoys his own product too much, or so the gossips say."

"And how does Davis Enterprises enter into this unhappy story?"

"Little brother—not so impatient, please." Walton finished off his wine, raised his arm in the air again, and snapped his fingers. It was clear that his civility did not include treating servants with respect.

"I plan on visiting the island and investigating this distillery business for myself. If what I have heard is true, perhaps we might purchase the operation for pennies on the dollar. It would prove to be a profitable enterprise. We could run it, or simply hold it for a year or so and double our money."

Gage was shocked. Never in his life had Walton shown the slightest interest in business matters.

"And do not worry about the costs, little brother. I have heard that if the operation is sold, a purchase price of under ten thousand dollars is all that would be required."

"Are you serious?"

"For the entire operation, plus acreage and slaves."

"Slaves?"

"I would think it is in our best interests to simply sell off the land and the slaves and operate the distillery as an independent unit. I knew you would be sensitive to the slave issue."

Gage could not have been more dumbfounded. "Well, of course I would never allow slaves to be owned by Davis Enterprises. Owning another person is just not done—regardless of what our Southern friends say. So there will be no slaves."

Walton smiled. For once it was not a sneer, but an honest, pleasant smile. "I thought as much. You can have time to consider . . . make further inquiries."

Is he being pleasant? Is this how brothers should act? Gage asked himself.

"No, Walton. I trust what you say. It's just that . . . that . . ."

"Unexpected, right? Not a head for business, right? I know."

Gage nodded.

Walton asked, "Then I have your approval to journey there? And the funds required? There is a ship that leaves in three days—a ship with decent accommodations that travels directly there and does not visit every island and port along the way."

"I . . . I . . ."

"I have surprised you, little brother, haven't I? So I should take your stuttering as a yes? I should begin my packing?"

"Well, yes, Walton, by all means." Gage regained his composure and continued. "This does sound like a grand possibility. But you must settle the slave issue before proceeding. Perhaps they could simply be given their freedom? Slaving is a nasty business."

Walton smiled one last time. "Perhaps that would solve it. Just be aware, little brother, that I am right about a great many things. You'll see. You'll soon see how right I am."

Walton's words hung in the still air until the maid reappeared with a fresh bottle of wine.

<hr />

The sudden shift in Walton's disposition lasted through his departure for the Caribbean. He actually asked if Gage wished to accompany him to the pier and, during the short ride, made pleasant conversation concerning the trip, the Christmas festivities he would miss, New Year's. In general, the two behaved as might any ordinary brothers.

Gage watched the handsome clipper ship slip away from the dock. The voyage would take no more than a few weeks in either direction. The ship's route would keep it in sight of land for virtually the entire voyage.

As Gage rode back to the family's home, he marveled at the change in his brother. *I trust this is the beginning of a new chapter for both of us. How wonderful these last several days have been.*

⟡

Walton stood at the stern rail and stared as Manhattan receded from the horizon. He took a deep breath of the cold sea air. Gathering his fur collar more tightly around his neck, he stepped unsteadily toward the bow of the rolling ship.

"It is miserably cold up here," he said to no one. "I hate this weather. But I can't stay in that miserable hole they claim is a 'deluxe cabin' for a minute more than necessary."

He huddled behind the large sea chest bolted to the deck. He reached into the folds of his coat and, after searching for a moment, extracted a fist-sized bottle of amber liquid. He unscrewed the cap and drained half in a long swallow, then turned again to face the wind.

"And in a few weeks, I think I shall have all the information I need. I do not trust Mr. French to do this delicate work. No, he is too clumsy. I will find out what I need. And when I do, my future will be most secure. Most secure indeed."

⟡

Gage called for the driver to stop the carriage a few miles from home.

"But, sir, there's a cold wind, and a man like you should be in a carriage, not on foot."

"And just what is a man like me?" Gage asked as he stepped to the curb.

"Well, sir . . . you know," the driver said, clearly embarrassed, "a man like your father. Not a man to walk in the cold, sir."

For a second Gage felt anger, then he shook his head."I won't freeze to death. And the walk will do me good, I am sure. Clear my head after all those smoke-filled meetings, don't you think?"

Emmett Tiller, the family's driver for more than a decade, was nervous. To allow his employer to walk the streets on such a cold and blustery day was simply not proper. "I could drive behind you in case you find the cold too biting, sir."

Gage put his hands in his coat pockets. "Mr. Tiller, that is plain ridiculous. I am capable of walking on my own. If I find my limbs growing numb, I shall slip into a restaurant or tavern to warm."

Mr. Tiller evaluated the street. "There may be some unseemly places, sir—Second Avenue is not as elegant as it once was. It would be best if I simply rode behind."

Gage's voice was now firm and nearly harsh. "Emmett, I will have no more of this. Take the carriage and go home. I wish to walk. It has been months since I have been alone. It will do my heart good. I will be fine. It is no longer your responsibility. Is that clear?"

Tiller swallowed. "Are you sure, sir? I would never forgive myself if something happened to you."

"I will be fine. I am sure. Now off with you."

Tiller hesitated, then switched at the reins. As the two bays set off on a steady pace up Second Avenue, Tiller turned many times to make sure Gage was not frantically signaling him to return.

Smiling at the man's persistence and loyalty, Gage began walking. He drew the scarf more closely about his neck.

It is cold out here, he realized. *I need to get moving.*

After walking a block, Gage was invigorated. Finally he was alone. The cold air felt good in his lungs. But after six blocks, the chill invaded his legs. At twelve blocks, his cheeks were numb, and his ears began to throb from the pain of the cold wind against them.

Well, I guess Mr. Tiller was right. And now when they find me, frozen on Second Avenue, he will be filled with remorse.

Gage laughed at the idea and stopped walking. He seldom ventured down this section of New York. His business was centered mostly uptown or in the warrens about Wall Street. The broad street was lined with three- and four-story buildings, nearly all apartments.

There was but a scattering of private residences. At the corner was a small restaurant and tavern. As Gage stopped and debated on entering, a patron exited. Pungent smells wafted into the chilled air, followed by a shout and a curse.

I like exotic foods, Gage told himself, *but that aroma is well beyond exotic and comes much too close to dangerous.*

Gage crossed the street and continued walking. He saw the shadow of a spire midway up the block.

If that's a church, then I can get warm there. They always keep the doors of churches open, don't they?

He hurried up the steps. It was not a large building. There were three sets of double doors at the entrance.

The middle doors were locked.

Then they'll find my frozen body outside a church. Won't that be ironic?

The right set of doors was locked as well. Gage hurried to the remaining doors. The left door opened. He slipped in and began flexing his hands and rubbing his arms, attempting to remove the aching chill.

Gage moved farther into the church. He blinked his eyes, trying to adjust to the darkness. The stained glass windows admitted little daylight, and the wobbly glow from a brace of candles illuminated but a small pool of space.

He put out his hand and found the edge of a pew, then slowly walked midway up the aisle. Even though the air inside was by no means warm, the feeling began to return to Gage's feet and hands.

He slipped into the pew and sat down, blowing into his hands for warmth. For perhaps ten minutes, Gage simply sat in the silence, staring at the small, trembling flames twelve yards in front of him.

I wonder who lights the candles, he finally thought. *I have not seen anyone, or heard anyone since I walked in.*

By now his eyes had grown accustomed to the dark, and he began to make out the rich colors of the windows and the simple carvings on the pews and altar.

"May I help you, my son?"

Gage literally leapt from the pew, falling into the aisle in a terrified heap.

"Oh my . . . I'm sorry. I did not mean to startle you." The voice came from the darkened rear of the church.

Gage turned in a flash to face the intruder.

"I'm Reverend Kenyon. John Kenyon. I'm the pastor here. I didn't mean to frighten you. I was . . . I was having lunch. I didn't hear you come in. I didn't expect anyone to be here."

Gage held his hands up.

Pastor Kenyon was a young man, around Gage's age, with a thin blond beard and wispy sideburns. But his eyes, a dark blue, were focused and intense.

"No harm done. You did startle me though," Gage said, bending to brush at his knees.

"Are you certain? I frightened you into a nasty spill."

"No, really, I am fine, Reverend Kenyon. And my name is Gage Davis."

Reverend Kenyon fussed about, nervously twining his fingers together. "Then, Mr. Davis, allow me to offer you a cup of tea. It will warm you. I have nearly a full pot in the kitchen. It would be no trouble at all."

Gage surprised himself by saying, "Well, that does sound good. A cup of tea would be very nice."

Reverend Kenyon beamed.

"Follow me, then. I'll get the tea. Sugar? Cream?"

"Sugar."

In a moment the two men settled into a pair of uncomfortable chairs in a small study overlooking the street.

"Reverend Kenyon, I have to confess something to you."

"I don't want to disappoint you again, Mr. Davis, but this isn't a Catholic church. I can't hear your confession. It's not what I do as a pastor, I'm afraid."

Gage laughed. "No . . . Pastor Kenyon, that's not the sort of confession I mean."

"Oh . . . then good, I suppose."

"I meant that I came into the church to escape the cold. I sent my driver home and thought it would be bracing to walk the last mile or so home. I'm afraid I overestimated my abilities and underestimated the power of the cold wind. It soon ceased being bracing and became downright painful."

"Oh . . . that sort of confession," the pastor said. He rubbed his hands together and looked away. "Then I have a confession as well. I was not having lunch when you arrived. I was sound asleep. And right in the middle of the time when everyone thinks I am working on my sermon."

Gage laughed again. "I won't tell if you won't tell."

"Agreed," Reverend Kenyon said.

Gage looked about the tiny room. Stacks of books canted into the corners, and five or six teacups were scattered about the room. Newspapers piled up by the desk, which itself was buried under an avalanche of papers, letters, and notes.

"It's quite a mess, I know that. But I seldom have visitors, so . . ."

"Don't be concerned. I find it interesting how people work," Gage said. "Every man has a different approach."

"I suspect that is true. Some of the fellows I went to seminary with were most fastidious—at least compared to myself."

"And where did you go to seminary, if you don't mind my asking?"

"A small school near Portland. I'm sure you have never heard of it. No one has. Walpole."

"You're right. I have never heard of it."

Pastor Kenyon sipped his tea. "And what do you do, Mr. Davis? If you don't mind me being presumptuous."

"I'm involved in a variety of things. . . ." *Just what do I tell people? What is it that I do exactly?* ". . . Investments, factories here and there, textiles, foundries, shipping . . . things like that."

Reverend Kenyon stared. His teacup rattled in the saucer.

"Davis? Arthur Davis?"

"He's my father."

"Oh my, oh my, oh my. I didn't realize that when I frightened you. I would never have brought you to this horrid, cluttered office."

"You know my father?" Gage asked.

"No. I mean, yes. I mean, I know him. Or I know of him. I read the papers. His name is mentioned quite often, you know."

Gage knew that. Anyone in a position of wealth or power became a standard target for reporters and newspapers. Even the *Post* took an occasional shot at the Davis family. Even his own name had appeared in several of the New York papers. The first time he saw those familiar letters, it gave his heart a jolt. Now he scanned articles searching for other mentions. He was not sure when that curious, solitary thrill would diminish.

"Don't worry about the cluttered office, Pastor Kenyon. There are industrialists out there who control vast empires whose offices are smaller and even more cluttered than yours."

"Is that true?"

"Indeed it is. You have heard of Joseph Aspdin?"

"I have . . . but I do not recall in what field of endeavor."

"He developed that cement . . . Portland, I think they call it. Made him a rich man. I called on him several months prior and had to fight my way through a maze of cartons and bags and books and all manner of debris. His desk was buried to the top with odd bits and pieces."

"Truly?"

Gage smiled at the pastor's amazement. What Gage took for granted, so many others could only imagine. With an appreciative and noncritical audience, Gage related other tales, from cluttered offices to meals eaten standing up, to a millionaire who bathed so infrequently that no one would sit next to him at dinners.

Nearly an hour had passed in pleasant conversation. Gage found it so enjoyable to sit and talk and not be worried over his choice of words or subjects.

When Gage noted the deepening of the shadows in the room, he pulled out his pocketwatch.

"I am afraid I will have to say my good-bye today, Reverend

Kenyon. I do have an appointment this evening that I simply cannot postpone."

"Oh yes, of course. I understand," Pastor Kenyon said as he rose. "I did enjoy our talk. When you are again in the neighborhood, please feel free to drop in."

Gage found himself nodding. "I would like that. I really would." He slipped on his coat and scarf. "Are there any carriage stands nearby? In spite of my stubbornness, I believe the cold would defeat me if I tried to walk the rest of the way."

Rev. Kenyon scratched his head.

"If I am not mistaken, there is a hackney stand two blocks to the west. It's either on Fourth or Fifth Avenue. I'm afraid most of the residents of this neighborhood, myself included, find a private carriage beyond them."

The two men walked to the door.

"And how long have you been a pastor here?" Gage asked.

"Ever since seminary. That's been four years now."

"And you enjoy it?"

Pastor Kenyon replied, in a softer tone, "I love every minute of it. The ground is hard—people today hear but don't seem to listen. Listening without hearing—that's the problem. I guess the city does that to a person. But in spite of the poor harvest, as it were, work here is good. There have been wonderful moments of joy. And if you ask God to bless your works, and serve him, then good things are bound to happen eventually, don't you think?"

Gage shrugged. "I don't know. I would feel most odd if I were to trouble God in order to bless a contract or a meeting. I don't think he would be comfortable in the soulless world of business."

Pastor Kenyon waited a moment before speaking. "Are you a believer, Mr. Davis?"

Gage did not show it, but he bristled at the question. "I believe in God. Only a fool doesn't. But I also believe God has his area of expertise and I have mine."

"Were that to be true, Mr. Davis, then I would be out of a job. God's place is everywhere."

Gage offered his hand. "That may be, Pastor Kenyon. But I am most sure God would prefer to not be thought of as an industrialist. I must offer my farewell for now. Perhaps I shall see you again."

"I would like that."

Gage grasped the door handle, then stopped in midstep. There was a flyer tacked to a board just inside the door. The words he saw made his heart hurt: NORA WILKES, IN A CONCERT OF SACRED MUSIC, THIS DECEMBER 19.

"Nora Wilkes? Is this a current flyer? Is she going to be at this church?"

"Yes, it's current. And she will be here. Do you know her? Miss Wilkes is a delightful talent. Her father and my father are acquainted back in Maine. She's really appearing here as a favor to my family, I'm afraid. A small church like ours would have no other way of having such a talent in concert."

"The nineteenth?"

"Yes, instead of our evening service, she will perform."

Gage blinked a few times, trying to adjust to this news. "You know . . . I think I have heard of her. In concert here you say . . . perhaps I will be in attendance that night. I do enjoy good music."

"Do that, please. I bet Nora would love to meet you afterwards. She is a most attractive woman. And still single, much to her mother's dismay."

"Then I will be here," Gage said, as if he had just made up his mind. "I will, indeed."

He turned from the pastor and headed toward the steps. The doors clicked behind him.

Nora!

As he stepped farther into the cold, a realization blasted at his thoughts as strongly as the cold that whipped about him. *The nineteenth! That's the same night as the Governor's Ball. If I miss that, Mother will drum me out of the family. With Father not well enough to be there and Walton gone, I have to be there.*

He stopped at the curb and glared into the gray skies.

The room sparkled like an elegant composition in the hands of a master painter. The men's black-and-white formal coats stood in stark opposition to the ladies' burgundy and scarlet and emerald green and Prussian blue gowns. The fat columns that ringed the long space were festooned with ropings of pine bough and graced with red velvet ribbons and ivory lace. By each stood a giant Christmas tree decorated with pearl garlands. From the ceiling hung a vast profusion of metallic stars, reflecting the light from flickering candles and hissing gas lamps. They rivaled the glorious brilliance of the stars in the heavens.

Waiters snaked through the crowds, holding polished silver platters groaning with quail eggs and wine, fruit cakes and rum, cheese and brandy. Hands would reach up, platters would dip, and lights would glint off the elegant trays.

Gage stood at the rear of the room, nearly hidden by a massive pillar. In front of him was the mayor of New York, who had propped himself against one of the pillars. A ribbon had come undone and was gaily draped about the man's head and ears. It was obvious the mayor did not notice. His affection for drink was legendary, and Gage watched as the mayor took three glasses from a passing tray, spilling nary a drop and returning two empty glasses in the time it took the waiter to pause.

Dinner—all three hours of it—had been served by a vast army of waiters and attendants in starched white coats. As soon as the last cup of coffee was served and consumed, another virtual army of servants swept through the vast hall, removing the tables and arranging the chairs to the side. As the tables were wheeled out, a full orchestra appeared on a raised podium as if by magic. An opening glissando of festive music flowed, and rounds of dancers took to the floor, weaving in and out among the waiters still carrying trays laden with drinks and sweets.

Gage leaned first to the left, then the right, and finally saw a flash from his mother's gown. It was trimmed with jewels, and her every move caught the light. Standing beside her was the governor of New

York. His wife, who had not been well for years, had taken a turn for the worse and had not attended this year's ball. Arthur Davis had been lucid for a few days at the beginning of the month but had slipped further into his own personal fog, so Isabelle was forced to attend without him. Gage could see his mother's head tilt back with laughter as she placed her hand on the governor's arm, holding it there for much longer than necessary.

Gage took out his watch. He nodded to a few acquaintances, calling out a greeting or two. A parade of dancers now filled the floor. Gowns adorned with imported lace swished against the floor as dancers swept past. Gage smiled and clapped politely as the first song ended.

He pulled out his watch again. Six minutes had passed. He peered toward the front of the room and saw his mother surrounded by several men. He could see her laugh, but a sea of music drowned out the sounds.

He stepped back and then, without stopping, turned, opened the door behind him, and slipped out into the hall. The door snapped closed, and the music instantly grew muted and hazy. He began walking, without looking to either side, trying to appear as inconspicuous as possible. A smile stole over his lips.

"Gage Davis!"

He heard his name from behind and yet did not stop. He recognized the voice from the chill in his neck.

"Gage! I know you heard me!"

He was trapped. He stopped and shut his eyes tightly for a moment.

"I knew you would be here. I saw you lurking in the shadows and told myself that you were planning on bolting. I could tell from your furtive manners. And I was right."

Gage turned, offering his sweetest, most innocent smile. "Why, Miss Brockhurst, what a pleasant surprise. I had no idea. What brings you to New York?"

Emily Brockhurst placed her hand on her hips and tilted her head like a schoolmarm about to give a lecture to an unruly student.

"Why, Gage Davis, if I didn't know better, I would think you are simply toying with me."

Gage appeared shocked. "Why, Miss Brockhurst, I am well aware that you are not a woman to be toyed with. Ever."

"You are such a scamp," she said lightly. "You knew I would be in New York this winter. I am staying with my aunt and uncle until spring. Then I sail to the Continent. I know you know because I wrote you four notes on the subject."

Gage looked lost. It was apparent to both in that moment that Gage never read any of her missives.

"Well, no matter, you silly man. I know you are possessed by business. I read the papers, you know. You are mentioned nearly every day. On your way to being a titan of industry, the *Post* said. A titan. And I can say I knew you when. And still do, right?"

Emily touched Gage's hand, letting her finger graze against his skin. It was far more forward than he expected or was necessary to get his attention.

He stammered out a reply, "I-I simply work for my father, Miss Brockhurst. It's nothing worthy of a newspaper report, I assure you."

She sidled up closer. He knew her gown, adorned with lace and pearls, had been imported from the Continent. The fit was very tight and the cut along her bodice verged on immodest.

"So you were attempting to sneak out, weren't you?"

"Why, Miss Brockhurst. My mother spent months and months organizing this affair."

Emily giggled. "I know. One of the gentlemen your mother is now talking with is my uncle."

Gage gulped. He felt every tick of the watch resting in his vest pocket. He gulped again.

"You were attempting to sneak out," she accused. "I know it now. There is a guilty look on your face."

"I needed to stretch my legs," he offered lamely.

"Gage, my sweet boy. You have lost the edge you had at Harvard. I no more believe that than I believe man will someday fly. But don't worry. I won't tell that you were leaving early–if you agree to make a deal with me."

She clutched his arm. "If you leave now, I will march in and tell my uncle that I came across my old friend Gage Davis slipping away from the ball. Of course, I will make certain your mother is nearby."

Gage closed his eyes. "And what will prevent you from doing that?"

"You must take me with you."

"But . . . but . . ."

"I know you are not seeing another woman tonight. Only a fool would schedule a liaison with a woman the same night as the Governor's Ball. Only a foolish woman would accept it as well. And you are not a foolish man, though you may consort with foolish women."

"But . . ."

"Take me with you, or your mother will know of your absence."

Gage stared at Emily. "Absolute silence?"

"Yes. I am nothing if not a confidante."

Gage knew otherwise, but he had no choice. If he waited, he would miss Nora altogether.

"Very well. I'll get our coats."

Emily offered a knowing smile in return.

I have no choice. Perhaps I can explain this somehow. Perhaps Nora will not wish to speak to me. Perhaps I will find the spark gone as well.

He slipped on his evening coat and hurried back to Emily with her velvet cape.

And what does Emily mean that I've lost my edge? I haven't.

They stepped out into the snow and Gage whistled for his carriage.

Have I?

⟨⟨❦⟩⟩

Gage had never been as captivated as he was that night.

Emily, as he expected, chattered the entire trip. By the time they arrived at the small church, the snow was past ankle depth. The concert had commenced only minutes earlier. He and Emily took seats near the back of the crowded church.

A sparse collection of pine branches attempted to adorn the front of the church. Watching Emily's eyes, he knew she considered the decorations pathetic. However, Gage was charmed by their simplicity and innocence. Even in the dim light, Gage knew no one in this audience possessed a gown, an evening coat, or a top hat. Yet everyone remained still, almost reverent, in their quiet appreciation as Nora played.

Most of the compositions were unfamiliar to Gage. A few sounded like hymns, but Gage could not be sure.

Midway through, Emily leaned over. "Just what are we doing here? Have you found religion? This is a church, isn't it?"

Gage ignored Emily's intrusive question and focused on Nora's music, her talent, and her beauty. He was not sure which of the three was most responsible for the curious ache in his heart.

After Nora finished her last piece, the congregation remained silent, in awe. Then Pastor Kenyon stood and began to applaud— softly, with decorum. As he took to his feet, the rest of the audience followed, and soon the entire church was filled with the sound of hands clapping.

"Gage, what are we doing here? I could have listened to music back at the ball."

Gage turned as if suddenly remembering Emily's presence. "Oh, I suppose I should have told you. Pastor Kenyon is an old friend of Joshua's. You remember my housemate?"

"The handsome one?"

"Yes," Gage replied, knowing he would never be called the "handsome one"—just the "rich one."

Gage searched for a plausible explanation and finally fabricated one. "It seems the pastor here asked Miss Wilkes to play this evening and told Joshua in a letter. Pastor Kenyon asked if I would attend, since Miss Wilkes is struggling to gain an audience. Then Joshua wrote and asked if I might take her cards and pass them around in the right circles. So I agreed to come and meet with Pastor Kenyon and this Miss Wilkes at the tea that follows. I hope you don't mind waiting with me."

Emily's surprised face showed a hint of anger. "You mean stay here? I thought we would be going out on the town this evening."

"Oh no, not tonight. I must apologize for not telling you sooner, but I think I will be tied up for at least an hour or two."

"An hour?"

"Or two. Again, Miss Brockhurst, I apologize."

"But . . . but . . ."

Gage tried his best to look as if an idea suddenly struck him. "Would you allow me to suggest something, Miss Brockhurst? While I hate to permit you to leave unescorted, I could ask my driver to take you back to the ball and then catch up with you later after this favor to a friend is taken care of."

"You would do that for me, Gage? That's a sweet offer from a gentleman. But how will you get back?"

"There is a carriage stand not far from here. I can be along when my business is concluded."

Gage could tell she was trying her best not to appear too enthusiastic over leaving what she considered a boring waste of an evening.

"Well, if it is no trouble, then I think that is the best solution. If you are sure I would only be in the way here."

"Absolutely. And I don't want you to miss any more of the ball than you have already," Gage said, escorting her to the door and whistling for his driver and carriage.

He waved as the carriage pulled away, the horse's hooves muffled by the snow.

And she said I have lost my edge. Rubbish, Gage thought as he smiled to himself.

⁂

As soon as Emily rode away, Gage spun about and ran back into the church. He brushed the snow from his shoulders and hair.

A large crowd had gathered about Miss Wilkes. Gage waited at the far edge, hidden in the shadows. More than a half hour passed until the crowd evaporated, leaving only Nora and Pastor Kenyon by the piano.

Gage stepped toward Miss Wilkes. "Nora," he said tenderly, "you played with grace and beauty. I have missed hearing truth expressed in music that way."

Nora blinked at the darkness. She leaned forward. Her hand fluttered to her throat. "Gage?" Her voice was softer than the fur of a rabbit.

Pastor Kenyon brightened. "Mr. Davis. You did come. I am delighted."

"Gage, it is you," Nora said, almost breathless.

"You two know each other?" Pastor Kenyon said.

"We do," Gage replied. "And I did not tell you I was coming because until this evening I did not know if I could. But I am so glad I managed."

"Then that's grand, Mr. Davis. Why don't the three of us head downstairs? The deaconesses will think we are avoiding their Christmas tea."

Gage stepped close and offered his arm to Nora. "Yes, Miss Wilkes, shall we? Let us determine if this tea rivals those in Boston and Cambridge."

Nora stood and took Gage's arm, gazing at him intently.

Gage could not tell if it was a smile or disappointment that showed in her eyes.

"The tea awaits."

CHAPTER ELEVEN

New York City
January 1846

FROM THE JOURNAL OF GAGE DAVIS

I have returned to my journal after months and months. I believe it would have languished on my desk forever had it not been for that cold day in December when Nora again entered my life. But my journey to this day is so convoluted, so Byzantine, that I am forced to write the particulars lest I confuse myself, let alone my biographer someday.

No pencils this time, but pen and ink. These days I feel less compelled to tweak at my father's sensibilities.

I could not have imagined a more odd scenario. Here are the characters of this little drama: Me, in a stunningly modest church, dressed to the nines, with top hat in hand. There is Pastor Kenyon, wearing vestments that need both cleaning and pressing. And then there is Nora, who was, quite simply, a crescendo of beauty–stunning in a simple bell-shaped dress of dark purple trimmed in lavender.

The rush of well-wishers quickly dissipated–the lure of food and drink does wonders to clear a crowd in a hurry. And we three remained, gathered about the church's ancient piano. I felt more ill at ease than a schoolboy badly prepared for an exam. Pastor Kenyon beamed and made small talk and offered introductions at least three times until we managed to explain that we had met and known each other back in Cambridge.

Not even a half year has passed since I received that sorrowful letter from Nora. But seeing her close like that brought an ache to my heart that was true physical pain, not just emotional hurt.

Nora, to her credit, was polite and civil. She inquired after my father, and I related the status of his current condition. She appeared to be genuinely concerned. She spoke some of how Pastor Kenyon and her family were related or intertwined. I must admit that I heard only a few words, being so captivated with simply watching her speak and being near her again.

The good pastor added what he could, laughing and knowing nothing of the pain I felt, and the pain that I hoped Nora felt as well. He went on and on about our meeting that night when I came in to escape the cold and he was sound asleep, et cetera.

"To think—one of the richest men in all of New York—on the eastern seaboard for that matter—enters my humble church and does not laugh at the frayed surroundings. A man of uncommon grace, I would say," is how the pastor phrased it.

I watched Nora's eyes as he said those words and could not find disagreement in them. Indeed, she nodded and smiled at the appropriate points.

How I wish that all my life and its entanglements could have been returned to their status before I received that dreaded letter.

The pastor then excused himself, saying that he had to tend to his flock, and "to get there before they eat everything, for I haven't had dinner yet."

After his departure, a terribly awkward silence filled the space between the two of us.

"You're looking well," she said finally.

"As are you, Nora. You played with genius tonight."

She looked away. Never comfortable with compliments, she often deflected them in the most self-denigrating manner.

"The audience was appreciative," she said. "That helps cover many of my shortcomings. And the sins of this piano, but I hate to fault the instrument."

"I did not hear a single false note," I said. "I was moved with your passion. It was obvious to all here tonight."

I had chosen the word *passion* carefully, to see if it brought a flicker of response to her eyes.

It did not.

After a long moment, she rose and said that she should appear at the reception.

I said I understood.

"It was so wonderful to see you, Gage," she said softly.

"And you, too," I replied. I thought I saw the flicker of hesitation before she turned away from me. But if so, it was for but a heartbeat.

And in the blink of an eye, she walked away into the shadows. When I heard the altar steps creak, I reached for my gloves, made my way down the aisle, and entered the world of cold and snow and wind.

Then, two days later, I received a note from Pastor Kenyon. I am copying much of it here.

Dear Mr. Davis,

(I have skipped three paragraphs of his opening lines.)

It was wonderful for you to be in attendance at Miss Wilkes's concert. I know all who heard it were blessed. And the church was blessed by your donation. I seldom, if ever, am informed concerning the amount anyone gives to the Lord, but the day after the concert, our treasurer came running into my office, out of breath, with an envelope in his hands.

He wanted to know if I knew a "G. L. Davis."

I said I did, and related just a bit of our meeting.

He then inquired as to your stability.

I replied that you seemed a stable fellow.

He shook his head as if he disbelieved my assessment of you. Thrusting your bank draft, issued to our church, under my nose, he inquired, "Does this check look like it was written by a sane man?"

I admit that the number of zeros was impressive, unexpected, and the likes of which have never been seen in this church before.

You are too kind. Please accept my thanks. It will help alleviate suffering for many families this winter.

But the real reason I write you concerns our mutual friend, Nora Wilkes. I had no idea you had been seeing each other in Cambridge. And like an idiot, I went on and on that night, offering introductions and the like. You must have thought me deranged.

Nora was unnaturally quiet and reserved that evening after her concert. She was about to retire for the evening (yes, I had a chaperone stay the night) and while she and I were alone for a moment, I asked about her past relationship with you. She related the tale in an abbreviated form, I imagine.

She grew quiet, and then I heard a sniffle and her soft crying.

I had no choice but to press on, as a man of God should do, and discover the root of her pain. She told me of her final letter to you and why she felt forced to write those cold words.

Now that I have written all this, I find myself in a corner.

Here are my options:

I could tell you if you find faith in God you could resume your relationship with Nora.

I could tell you that Nora holds in her heart a glimmer of hope for your relationship.

I could tell you that she has wept over seeing you again.

(I am certain she never expected me to write this letter to you. If she knew what I was doing this moment, she would be as angry as a group of wasps in a nest hit by a rock. So for heaven's sake, and mine, never mention a word of this to anyone.)

And thus, I find myself in a predicament.

Nora is a treasure of great worth. I am sure you know that. Yet she is firm in her faith, and I am sure that a suitor must share her faith and belief in God.

Mr. Davis, forgive my presumptuousness—but this too is the mark of a

*pastor. Often we must ask the hard question, risk offense, risk being rude—
in order to serve the Lord as his disciple and witness.*

*You can make things right with God, you know. It is not a complicated
matter. Surrender yourself to him. Accept his lordship of your life. Take the
gift of salvation.*

*I am botching this, I know, but I have written far too much to discard
and start again; my hand is cramping up. And yet I know you both can
have what you want.*

*No doubt this is too much to accept in a simple letter. Ponder what I
have said. Come to see me. I would call upon you—again, that is the mark
of a pastor set to increase his flock—but I realize that a man like yourself
finds private moments scarce.*

*And after our long, teary talk, Nora admitted that her heart has been in
turmoil since you and she parted ways. Often God uses a heart in turmoil
to move his children to a different place and teach them.*

*This is what I ask you to do. Write to her. She will be shocked, to be sure, but
in a happy way. Tell her the news of your life. She was concerned over the
health of your father. Write as if you are talking to her. Perhaps in this way
you will both learn from each other. And is not wisdom gained in small steps?*

*Perhaps she can help guide you on your journey to God. And, Mr.
Davis, forgive my boldness here—again, the mark of a pastor—but every
man now alive will one day face God. It may be at Judgment Day; it may
be prior to that. To ignore God is to have chosen unwisely. Don't be unwise.*

*Forgive this long letter. I am afraid that I am as long-winded in letters
as I am in the pulpit.*

*Our church will pray for you and your father. You will both be lifted up
through our humble prayers.*

*Thank you again for your gift. If you choose to attend some Sunday
morning, we do not expect a similar gift. Unless the Lord leads you . . . and
there I am being a pastor again.*

With regards,
Pastor J. Kenyon

A most curious letter I must say. I have read it so very often—stopping to read and reread the part of Nora's tears.

And now, after hours of writing, I have a sheet of my personal letterhead before me. I will follow the pastor's advice. I will write Nora a letter.

Yet I cannot do what she and Pastor Kenyon want.

She is calling on me to sacrifice so much—to give up everything and follow her faith. "Give up all and follow me." Is that not what the Lord commanded? Such an order is so permanent and drastic—I do not think I can give up that much.

But for a woman like Nora . . . ?

For the first time in months, my heart feels unburdened and light—as if all the troubles of business have been placed into their proper perspective.

I have never hoped without cause before, and I have never allowed hope to twist the truth of reality. Yet if she receives this letter and responds to it, then there is great reason to hope.

March 1846

"So the distillery, while it had great promise, has been allowed to deteriorate much too far. There was rust on the boilers, some buildings were near collapse due to the beams rotting out. If I had found out about this potential investment a year earlier, perhaps it would have made sense."

Walton leaned back on the couch in the formal drawing room. His fair skin had been burnished to a nut-brown tint, yet his ears and neck were more red than brown. He had not shaved in weeks, claiming that his skin had grown too sensitive for a blade.

When Gage first laid eyes on his older brother, on a blustery gray morning at the south docks, he laughed and called him a pirate.

Rare for Walton, he offered a laugh in return. "I feel like a pirate, little brother," he called back from the ship's rail.

And now back at the Davis home, Walton described his trip to Hispaniola. "First—the food is barely edible," he said, munching on a cold slice of lamb roast. "During the entire trip, I daresay I consumed one palatable meal. Accommodations are even worse than the food, with roaches the size of your palm and biting insects and buzzing whirligigs so thick, one might think a child could be carried aloft by them."

"But what of the natives? How do they cope?" Gage asked, listening eagerly. "Surely the landowners must have found a way."

"They do. It's called rum. Spend your entire day half filled with the stuff, and no amount of whirligigs are bothersome."

"Walton, is this really true? Surely not everyone is drunk all day. There must be other ways to cope."

"If there are other methods, I have no idea, Gage. Perhaps there are. One positive thing about the island is that the vistas are quite beautiful—sea and sand and rocks and glorious sunsets and the like—and the weather is remarkably fair and even. But I would as soon live there as I would live on the moon."

Gage shook his head. "That is regrettable. I had hoped that this would work out."

Walton offered an odd smile in return. He paused, then took another bite of lamb. He washed it down with half a glass of wine.

"Well, little brother . . . Gage, there are other opportunities. This is the land of unbridled chance, you know. And in a few days, after I wash the salt from my hair and clothing, I have another possibility to investigate."

"Truly?" Gage asked. "Back in the islands?"

"Heavens no," Walton said, laughing. "This is in America. I heard some amazing things while on ship. This possibility has to do with shipping. A sailor I met on board told me a story that he heard from the most reliable sources."

"Shipping?"

"From the islands to Portland."

"Portland? Portland, Maine?"

"Indeed. Next week, if you think it acceptable, Gage, I would like to travel to Portland. I would like to pay a visit on a shipper there— who might be thinking of getting out of the shipping business."

"Retiring?"

"Something like that."

191

When Gage nodded, he failed to notice the twisted smile that graced his brother's face.

✦

Walton paced about the attorney's office. The only noises were the crackle each time the man turned a page and his mumbling as he read to himself. At last he flipped the last page and looked up at Walton.

"So, tell me, what does that legal confusion truly mean?" Walton asked. "Or is it a secret that attorneys only reveal after they get their slice of my father's estate?"

Horace Cochrane snorted, "And for that, I am adding another hour of time, regardless of what I tell you now."

Walton impatiently answered him with an angry wave. "So add it to your bill."

"I will add that amount," the attorney replied.

"Whatever. Just tell me if it's in there."

"It is. Paragraph 15, subsection 4, clauses B and C."

"Spare me the directions. Just tell me what's in there. In plain English, if you would be so kind."

The attorney, a gnomelike man with meaty hands, again skimmed over the document.

"It's filled with all the standard clauses found in most last wills and testaments—especially for someone with your father's assets. He has made certain that his heirs are well-taken care of . . . unless."

"Unless . . . unless what?"

"It says here that anyone on the board of Davis Enterprises must be a person of unimpeachable character. That if convicted of a major crime or offense, then that person shall be removed from the board and denied any rights of further inheritance."

"Does that mean what I think it does?"

Cochrane blinked and scrutinized Walton. "If you are convicted of stealing or adultery or fraud or any number of offenses, then you're out."

"That includes stock manipulations?"

"It does."

"And they don't get a single dime if they get caught?"

"That's right."

Walton let the information sink in, then addressed the attorney. "Add a full day to your bill. I'll see that it gets paid."

The faces of both men revealed an identical sinister smile.

❧

The rehearsal hall smelled of old paper and canvas. Walton would have opened the windows, but spring in Portland could be a time of cold blustery rain. The windows rattled from the wind. He could see the white, choppy waves in the harbor. He shivered.

"I shall never get warm again."

Just then the door at the far side of the hall opened. A young woman in a bright red coat entered. She had a thick portfolio under her arm. She looked in Walton's direction and smiled. He did not return the smile. She hesitated a moment, as if waiting for Walton to walk towards her. He did not.

Her footsteps echoed in the deserted hall.

"Mr. Dennler?" she asked.

Walton had to think a moment to remember that was the false name he had provided her agent. Nora extended her hand.

"I'm Nora Wilkes. Mr. Arthurs said you were interested in perhaps booking a tour with me this fall."

Walton nodded.

"And he said you requested a short performance."

Walton nodded again. She removed her coat, and Walton tried not to let his eyes give away his thoughts.

My word, she is a pretty one. Very, very pretty indeed. I'll give this much to my little brother—he has good taste when it comes to women.

Nora untied her portfolio.

"Is there anything particular that you would like to hear? Some Bach? Vivaldi? Sacred music? I do have a complete repertoire if you would like to look at it, Mr. Dennler."

He smiled.

No sense giving away too much beforehand.

"No, just select a piece or two–short ones–that you like. I'll just sit over here and listen."

He placed a chair so that Nora was between him and the light from the window. She would be less likely to see his face and eyes as he stared.

After the last few notes faded into silence, Walton stood and clapped.

"A most marvelous performance, Miss Wilkes. I had heard you were talented, but I had no idea."

Is she blushing?

"Thank you, Mr. Dennler. You are most kind. This hall is too empty to do justice to the music."

"You must not be so modest, Miss Wilkes. You are a talented player. And a most attractive one as well."

Now she is blushing for certain.

Walton felt at his breast pocket. The thick document was snug against his heart.

I don't believe how excited I am. My heart is literally racing.

"Thank you again, sir."

Walton waited, allowing his eyes to roam over her face without censure. She watched a moment, then stared at her hands still resting on the keyboard.

"You're welcome," Walton said. "But I am afraid I am not here to book a concert tour. However, I do have big plans for you."

"Plans?"

Walton rubbed his chin with his hand. "Indeed." He reached into his pocket and pulled out the thick parchment. "But I have something to show you before I explain your part in my little plan. And once I explain this, I am sure you will be eager to cooperate."

Nora looked up, a hint of cold fear in her eyes. Walton saw it and smiled.

"Do you know what this is, Miss Wilkes?" he said as he held the parchment in front of her.

194

She did not speak. She glanced over her shoulder, her eyes quick to focus on the only door to the hall.

"Miss Wilkes, you offend me. I am not a threat to you. I will not harm you physically. I promise that on my father's future grave. Do you believe me?"

Nora offered a nod in reply, but the fear did not leave her eyes.

"Your father is involved in shipping, is he not?" Walton asked.

"My father? What does he have to do with this?"

"Everything, Miss Wilkes. And in due time I will explain."

She stared hard at Walton, trying to understand. Finally she answered. "He owns a few ships, yes."

"And the *Walpole* is one of them?"

She nodded.

"You were there when they launched her, weren't you?"

"Listen, Mr. Dennler," Nora said, standing up, "this is making me very nervous. If you are not interested in my performance, then I think I should leave."

"Sit down!" Walton shouted, the vein in his forehead pulsing. He glared at Nora until she slowly sat down. Walton wiped his hand across his mouth. "I am interested in your performance. Very interested. Only it has nothing to do with how well you play the piano."

Her eyes never left his. He could see her arms tense as if waiting to fend him off.

Walton took a deep breath and stepped back. "Your father owns the *Walpole*. It makes the run between the Mediterranean, the Caribbean, and Portland."

"So? What concern is that of yours?"

She's a bit of a fighter. That's good. I like that.

"Well, Miss Wilkes, you may not know, or indeed not care, as to the cargo that this ship of your father's carries. Sometimes it is olive oil from Italy. Sometimes it's wine from France. Sometimes it's sugar from the islands. Sometimes it's rum."

"So? Again, Mr. Dennler, I must ask why you care. And if you don't tell me, then I shall just leave." She grabbed her music. "And you should consider yourself lucky that I don't alert a constable."

"Sit down!" he shouted again with even greater volume than before. She glared at him and obeyed.

He tossed the parchment into her lap.

"I'm enjoying this game, but I think the time to ante up is now."

She unfolded the document.

"It's a signed manuscript from the Spanish governor of Hispaniola. It has the king's seal. It's in Spanish, Miss Wilkes, so you won't be able to read it."

"And what does this have to do with me or my father?"

Walton laughed. "On a recent voyage–last spring to be exact–the *Walpole* entered the harbor on its way from Africa. On board were nearly seven hundred slaves."

He enjoyed watching Nora flinch at the word.

"Oh yes, occasionally the *Walpole* trades in slaves. It's all in the document."

"My father is an honorable man. He doesn't do that."

Walton laughed again.

"The governor says otherwise. And slaving is legal in the islands. Now I understand that business is business, and sometimes you can't let personal ethics stand in the way of profit. But you know, Miss Wilkes, that's not the true horror of the document. You see, it appears that the Spanish governor raised the docking fees just hours before the *Walpole* slipped into the harbor. He doubled the tax on slaves as well. It's clearly a case of a petty tyrant gouging the market– but that's not my problem–nor yours."

Walton stopped and walked closer to Nora. He saw her wince and was surprised at how good it felt to see her fear.

"The good captain refused to pay the doubled fees–nearly a thousand extra dollars, I am told. He wasn't sure if such additional funds would be paid by the owner of the ship. So he sat in the harbor, waiting for the governor to lower the fee and waiting for the boat's owner to respond. The governor sat in his palace and waited for the ship's captain to pay up. Neither did. Neither man gave way."

Nora appeared angry. "So! What does it have to do with my father?"

"There is a note in the document you hold in your hands. It's a translation of a letter your father sent to the ship's captain. He said never to pay the increased fee—that the governor would back down and that Spaniards were a race of cowards."

Walton leaned against the piano. "A little shocked to hear such words from your father? Well . . . maybe not. We all have our prejudices, I suppose."

He turned to face her. "You know what happened then? Both sides eyed each other and refused to give in. In the game of chess, they call this situation a stalemate. Neither side can win. But unlike a chess stalemate, this situation proved to be different. Time doesn't count in chess—but it did here. Neither side was strong enough to win—right away. But food began to run short on the *Walpole*. Your father refused to let the captain send for more. He said the governor would capitulate soon enough. He said that a thousand dollars was a lot of money."

Walton grinned and rubbed his hands together. "You know slaves aren't that strong to begin with. And now they started to die. Such a perishable cargo. It took your father five weeks to realize that he wasn't going to win this battle. And in that five weeks more than five hundred bodies were dumped into the harbor at Hispaniola. Imagine the stench. Five hundred dead slaves—and a large portion of that number—more than one hundred—were infants and small children."

Nora stood, her eyes flashing in anger. "My father did no such thing! That's a lie! You are lying about all of this!"

Walton did not look surprised by her outburst. "I knew you would think that. Look on the last page. I had the document translated into English. The translation has been notarized. It's authentic."

Nora tore to the last page and scanned the words. Her face appeared to crumble and fall. Slowly she folded the document and laid it on the piano.

Walton waited, knowing that the impact of this sudden truth would take time to sink in.

After several minutes, Nora looked up at him. There were tears in her eyes. "What do you want? Why did you tell me this? What can I do about it?" Her voice cracked and trembled.

Walton drew his chair close and sat down. "I know it may be a shock to learn the truth of one's father. It was for me as well. You have my sympathies." Walton licked his lips. "Your sadness notwithstanding, I do have a request for you."

"What?" Nora asked. It was apparent in her expression that she feared what he would say next and seemed to be calculating her response to an assault on her virtue, her innocence.

"I am certain you do not want this information spread about. Your father is an elder at his church, isn't he? What would the pastor and the rest of the congregation say if they heard this horrible news? And your mother? What would her friends say if they knew? And you, Miss Wilkes, who would have you perform in concert? How many bookings would you get if they found out your father was the sort of monster who would let even one child—let alone so many of them—die for a lack of a thousand-dollar tax? How greedy and heartless can one man be?"

Nora appeared to shrivel in pain. "What do you want me to do?" Her voice was small and hollow.

"In order to make this stay hidden—and I can do that—I have one request."

"What is it?"

"I want you to allow my brother to court you."

She looked up, incredulous.

"What?"

"Gage Davis. He's my brother. My name isn't Dennler. It's Davis."

"Gage is your brother?"

Her eyes mirrored her desperation.

"And he must never know any of this. If you tell him, then I will tell all of Portland the truth of your father."

She stared at him. "I don't understand. Why? Why do this just so I will see your brother again? None of it makes sense. Why do you care?"

Walton grabbed her hand. She attempted to snatch it away, but his grip was tight. His words were cold with calm fury. "Listen, Miss Wilkes. My brother has usurped my rightful position. And I believe he is committing stock fraud. I want you to find out more. He is enamored with you—with good reason. He'll tell you every secret he knows. A woman can do that to a man."

Nora shut her eyes and shuddered.

"Listen, Miss Wilkes, I am not saying that you need to take my little brother to your bed. Far from it. Gage is a gentleman. He would not expect that from a woman with your breeding and style."

Nora opened her eyes. Tears had begun to form.

"You want to protect your father? Maybe he doesn't deserve it. But if he falls, your mother will fall just as far. And she's innocent. And you'll fall too, Miss Wilkes."

Walton dropped her hand and stood up.

"I'll allow you a day to think about it. You can spare your family so much pain, Miss Wilkes. It's your choice. My brother's head in exchange for your parents' honor."

Walton picked up his coat, swung it about his shoulders, and began to walk to the door. Sleet began to splatter on the windows. A thick canopy of clouds descended. The town was lost in the shadows of the gray afternoon.

"We will meet again tomorrow. Noon. At this hall. Alone. Be prompt, Miss Wilkes. I appreciate people who are prompt."

<hr />

Walton sat at the piano, plunking away a cold, tuneless melody.

He stopped when he heard the latch of the door. Standing in the doorway, wearing the same red coat, was Nora. She looked older this morning, Walton thought, as if the night's turmoil had added years to her face.

No matter, truly, for she is still a remarkably beautiful woman.

She stepped into the hall. Her footsteps echoed. She stopped midway in the room. She looked up at Walton.

"I'll do what you ask," she said, her voice trembling.

Walton could not help but smile.

CHAPTER TWELVE

Portland, Maine
April 1846

As he left Portland, Walton could not recall ever being happier. No Christmas or birthday or family outing came close to the near-euphoric feeling that took residence in his body. He whistled as he walked to the pier to board the clipper ship headed to New York.

Before he had left Nora that morning at the rehearsal hall, she had answered his questions with a flat, expressionless monotone and agreed to resume her relationship with Gage.

"I know this revelation has been a shock to your sensibilities, Miss Wilkes," Walton had said. "I do not expect you to be chipper so soon, perhaps, but you had best find a way to mask your lack of emotion. If you are not your old self, Gage will know. He is a smart lad. If I hear that he suspects anything, then you, your mother, and your beloved father will soon be scorned by all of Portland. People on the street will point to you and whisper, 'There goes the daughter of a murderer.' So it is in your best interests to do what you must do to make Gage believe all is wonderful. Gage will write to you. I am sure of that. He is not a man to give up on a conquest. You are much too beautiful a prize to simply walk away from. I have seen him pacing about. If he doesn't write within the month, you must notify me. If he refuses to move, you will have to take the initiative. But I am sure communication will begin. When that happens—he must not suspect anything amiss. Anything at all. Do you understand?"

She had glared at him. Her eyes were red and swollen.

"I understand," she said softly. She wiped her nose with a rose-colored handkerchief. "And rest assured that I will despise you to my grave. I give you my word on that."

Walton had placed his hand on his heart. "You wound me, Miss Wilkes. You cut me to the quick." And then he had loomed closer to her. "Let me tell you a secret. I don't care. I truly don't. Your feelings towards me are so inconsequential as to be meaningless."

He had stood and gathered up his coat.

"I will be in touch, Miss Wilkes. You have my box number for correspondence. And when you come to New York, you know how to contact me, correct?"

"I am not planning to come to New York. I cannot afford the trip."

Walton had smoothed out his scarf.

"You will not have to. Once you begin to pursue my brother, he will find a way to get you closer. The right word from him, and you can have your pick of a hundred parties and performances among New York's elite." He had then completed the last button at his throat. "You see—that's an unexpected benefit to this. Gage will help make you rich."

And with that he had turned and left the rehearsal hall.

❦

When Walton exited the hall, Nora slumped on the piano bench. A moment later, she began to sob and buried her face in her hands.

New York City

Walton returned home from Portland in an ebullient mood. He was so jaunty that even Gage commented on his positive disposition, calling it infectious. One quiet afternoon Gage found himself alone in his office with not a single pressing appointment or task. He looked around the room, paced a few minutes, stared out the window, leafed through several new books, sat behind his desk, and sighed.

I have delayed this long enough.

Gage removed a piece of stationery from his desk. It was the color of dark ivory and embossed at the top with a delicate monogram: GLD. He picked out a pen, dipped it into the inkwell, and began to write. He penned the opening words, "My dear Nora," then stopped and looked at it.

Is it too personal for the first letter?

He quickly agreed and crumpled the paper into a ball. Before an hour had passed, a small mound of crumpled balls of paper lay in a heap in the corner.

"Blast it all," Gage muttered. "It's a simple letter. Why can't I get it started?"

He reached over and tugged on a bell cord. He could never hear its ring, yet in an instant, Edgar entered the room.

"Sir?" he asked.

Gage looked up at him with rare helplessness on his face.

"I can't do this."

"Do what, sir?"

"Write this letter. To Miss Wilkes."

"I see. Should I call on someone to offer assistance?"

Gage crumpled yet another sheet of paper.

"No, Edgar, that's not what I want."

Edgar waited in silence for Gage to continue. After a few minutes, it became apparent Gage was not speaking.

"Sir . . . is there anything I can get for you? Perhaps some tea?" Edgar prodded.

"How would you start this letter, Edgar?"

"Sir, such a question is beyond the bounds of my responsibility. It is a personal matter."

When Gage sighed, Edgar said cautiously, "Sir, did you not see Miss Wilkes at Christmas?"

"I did."

"And did not that Pastor . . . Pastor Kenyon . . . indicate a letter from you to this young lady might be well received?"

"He did."

"And what month is it now, sir?"

Gage actually glanced at the calendar.

"April."

"And how many months have passed since Christmas?"

Gage let his head drop onto his hands. "It's hopeless. You're right. I have waited too long. I can't write now. She'll think it horrible of me that I did not write sooner."

Edgar brushed off a speck of lint from his lapel. "Sir, why did you not write before?"

Gage lifted his head and stared at Edgar. "Well . . . I don't know exactly. I was afraid she would throw it away. I was afraid I would say the wrong thing. I don't know—all that sounds so cowardly."

"Indeed," Edgar said softly, without judgment. "I think an apology would be a sound beginning. Offer no excuses. Just an apology. Then you share what news she might find interesting. The opera opening. The painter that you met. The Dickens book that might appear in the *Post*. Things of that nature."

"An apology? That would work?"

Edgar actually smiled. "I have no way of knowing, sir. No man does. But it appears to be your only choice."

Gage brightened. He placed a clean sheet of paper before him, dipped his pen in the well, and began to write.

As Edgar reached the door, Gage called out, "Thank you, Edgar."

Edgar gently nodded in reply.

From his second-story bedchamber, Walton noticed Edgar on the street below as he walked away from the house. A moment later a slight tapping sounded at his door.

"Come in," he barked.

The door opened, ever so slowly. It was Margaret, one of the upstairs chambermaids.

"Sir?" she said, her words edged with fright.

"What?" Walton called out.

"I . . . you . . . well . . ."

"What is it, you silly woman? Spit it out. I don't have all day."

She cowered visibly and took a step in retreat.

Suddenly Walton became aware of the connection.

"Was Edgar carrying a letter when he left just now?"

Margaret nodded. "He left Master Gage's office, and I saw him slide something white into his breast pocket. Looked like a letter."

Walton smiled. He reached into his vest pocket, took out a five-dollar coin, and tossed it towards the door. It clattered and rolled into a corner. Margaret knelt down quickly and retrieved it.

"Thank you, sir," she whispered as she hurried out.

"Wait!" he called. "I want you to go down to Gage's office right now. Tell him that Edgar wanted you to clean up."

"But, sir, that room is not my duty."

"So? Just who is in charge here? Me or you?"

She lowered her eyes.

"Make sure you gather up all the paper on the floor. Gage could not write a letter like this on the first draft without making a few false starts. I want to know for certain."

Margaret nodded, then snapped the door shut.

In less than ten minutes, Walton ran to the door in response to the same sort of tapping that had announced the maid earlier.

Margaret held out a crumpled sheet of paper. Walton took it, closed the door, and unfolded it. The paper contained only three words: "My dearest Nora . . ."

And with that Walton began to laugh with joy.

Portland, Maine
April 1846

My dear Gage,

How delightful to receive your letter.

Of course I forgive you for not writing sooner. Actually, it may have been for the best. I was so very busy in January and February that I scarcely had time to rest. And to be truthful, the time between our meeting in New York and your letter gave me much time to ponder and reflect on my life—both social and spiritual.

Of course it would be wonderful to discuss such matters further together.

I am so saddened about your father's condition. My father's sister-in-law's mother is much the same. The doctors offer no hope, and her behavior has become exceedingly difficult. I write this not to be pessimistic, but to simply share your concern and let you know that I care and will pray for your father's health.

It appears you have found great delight in the business world. Gage Davis— captain of industry! How noble and exciting that sounds. I shall be able to tell others that I knew you when you had just begun. The business you describe about the telegraph is most intriguing. I, too, have read some on that matter. The world will begin to shrink to a small size when we can communicate in an instant over a wire. And this new device that you described appears to offer even greater changes. Is this the same inventor that you mentioned to me once back in Cambridge?

All is well in Portland. Perhaps someday I might arrange another perfor- mance in New York. If so, perhaps we could meet again. We have much to talk about.

With fond regards,
N. W.

Nora was glad that Gage could not see her as she wrote, for despite her cheerful tone, she smiled not once during the entire letter.

FROM THE JOURNAL OF GAGE DAVIS

She has written back!

A modest little letter—but she has written back. It offered such hope in a situation that I thought hopeless.

She has mentioned that travel to New York might be accomplished if only she had arrangements for concerts. I will send a few notes today and by the end of the month I would think Nora would have more concert offers than she has free dates.

Portland, Maine
May 1846

My dear Gage,

I am overwhelmed. I have on my desk before me a tall stack of solicitations for performances. These would provide months' worth of bookings. I am elated.

Is there any reason why all of these wonderful invitations are from New York City? Not one comes from any other part of the country.

Can you even imagine the odds of such an arrangement?

Gage, you sweet dear—I know that many of these offers came as a result of a gentle nudge from you. And I am not offended in the least, but grateful for your help. How else would I be able to enter the world of New York's high society?

Playing church recitals is fine—but I want more than just that. And with your help, I think I will achieve it.

It will take me several weeks to tidy up matters here in Portland. I must correspond with all those who made offers to me and set firm dates and the like.

Then I will pack my bags and head to New York City.

Perhaps you can suggest a temporary residence for me there? The Wilkes's clan, while extensive, has no branches in New York. I have heard of room-

ing houses that only rent rooms to women. That sort of arrangement would satisfy my mother, who thinks New York is a virtual den of iniquity.

Thank you so much, Gage. I had forgotten how much I enjoyed our time together. Now, when we meet again, I will have to show my deep appreciation to you. And you must allow me to reciprocate your great kindness to me.

Until then, I remain, a faithful friend, and more,

N. W.

Leaving Portland was not as simple as Nora imagined. Because of Gage's help, she had more than fifty concert dates scheduled for the fall and early winter. Some were simple piano recitals; some were part of a larger evening of entertainment. She had spent much of the spring making arrangements, signing contracts, and handling logistics of piano moving and the like.

Gage wrote more than ten letters in the interim. He wrote that he had located a wonderful women-only residence only a few blocks from his family's home. He had taken the liberty of reserving a suite of rooms on the third floor that overlooked a pleasant park.

And now Nora stood at the rail station offering final embraces to her parents. She hugged her mother with great fervor. "I will miss you so very much," she whispered as she held on for a long moment.

She offered her father a more reserved farewell. A quick hug, a simple good-bye, and she stepped aboard the train headed first to Boston, then New York.

She had watched her father's face carefully the last several months for any hint that he could be the author of such a tragedy that occurred in Hispaniola. At first she refused to believe it. Her father had always been an ideal man—caring, compassionate, funny, and gentle. He would never have authorized such a horrific action.

But as she listened and watched, she began to doubt her original assessment. In business matters, he was quick and cutting and tolerated little discussion. He made decisions in an instant, and rarely if ever backed away from them, even if proven wrong.

I hate to admit this—but I believe the evil that Walton told me. And I hate myself for that belief.

What sealed her belief was a trip to the Portland library.

She found a small article in a New York paper from a year prior. No more than a hundred words long, it described a situation on a slave ship in the Caribbean in which hundreds of slaves starved to death. No names were mentioned, but the few details matched the story that Walton told her.

As the train began to chug away, Nora offered her parents a final wave. She smiled widely and did not let on how much her heart hurt.

I am to honor my parents, she thought, *so that my days are long on earth. That is a commandment with a promise. But how far does that honor extend? Do I overlook what my father has done? And if I do not, if I say no to Walton, then it is my mother who will be most pained and injured. Father has a thick skin from his years in business and politics, but Mother has none of that sort of internal toughness. If someone were to speak ill of her, she would be wounded to the quick. And if such news were to come out in the open, it would not be one person speaking ill of her—it would be the entire town. I know it would.*

It would make no difference to the gossips that my mother had no part in such a tragedy. It would make no difference to them that my mother was innocent of all wrongdoing. She would be painted with the same evil brush as my father.

And she would never recover. It might even be the death of her.

I am least concerned of my fate. I trust that my faith will see me through regardless of the sins of my father.

Indeed, Father has sinned greatly—though he is still a man worthy of respect and honor.

I will do what I need to do to keep their secret hidden. I will do what I need to do to prevent the truth from ever being known. If this is a sin, then so be it. I will ask God to forgive this sin, for I am protecting a weaker soul.

The train conductor's calling for tickets interrupted Nora's reverie. She reached in her bag and presented hers to him. He smiled and touched the bill of his hat as he walked on.

If he knew the pain I felt, he would offer no smiles. If he knew the truth, he would offer no polite mannerisms. No one would.

And the train rolled on, faster and faster, closer and closer to New York.

In New York one young man waited with great anticipation for Nora's arrival.

CHAPTER THIRTEEN

New York City
January 1847

You have made the *New York Post* once again," Gage said as he folded the newspaper in half, then half again, and pointed to a small article near the top of the page devoted to culture and entertainment. "It says here that a young and very beautiful Nora Wilkes–I like this reporter already–has dazzled her audience with her talent and verve."

Gage smiled at Nora, who was seated across from him at Blake's, an expensive restaurant situated between his home and Nora's hotel.

"You have verve," he repeated. "I think that's why I like you. It's your verve."

A twinkle in her eye, Nora shook her head. "Gage, you are an impossible man."

"No . . . now it all makes sense. It's been your verve that caught my eye. You womenfolk just don't realize how important verve is to a man." Seeing that he had made Nora blush, just a little, he laughed and dropped the paper on the table.

"I had no idea verve was so important," she replied, playing along.

"There are men who live for verve," he said. "But the verve

question aside, this is still a glowing review. That should make you happy."

"It does. I am always grateful—and a little surprised—that the newspapers consider me worthy of such reviews."

"Worthy? Why, you are the talk of the town. To have you perform at a party is quite the coup."

She sipped her coffee. Gage glanced at her plate, hoping he was not obvious. She had barely touched her soup and now had left most of the roast beef uneaten. He would have sent the meal back for her and insisted that the kitchen prepare her a new meal that was more to her liking. He had done so the first few times she consumed only an additional bite or two. But Gage knew that an action like that embarrassed Nora. If he questioned her now on the taste of a meal left uneaten, she would insist that she simply had not been hungry. Gage had been unconvinced by such an explanation and remained concerned. Yet he found no possible solution to the situation.

Perhaps it is simply because of the pace of her life in New York, he reasoned.

Nora had been exceedingly busy from the first day of her arrival from Portland. Her success far surpassed the initial bookings that Gage helped arrange. She could have given two performances a day, seven days a week, if she had so chosen. The first months of fall she had done exactly that, but now that winter had arrived, she actually began to decline bookings.

She said that she was often weary, more often as of late. So today she had scheduled not a single appointment or performance. Gage seized upon this rare inactivity and insisted that they share lunch, then spend the rest of the day together.

He leaned back in his chair and grinned. "Then what shall we do today? These next precious hours are ours to spend as we choose."

Nora looked lost in thought, then simply shrugged. "You have taken me to every exhibit and art showing in the city. There are no afternoon performances that either of us would wish to see. The circus will not be in town until next week. The weather is too frightful for a walk in the park. And we have already eaten lunch . . . I am at a loss to suggest a possibility."

Gage covered her hand with his. "Perhaps we are burning candles at both ends. It does seem like forever since we had a time not consumed by business, a performance, or some sort of engagement."

She offered a wan smile in reply.

A gust of wind rattled against the windows. A biting mixture of snow and rain lashed through the air. She stared out at the gray sky.

"And it is not the day for a picnic, that is for certain."

Gage nodded, then stopped. He turned to face her and smiled. "Now that is a grand idea."

"What is?"

"A picnic."

Nora laughed. "Even for you, Gage, that would be a most difficult feat to arrange."

"I think it can be done. Do you trust me?"

She looked away, then replied, "Yes, I trust you."

Gage thought he heard a subtle hitch in her words but ignored it.

"Then I will send a carriage to your residence for your warmest winter hat and coat and mittens. I will hurry home for all the other accoutrements. If you will be so kind as to wait here, I will send a carriage for you in less than one-half hour. Have a dessert. Order another pot of coffee."

He stood and threw his coat over his shoulders. Nora would have objected to his quixotic suggestion, but part of her was intrigued as to how a picnic might be fashioned in the middle of winter.

"A picnic you will have, my lady, if a picnic is what you desire," Gage said, and then bowed, dipping almost to the floor. He rose laughing and ran from the table.

Within the hour, the Davis carriage pulled to a stop outside the restaurant. The driver, wrapped in an enormous Indian blanket, jumped to the street. He escorted Nora, holding an umbrella over her to keep the snow away.

"Where is Gage?" she asked him as he closed the carriage door.

"He said he will meet you. That's all I know." He then handed her a thin envelope. It had *Nora* written on it—in Gage's slash of handwriting.

She tore it open. Inside was a single train ticket. The destination was Southampton.

"Southampton? In this weather?"

But the driver did not answer. He was lost again in the folds of his great red blanket.

❦

Nora was as tired as she had ever been. She settled back, snuggling into the fur robe over her lap. And she allowed herself the barest of smiles.

The driver had transported her to the proper train and to her individual compartment. The tracks to Southampton had been finished for a few months and the journey now consumed less than two hours, rather than nearly a full day.

Several minutes after Nora boarded the train, the car lurched and the station resounded with the engine's cough and chug. The train breezed past the crowded streets and soon began to clatter along the now-barren farm fields of Long Island. The rhythm and gentle swaying caused her eyes to drop. In five more minutes, she was sound asleep.

She awoke as the train pitched to a stop. The depot sign read SOUTHAMPTON. And unlike the dark bluster of the city, the station was drenched in sunshine.

She stepped off the train. An elderly man standing by a large carriage held a hand-lettered sign bearing the words MISS WILKES. Minutes later she and the carriage were swaying down a quiet country road. To her left was the slate sea, tossed by the cold wind. Clumps of sea grass bent and swayed.

Certainly he can't expect a picnic outside. We would freeze to death, she thought.

The carriage slowed and turned onto a driveway hidden by massive oaks and lindens. The long drive led up to a gray-shingled house that appeared to go on forever. A sweeping porch, with white pillars and rails, surrounded the structure. The house faced the sea, and Nora thought there might be a hundred windows now barred by closed sets of shutters.

The carriage stopped, and the driver escorted Nora up the stairs and opened the front door. Several rooms radiated from the entry, each with a collection of furniture hidden by white canvas throws.

"Upstairs, miss," the driver said. "Mr. Davis said he would wait for you upstairs—and to the right—down the long hall."

Nora offered a puzzled look in reply. "Up the stairs?"

"And then right. Keep walking—it's a long hall."

She ascended the stairs, hearing the door shut behind her. Smiling, she reached the landing. Shaking her head, she realized that the walk would be long indeed.

At the very end of the hall, after passing what seemed like fifty closed doors, Nora came to a set of double doors. She paused, unsure if she should knock, or simply enter. She chose to knock.

"Welcome to your picnic, Miss Wilkes," Gage called out, and the doors swung open.

The massive fireplace at the far end of the room held a huge, cheerful blaze. The shutters had been opened, and the room was bathed in sunshine. The windows revealed glorious views of the sea. A huge blanket was spread upon the floor, and wooden porch chairs were scattered about. A picnic hamper lay at the middle of the blanket, with two ends of bread loaves peeking out from under the lid.

Nora could do nothing but laugh. "How did you manage to do all this?" she said, utterly delighted.

Gage took her hand and led her to one of the porch chairs. "It was not easy, but I do not want to reveal my trade secrets. And since this room offered the best view in all of Long Island, I could think of no better place for an afternoon picnic."

Nora sat down. The space was surrounded by windows through which she could see the beauty of the deserted beach. A few gulls swooped in the chilled air.

"And it will be peaceful out here. No one will bother us. There will be no concerts or impromptu meetings. I had my driver take every book from your room, hoping there would be a title not yet read. And I brought some of my own, as well as a handful of newspapers I bought at the station. I managed to catch the train just before yours. Had to run the last twenty yards with four servants in tow, who were carrying all manner of things. I hope everything made the train. Now we can listen to the wind and the snap of the fire and simply relax for the rest of the day."

Nora stood and embraced Gage. "You have no idea how delicious this all sounds. You are such a wonderful man. So romantic."

It was Gage's turn to blush a little. "Is it too warm in here for you?" he stammered.

"No, I like not needing a shawl. It's fine."

"Do you want anything to eat? Or drink? The cook actually packed three hampers with what food he had on hand. I wasn't sure what you might like."

"Gage, you are so sweet. This is such an unexpected treasure. But right now, let's take advantage of the quiet. Sit here with me, and we'll read together. You can read the newspaper, and I'll read that book by Dickens you have raved about."

He smiled and clasped her hand, then sat in the chair next to her. And as he read the papers, he kept glancing at her profile, the gentle arc of her throat, her full lips, and her soulful, deep eyes, wondering how he was going to tell her what he needed to say.

***

"Dinner was marvelous," Nora said.

"I'll send your compliments to the cook," Gage replied as he began to gather up the dishes and glasses and place them back in the large wicker hamper.

"Let me do that."

"No," Gage replied. "You are my guest, and I am serving you today."

The afternoon sun had faded to a thin sliver of red at the edge of the sea. The wind grew calm.

"When will we have to leave?" Nora asked. "Or did you plan on holding me captive here till spring?"

"Don't tempt me, Nora. I have to admit the idea has crossed my mind."

"But you didn't pack enough food to last till then, did you?"

Gage laughed. "Drat! I've been discovered." He checked his pocketwatch. "We have an hour left. Then we'll have to head back. It will be late, regardless."

"Well, I have not had such a peaceful and relaxing afternoon since . . . since before I came to New York. Thank you again, Gage. You knew exactly what I needed—even before I did."

Smiling, he closed the lid of the hamper. Then he said quietly, "I have something to tell you, Nora. I have been putting it off for a while."

"Is it something about your father?"

"No, he's the same as he has been."

She appeared flustered. "Is it something about your brother?"

He tried to hide his scowl. "No, although as of late, he has almost been civil to me."

"Then what?"

"I have to leave for a few months."

Looking stunned, Nora finally managed, "Where are you going?"

"Philadelphia, Pittsburgh, Cleveland . . . a lot of places."

"Why?"

"I should have gone last fall—but that's when you came back into my life, and I couldn't bear the thought. So I postponed the trip. Davis Enterprises owns foundries in Pittsburgh and a carriage works in Philadelphia, and we have some shipping concerns in Ohio—there are a lot of things that need my oversight."

Nora nodded, then gazed off into the fire. "I understand, Gage. You shouldn't have felt guilty about telling me. You have a company to run, after all. I know that."

He stood and walked to the windows. "But it's different now. Before I would find the idea of this trip exciting—another experience, another adventure. Now I simply dread the thought of leaving you all alone in New York."

"I'll be fine. I suspect that if I need anything, I could call on Edgar. Or is he accompanying you as well?"

"Edgar. No, he's staying. Someone needs to watch over my father, and it is clear that no one else seems to care."

She stood and placed her hand on his shoulder. "Gage, don't worry about me. I am a grown woman. I will be fine."

"Are you certain?"

"I am."

She hesitated, then embraced Gage for a very long time. She leaned against him, looked into his eyes, and then kissed him. He returned her kiss.

They held each other as the sunset colored the room scarlet. Then Gage stepped away.

"We should get ready to depart. We don't want to miss the last train. And even though the idea of spending the evening with you is so desirable, I will not compromise your good name for the sake of a missed train."

"And I admire you all the more for that, Gage," she replied and kissed him again with even greater enthusiasm.

He stepped away and almost stumbled as he scrambled for the picnic hamper.

The train was nearly empty as it chugged away from Southampton. Gage and Nora had wrapped themselves in several blankets borrowed from the Davis summerhouse. Though the winds had diminished, the temperature had fallen. The train car was heated, to a degree, by a large stove at one end of the car. On cold days, it was more comfortable to ride in the second-class cars—one big open space could be easier to heat. The private compartments seemed to be insulated from any warmth.

Gage placed yet another blanket over Nora's shoulders.

"I'm fine, Gage. It is not that cold. I've lived through Portland winters, remember?"

"But that was before you met me, and now I feel responsible. I will not allow you to catch a draft on my watch."

She buried her head in the thick blankets. Then she peeked out at the dark landscape. The car rocked and swayed as the moonlight colored the farmland silver.

"It feels like we are the only two people in the world, doesn't it?" she said softly.

"Yes, and I am overjoyed that you are the other person."

She blushed and looked back out the window. "So tell me again of your trip out west. It does sound most exciting—and exhausting."

Gage related many of the stops he had planned to make. There was a wagon maker in Philadelphia, foundries in Pittsburgh, an interest in a large coal-mining operation in West Virginia, a ship-building concern in Cleveland, a canal and lock operation in Pennsylvania, riverboats on the Ohio and Mississippi River, a dry dock in Ohio.

By the time he had finished, Nora was amazed. "And you keep all those investments orderly in your thoughts? I admit that I am already hopelessly perplexed."

"There are some who seek to control all of one industry," Gage explained. "I consider that a great risk. If that segment should falter, then the entire company falters as well. As a result, we have always attempted to own small pieces of many industries. That's why there are so many stops on my trip."

Nora averted her eyes, then asked, "What of that telegraph invention you wrote of in your letter? What has come of that?"

Gage leaned forward. "That is another reason I am making this trip. To scout out locations and offices that would benefit from using this new invention. And to think, once Shirdler perfects his concept, Morse will be left in the dust."

"Morse?"

"That other fellow. He managed to get the government to fund his work. So the fools in Washington run a telegraph line from

Washington to Baltimore, of all places. My taxes are used to pay for a private invention–remarkable cheek if you ask me."

"And this Shirdler fellow, his idea is better?"

Gage could not help from smiling. This was one of the few times that Nora had shown such a keen interest in his work.

"Much better. And what is remarkable–at least for Davis Enterprises–is that we have not risked a single dollar of our own money on this investment, while still maintaining majority ownership."

Surprise showing on her face, Nora asked, "And how can that be? How can you own something if you haven't paid for it?"

Gage peered about, worried about being overheard. He was immediately satisfied that no one was listening.

"Let's say a company is worth a hundred dollars. And there are a hundred shares of stock."

"But isn't it worth much more than that?"

"Well, of course, but a hundred dollars is an easy figure to understand."

Nora nodded.

"The company needs another hundred dollars to finish the invention. So for two hundred dollars, a man could buy the company."

"And that's what you did?"

"Not exactly. We raised the hundred dollars for research, then another hundred dollars for the real worth of the company, and then claimed that there was still a hundred shares to sell. But all the while, we have a contract with Shirdler that claims we have a 50 percent interest in all his royalties and assets forever. We sold shares of 100 percent of the company–actually more–while still owning half the company."

"I'm confused."

"It's more complicated than this, I assure you. What it means is that for our ability to raise money, we were paid half the worth of the company."

The delicate lines about Nora's eyes deepened. "I'm still confused."

"Don't be. I understand it, and that's all that matters."

"But . . . but isn't that a little illegal?"

Gage lowered his voice and offered a most curious, wry smile. "Not exactly. With the advance of business today, one raises capital in any manner possible. What we did is perfectly acceptable these days. And since this company will be so successful, it really doesn't matter how much we sell. Every investor will get double their money back."

Nervous, Nora whispered, "Are you sure you can't get into any trouble for this? It sounds . . . wrong."

Gage shook his head. "It happens all the time. No one will mind, as long as money is to be made. And no, sweet Nora, I will not get into trouble for this."

When he took her hand in his, he was surprised at how cold it was. "That is, as long as you don't tell anyone," he said, laughing. "You're not going to tell anyone, are you?"

She laughed and shook her head no.

❦

The bell of the grand Presbyterian church on Fourth Avenue tolled. It was black as pitch in Nora's room. She counted. "One, two . . ."

And then the bell was silent.

She lay on her bed, fully clothed, still wearing the heavy woolen coat she'd worn on the train ride home.

At the end of the day, Gage had escorted her to the door of her building, and she had allowed him to kiss her one last time. With his strong, warm arms around her, she had returned his embrace. For the first time that day she felt a glimmer of hope.

He had smiled at her and whispered in her ear, "This was the most perfect day of my life. You cannot imagine how wonderful I feel."

And with that he returned to his carriage. She waved to him as it rode off, then she turned slowly and walked to her dark room. She did not light a lamp but threw herself on the bed and lay there, praying that sleep would free her.

It had not.

She stared out the window at the dark city. A faint light shone off the wet cobblestones from the lamp at the street corner.

She sighed and felt the first sting of a tear.

I am falling in love with him. I cannot seem to stop my heart. I tried, I really tried not to love him, and I have failed. I open my eyes, and I see his kind and loving face before me.

She fell to her knees.

Lord, I know he is not a believer . . . and I know that what I feel for him goes against your Word, but I cannot help it. He is such a kind and generous man. He is so giving and gentle. He is more the Christian than many true Christians. Lord, that must amount to something in your eyes.

She began to cry.

But I know that being kind is not enough to make someone your child. And now he has told me too much about this Shirdler person. And I will have to tell Walton. I have no choice. He will not remain patient for much longer.

Her sobs caught in her throat and her chest hurt.

I must sacrifice the man I am beginning to love—or my parents who gave me life.

Lord, this is not fair. You have no right to place me in such a horrible quandary. Surely there must be some manner of escape. Surely you cannot mean for me to make this choice. You cannot ask me to forsake Gage . . . or my parents . . . or you.

God, I don't understand.

She bowed her head and remained silent for a long time.

In the darkness, the church bell rang again.

"One . . . two . . . three . . ."

CHAPTER FOURTEEN

Shawnee, Ohio
February 1847

Gage!"

"So I have surprised you?"

Joshua stood at the doorway to his parsonage in Shawnee, Ohio, his face a mask of confusion. It took nearly a full minute until he found the power of speech.

"Surprised does not begin to describe this. What in the world are you doing here? Why are you in Shawnee?"

"Tell you what, old friend. Invite me in out of the cold, and I'll tell you the entire tale."

Joshua stammered an apology as he escorted Gage to his most comfortable chair, just by the fire. He tossed two more logs on the flames, then fussed about in the kitchen, heating water for coffee, scraping together enough odds and ends for a decent meal.

"Don't go to any trouble. I'm sure I can get a meal at the inn later."

"Nonsense," Joshua called back. "You'll stay here with me. The inn might be acceptable to some, but not to my friends."

Gage smiled as he picked up the mug of steaming coffee.

"It is good to see you, Joshua. I had no idea how much I missed you until this very moment. It has been almost two years, and that is too long."

Joshua drew a three-legged stool close to the hearth.

"It has been a long time," he said softly. "Like you, I suspect I did not truly appreciate all that I had at Harvard. Now it is gone, and that part of our lives will never be replicated."

"Carefree, without worry, without stress," Gage said, offering explanation.

The two old friends let a warm, comfortable silence fill the room. The fire hissed and popped. Outside, the wind increased and rattled at the small windows set in the logs.

"So tell me, Gage—why *are* you in Shawnee? Of all the people in the world I would have never expected to see at my doorstep, you are number one or two."

"And Hannah was number one, I imagine."

Joshua stared, appearing incredulous. "You know about her visit here? How?" he whispered.

"Philadelphia was on my route. I stopped in for a visit. I saw her before she left. She said she was calling on you. I imagined her visit was the talk of the town."

Joshua's eyes clouded with a quick pain, then it was gone. His voice found a cheerful, positive note. "It's not that I am prying, but everyone in my congregation—no, let me amend that—everyone in all of Shawnee will want to know why you are here. And it is not simply because you are the richest man to ever visit this town. They expect a full report on any stranger within the town's boundaries."

"Every visitor?"

Joshua nodded with a smile. "Yes. Not just fancy lady visitors. Shawnee is not on a par with New York in the number of diversions that one finds. A visitor is such a rare treat that each must be savored. So you had best share all the news with me."

Over the next hour and three additional mugs of coffee, Gage divulged all that he could of his travels so far. He had Joshua enthralled at his descriptions of the foundries and the mills. It was not that Joshua had never traveled, Gage thought later, but the reason for his rapt attention was that he imagined he might never travel again. His questions about New York and Pittsburgh were of such a wistful nature, so colored with yearning, that Gage could almost feel the wanderlust in each query, each comment.

He waited until the end of his travel account to return to the subject of Philadelphia and Hannah.

"So you saw Hannah before she left on her tour. How did you find her? What did you make of her plans?" Joshua asked.

Gage knew that Joshua was desperate for additional news of her while knowing, deep in his heart, that the news might be painful.

"I thought she was our old Hannah from Harvard. But remember, I could only visit for an afternoon and evening. My business in the city was complete, and my itinerary did not have me departing for another day. I hoped she enjoyed my visit."

"And she didn't?" Joshua was surprised. "She didn't mention that you called on her."

"I don't think she would. I think I said some unsettling things to her. But she can be a most clever actress when the situation requires it," Gage said, then immediately regretted his words.

"An actress? What do you mean? Of all the women I know, she possesses no guile whatsoever."

"It's not guile, Joshua. And I don't mean to impugn her honor or intentions."

"Then what?"

Gage realized that Joshua was now very angry and very hurt.

"I'm not certain I can tell you all this and not allow the situation to be colored by either of our hearts," Gage answered.

"My heart? What do you mean, my heart? How would that color this story?" Joshua's voice had become thinner.

Gage swallowed and stared at his hands. "I know that her friendship meant a great deal to you. Let me leave it at that. But her current situation is what I was referring to. Her life is probably much different than what you imagine. During my very brief stop in Philadelphia, it was my distinct impression that she was greatly embarrassed for both her parents and their present difficulties."

Joshua knitted his brow together. He knew something of what it was to be embarrassed by others, to be ashamed to see one world overlap another. "But I thought her parents were of the best families in Philadelphia. How could they embarrass anyone? Is it simply that they are less rich than they once were? How could that make such a difference?"

Gage shrugged. "When I called upon her, I had no idea of what I'd find. I mentioned to you the financial problems her father has encountered. Financial reversals can take their toll. People who are used to having it all do curious things when that river of money dries up to a trickle."

Joshua interrupted, "But as I once said, Hannah had the look of prosperity about her at all times. She had never appeared to want for money—even if she did wear fashions from a year prior."

"Hannah had the protection and comfort of her trust fund. Such a fund, meager as it might have been, insulated Hannah from all manner of trouble." Gage stood, stretched, then stepped closer to the fire and warmed his hands, only inches from the flames.

"You are painting a most somber portrait of the matter, Gage," Joshua said.

"No more somber than reality. The family manse is an imposing structure—a vast, two-story brick Federal house, situated on perhaps three acres of land just a few miles west of downtown Philadelphia. The neighborhood itself has seen better days, and the vortex of society has moved several miles away. The families that remain either have chosen to take a stand against the decay or are unable to move on. Hannah's parents are in the latter category."

Gage sat back down. "The house was showing tatters. The entire place cried out for paint. Dried tufts of grass remained in the walk. I saw several windows broken or cracked and not replaced. The chimneys had lost bricks for want of tuck-pointing. On one side of the coach house was a carriage with a broken axle. It appeared as if it had been there for several years. It had the look of a house in which hope for a bright future had simply evaporated."

"Surely it was not that bad. Don't they have relatives who are still wealthy?"

"And if you had money, would you gladly give it to someone who squandered their share?" Gage stopped and scrutinized Joshua's pained expression. "Well, I suppose you would, but there are not many like you, Joshua. There are not many people who would give out of their good nature."

"I think there are."

"Perhaps in some circles. Maybe because you have this unbending faith. There are other families, who, even if they are churchgoing, do not ascribe to those attributes and characteristics."

Joshua looked away, not wanting to confirm Gage's opinions.

Gage continued, "I was invited in and offered refreshments, as any person might offer to a guest. But, Joshua, there was not even one servant left in the house to fetch tea and biscuits. Hannah herself marshaled about the kitchen—much like you have done tonight."

"And that is an offense?"

Gage replied in haste, realizing that he had come close to insulting his host. "That is not what I meant. But a family like Hannah's— well, to not have a servant is a very drastic thing. It means that whatever money they might have had is truly at low ebb. Of course they have been acquainted with our family over the years—at least by reputation. And I must say that her parents looked at me as if I possessed a rope and they had fallen into frigid waters. I am sure I was considered a possible suitor for Hannah."

"And you're not, right?" Joshua replied quickly.

"No, indeed I am not—and never have been."

He paused. "I am not saying that being without riches is wrong. But having riches and then losing them is a much different matter. I know I can be frank with you, Joshua. I know you have limited means. And I see a clear nobility about you because of that. But you were never rich, never privileged, never had a small army of servants. If you had them and suddenly they were gone—you might act very differently."

After a silence, Joshua replied. His voice was soft. "I understand what you're saying. I do. But Hannah was different. She valued the heart. She valued the soul. She was not simply interested in wealth."

"You're right, Joshua. Hannah is a rare person. But she also knows that her parents see her as a means to regain their standing. If she marries well, then they can once again climb back up—at least partially."

It was clear Joshua found it hard to hear those words. He stood and walked to the window, staring out at the ghostly fields of snow. He didn't say anything for several minutes, and Gage let him remain silent.

"So she'll marry that other fellow? The one she told me about? Robert Keyes?"

Gage shrugged. "I'm sure her parents would be overjoyed if she did. She is a most beautiful woman. Keyes would be a fool to let her get away, even if she is now poor by his standards."

"And he'll wait until she attends Oberlin College? He'll wait that long?"

Gage stood and filled his coffee cup from a kettle resting near the coals. "She'll never go to Oberlin."

"But she said she was," Joshua answered. "Upon leaving here, she was on her way to visit the campus."

"The trip was more to escape her parents for a while and to tweak their restrictions. She must rail at what they expect from her."

"She won't go to Oberlin? Is that the truth? She'll wind up wasting her God-given gifts?"

"I suppose one could debate how she might waste her talents—and how she would use them as a doctor—being a woman and all. But no, she will not go to Oberlin to waste away in the middle of Ohio for four years."

As he spoke those words, he regretted them immediately. Gage could see in Joshua's eyes that he felt those words were aimed at him, as well as Hannah.

"Joshua . . . I did not mean that. . . ."

Joshua tried to laugh. "I know. I know you did not. But here I am, in the middle of Ohio as well."

"Joshua, you must not think that. I don't think that of you. Honestly I don't."

Joshua returned to the stone hearth for warmth. "No matter, Gage. I am serving the Lord here. My life is rich and varied. It truly is. I find many challenges and rewards in serving this small church."

"Then you must ignore my clumsiness. You must ignore the rambling of a man made weary and foolish by travel."

Joshua placed a kind, steady hand on his friend's shoulder. "You must forgive me as well. I have kept you from sleep. I can see you are tired. Let me show you to the bedchamber. We can talk in the morning."

Gage searched Joshua's eyes and saw no anger or bitterness. "I would like that, my old friend. You have no idea of how wonderful a cozy bed sounds to me now."

⁂

Gage awoke before dawn. It was the sheer absence of noise that brought him out of his sleep. In New York, there were always sounds filtering into his room, sounds of carriages and calls from vendors, and shouts from workers. And traveling brought its own sounds, from fellow travelers to servants and scullery help. Sleep was often interrupted by the clang of chamber pots being emptied or logs being dumped into fireplaces.

But here in Shawnee, none of that existed.

He rose as quietly as he was able. Joshua slept on a mattress of blankets, piled in the corner of the bedchamber. Joshua had insisted on providing Gage a good sleep in his bed and would tolerate no discussion. The snow-covered landscape reflected the moonlight and Gage found his way easily. He took a candle with him and gently closed the bedchamber door. He added a few logs to the fire, taking care to remain silent. The wood quickly took to flame from the remaining bed of coals. Gage lit the candle and examined the large room.

The furniture was rough, but of good quality. A bookcase filled one small wall and held more than a hundred books. Gage pulled some out; most were theology books and the like. A few well-worn ones were tales of adventure and exploration, such as Kirkland's *Western Clearings* and *A New Home–Who'll Follow?*

He slipped into the kitchen. Joshua owned only two plates, two cups, and two sets of mismatched silverware. It was apparent Joshua did little entertaining in his simple abode.

Gage walked back to the fire and propped up his feet, clad only in stockings, a foot from the flames. The bare stone and wood of the floor were quite cold.

This is a most spartan home, he thought. *I would not have imagined such a bare existence for Joshua. He was in my home and now he is here— how huge the difference in our lives! How does he maintain a pleasant and cheerful attitude?*

Gage found the coffeepot and filled it with water from the bucket by the sink. He rummaged about and found a small amount of coffee in a tin.

Do I take the last of his coffee? Maybe he just does not drink it often. Well, no matter. I'll slip some bills in one of his Bibles. He'll never take it if offered directly and this way, he'll find it after I am gone.

In several minutes, the water was steaming, and Gage sipped the hot, rich liquid.

And he has not once mentioned the condition of my eternal soul. Perhaps he is slipping as well in that regard. I'll have to scold him about it when he wakes.

And as if on cue, the bedchamber door creaked open.

"What are you doing up?" Joshua asked with a yawn.

Gage jumped, startled. "You need to provide me some noise and clatter. The country is too quiet for a city boy."

Joshua poured coffee into the other cup and tossed a thick, rough blanket near the fire. His hair was a wild, blond tangle, and he made no effort to comb it back.

"You look like a wild Indian," Gage said, laughing.

"And you have seen an Indian?"

"I have seen pictures."

"And how many blond Indians do you think there are?"

Gage chuckled further.

"Besides, the residents of Shawnee are not the type to be impressed with personal grooming, since there are quite a few of them who simply do not own a comb or brush," Joshua said, smiling.

"Truly?"

"A cow doesn't care what you look like," Joshua said straightforwardly. "You want some breakfast?"

Gage shook his head no. "The coffee is fine."

After a moment, Joshua cleared his throat. "Gage . . . I had hesitated last night to bring up this subject. Maybe the talk of Hannah distracted my thoughts. But I must return to it. What about you and God, Gage? What of you and your faith?"

Gage laughed with gusto. "I am not laughing at your question—but because of my great relief. I thought you had forgotten. That would be so unlike the Joshua I knew back at Harvard who used to ask me such questions for a pastime. I was worried you had given up on me, not having demanded a recount of my churchgoing activities these past years."

"Well . . . are you ready to answer yes?"

Gage sipped his brew. "No . . . but I must thank you for asking."

Joshua looked about. "If I had a pillow, I would throw it at you. But it's too cold to go back into my room to get one."

"Thank heaven for small favors."

Joshua shuffled even closer to the fire. "Gage, I know you have made light of this subject in the past, but we both know it presents no levity. You do need to be concerned. Man does not live for just riches. You'll find that empty."

"And being poor offers a spiritual blessing? Is everyone without money closer to God?"

"No, they aren't. But money clouds a man's life, Gage. Think about what you said about Hannah's parents last night."

Gage opened his palms in confusion. "They were happy when they were rich and now that they are poor, they're miserable. It proves what I have always said. Money may not buy happiness, but it offers one great, comforting insulation against the hardness of the world."

Joshua shook his head. "That's not what I meant. A man can be happy being rich or poor. The happiness comes from his heart and from God's love, not money or possessions. What would happen if you lost all you had, Gage?"

Gage smiled. "That will never happen, Joshua. There is too much to lose it all." Then he said wistfully, "I miss talking to you, Joshua. Remember how often we talked about matters like this? How I miss that."

"And there is no one at home you can talk to?"

Gage snorted. "No."

He thought about his brother, then his father. He wanted to tell Joshua, but he hesitated. He wanted to tell him about Nora, but he could not find the words to begin. It was as if it were all too complex and complicated to describe. His heart hurt over his father. He felt alone in business. It was only Nora who offered him hope and love.

"There is this . . ."

And then he stopped.

"Yes?" Joshua said, expecting more.

"Never mind. It's not important."

Yet in that moment, Gage felt a shift in heart. All the while Joshua had encouraged him to consider God, Gage had fought against it, thinking that to admit spiritual need would indicate a weakness in his heart. All the while Nora nudged him to consider his faith, Gage had fought against it, thinking that a man does not admit that need before a woman.

But now, in this chilled, drafty, ill-furnished cabin in Shawnee, Gage saw his life—for an instant at least—with absolute cold clarity. He had pushed away Joshua. He had pushed away Nora—all because they saw something in him that called out for permanence, for substance.

Now he did not have Joshua nudging him at every opportunity. And Nora seemed to all but ignore such matters since moving to

New York City. Nevertheless, Gage found himself in the most odd situation—considering faith in a new light.

"There is this . . . you said," Joshua asked. "A preacher? A woman? Who?"

Startled alert by his accurate guesses, Gage shook his head no.

"No . . . it's no one. But I am thinking about all the things we talked about, Joshua. Maybe now that no one is urging me, I can see things a little clearer."

Joshua leaned closer. "Do you mean that?"

"I do. Things are happening in my life. Good things. Good things that I could never have imagined. Doesn't that mean that God is . . . I don't know . . . that God is directing me? If being successful is God's way of showing favor, doesn't that mean he might be favoring me?"

"It could be," Joshua said, sounding concerned. "But don't think that riches mean God is blessing you. I've told you before that God allows rain to fall on the just and the unjust."

"But so much rain, Joshua? Surely that means something."

Joshua pondered his answer. "If being wealthy and being a success gets you to find God, then, perhaps it is all part of his plan."

"Well, if that's part of his plan, then I heartily endorse it," Gage answered.

<hr />

As Gage left Joshua's, he offered his friend a free ride on one of the Davis riverboats that plied the Ohio and Mississippi Rivers.

"Are you serious?" Joshua asked. "I have always wanted to take a ride on the river like that."

"Of course I am serious. Mention my name, and it will be taken care of. As short or as long as you wish."

"You are serious, right? I won't get there and have them laugh at me?"

"Good heavens, no. One free passage is the least I can do."

Gage took his business card and inked the words: "Valid for one free ride—to wherever and back the bearer so chooses. G. Davis."

He handed the card to Joshua with a grand gesture.

"And I can go as far as I want . . . the whole way to Cincinnati?"

Gage smiled as he offered Joshua his hand in farewell. "Just mention my name, and you could take it the whole way to New Orleans if you'd like."

As Gage studied his friend's eyes, he knew in that instant that Joshua would take him up on the offer.

"New Orleans," Joshua replied, as if his words were lost in a dream.

CHAPTER FIFTEEN

Washington, D.C.
May 1847

Jamison Pike worked his way through the crowded room. Several people stopped him as he made his way to the buffet table, offering him congratulations on his most recent series of articles for the *New York World.* Jamison had had a grand time over the past months, sleuthing about the docks and the waterfront, investigating allegations of bribes. One high-ranking city customs official had already been dismissed as a result of his series of articles, and there were rumors of more to follow.

It had been quite the accomplishment for a reporter so recently out of school.

The celebration was for the dedication of the new Smithsonian Institute. Jamison was not on assignment, but reporters and journalists were notorious in their quest for free meals. As a result, Jamison gleefully joined the hunt and found his way to wrangle invitations to scores of events such as this.

He had spotted Gage the second he walked in. He elbowed and dodged and slipped along until he got close to his old friend.

"Gage!" he shouted. "Over here!"

Gage turned, scanned the faces, and grinned.

"Jamison," he called back. "How's the free food?"

"Good. You realize that no celebration is complete without a buffet table and a gaggle of reporters."

The two shook hands.

"How have you been?" Gage asked. "It has been months since you stopped by. We need to stay in touch. You're the only one from Harvard I see more frequently anymore."

"I've been busy."

"So I've heard. By the way, don't hope to get any invitations from the mayor anytime soon. I met him yesterday, and he directed several unique curses at you and your possible future offspring because of your stories on the dockyards," Gage said, chuckling.

"I wrote what I saw. It was the truth."

"He said it was a great embarrassment. He wanted me to pull strings and boot you off the paper."

"You said no—I hope."

Gage tilted his head back and exploded in laughter. "Jamison, you should expect more of me than that."

Jamison was relaxed before but now looked a little more relieved.

"I told him no—but said I would take his suggestion under advisement."

It was Jamison's turn to laugh. "Gage, he's a politician. Does he expect special treatment?"

"No, I don't think he does, really. But he was wounded and wanted me to know it—so maybe the next time we would go easier on him. And he more or less offered me a tip in the future in return for favors."

"And you accepted?"

"I said I'd take it under advisement," Gage continued lightly. "Just don't expect an invitation to tea anytime soon."

"I won't, I assure you. . . . Some party, eh?" Jamison asked as he scanned the crowd for prominent politicians.

"This town fairly oozes with money to be made and power to be wielded," Gage answered. "You'd never know there was a war going on in Mexico."

"They say Zachary Taylor and Winfield Scott are aces when it comes to soldiering," Jamison replied.

"I read about the routs in Vera Cruz and Buena Vista. Your editor said the war should be over in a fortnight or two," said Gage.

"So he says. And then we get Texas and all those wide-open spaces for cattle. You into raising cattle, Gage?" Jamison asked with a smile. "As if you needed any more ways to get rich."

"I do think of other things besides making money, you know," Gage said, winking.

"Such as . . . ? Could there be a woman occupying some of those thoughts of yours?"

"Are you that good of a detective? You may find the clues sparse."

"A challenge offered," Jamison replied. "It might be a good day after all." His expression suddenly grew dark. "Gage, can I talk with you?"

"Go ahead and talk."

Jamison looked around. "Not here. Someplace a bit less noisy and . . . less conspicuous."

Intrigued, Gage replied,"You make it sound so sinister. Have you been hiding in the shadows collecting evidence for too long?"

"Gage, I'm serious," Jamison replied. Motioning for Gage to follow him toward a door on the far wall, they wormed through the crush of people about the buffet.

They made their way through the double doors and found themselves on a long, empty balcony overlooking the street below. Dusk was falling, and the air felt brisk with the rich chill of spring.

Jamison stared out at the streets and the lights as the carriages and wagons clattered by. "I can see why you love New York. Compared to this town, there is so much going on–I sometimes am reluctant to go to sleep because I know how much I will miss."

Gage nodded. "The hustle and bustle can be infuriating, but there is no city like it in the world. . . . But I know you didn't ask me out here to compare cities. So what is it?"

Jamison turned to face him. "Gage . . . I have heard things."

"Heard what?"

"Things that I don't believe."

"Don't believe? Then why tell me?"

"Because the stories have to do with you. That's why I don't believe them."

"Me? About me?"

Jamison checked around as if making certain no one had slipped out on the dark balcony behind them. "Listen, Gage, being a reporter . . . well, you start to hear all manner of stories. People are beginning to pull me aside and tell me amazing tales. No reporter worth his salt believes everything he is told—but we are paid to listen. An accountant tells me about his employer who is cheating on his wife and his books. A clerk seeking revenge tells me about his boss who passes out great sums of money under the table. People seeking retribution or revenge often stretch the truth—or make it up if need be."

"Jamison, I understand how the system works. Remember that we own part of the *New York World*. I have friends who work there."

"I know you do. And I wanted you to know that I'm not some cub reporter who runs about like Chicken Little claiming the sky has fallen."

Gage waited for an explanation.

"I have heard stories about that invention you represent—the one purported to make the telegraph obsolete. Someone is claiming you have oversold the stock in this venture by 100 percent. I have heard that the invention itself has yet to be finalized, but investors are handing you money because of your reputation for an honest deal."

Gage inhaled and paused before replying. "The story is untrue," he finally said flatly. "Absolutely untrue."

Jamison breathed out with great relief. "Then I am satisfied that this story was simply a prevarication. I will assign this tale no further credence."

"You do that, Jamison. Although there *is* an invention and I have helped represent the company and its stock—just as I have represented stock in the past, everything is aboveboard and perfectly legal."

Jamison stared at his friend in the waning light. "Then I am satisfied."

Gage turned, almost abruptly. "We had best return to the party. I have a few people I need to see."

As he took hold of the latch, he studied Jamison one last time. "If I asked, would you tell me where you heard this story?"

Jamison swallowed. "I thought you might ask. And I agonized over my answer."

"Which is no, correct?"

"Yes, I won't tell you. I will not name names."

Gage's hand remained on the latch, but he did not open the door. He looked away and asked in a small voice, "Was it my brother? I am not asking for a name. Just a simple yes or no. I deserve that much. I do. And you know it. Was it my brother?"

When Jamison at last answered, his words were almost whispered. "No. And do not ask me any more questions. I don't want to damage our friendship like this."

Gage nodded. As he turned the handle, the noise of the party hit them as a wave in the ocean.

❧

New York City

The tavern was nearly deserted.

How does this man find only the empty bars in all of New York? Are they so because he frequents them? Is the alcohol tainted? Walton thought with a sneer.

He blinked several times. It was dark outside, but even darker inside. The dank interior smelled of rotten canvas, stale beer, and hopelessness. A trio of anemic lanterns glowed in a far corner. Walton stopped at the bar, ordered a whiskey, then found a table in the middle of the room.

Tentatively, he sipped his drink. If it were tainted, he could detect no discernable poison. He took a longer swallow. He enjoyed the warm feeling as it spread down to his stomach.

The thin reedy moonlight poured in as the door opened. Mr. French ambled in. He waved to the bartender, who was already filling a fat glass with whiskey. After Mr. French took it, he slumped down across from Walton.

"So why are we meetin' tonight? I thought I told you I was busy," he snarled. "I skipped a dinner on account of this. Invited by a real reporter. He said he's writing a story of sailing and wanted to talk with an old salt like me."

Walton waited a full minute until he spoke. His words were as cold as a lead sky in winter. "Mr. French, I do not consider your schedule—or any of your personal reasons—to be worthy of wasting my time. You do remember where your money is coming from, don't you? Or has the whiskey addled your weak brain?"

Mr. French sat up and licked his lips.

"Listen, don't belittle me, Mr. Davis. I ain't got time to be pushed around by the likes of you."

Walton glared, then spoke in a pleasant tone, but with an iron firmness. "Don't threaten me, you swill-drinking swine. If you say one more word, I will have your throat cut before the moon sets. I now am acquainted with men who will do the job for ten dollars. If I leave here unhappy—you're a dead man, Mr. French."

Kicking back his chair and clenching his fists, Mr. French hissed a reply. "I know such men too. It could be your throat that's cut."

Walton turned his head to the side and replied in an even, calm voice. "No, it couldn't. Whatever money you would offer, I could double it. And everyone knows it. A word of advice, Mr. French— don't start a knife fight with a man holding a gun. And that's what you're about to do unless you sit down and shut up."

Mr. French looked about the room, as if hoping to see a friendly face. There were none. He muttered a curse to himself, kicked at the chair, then settled back down with a thump.

"Thank you, Mr. French," Walton said. "Now that we have that little misunderstanding settled, shall we begin?"

Mr. French grunted a yes.

Walton downed the last of his drink and slid the glass to the side. "I believe it is time to put our plan in motion."

"Tonight? I said I was . . ." Mr. French swallowed hard, winced, then added. "It can be tonight, I guess."

Walton stared at him. "It doesn't have to be tonight. Any day this week will do. As long as the job is done by next Monday."

Mr. French took a long drink. "And you just want us to . . . how did you put it . . . to 'encourage' him to leave?"

"That is all I think it will take. But don't be coy. Let him know what remaining in town will entail. Offer him the incentives we discussed."

Mr. French began to laugh. "Incentives, sure, I remember them. We'll offer him all the incentives we got."

Smiling, Walton stood and removed a thick envelope from his breast pocket. "Now here is your payment. Do a good job and there'll be more. A lot more."

Mr. French grabbed the envelope and stuffed it into his coat. He swallowed the remaining whiskey and walked off into the darkness.

Pulling up the lapels of his coat around his chin, Walton exited the tavern and meandered along the dark streets. He did not have cause for hurry. In fact, he stopped at several displays in the shop windows along his way, peering into the darkened interiors.

For the first time in years, he began to whistle a tune from his childhood. He could not recall the song's title, but it was bouncy, cheerful, and matched his mood to perfection.

Over the last several months, Walton had carefully assembled a great many facts. He found, in Gage's locked desk, a copy of all the investors in Shirdler's scheme. He spent weeks visiting each one of them. He operated under the guise of determining which manner of dividend payment each party preferred—bank draft or money transfer.

It had been a simple matter to begin to add up the figures. Gage had sold more than 100 percent of the company, much more. Each man claimed to own a certain percentage of the invention—and those numbers quickly swelled past the 100 percent level. Walton realized that it was a common occurrence, especially with fast-developing companies focusing on new inventions. To be safe, the underwriter often added a percentage or two and kept that amount for himself, over and above any underwriting fees. If successful, the profits would secure any dividends needed to cover the percentage above 100. If the scheme was unsuccessful, every investor would lose their money, and no questions could be asked. In either scenario, no one would be the wiser. And the underwriter would be that much richer.

This week Walton had made appointments with three solicitors, all selected at random. He employed a false name with each, not wanting to arouse any suspicions. Walton carried a single sheet of paper with him in which he had outlined the particulars of his brother's scheme. He mentioned no names, for he was aware that the solicitors would love to participate in any manner of litigation.

Each attorney read the letter and without exception claimed the action was clearly criminal. Each man stated that the underwriter could be sued for stock fraud and deceptive practices by misrepresentation.

"Would the underwriter go to jail?" Walton asked each of them.

"Do you have a witness to this plan?" each asked.

"There is an associate who has heard the scheme discussed in detail."

"And this associate would testify in court?"

"This person would love to tell the story," Walton had replied each time, holding back his smile as he imagined the beautiful Nora Wilkes squirming on the witness stand.

All three solicitors then answered that if the facts were true as presented, and if there was indeed a credible witness, then the underwriter would most likely spend years in prison. Holding back his glee, Walton paid each man in cash and left, whistling that same jaunty tune.

And now, as Walton walked home, he realized that he was only days away from becoming the president of Davis Enterprises. The thought rushed through his body in a wave of pleasure.

There was no one who could stop his plan. Not Gage, not his father—no one.

Just that morning, Walton had stopped in his father's room to make certain. It had been nearly two months since the two men had seen each other. Walton was shocked at his father's appearance. In the span of less than a single year, Arthur Davis had disappeared, leaving another person in his stead—living in a hollow shell. From a distance, he appeared as hale and hearty as always. But drawing close, the change became obvious—especially in his eyes. Only a year prior, the dark gaze, the piercing look was legendary. But now his eyes were vacant and blank. As Walton talked to his father, without receiving or expecting any reply, he could see scatterings of terror sweep across his father's visage. It was as if every few moments, Arthur Davis became aware of who he was and just how lost he had become.

Walton knew that, short of a miracle, his father would never utter a single coherent sentence again.

And Walton did not believe in miracles.

Walton arose early on Monday morning. He had trouble sleeping the night before and walked to a coffee shop at the end of the block. He ate two rolls while he read the morning edition of the *Post*.

He folded the paper under his arm and sauntered back to the family home. He walked up the front steps, tossed the newspaper onto a hall table, then, without knocking, entered Gage's office.

Gage looked up from his desk. "Walton, you're up early. Something on your mind?"

And then Walton smiled. "Yes, there is, little brother."

Gage expected Walton to continue or to ask for an increase in his spending allowance. Instead Walton walked to the window and gazed out at the garden beyond.

"Well?" Gage asked.

"Well, indeed," Walton replied without turning around.

Gage sighed deeply. It appeared as if his brother was slipping back into the pattern of bait and torment. Gage had decided months ago that if such a change occurred, he would have no part of playing the game any longer. "Walton, I am busy this morning. If you want something, just ask. If you came in to waste my time, then I must ask you to leave." Gage kept the anger out of his words.

Walton held back a laugh and moved to sit in the chair opposite his brother's desk. From his pocket he withdrew a thick packet of papers. His eyes grew cold and his lips narrowed. His words were chilled and dark. "You shall never order me around again, little brother. Never."

Gage held up his hands. "Walton, I am sorry if I offended you—but I simply must ask you to stop wasting my time. I am a busy man, and I must get on with my work before I go to the office today."

Walton offered a hollow laugh in reply. "You're not going to the office today, little brother. You're never going back to the office again." Walton's ominous warning brought Gage to attention.

"What on earth are you talking about? Not go to the office? Since when do you have any control over my actions?"

"Since now, little brother. Now I have the power."

Gage laughed. "Power? Walton, you forget who runs Davis Enterprises. I have the power."

Walton stood up, threw the papers on Gage's desk, and shouted, "Not anymore!"

Gage jumped back in surprise, then gathered up the papers. As he began to scan them, he felt a chill in his heart. He read the first page, then the second, then the third. Finally Gage looked up. He tried to appear as if he were unconcerned, but he knew he failed. "This will never hold up in court. Every new company I know of has been oversold."

"Perhaps, Gage, but I have your list of investors. I am sure they will not be happy having received only half of what they paid for."

A bead of sweat trickled down Gage's back. "It isn't that much money. Davis Enterprises has more than enough liquidity to cover this insignificant detail."

Walton countered. "Little brother, did you ever read our father's will? In it, he has specified that if dead–or incapacitated–which he is, then whoever is in control of the company shall be of 'good moral character.' "

"I have good moral character," Gage replied, his voice low and calm.

"It appears you have committed a crime. Several lawyers whom I've consulted have determined it to be stock fraud, plain and simple. That means you, little brother, are a criminal in the eyes of the law and . . . well, should be booted out of the president's office."

Now sweat appeared on Gage's forehead. He shuffled through the papers again. Events seemed to be spinning out of his control.

"You can read everything a hundred times, Gage, but I think what we have here is airtight. I know several attorneys who would love to offer me help."

Gage studied his older brother. "You can prove no ill intent. It can be claimed as an oversight by an accountant or clerk." It was true that several cases of this type were dismissed from court for just such a defense.

Walton smiled. "Do you remember the train ride you took back from Southampton with a certain Miss Nora Wilkes?"

Gage closed his eyes. The world he had carefully crafted was beginning to splinter. "What do you know of her?"

"Many things, little brother. I know you told her all about your scheme to oversell the company. Tsk, tsk, tsk–you should know better than to tell a woman anything in confidence. They simply cannot keep a secret."

Gage stood up, the vein at his temple throbbing. He sputtered, trying to control his anger.

Walton did not move, except to raise his hand. "Gage, you should not be angry with me. It's she you should be angry with. She is the one who caused you to be found out. She is the witness to your perfidy."

"That's not true. You know it's not true."

Walton sat back, a smug, satisfied leer on his face. "I win, little brother. I win for a change."

Gage could not believe any of what was occurring. He had to find Nora. She would tell him it was all simply a misunderstanding. He could salvage his life. He could hang on to the treasure he had amassed. She was the key.

He ignored Walton's harsh laughter as he grabbed his suitcoat and ran from the room. Waiting for the carriage to be readied would be worse than torture, so Gage began to sprint down the street, his elegant coat flapping as he ran.

Gasping, he leaned against the desk in the lobby of Nora's residence.

"She's not here, Mr. Davis. She left an hour ago and told me she would return by noon."

Gage was only steps away when the woman behind the desk called out, "Did she tell you where she was going?"

Gage spun around. "Going?"

The woman pointed to the pyramid of luggage to the side. "Those are her things. She's leaving this afternoon."

Gage turned and ran, jumping three steps at a time. Less than fifteen minutes later he was at the door to Shirdler's laboratory. Usually the room was filled with noise and a tracing of acrid smoke, but today Gage heard nothing.

He pounded on the door. There was no answer. He called out and heard no response. He stepped back and raised his right foot and kicked the lock. Then he offered a second and a third kick and the door splintered open, banging against the far wall.

Gage took a step inside, then stopped and stared.

The room was empty. Work benches were littered with a few beakers and broken tubes and wire. But everything else was gone—as if Shirdler had never existed. Wide-eyed and frightened, Gage ran to Shirdler's private office.

If I can find Shirdler, I can make this right. We can agree on a different number. We can call the amount already sold as the total stock offering. All he needs to do is to agree. He'll have to agree. . . .

Gage found himself staring at a deserted office. A few papers lay scattered on the floor; others lay in a pile on a shelf. A cabinet was left open. The desk sat at an angle in the corner, its drawers open. An overturned chair cluttered the middle of the room. Gage spun about, shouting Shirdler's name.

He was not aware of how long he stood there.

"Who are you?"

Gage jumped.

"Gage Davis. I'm looking for Shirdler. Who are you?"

A beefy man in a tight suit hulked into the room. "I'm the landlord here. I came to collect the rent. I can see somebody left in a hurry."

Gage closed his eyes. "I don't suppose he told you where he was going."

The beefy man shook his head. "No . . . but nobody leaves like this unless they're hiding something—or running away. I sort of figured that fellow was doing both. Something about the way he sulked around here."

Gage kicked a glass beaker on the floor. It rolled, making a hollow sound.

"The fellow owe you money, too?"

Gage looked up. "Something like that."

A few minutes later, Gage hailed a carriage and gave the driver Nora's address. As he rode, a blackness descended upon his heart.

If I could have found Shirdler . . . maybe I could have salvaged this. But not now. With him gone, investors are going to scream a swindle. They'll say I was in on it. Then somebody is going to start adding up numbers. And when that happens . . .

He held his head in his hands.

I have been caught. It's true what Walton said . . . I could go to jail for this. I can be removed from the company. I can't let that happen.

He wanted to call out to God . . . to someone . . . but he thought there would be no one who would listen. He opened his eyes.

I need to see Nora. I need to talk to her. What Walton said can't be true. She would not betray me like this.

The carriage jerked to a stop. Gage ran down the block and into Nora's residence again. This time her luggage was gone.

"Where is she? When did she leave?" he shouted.

The woman behind the desk looked surprised. "Didn't you pass her on the steps? The driver just took her last bag out as you ran in."

Gage jumped all the steps this time and banged through the doors. Frantically he scanned the street for a departing carriage. At the end of the block, he caught the fleeting sight of a carriage's luggage rack as it turned the corner. Gage began to run.

Midway along the block, his steps carried him abreast of the carriage. He shouted out Nora's name. Framed by a tiny window in the rear seat, he saw Nora's face. Her eyes were red, and tears streaked down her cheeks. Her face, suddenly gaunt, was a mask of pain.

"Stop!" he called out. The driver ignored him, and the carriage clattered on.

In that instant, Gage knew. Gage knew everything.

Nora had sacrificed Gage. Nora had told Walton everything. Whatever the reason, Nora had effectively destroyed Gage's life.

Gage slowed, stumbled once, then began to walk.

"Stop!" he cried one more time, knowing the carriage would not stop.

He lurched to the street, then stepped off into the gutter. His sides hurt from running; his thoughts swirled like a hurricane.

And his heart had been torn in two.

He lowered his head, oblivious to the pedestrians and carriages flowing about him. Gage looked up, staring into the heavens as if he expected to see something. Then he lowered his head again and closed his eyes.

Chapter Sixteen

New York City
May–June 1847

Gage stood in the street for a long time after Nora's carriage rolled out of sight and south along Fifth Avenue. He presumed she was headed to the train station. He knew he could have found a faster carriage. He knew he could have followed her to whatever her destination.

But just as sure as he could follow her, he was just as sure that to do so would be futile.

Maybe she has a reason for why she told Walton. But whatever the reason she had to justify this, how could it lessen the pain in my heart? How could I trust her ever again? No . . . she is right to leave. And I am right to let her go.

Gage walked slowly down the block, not knowing in which direction he was going. By early afternoon, Gage found himself at the banks of the Hudson River, on the far west side of Manhattan.

He walked out on a pier and sat down. The breeze flowed up the river, and ripples of water caught the afternoon sun. A flock of gulls circled and flashed in the bright sky. Yet Gage hardly noticed any of his surroundings; he was barely aware of how he had made his way to this spot.

He replayed the confrontation with Walton a hundred times, searching for a weakness, a solution. Each time he considered an avenue that might lead out of his predicament, another problem would arise that had no solution. He considered paying his investors off, but with what? Walton would not allow that without a fight. If Gage were removed from Davis Enterprises, there would be no access to cash. He had only several thousand dollars in his own personal account. He considered fighting Walton in court, but if Nora had agreed to be a witness, Gage's story would be doomed before he uttered a single word. How could a judge not believe the words of such a beautiful woman?

Despite considering a hundred solutions—some of which might prolong the inevitable for months, if not years—Gage experienced an epiphany of sorts while sitting on the pier that spring day.

Gage realized he was exactly what Walton had accused him of being—a thief.

One might dress up Gage's actions over the past months in polite and precise terminology. One might say it was an accepted business practice. One might argue that the money involved was nearly inconsequential. But none of those rationalizations changed the reality—Gage had committed a crime. And what hurt worse was that Gage's potential reward would never have amounted to more than a few thousand dollars.

If Shirdler had not disappeared and if his so-called invention had been a success, the reality was that Gage would not have become noticeably richer. There would only have been some more dollars in his bank, for certain, and the thrill of beating out other businessmen.

But would he have been 2 percent more wealthy? 5 percent? Certainly no more than that.

And for that small amount, Gage had risked his reputation. He had gambled so much of his life to win a paltry amount.

And he had lost.

Gage Davis had lost it all.

He lowered his head, trying to quiet the voices shouting recriminations in his head. He didn't hear a schooner slide by, with bells tolling. He didn't hear the caw of the gulls as they followed a fishing tug. He didn't hear the shouts of the teamsters, stevedores, and dockworkers as they unloaded a clipper ship three piers down.

All he heard was that voice inside him, berating his stupidity and foolishness and greed. Tears welled up, but he forced them back.

He might cry over a death or an illness, but shedding tears today would be crying over a half-witted and senseless action of a man who should have known better.

Gage rose stiffly from the wooden pier. He drew in a great breath, feeling the bones of his back creak into place. "I know what I must do," he whispered to himself as he noticed the position of the sun. Then he turned and began to walk toward home.

⁂

"I'm a compassionate person," Walton said, stretching his arms open. "I never said you would have to leave tonight."

Gage offered no reply. He had returned home to admit defeat.

"All you have to do to avoid prosecution and humiliation are two simple things," Walton continued.

Gage waited, unwilling to give Walton the satisfaction of supplication.

Walton rubbed his hands together. He was as joyful as a child on Christmas morning standing before a mound of wrapped gifts, all addressed to him. "Well, I can see you are not going to ask. No matter. It will not affect my satisfaction one bit."

Walton was seated behind Gage's desk. Already he had reorganized things, moving a lamp to the opposite side, removing a vase, and placing all the papers in a neat pile. He opened the top drawer—the drawer Gage had left locked.

Walton looked up. "I found an extra key, little brother. I didn't want to damage such a wonderful piece of furniture."

He extracted two sheets of paper. "The first paper is a simple document I would like you to sign."

"What is it?" Gage asked, his voice expressionless.

"It states that you are officially renouncing all your ties to Davis Enterprises and that you have resigned as president as of today."

Gage extended his hand, and Walton passed the paper to his younger brother. Gage read through the short document, then without saying a word, placed it flat against the table, picked up a pen, dipped it into the inkwell, and scratched his name on the bottom line. He handed it back to Walton, who took it, blew upon the signature to set the ink, and slid it back into the top drawer.

"And the other paper?" Gage asked wearily.

"Well, as I said, I am not a man devoid of feelings. And this document will prove that."

Walton tossed the paper at Gage. "I'm providing you with ten thousand dollars. I want you to leave New York City and agree never to return."

Gage shut his eyes, struggling to prevent his anger from exploding. "You can't ask that! I have a right to see our parents."

Nodding, Walton leaned back in Gage's old chair.

"Of course you do, Gage. It is quite clear that our dear old mother does not epitomize the self-sacrificing noble image of a mother that literature holds as ideal. Her only comment in all of this—and I did talk to her about it—was that she requested an increase in her monthly stipend. I agreed on that point, and she is now quite content. And as for Father—well, it's clear to me that he is unaware of who he is, let alone who you or I are."

Gage slapped his hand on the desk.

"Wait, little brother. I am willing to compromise. Come back to New York twice a year. Stay each time for three days—but do not announce your coming to anyone. And if Father should pass on, then, by all means, feel free to attend the funeral."

Walton scrawled a visitation clause in the margin with angry strokes, then pushed the paper to Gage. "I'd like you to sign now, please."

Gage wanted nothing more than to leap over the desk and

pummel his brother soundly. But he closed his eyes and instead signed the paper.

"Well, then, all is settled, isn't it?" Walton said, his voice oozing with false sincerity and warmth. "I'll have the bank deliver your money tomorrow. You can leave town by the end of the week, can't you?"

Gage stepped back. "How can such a monster like you be my brother?" he snarled.

Walton opened his eyes in mock hurt. "But it was not I who broke the law, Gage. Remember, *you* are the man who jeopardized everything with your greed. Not me. I am the innocent party in this sordid affair. I knew nothing about your deceit and treachery."

Gage stormed towards the door.

Walton called out, "I just pray that I can rescue the good name of Davis Enterprises."

Gage turned and glared at his brother. *How ironic,* he thought. *The likes of him being viewed by all the world as the pious one.*

"How did you force Nora to turn against me?" he demanded out loud. "What did you hold over her?"

Walton reacted with that same, infuriating mock surprise. "I did nothing, little brother. She is, after all, a woman of fine pedigree with strong moral values—a devout Christian—or didn't you know that? Do you think she could sit idly by and let you steal money from others? Do you think you could sin like that and not have your action prick at her conscience? She did what any moral woman would do— she offered to tell the truth." Walton chuckled, apparently enjoying every moment of his brother's torture.

"I may have nudged her a bit. But it was only a nudge, I assure you. I showed her a newspaper clipping or two. A document. A nudge." Walton offered a tight smile.

Gage's eyes pierced his brother. Then he opened the door and walked out of his office in Davis Enterprises for the last time.

"Gage, what can I do to help?" Jamison asked.

"There is nothing, old friend. You warned me, and I was too

proud and too foolish to listen. You have done more than anyone—and I ignored your offer. I'm sorry I . . . lied."

The two were seated in a confectioner's store several blocks from the train station. Gage had sent word that Jamison must meet him.

It took less than an hour to relate the entire story.

"You could fight him, Gage," Jamison said. "You could win. Things like this go on all the time in business. In fact, it is almost accepted behavior."

"Almost does not make it legal."

"But, Gage—with your connections—surely there is a judge or attorney who could nudge the right people. Walton would be out on his ear. Call in a few of your favors."

Gage swirled the coffee in his cup. "And confront one crime with another? Didn't you crusade against bribes to City Hall?"

Jamison looked away. "But they weren't friends. You are. I don't want you to leave like this."

Gage dismissed the thought with a gentle wave. "I'll be fine. Just promise me that you'll do what you can to maintain the good name of Davis Enterprises. I'm asking you one last favor. Don't write what you know about this. Don't tell others the truth. I want my father's name protected."

Jamison nodded. "I'll do what I can. Without you fighting your brother, this story will be much less appealing to any editor. And I'll spread the word. I would wager that this news doesn't get closer to the front than page six, and it will be below the fold."

"Below the fold?"

"On the bottom of the page. No one reads those stories, really. Not even the editors, I think."

Gage offered a weak smile.

"What will happen to the company?" Jamison asked. "You always said that Walton had no interest in it."

"Walton may be a horrible brother, but he is intelligent and crafty. He'll make an adequate businessman—although not necessarily an honest businessman. And there are so many talented people within the organization. I don't think Walton will be able to destroy it, even if he wanted to."

Gage sipped the last of his coffee and pushed the cup to the side of the table. He checked the time on his pocketwatch. "It's an hour till my train leaves. We should say our good-byes."

"You never told me where you are going," said Jamison.

"I'm not sure myself. West, I think. I'm heading to Chicago, then south along the Mississippi to New Orleans. By the time I get there, I should have some idea of what to do with the rest of my life."

"And you're never coming back to New York?"

"I don't think so. My father doesn't know me anymore. I stopped in his room just before coming here and he didn't respond."

"Gage, I'm sorry. I know how much you loved him."

"I did and still do. And I've lost him without losing him. He's all but dead—and there's no funeral, no ceremony."

"Are you going to write to Hannah about this?" Jamison asked.

"No. I hadn't planned on it."

"Then I won't tell her either."

Gage tilted his head. "Do you two write each other often?"

Jamison averted his eyes. "Define *often.*"

"More than once a year."

Jamison couldn't help but smile. "Then we write often."

Gage leaned forward. "Jamison, I have heard she is all but engaged to Robert Keyes. You knew that. It was reported in your paper."

"And if she is engaged, does that mean she has lost the power of writing?"

"Well . . . no, but . . ."

"But what?"

"I just never thought you two had that much in common."

Jamison laughed. "We don't. We spend most of our time simply illuminating our differences."

Gage smiled. "Thanks, old friend. Now I can leave on a happy note."

"Keep me posted as to your location. Drop a note to the newspaper. They'll pass it on to me wherever I am."

"Wherever you are?" Gage asked. "Why? Is the *World* sending you someplace?"

"Not that I know of. But they might. I keep volunteering." Jamison grinned.

"Then good-bye, friend. I'll write. I promise."

Jamison stood and embraced Gage in a great long hug.

"I have heard that promise from your lips before. This time you had best mean to keep it."

"I will, Jamison. I will."

Galena, Illinois

Gage stood on the pier and listened. The Mississippi River surged underneath the warped and canted boards, its muddy waters only feet from where he stood. Rain had followed him on the entire trip from Chicago. The Galena River had risen, and the small canal boat had quickly covered the distance to the Mississippi. So swift was the river's flow that the larger riverboat on the Mississippi had cut a full three days off the normal sailing schedule. Patches of low-lying farmland had been covered with brown water as the boat floated past.

New Orleans, Louisiana

They entered New Orleans at nightfall. Tying up at the dock, Gage jumped to the pier, anxious to stand on firm ground again. But he halted as shouts and a loud crash of music poured out from one of the taverns that lined the streets by the dock. Gage motioned for a stevedore to help with his few bags.

"Where's the best hotel in town?"

The black man rubbed his chin. The light glinted off a gold earring in his right ear. "Well, sir, that be a puzzle. I don't believe New Orleans got a best hotel. They all be bad if you ask me."

Tired and dirty, Gage desperately wanted to sleep in a bed not infested with weevils and bugs. "Well, then, what's the most expensive hotel in town? Where the rich people go?"

"Well, dat be easy, sir. Da Crescent Moon."

Gage eyed the stevedore. "It's just a hotel, right? I don't want to pay for more than I use."

The stevedore offered a wide smile in reply. "Yes, sir. Da Crescent just be a hotel. You want any extras, you come ask for me. Ask for Anton LeMark. Dat be me."

Gage pointed to his bags. "Anton, if I want anything, you will be the first person I call."

Anton grinned and hefted the luggage. Gage followed Anton as he made his way down the street. Crowds of people spilled out from the taverns and restaurants and milled about, laughing and dancing. Gage sniffed the air. The fetid, humid smell of the river was coupled with a hint of bourbon and gardenia and cheap perfume.

"Anton," Gage asked as they turned onto a quieter street, "what's the occasion?"

"Occasion, sir?"

"For all the partying."

Anton laughed. "Ain't no occasion, sir. Be like dat every night 'cept Mardi Gras. Den it be even worse."

Anton walked down another narrow street. At the end was a pair of gaslights.

"We be at da Crescent, sir. Most expensive place I know in these parts."

Gage reached in his pocket, pulling out a five-dollar gold piece. Then he thought for a moment and slipped it back in his pocket. Instead he took out a silver dollar.

I keep forgetting that I am no longer a rich man.

Gage gazed up at the cool white marble facade of the Crescent Moon hotel. Inside, behind the desk, stood an elegant black man in a starched white coat.

But tonight, I will pretend that I am still rich. It will be a lovely dream.

During his journey to New Orleans, Gage had spent very little time thinking of anything. Most days found him on deck, staring blankly at whatever scenery passed by the boat. If it rained, he sat in his cabin and stared out the window. Occasionally he purchased a newspaper, but he would hold the paper open for an hour and then realize that he had read either no words, or the same headline over and over and over.

It was as if New York and Nora and Harvard and Walton had simply never existed. He did not sink into despair. He did not enter into planning for the future. He simply was. Time flowed around him as he journeyed.

One evening, as he stared blankly at the stars, he imagined himself as a caterpillar. He was now in a cocoon and would soon emerge as some other creature with a new life.

Now that he was in New Orleans, he began to realize he would have to do something with his life. Granted, his bank account might let him live without working for years and years—but that was not an existence that offered any promise or joy.

He decided to remain at the Crescent while in the city. Anton may have deemed it expensive, but it was a quarter of the cost of a modest New York hotel. Gage checked a few other hotels—but none were as clean or as quiet as the Crescent.

Summer in New Orleans was not the season to explore. A thick, almost crushing blanket of heat and humidity covered the city. By the time he walked three blocks Gage was drenched with sweat.

So he would walk in the early mornings—just as the hint of dawn colored the sky pink. Vendors and cafés offered thick coffee and wonderfully delicate pastries. He heard French and Creole spoken, languages that sounded as close to music as speech can be.

One morning he found himself staring at the Mississippi. He stopped at a small café and sat outside, reading the local newspaper. When he happened to look up, he noticed that on the riverbank just south of him lay a mound of equipment, seemingly tossed into a haphazard jumble. The pile of rusted metal and canvas and wood was as tall as three men and hundreds of yards in circumference.

Gage motioned to his waiter. "What's that over there? Did a riverboat go down?"

The waiter laughed. "No, sir, not exactly."

"Then what is it?"

"That be a pile of stuff those poor Northern fellows never got around to taking with them out west."

"What? What poor fellows?"

"Anyone from up north going west—who wants to avoid fighting Indians by taking the water route—comes to the Crescent City—like you. Plenty of boats from here go west—and a lot of 'em filled with Northern boys."

"But what does that have to do with all that junk?"

"They bring it with them. Then they find out how much it costs to take it the rest of the way, and they leave it here. Boat captains get used to it now—and they just dump it over there."

"And it just stays there? Perfectly good equipment?"

"Sir, you think I got any need for a plow down here? I start to plow this dirt, and water comes up. It might be worth something up north, but not down here."

Gage put his paper down. He stared at the pile of equipment. Three gulls swooped down and landed on what Gage thought might be a farmer's harvester machine.

He closed his eyes—and felt the tight wrapping of his cocoon begin to rip and his new wings unfurl in the cool air of the dawn.

CHAPTER SEVENTEEN

California Coast
November 1847

Gage, holding on to the ship's aft railing, could not recall ever being as sick as when he first saw the coast of California. As a boy and young man, he had sailed hundreds of times in the often-turbulent waters of Long Island Sound and from Manhattan to Southampton in rough weather. Until this last stretch of sea, Gage envisioned himself as a seasoned yachtsman.

The breeze was from the west, the swells were unusually high, and the ship rolled down each trough as it pitched aft to stern as well as port to starboard.

"It's the combination of movement that has done me in," Gage shouted to the ship's captain, just before he ran to the rail for a third, then fourth time.

After another hour of pitching about in the heavy chop, the captain shouted out, "There's the coast, Mr. Davis. That's California. We've done it."

Weakly, Gage raised his head. Off to the east, perhaps two miles, lay a band of purple hills, mottled by the shadow of mist and clouds.

He blinked his eyes several times, reached down into the spray off the hull and wiped his face with the saltwater, and stared again.

Finally, Gage thought. *This is one voyage I hope I will never have to endure again.*

The captain set a course closer to shore and by midafternoon, the winds tapered to a gentle breeze, and the wave crests softened. Gage managed to down a cup of lukewarm tea and a few biscuits, and he began to feel almost human again.

It had been an arduous journey, and the entire crew seemed to offer a collective sigh of relief now that their destination had come into view.

Gage's steps were still tentative, but he made his way to the bow of the ship, carrying his journal with him. He was encouraged by the smiles of the men as he passed. He gathered up a spare jib sail for a seat and reclined against the forward hatch, out of the wind. He took out a pencil and smiled.

I have come full circle–pencil, then pen, then pencil again.

Before he began to write, he reread several of his entries from the last months.

FROM THE JOURNAL OF GAGE DAVIS
AROUND THE HORN AND BEYOND

Traveling to New Orleans has been a great adventure. America is indeed a land of bounty and beauty. It is one thing to read about the west and the rivers and the mighty land–it is another thing altogether actually to experience the breadth and width of the land as one travels.

The Mississippi–how could a writer accurately describe the power of the great river? I have read in some account that the natives along its banks called it the "Father of Waters." It is an apt description. Sometimes muddy, turbulent, and dangerous, sometimes languid, slow, and peaceful, the river carried me from my old life–to the spot where I began my new life.

I am attempting not to dwell on the past, though that task is hard–perhaps the most difficult task I have ever faced. At night, as I tumble across that invisible divide that separates sleep from consciousness, I see Nora's face. Sometimes the image is her tearstained face that I glimpsed as the carriage hurried her away for the last time, and other times it is her face marked with laughter and gentleness. Yet more often, more painfully, the image is that of her face creased and twisted with evil laughter.

That sound of pernicious, malevolent glee awakens me. Then for hours I struggle to find the sweet relief that sleep provides. In the darkness I brood, growing bitter and angry as the night deepens.

As one might determine by my words, I am not yet over the pain.

My brother's treachery can be explained—if not all but expected. I should have seen his actions and his plotting long before they exploded.

But I was a fool to believe in brotherly loyalty and *bonhomie*.

Walton's duplicity cost me everything—but that loss was nothing in comparison to the pain Nora inflicted on my heart. How treacherous a woman can be. How completely the destruction of a man can be accomplished by a meek and gentle woman. The devil has the power, it appears, to assume a pleasing shape.

Yet I am fortunate in some regards. Nora inflicted a grave wound on my heart—but not a mortal wound.

I will recover. I will be stronger because of what she has done to me.

That is my vow.

But I have digressed. I must return to the rubbish pile.

The rubbish pile on the bank of the Mississippi, that is.

Seeing that discarded pile of rubbish—some of it nearly new merchandise—on the edge of the river was the start of a great awakening.

I made further inquiries and discovered how common the practice is. Settlers and explorers and farmers continue to head west—the trickle of faces growing—and I imagine it soon to be a torrent. It is obvious why these honest folks discard some of their prized possessions. At some point on this long journey, Grandmother's revered heirlooms become so much dead weight. How useful will a portrait of a long-forgotten relative be? Other items are much more difficult to explain. Why would a farmer, bent on planting cotton in California, discard a cotton gin on the muddy banks of the Mississippi? Some items are reclaimed and resold—but many are simply left to rot in the rain.

I have been told that many decisions come down to a simple matter of money. Some settlers leave on their journey with scant resources. When they arrive in New Orleans, or other ports of embarkation, they find that their money can purchase the shipping tariff for their goods *or* the cost of a ticket for themselves—but not both.

What would I do in that situation? Begin the journey with more money, to start. But if I could not add to my resources, I would buy a ticket for myself, thinking that the abandoned items can be replaced at the end of my journey.

This is a situation that never arose in a Harvard business class—what to do with free goods?

While I am not rich by any means, I do possess a handsome stake. Walton gave me a pittance to leave New York, and I had some funds available to me that he knew nothing about. I suppose I could live out the remainder of my days on these monies, providing I squelch my desires for the better things in life.

But I do not choose to follow that path. My desires are an integral part of me.

I found a ship (New Orleans is stocked with ships) that was older, but still quite serviceable. She is a sturdy vessel with an amazing capacity for freight. For three months, I met every riverboat heading south on the great river. I passed out handbills. I blanketed the docks with posters. I told everyone I met my intentions.

I was buying what the good settlers were bent on discarding.

Was I foolish to offer cash to what would soon be free? No, because now I had first choice and a steady supply.

And instead of relegating these items to the trash, I offered but a small percentage of their worth. Settlers and farmers and the like flocked to me with all manner of material. There was much I would not purchase—like the portrait of anyone's long-dead Uncle Mortimer. But cloth and quilts I purchased. Farm implements I purchased—often the equipment had never been used. I bought lanterns and barrels and silverware and mirrors and plows and nails and tools.

In the span of weeks, the cargo hold of the ship was overflowing.

It was then I calculated my finances. If careful, I could buy a second ship as well as purchase cargo.

I did.

I found captains for both vessels who were willing to take the voyage and locate eager crews. While the fellows I was forced to hire may not be the most law-abiding and civil of men, they do not appear to be dangerous.

At least on a regular basis.

In mid-August, my two-ship armada set sail for the western edge of the Americas—specifically, San Francisco.

The voyage out of the Caribbean was uneventful, as was most of the journey down the coast of South America. I cannot say that the weather was always fine, but we made good time. The farther south we traveled, the colder it became. Of course we all knew that fact, but it was odd to experience nonetheless. We stopped in ports only out of necessity to replenish food and water stocks. I imagine any port in the world is the same—high prices for inferior material.

We managed to slip into the port of Ushuaia in Tierra del Fuego just as the biting, angry wind behind a huge gale arrived. The gale brought forth a full blizzard. They call it the "land of fire," but the winds howled so during our stay, I don't see how any fire could remain lit. The locals thought us mad for attempting this voyage in winter—but they agreed the weather in summer is no more predictable.

We rode out the storm while lying at anchor for two weeks. The sun was a welcome sight when we at last glimpsed it again, though it did not affect the freezing temperature in the slightest. Since it was winter, the sun was visible only for several hours.

The captain admitted that a winter traverse was a gamble, but we pushed off and headed round the Horn—and made it through without a problem—much to the relief of the crew. Sailors who have made the trip tell of storms that stir the ocean and build waves a hundred feet tall. They tell stories in which the gales dash ships to the rocks, as if the crafts were no more solid than matchsticks.

Much to our delight, our trip north was as uneventful as the trip south—save the increase in temperature.

I suspect I should mention more of the wondrous sights I have seen on this journey, but I have read that to capture the moment is difficult—better to wait and write about the sights and sounds that had been most memorable on the voyage.

Both ships remained sound and seaworthy during the entire voyage. Two of the crew sickened and passed on as we headed north—but the captain claims such deaths are a normal occurrence and that ships often lose a full quarter of their crew.

Watching their bodies tumble into the sea was a sobering experience for me, since both fellows were not much older than myself.

And now, after months of deprivation and toil and death, we are in sight of the land called *California*.

The captain had told me much of the comings and goings of the territory. I was vaguely aware of some problems there with the Mexicans, but I admit I did not pay much attention to the story, since it was as close to me as the moon. I knew there were disputes over the territory—but no one paid it much notice.

As I understand it, the Spaniards claimed the land first, setting up a string of missions along the coast. Then the Mexican folks sort of claimed it by default. Then there was this fellow Fremont who began to stir up trouble between the Mexican folks and the Americans who lived there, claiming that California is a republic. Sometime in the summer of '46 the navy sailed into Monterey, set up shop for Washington, and then named someone to be civil governor of California. Things heated up down south and in Mexico. But from what the captain's heard, the north—where we're going—is as peaceful as a Sunday afternoon. Some of the Californios—the Spanish folk who stuck around—might be a bit upset, but not enough to cause trouble—especially since one of the American generals offered them all pardons.

A smart businessman can make money no matter who's in

charge—but I'd rather have the United States government handling things.

As we sailed closer to our destination, I spent hours poring over the map in the captain's possession. The map was of good quality and showed nearly all of California's coast, the mouths of major rivers, suitable bays and landing spots. It was clearly drawn by a navigator, because little detail was noted concerning the land's interior.

I inquired of the captain as to the nature of the harbor of San Francisco. He explained that it was a large, well-protected bay. The hills about the bay angled sharply up. Two narrow spits of land guarded the entrance to the harbor.

"It's the prime spot in the northern territory," the captain related. "You'll find that every ship calling on the territory will anchor there."

"Every ship?" I asked.

He said yes, and that the harbor is often so crowded with ships, it is possible to walk across the bay on the decks of a hundred ships.

That comment drove me back to the map.

I noticed a great half-circle of a bay perhaps a hundred miles to the south of the bay of San Francisco.

The captain looked at the map. "I have anchored there in the past. It's a fine harbor. Right there is a small fishing town called Monterey. There are several docks built into deep water. You can't call Monterey a city—it's more like a village."

I asked if any knew if settlers and immigrants made it a spot to disembark.

"A fair number do," he answered. "Not as much as San Francisco. But Monterey just finished a large customs house, so I suspect they're ready to handle anything."

I studied the map for the rest of the day. Then I decided.

"We're landing in Monterey, Captain," I said. "Can you set your course there?"

The captain was a professional. If he was surprised or dismayed, he showed neither.

"We can do that, Mr. Davis. And we'll be there, God willing, before nightfall tomorrow."

As we spent that last night at sea, I turned the question over and over in my mind—is it better to be a small fish in a large pond, like what would no doubt occur in San Francisco, or a large fish in the small pond of Monterey?

I decided I would prefer to be noticed right away. Toiling in obscurity has never been the Davis way.

It was just as dusk colored the hills red and umber that I first glimpsed the town of Monterey. The captain was right—no more than a hundred dwellings ringed the quiet harbor. A handful of docks and warehouses leaned and tilted about the shorefront. Myriad fishing boats bobbed at anchor as we drew close.

Since no one was expecting us, no one was at the docks to greet us.

We tied up the vessels securely, our journey complete. The crew took off for the nearest tavern, which was their normal course of action at every port of call. Yet with the end of the voyage all displayed a greater urgency to find a source of unlimited libation.

Darkness fell. I was the only man left on the ship. An hour after sunset, a full moon rose over the placid waters of the bay, the silver image reflected like a ghostly, rippled beacon. I sat, drank coffee, and waited anxiously for the sun.

My new life had begun.

❦

Monterey, California
December 1847

The first day in California waters, Gage awoke moments past dawn. As he stepped to the main deck of his ship, what he saw offered no surprise. The captain and most of the crew sprawled about the deck, some of them moaning softly, some lying with an empty bottle or two snuggled in their arms.

He knew from past experience that nothing short of a storm would awaken them. Gage climbed down to the dock, waved to a trio of fishing boats headed out to sea, and set off to find breakfast. From his left came the barking and grunting of a small group of seals, basking on an outcropping of rocks. A slight breeze from the ocean brought a hint of warmth.

If this is winter, then I most wholeheartedly approve, Gage said to himself, smiling.

A rutted path from the dock led to a long, two-story building. Gage peered in through the closed windows.

If this is the customs house that the captain mentioned, then they have a most relaxed manner of greeting incoming ships.

He tapped at the door and waited. He expected no one to answer and was not disappointed. He turned and sniffed the air. Someone close by was cooking. His stomach growled. For more than three months he had lived on biscuits, cheese, fish, and canned beans. There had to be a restaurant nearby.

He began to walk up the hill, where tracks radiated away from the bay like a spiderweb. Along the path was a scattering of cottages and homes. He walked to the north a quarter-mile or so and came to a more defined road. A few larger buildings faced the wide street. One appeared to be a tavern or restaurant, but its doors were shut and the blinds drawn tight. Another was obviously a livery. A third building stood alone—a trim two-story structure, with a balcony protruding over the covered front walkway. Gage walked up and peered in—it was deserted. A few tables and chairs lay in the empty darkness. There were no other signs of habitation.

Must have been a tavern that failed, Gage thought. *Might be suitable for my needs.*

At that moment, he heard a door slam and shards of conversation. Just around the corner, towards the bay, stood a rambling shanty constructed of weathered wood. From the smell, Gage knew that he had found his restaurant.

He entered and took a seat near the window. There were perhaps ten men there having breakfast, and every one stopped to watch as he walked in. They silently examined the newcomer and then, a heartbeat later, almost as if on cue, returned to their meals. The hum of conversation continued.

A young woman came over to his table. "You on board one of the two ships in the harbor?"

Gage nodded. "I take it everyone else here is a regular."

"Yep," the serving girl replied. "You ain't a settler, I know that. You ain't got a settler's look."

"What do settlers look like?" Gage asked.

"I don't know exactly. More in a hurry to get somewhere. Sort of frantic. And poor. You ain't poor."

"I'm not?"

"Nope, it's your clothes–they're much too nice for a poor man– even if they ain't been washed in a few weeks."

Gage smiled. "Hard to wash them in salt water."

The serving girl nodded knowingly.

"Do you get many settlers through here?" Gage asked.

"Quite a few," the serving girl replied. "When they land here, they don't stop long. They may spend a day getting rid of their sea legs– then they head east. But there ain't been any new ships stopping here for the past few weeks. Things have been slow."

She peered out the window when she spoke, as if expecting a ship to arrive at any moment. "So what will you have?"

Gage rubbed his hands together. "I've been at sea for months. I have dreamt about this meal for a long time. Bring me a portion of everything you have–eggs, bacon, grits, potatoes, mush, johnny-cakes–whatever you're serving today, I want some of it."

She laughed.

"What's so funny?" Gage asked, wondering if he had said some-thing foolish.

"Don't worry. It's just that every sailor orders pretty much the same breakfast. All of them ask for a serving of everything. Don't worry; we'll fix you up fine."

Before fifteen minutes passed, a huge tray of food was brought to Gage's table. For a second or two, he simply stared and inhaled the aromas, then proceeded to dive into the meal with unbridled enthusiasm.

After an hour-long repast, Gage forced himself to leave the table.

He left a nice tip for the serving girl—not as rich as once was his preference—but Gage no longer had unlimited finances.

She told him that the deserted building had been a tavern, but the man who had been renting it had not been seen for months. The owner was just now starting to look for a new tenant. Gage realized that to build his own building would require too much of his precious capital.

He sought out the owner, and before noon, they had struck a deal to rent the building for the next two years.

By the end of the week, Gage was nearly in business. He had the place cleaned and the first floor painted. Upstairs, at the rear of the building, lay a large storage room. At the front of the second floor was a small apartment with windows that overlooked the bay. There was a glass door that led to the balcony and a panoramic view of the entire area.

The crew from the ships unloaded the cargo, then wagon by wagon hauled the items up the hill and brought them into the store.

Gage hired a sign painter who produced a huge board that was installed on the second-floor facade. It read: GD ENTERPRISES. ALL MANNER OF NECESSARY GOODS PROVIDED AT MOST REASONABLE PRICES. GENERAL MERCHANDISE OF HIGH QUALITY.

As he worked, and as deliveries were made, a small crowd of local citizens stood in a wide circle watching the activities. Gage made a point of introducing himself and telling everyone of his intentions.

Officially Gage opened his store on the second Monday after he arrived in California.

He cleared $2.17.

FROM THE JOURNAL OF GAGE DAVIS

I cannot believe it!

$2.17!!

While I did not expect a landslide of business the first day, I did expect more than $2.17.

That same evening, I sat on my balcony and watched the stars. Each pinpoint of light reflected by the black water made me feel lost

271

in the vastness of the heavens. How small I felt. How insignificant and unimportant.

As I contemplated my location in the celestial emptiness, I realized that the worst result of my decisions might be losing all my money. If that happened, my life would not end. I would be poor, but with breath and mobility in my body. I would still be young. I would still be smart–at least by Harvard standards. I would still have an unlimited future.

As I stood there and began to count my blessings, I heard Joshua's voice in my ear, telling me that is what a Christian must always do. Furthermore, Joshua insisted that God asked for more–and that it was more than I was able to offer.

I came to no conclusions that night, but I was resolved. I would endeavor–to the best of my abilities and skills–to make this effort a success.

I awoke the following dawn and looked to the west. At the horizon I saw the jagged profile of a clipper ship, tracking on course for Monterey Bay. It anchored, and by noon all passengers had been unloaded. Nearly a hundred souls passed through the doors of GD Enterprises that day.

And to my great surprise and relief, my two-day sales total stood at $518.45.

I had made the right decision after all.

At the end of that week, after allowing my two ships to remain at anchor for nearly three weeks, I instructed both captains to return to New Orleans. To turn around so quickly, they demanded concessions I was forced to grant. They sought an increase in their shares of the business, as well as increased shares for each crewman. And I had to give them letters of authorization to use my remaining funds from a New Orleans bank to purchase new materials. I immediately discovered I had bought short supplies of several categories of goods. I needed more sewing notions, staple foods, bolts of fabric, heavy canvas, farm implements, and a long list of other items.

If the winds were favorable, both captains said they could return within the span of five months.

If possible, I told them, they should seek out a third ship for our plucky little armada.

My ships and my future sailed out of sight a few days before Christmas, under a warm sun and a strong wind from the west.

I was set to celebrate this holiday for the first time in my life by myself. I had been in Monterey less than a month and while acquainted with many citizens, I felt no strong kinship to any.

But on the night before Christmas, I heard a tapping at my door. It was Dortha, the serving girl who provided me with my first meal in Monterey. "Come on, Mr. Davis. A group of us are gathering at the open space by the docks. It's Christmas Eve, you know."

She would not listen to any of my objections but nearly dragged me the half mile to a wide grassy area just north of the customs house. A small bonfire blazed. Although the temperature did not require the additional heat, the smell and sound and sight felt right for a Christmas gathering.

Perhaps sixty people gathered there—mostly menfolk. Besides Dortha, I had met only two other single women, and no more than twelve married ladies. A bottle was passed about, and I would have felt odd to refuse. It was a thick, warm rum punch, with spices and a hint of clove. I coughed as I took a polite drink and was slapped on the back by another fellow who laughed at my reddening face.

One fellow started singing, and the rest joined in. Even I, who possess no singing voice of note, participated.

It was clear that every one of us standing around that fire had left someplace to journey here to California. Every man and woman had left family, friends, and all that was comfortable to trek or sail halfway around the world to begin a new life.

As I recognized that fact, I began to feel a kinship with these lonely and alienated men and women. Our shared bond was being forged out of a need for being connected, of feeling part of a place. We were all celebrating, in our own way, the building of a home.

The evening ended with a warbly but heartfelt rendition of "Silent Night." Our voices lowered, almost as if in reverence to the feeling that I think we all shared—that we were home—such as it is. The words *All is calm, all is bright* have never been sung with as much passion and feeling as I heard that night. We, immigrants and travelers all, gathered about a crackling fire, within sound of the sea edging at rocks and sand, under the starlit skies of the territory of California, and celebrated finding a home in that song and in this season.

CHAPTER EIGHTEEN

Monterey, California
August 1848

Gage would claim later that he had never been so frustrated, anxious, and yet invigorated as he was that summer in Monterey. No longer could he lean on his previous incarnation—the life of a rich, handsome businessman, destined to take over the family concern. No one in Monterey knew of his history or of his family. That Arthur Davis would have been listed as one of America's most wealthy men meant nothing to anyone in this village on the warm Pacific waters. He had to compete with other traders and importers as simply one more fellow in business—and not the son of a financial titan.

Gage was certain some people did know of him—or his father—but were most adept at remaining unimpressed. Even when he emphasized his last name, most folks would only nod, with nary a tad of recognition or deference.

Yet no man's reputation proved to be of consequence in light of events that had already happened but were soon to be made public.

Late in the month of January of 1848, after Gage had been in California for less than three months, a most serendipitous discovery was made—one that would forever change the face of America.

By Sutter's Mill, not more than a four-day ride from Monterey, a worker building a second mill on that river crossed the current and stumbled on a tiny piece of glittering metal. That first piece of metal could have been hidden by a man's thumb—yet its presence would uproot and transplant thousands upon thousands of young men from all over the world.

That small glistening object turned out to be gold—nearly 100 percent pure. It lay there in the rushing, cold water, free for the taking, as if asking for man to bend down and pluck untold wealth from the very arms of the earth itself.

Word of the discovery spread through the territory, but not as fast as Gage would have thought. It was midspring before he heard the news. The story had been carried from San Francisco to Monterey by a sailor who stopped in Gage's store for canvas and happened to overhear a reporter in a tavern who had heard it from another reporter who had heard it from a man who had claimed to have been by the river the first day the yellow metal was found.

Gage knew that the links of this story were tenuous at best, but in business, a man who waits for all the facts to be gathered is often the man who is last in line.

Later that same month, Gage heard that the news of the discovery had found its way into the local newspaper—yet so few people believed what was written that the report was all but discounted.

It might have been fiction, Gage thought, but such tantalizing fiction would definitely elicit a response. Free gold would be too much of a lure to be ignored, even if it was overstated.

Gage knew that the time to move was now.

Men fought battles and died over less concrete news than this. Gage knew how men's hearts yearned toward riches and wealth. He knew because his own heart yearned toward the same goal. He felt it more closely now because, even at his young age, he had already lost an entire fortune.

In spite of his own longing, Gage reacted calmly to the news and spoke to very few about what he had heard. But he did act—and quickly sought out every ship captain who anchored in the calm bay. He told each of them he would buy whatever they could bring him—cloth, picks, shovels, flour, sugar, soda, coffee, dynamite—anything and everything.

If they all returned with their promised cargo, Gage would be brought down to the nubs in terms of available cash. He had carried with him enough gold and script for three years' worth of business. But his plan had suddenly required condensing. He immediately sent word to New Orleans to have his savings transferred to California as soon as possible.

In practical matters concerning his business, what Gage could find for sale, he bought.

Gage faced frustration every day over the paucity of materials and goods for his store. In New York, he could walk down the street and find ten or so stores making and selling hats and an equal number selling cigars or men's suits. But here in California, in the sleepy village of Monterey, most items could not be found at all—unless they were imported to the territory. Gage could travel for miles and not find multiple sources for anything other than fish.

By midsummer, in the quick span of six months, Gage heard San Francisco had nearly doubled in size. Ships were being abandoned in the harbor as crews took to the interior as soon as their anchors were cast into the water. Merchants did not have time to construct actual buildings of stone and wood, so instead they set up canvas tents to sell their wares to the new flood of immigrants.

As Gage examined his store and stockroom, he began to get nervous. He had sold perhaps 50 percent of his original shipment—and at a huge profit—earning nearly ten times his initial outlay. But after these goods were sold, the shelves in his store would be bare. The stock he hoped was in transit would not arrive until fall at the earliest.

Every morning he arose, made a strong cup of coffee, walked out onto his balcony, and scanned the bay and the horizon of the Pacific beyond. His eyes sought out the image of any sailing vessel that might have extra cargo. Most mornings, he was disappointed. All he would see were the waves glinting back the first gold hues of the sunrise.

Monterey had grown as well, though not as fast as San Francisco. Twenty-four new families had already settled on the hillside, and every day brought with it the sound of sawing and hammering as houses sprang up. Gage bought the land parcels on both sides of his rented building, along with several others that directly faced the harbor.

On this day Gage had brought his coffee and a New York paper, now nearly five months old, with him to the balcony. The paper had been carried by a sailor who had been delighted to receive a full dollar from Gage, who was happy to pay that price for some news from home. Gage also had a recent copy of the *California Star*. The headline claimed that old Zach Taylor, the Whig, was running for president. Gage truly did not care who won. As far away from Washington as he was, the news had but a trifling effect on his daily operations.

Scanning the bay, he saw no new ships. A small part of his heart winced in pain. It was a most familiar hurt.

As he neared finishing the front page, a voice cried up from the street. "You Gage Davis?"

Gage lowered the paper and peered over the railing. "I am. Who's asking?"

The fellow in the street wiped his mouth with the back of his hand and shouted back, "Carty Todd."

"Carty? What's the name short for?" Gage queried.

The fellow shrugged. "Nothing, I guess. Carty is what my ma called me, and I never thought to ask if there was any more to it."

"Well, then, Carty, what can I do for you?" Gage asked magnanimously. "You need supplies? I can open the store, though I generally wait till 9:00 A.M. or so."

Carty hung his head for a moment, then straightened back up. He squinted. "No . . . I ain't buying, exactly. I got sort of a business proposition for you."

Gage leaned forward to study the fellow more closely. It was certain that Carty Todd did not look the part of a businessman. But Gage knew better than most of the absolute serendipitous nature of good fortune, so he stood up and headed for the stairs.

As he let Carty in, Gage sniffed the air, trying not to be obvious. Carty required a bath, and it would help if he refrained from consumption of cheap liquor, Gage thought.

Aloud Gage asked, "Would you like some coffee?"

Carty nodded. "I'd be obliged. Been a while since I ate."

Gage brought out coffee and a plate of hard rolls and honey. He waited in silence, sipping his coffee, reading his paper, as Carty ate his way through the entire plate.

"Thank you kindly for the food," Carty offered at last. "I weren't expecting none of it, but like I said, it's been a while since I had three squares in a day."

"My pleasure," Gage replied. "Now, tell me about this business proposition of yours."

Carty wiped his mouth with the back of his hand again. "I ain't what you might call your typical businessman, Mr. Davis. Not at all."

"Then what are you?"

Carty stared at his hands before responding. "I was a sailor. Now I'm . . . I'm sort of an ex-drunk."

Gage tried not to appear surprised. It was what he assumed Carty to be, but he never imagined any man would admit to such a failing. Finally, he asked, "Then, what is it you're offering?"

"I think my drinking days are over," Carty said. "I hope and pray they are, in any case. Been two weeks since I tasted anything of the drink. I know I smell of it, but these clothes are the only ones I got. Haven't had a chance to wash 'em."

Gage nodded.

"Listen, Mr. Davis, here's what I need to say. I see you got this fine store here. Being a sailor before, I know how hard it is to get merchandise to this territory. You wait and wait, and sometimes it never gets here. Ships sink, or a captain gets a better offer in another port."

"You're right about the waiting," Gage affirmed. "Every day I look out to the horizon for three ships on their way here from New Orleans."

"Yes, sir. I know how that must be," Carty said. His voice grew soft. "I ain't got no special talents for you, Mr. Davis, but I do know ships. I worked on a lot of ships. I know the captains and the like."

"And that will help me how?" Gage said, puzzled.

"The big ships be going up to San Francisco first. They know that be the place most likely to sell what they got. Some stop here in Monterey, but not that many."

"That I know, too. We usually get what didn't sell in San Francisco."

Carty rubbed his hands on his legs. "Here's what I know. Most vessels on their way north stop at the missions in San Diego or San Pedro or even Santa Barbara. There ain't many people living round there. They sell a little and head north."

"Carty, that's interesting, but so far you haven't told me anything I don't know already."

Carty tried to smooth back his stringy, greasy hair. "Stopping a ship takes time. Captains hate to take time. Always in a big hurry to get to the next place. They waste a week down south and then get in a knot making it to San Francisco in a hurry. Now sailors like any stop 'cause it gives them a chance to go out and sample the local drink."

Carty stood and gazed south, as if lost in a bittersweet memory. "Mr. Davis, I can get down there—down to San Pedro and the rest—I know the way. I can tell every ship captain that ain't under contract to let them know that I got a customer in Monterey who's buying what they're selling. Rather than sailing right past here, I can get the pick of goods for you. Monterey gets first pick instead of last."

Gage sat further forward. All of a sudden Carty's idea made great sense. Although it was not a guaranteed supply, it would be so much better than he had now.

"But, Carty, why would they listen to you?"

Carty looked pained. "Some might not. Some of 'em may remember me being just another drunken sailor. But if some of 'em see that I ain't drinking anymore, I bet they would take the chance and stop. That gives you merchandise to sell."

Gage did not want to show how excited he was about the idea. Seasoned by hundreds of business meetings in New York, he knew that one never gained the advantage by letting on too much.

"Carty, why did you pick me?"

He shrugged. "Ain't no one else in town doing what you're doing. And I weren't sober much before this."

"Well, Carty, you're an honest man. I like that. And since you're being honest, I need to ask, what's in this for you?"

Carty's watery eyes focused on Gage. "I just want a fair wage, Mr. Davis. A dollar or two a week maybe. I don't know nothing else than sailing, but if I go back on a ship, I go back on the bottle. I know that for a fact. And if I go back on the bottle, I'm no better than a dead man." He sniffed loudly, then said, "I'm better than that . . . a good sight better."

Gage nodded. He knew he would be risking nothing to add Carty to his employ; but there was a huge profit to gain if his idea worked.

"Tell you what, Carty. Let's give this a try. But that couple of dollars a week . . . I don't know about that."

Carty shuffled about. "I guess . . . I guess I could take less, Mr. Davis. I don't want to go back on the bottle."

Gage replied immediately when he saw the pained confusion on Carty's face. "No, Carty, that's not what I mean. It was a bad joke. A couple of dollars isn't enough. From today on, you're working for me at ten dollars a week. And tell you what else. I have a suit downstairs that looks like it might fit you. You're taking that as part of the deal. And we're burning what you're wearing now. I'll not have any employee of mine offend people just by being upwind. And you take a bath. Maybe on a regular basis as well. You have all that?"

"Oh, yes, Mr. Davis. I'm sure I have it."

Carty extended his hand, and Gage shook it firmly. Gage thought he saw the sunlight glint off a tear, but Carty raised his hand and wiped his face once again.

<hr/>

Carty Todd proved to be of such importance to Gage's business that after only three months, he presented Carty with a bonus of a hundred dollars—with a promise not to spend it on liquor.

Carty sniffed loudly, took the money, and extended his hand. "You believed in me, Mr. Davis. No way in the world I could betray that trust. I ain't never going to drink again; you can be assured of that."

Carty had intercepted nearly a dozen ships in his first weeks traveling up and down the southern coast of the territory. Not every captain believed his story, but enough did. And not every ship would sell all its cargo at once—much to Gage's dismay. They had a route to follow and wanted to keep their customers happy from San Diego to the San Juan Islands up north.

But he now had an increased source of goods to sell.

And he began to sell everything. His customers had a huge appetite for what Gage was serving.

Gage knew, and all of Monterey realized, that they were not the key port to disembarking miners—San Francisco was. But if Monterey was not key, it was close. A ship might carry two hundred and fifty men, all bent for the gold fields. Some were marvelously equipped, even down to pack animals, tents, fine china, and linen. Others carried little more than a blanket, coffeepot, and what they wore on their backs.

As the men left their ships and began to hike inland, most of these men stopped at GD Enterprises. One could almost smell the air of desperation about them. Gold was waiting in the hills for them to find it and return home rich conquerors. They felt it was their destiny, but their dreams were often poorly equipped. They would open their purses and count out dollars in pennies and nickels. They would buy a sluicing pan, a pick, a week's worth of supplies, and return to the street, following the stream of men heading inland.

Gage watched their eyes as they shopped and paid for their

meager purchases. He noticed both a grim determination and something else—the hope that the American Dream finally included them. Although Gage had known wealth and privilege, it was obvious most of these men had not.

But now, through a simple fluke of nature, everyone could dine at the same table; everyone could share in the bounty of the land. The draw and the allure of gold were powerful indeed.

A farm boy from Ohio or Iowa or Pennsylvania, with no education and limited prospects, could look forward to not much more than living and dying on the same piece of property his father lived and died on. He faced lean years, and then leaner years—but seldom years of unfettered bounty. A farmer did not possess that sort of future. Too much rain, too little, a blight, a hailstorm—all conspired against him. But with gold washing about in the streams, that same farm boy could return a master of all he surveyed. He could return a new king, with gold pouring from his pockets. He could laugh at the vagaries of weather and fate. Heading to California, pick and shovel in hand, might be his only chance to break the iron tether that the land imposed on him.

Or he could return to Ohio poorer and broken—with nothing to show for his work.

Such is the risk of dreams, Gage thought.

And as Gage watched closely, his conscience was being tugged and tightened as these young men wandered about his store, touching more expensive items, their eyes saying, *Someday.*

Gage knew without knowing anything about mining and gold and prospecting that most of these men would fail.

But what great faith they had on their way to the American El Dorado.

December 1848

The sun sank below the Pacific in a glorious shower of purple and crimson, highlighting the hills about the bay with a velvet fire. At sundown, the winds stilled to a whisper. Then, as the light slipped away from the horizon and the night edged west, the winds shifted. Now they whispered back to the sea, the hills and canyons carrying scents of pine and mesquite campfires.

Gage and Carty sat quietly on the balcony over the store, watching nature's final lighting of the day. A blanket of stars slowly pricked into view and on this moonless night, soon dotted the heavens with uncountable flickerings.

For a breath the air was still. Then a chorus of crickets began, and from the bay the barks of the seals punctuated the night.

"Carty," Gage said, breaking his silence, "how long will you stay this time? You know you are always welcome to rest here for as long as you want."

"And I appreciate that, Mr. Davis. I do. But I find that if I stop working and stay in one place too long I start hearing the voice of the devil behind me. He don't talk as much when I'm busy and on the move. But when I sit for a spell, he'll start whispering such enticing things in my ear."

"Devil?"

"Devil, indeed, Mr. Davis."

"You believe in devils?"

"Well, I didn't use to. But now I found God, I sort of have to. The Bible says there is a devil—so I have to take God's word on it."

"You didn't believe in God before?"

Carty wiped his mouth with his sleeve. Even in the dark his nervousness was loud and bright. "I did, Mr. Davis. But then again, don't everyone believe in God?"

"I do."

"Well," Carty replied, hesitating a bit, "I thought I did. I mean, I sort of believed in God. But it wasn't till I stopped being a drunk that I . . . well . . . that I had to give up myself and let him be God. And it was God that got me to stop."

Gage tilted his head, not understanding.

"Mr. Davis, I ain't the one to be explaining this right. All I know is that when I was a drunk I knew there was a God, but I never allowed him to help. I listened to the voice calling me into the bottle. Now that I'm sober, I let God lead my life. But when I slow down too long, that's when I hear that voice and get tempted again."

A memory of a late-night discussion with Joshua Quittner caught Gage unaware and his heart tightened over the loss of contact with his friend.

"But I thought God fixes all that, Carty. Doesn't he make the cravings go away? That's what I've heard others say."

Carty shrugged. "I wish I was like those others, then. But I ain't. The cravings are always with me."

Gage laughed softly. "Carty, you're not making sense."

"Mr. Davis, I know. It's like when you leave a beautiful woman because you know she's all wrong for you. Then it's no use spending your days pining after her beauty when you know she's no good. No use making more heartache than you already have. All I'm saying is that if I stop working for a long time, I'm going to have to really battle with the devil over my wanting to drink. I don't want to do that. God is powerful, Mr. Davis, and he can do what he likes, but old Carty here, well, he ain't always so powerful. It's better for me if I just don't stop long enough for the devil to tempt me with drink. So I keep working, I keep on the move. Better for me the devil shows up a day after I'm gone. You understand what I'm trying to say?"

After a long silence, Gage nodded in the dark. "I think I do know what you mean, Carty. I think I do understand."

Monterey, California
December 31, 1848

Dear Edgar,

Happy New Year and greetings from the California territories. I'm not sure how much longer I will be able to write that—there is a large contingent of folks out here lobbying to the Federals to make the territory a state. If General Zachary Taylor lands in the White House, the Californios will get quiet, and we'll get to be a state. I think the chances are good.

Most businessmen would welcome statehood–it would provide a legal structure here. Right now things are chaotic at times with one territory governor saying just the opposite of what the former one said. And the territory certainly could use judges and policemen. Monterey is peaceful, but I have heard stories about the gold fields–where men have shot each other over a few yards of riverbank. No man should die over such things, but it occurs with frequency, I am told.

Business is booming. Each day it seems brings another ship heavy laden with men on their way to find gold and their fortune. We had a ship from China dock the other day. Some of the men wore their hair in a long pigtail down their back. Only a handful knew the barest amount of English. And despite the fact they are a small race, they carry loads that would make a normal man stumble and fall. Hundreds of pounds of gear and material are loaded on their shoulders, and with nary a complaint, they head off into the interior.

Every miner-to-be who lands in our little bay has to travel past GD Enterprises on his way to the inland rivers. My associate, Carty Todd, has ensured me a steady supply of merchandise, and that action has been key to my success. My inventory seldom lasts longer than a month, so great is the demand. The men buy everything. I hesitate to mention the profit I am making on each sale–it is so paltry compared to the profits my father used to make.

And mention of my father brings me back to the painful reality of things.

Thank you for your recent letter. I am glad that my father is in no pain. How sad, though, to realize that he is unaware of all but his basest needs. Perhaps it is a blessing in disguise. He cannot feel depressed over what he has lost if he cannot recognize the loss.

I am not surprised over Walton's performance as head of the company. As he forced me out, I realized that underneath his anger and treachery, there lay a ruthless businessman of the first order–no compassion, only interested in himself, viewing all competitors as mortal enemies.

I am only being partially truthful–it does hurt me to know that such a man is running a company that stood for quality and integrity–but there is nothing I can do to affect the situation.

You mentioned that a letter had come for me with a return address from the Boston Female Medical School. I had no idea that such an institution existed, so it must be newly opened. Please open it, as I am anxious to know if it is merely another solicitation for donated funds to Davis Enterprises or if it might be from Hannah Collins. If it is from her, you must send it on by special messenger.

I am in the process of scouting out new locations to set up retail operations. I would prefer to do my own manufacturing, but as of now, California is so lacking in skilled engineers and builders that I must be content with buying and reselling. I hesitate to enter into the market in San Francisco since it is already crowded, but since I have a more secure supply, I may be able to compete very handily. My three ships have returned from New Orleans with a great many items in high demand. We will unload, warehouse the materials, then I shall send them back again on the very long circuit.

Edgar, I am so glad I am able to write to you. You are a link to my past that I thought was gone forever. Did you ever think that I would fall so far from grace—and become a simple shopkeeper?

Well . . . perhaps not just a simple shopkeeper, but a rich one.

I send you all my regards. Please say hello to my mother for me.

You may ignore Walton as you see fit.

Perhaps one day I may be wealthy enough to send for you.

When I build my mansion in San Francisco, I will do so.

Yours truly,

G. Davis

The village of Monterey and its inhabitants entered the year of our Lord 1849 lost in a swirl of thick fog. Early on New Year's morning, Gage walked out to his balcony in the morning and felt as if he entered a dream. The whiteness about him was so complete that in the span of a few steps he turned and nearly lost sight of the door through which he had exited.

He put his coffee cup on the table and swung his arms about as if thinking he might cut a swathe through it. He smiled as he actually saw eddies and ebbs of the fog follow his movements.

"I have never seen such a complete whiteness," he said aloud, though he knew no one else was listening. "I used to awaken to a New England winter blanket of snow, and now there is this."

He sat at his table and listened. Birds must have remained on the ground as well, for he heard no sound, not even the bark of the seals, nor the splash of wave on rock.

He sipped his coffee, ate his rolls, and stared out into the bright nothing.

I do not think I will have any customers today, he thought. *And since so many will awake with a New Year's headache, I may not see anyone till this afternoon.*

Gage had been invited to two celebrations in the village set to mark the advent of the New Year–and had declined both. After writing to Edgar, a sense of deep melancholy surged over Gage much like the fog swept over the bay. Gage had written the truth of his business and the talk of statehood, but he did not write of the gnawing edge of pain in his heart.

He was making more money than he ever thought possible from a simple retail operation. Yet, on his way to becoming a success in the territory, on his way to building a second and perhaps third store, he felt loose and unconnected to life.

He stood up in the fog and slipped back inside. He returned a moment later, carrying his journal and a bright lantern.

FROM THE JOURNAL OF GAGE DAVIS
JANUARY 1, 1849

I have left one life–or been forced out of it. Life in New York seems like a dream to me now. All my years as a youth and young man I expected to be at my father's side, working in business with him. I never had another dream. I would be rich and powerful. And for a brief moment, I had the dream in total–then was willing to risk it all by being greedy and foolish.

Perhaps God determines who truly realizes their dream on the basis of their innate worthiness and righteousness. I suspect both were lacking in my heart.

But such is the fickle nature of dreams. Such is the fickle nature of a man's heart.

What I have lost, I have attempted to find again. I have begun my new life with great success. I suspect that California has always been my destiny.

I know no man can see the future—neither do I have that gift—but some things are most obvious. I have no doubt that I will soon be the wealthiest man in Monterey—but such a task is easy since the pool of competitors is so shallow. And if my experience counts for anything, I believe I will be able to duplicate that success in San Francisco. If I add two new stores, or three, or four, then I will be that many times as successful.

It is a most simple calculation.

But . . .

Carty's confusing words about women and drink a few weeks ago have brought me a great deal of unexpected pain. While Carty made no sense at all, the fact that he spoke of women and love and heartache brought all the memories of Nora back into my thoughts again.

I had believed I had forgotten all that pain; it is clear that I have not.

I still see her face smiling, her eyes dancing with joy, her hair framing her perfect features—even as I write this. How can that be—after the evil she did to me? Why do I still find my thoughts turning to her?

And even if I do think of her, I know there is no possible way I shall ever see her again. I am sure she returned to her family in Portland.

And, as anyone can see, Portland and Monterey are as far apart as America can make things.

No, I do not expect to ever see her again.

And as much as I want all this activity and money and probable power, it simply seems as gossamer, and just does not satisfy.

How I hoped that it would.

I have found my gift, and that gift is to take disadvantage and make money in spite of it. I have the gift of business, just as my father told me years ago. It is in my blood.

And now that I am using that gift and making money, I am finding it leaves my soul empty and cold.

And that knowledge brings me no joy—only wild despair.

For if this is my future, where will I find contentment?

And worse yet, where will I find love?

And in this mood, I enter the New Year.

Monterey, California
February 1849

The last customer left the store just as Gage's new clock struck the sixth chime. It had been a very busy day for both Gage and the two young men he had hired to assist him in the details of running a store.

He was about to lock the front door for the night when a man in a bright green coat placed his hand on the latch.

"We're closing, friend. Something you need in a hurry?"

The gentleman stared hard at Gage, then smiled. "You're Gage Davis, aren't you?"

"I am. And do I know you?"

The stranger stepped back, extending his arms to allow Gage a better look.

Gage shook his head. "I'm afraid I don't recall. . . ."

The stranger in the bright green coat then laughed, bent to his knee, assuming a most dramatic pose, and in a loud voice called out, " 'But, soft! What light through yonder window breaks? It is the east and Juliet is the sun!' "

Gage's two assistants had gathered behind him, peering at the stranger who called out the dramatic words.

When he had finished, Gage laughed and applauded. "Charles Thornton! I didn't recognize you without your costume. How are you? And what brings you from Harvard to here? I thought you were on your way to a career upon the New York stage?"

Charles stood up, dusted off his knees, then shook Gage's hand. "I was on my way indeed, old friend, until there was this most unfortunate incident with a most delectable woman, who just happened to be the wife of the theater owner. I thought California was a better place to open than in prison. And I am in Monterey due to the capricious nature of the sailing vessel and a most ill-tempered captain who demanded payment in advance for any further travel."

Gage blinked. "Prison? Truly? You were threatened with prison in New York?"

"Well, no . . . but I could not even get a small part after what transpired. So I have come west, with several trunks full of plays, costumes, scenery, and a half-dozen actors I encountered along the way who were not quite polished enough to be welcomed in New York. I thought the pool might be shallower out here."

"You would be most accurate in that estimate," Gage said, chuckling.

Charles stood back and brought his hand to his chin in a dramatic, contemplative pose. "And, pray tell, why is Harvard's young industrial titan in a most out-of-the-way village like this? Picturesque and peaceful no doubt, but a world away from New York. I must inquire as to the means and machinations that brought you here as well, old friend."

Gage smiled. "I think we both were threatened with the same possible punishment. But for much different crimes, I will hasten to add."

Charles appeared most surprised. "Is that the truth? Well, I must have missed that delectable bit of gossip before I so quickly departed from Gotham."

"Well, Charles, let me invite an old Harvard chum to dinner, and I will tell you all about it—as long as you tell me of your story as well."

Charles bowed to the waist with a flourish. "Ah, the gentleman doth drive a most penurious bargain. But since perchance I have this evening without encumbrance, I shall deign to dine with thee. And for such a fee, I will entertain thee with much news, and yea, much gossip from Gotham, that will fill your mind with wonder."

Gage laughed at his theatrics, clasped him about the shoulder, and led the way upstairs. "And where is the rest of your entourage?"

Charles turned and pointed to the harbor. "Do you see that ship? They are there—more or less hostages of the captain—and he has vowed not to release them until a certain matter of fares is dispatched."

Gage laughed again. "How much arranging do you require?"

"Well, it is not much," Charles said contritely. "No more than fifty dollars."

Gage reached into his wallet, extracted several bills, and handed them to one of his assistants. "Bail them out and bring them back here, if you would."

The assistant frowned at Gage for a moment, as if he had taken leave of his senses, but then headed down the lane to the bay.

Later that evening, after a hearty meal and much conversation and laughter, Gage bid his new friends good-night. They took to sleeping amidst the counters and tables on the first floor, since Gage's Monterey home had no provisions yet for overnight guests.

As Gage went to bed he wondered how it was exactly that he had become the majority owner of The Thornton Players, the first theater and vaudeville company to be formed in the grand territory of California.

FROM THE JOURNAL OF GAGE DAVIS
NOVEMBER 1849

General Riley, our old territorial governor, is not a patient man. He called for a convention in Monterey back in September, and the next thing we know the delegates created a state government—without waiting for congressional action. In October they adopted a constitution, and today we all got to vote for it. That's a fast turn of events by anybody's standards. We picked a governor and state fellows and voted against slavery. Feels good to be part of the state of the union. That's one of the things I really like about California—people here aren't afraid to take matters into their own hands when they decide something should be done a certain way.

And we move fast.

CHAPTER NINETEEN

Monterey, California
April 1850

A sunburned Carty Todd stepped out onto the balcony carrying a coffeepot and a two-month-old copy of the *New York Post*.

Gage looked up in pleasant surprise. "Carty! I didn't think you would be back so soon."

"I didn't either. I planned to ride my horse back the whole way from San Diego to Monterey, but that little sloop—the one anchored in the bay—had room for us both."

"An empty ship in these waters?" Gage asked, surprised. "Isn't that a rarity these days?"

"Mr. Davis, he's a new captain. He sold everything in San Diego. Then he thought he would head up the coast to seek out new customers. I told him I would introduce him to the only man he would need to know—if he gave me and my horse a ride."

"You drive a hard bargain, Carty—especially since you knew that he really doesn't have to meet me," Gage said, grinning. "The only person he truly needs to meet is you."

"Well, he doesn't know that, does he?"

"Where's the fellow at?"

"He's still at the dock tying up. He'll be up shortly."

Gage poured a fresh coffee for himself, then one for Carty. In the months they had been together, Carty had gained twenty pounds. His skin was no longer blotchy, and he looked healthy and fit.

"I've interrupted you, haven't I?" asked Carty, apologetically.

"No, not really. I am just finishing a letter to an old . . . an old friend in New York."

"Then finish it, Mr. Davis. I'll sit here, drink my coffee, and be real quiet. Maybe I'll read your newspaper if you don't mind. I know how it is to have somebody else rumple the paper beforehand. I'll be careful."

Gage smiled. He was most particular as to who read his paper first.

"Go ahead, Carty. For you, I shall make an exception."

Gage dipped the pen in its well, added a few lines, then signed it with a flourish. He blew on the ink to dry it, then shuffled the papers back in a neat pile and read what he had written.

Monterey, the Territory of California
April 1850

My dear Edgar,

I must ask you to forgive my tardiness in responding to your letter. While I admit that busyness is never an excuse, I have been so very, very preoccupied these past several months. When I have a moment to spare, I find myself simply stretched out on my balcony, staring out across the blue and green expanse of Monterey Bay.

This peaceful setting is betrayed by the general confusion and bedlam that is California today. Miners and immigrants are everywhere. People arrive daily—all in search of their fortune. Only two years ago, I am told, less than a thousand people lived in San Francisco. Today, if I am to believe the most recent newspaper, more than a hundred thousand people call that town home. A third of them arrived by sea and nearly half made the arduous trek overland, according to the report. Someone also counted at least three thousand sailors, now living within the city limits, who had earlier deserted their ships.

Such explosive growth has never been seen in all of history, I am sure.

When I wrote last, there was but a single store operating under the banner of GD Enterprises. Now there are four: Monterey, San Francisco, Sacramento, and one on the American River near Sutter's Mill. The operation in San Francisco is huge—nearly a full city block. Some of the structure is wood frame, but due to a dearth of carpenters and milled wood, the rest of the building is constructed with stones, canvas, and rope.

I have chosen the peaceful village of Monterey as my headquarters and avoided many headaches and congestion.

I am sure you heard that President Taylor confirmed the discovery of gold when he addressed Congress last year. Newspapers here made much of his quote—and it even has appeared in the most recent issue. "The accounts of the abundance of gold are such an extraordinary character as would scarcely command belief were they not corroborated by authentic reports of officers in the public service."

His words set off a wave of reaction . . . no, an actual flood—at least in California. I spoke of sailors deserting their ships, but not only ships suffer from the problem of desertion. Even the California Star *has shut down for a time as all its reporters and pressmen took off for the gold hills. A second operation, called the* Daily Alta California, *is now publishing—using a steam-powered press, of all things.*

The only manner to survive these times is to offer wages that, on the surface, seem simply ludicrous. I am paying three and four times the average wage for a clerk, as well as crews for my ships. I have been lucky—not all men believe the promise of gold. I look to hire cynics and realists. They know that the first man to the river may get rich, and the second and third perhaps—but not the man who is the one-hundredth in line.

I am not saying any of this too loudly, of course, for my business is now predicated on the suspension of all rational thought.

Speaking of suspending all rational thought—over the past few weeks a group of would-be politicians met in Monterey. I opened up my home to some of them. They squabbled and argued so many things, but did agree to a state motto—Eureka—meaning, "I have found it."

Appropriate, with the gold and all that, don't you think?

I have rambled on. I suspect my chaotic writing is due in part to my chaotic schedule. I meet customers, I argue with customs officials, I bribe captains and promise crews larger and larger bonuses to remain on board, I scout out land, I oversee construction, I am part of a group setting up a bank—one could never achieve this level of experience back in the crowded streets of New York.

I have heard talk of a group headed by a Mr. Degrand that seeks to secure funding and legislation required to bring a rail line to San Francisco. A few business folk here claim he is honest, but I remain unconvinced. Edgar, could you do me a favor and make a few discreet inquiries as to his background and intentions?

I am building my house on the hill. Edgar, I may have need of you yet. I purchased for a pittance a most pristine section of high ground, perhaps a half mile from the harbor. No one had tended to the land in years, so it had been wild and overgrown—with even several feral pigs in the underbrush. I scoured the countryside for carpenters and located a smallish crew. They began excavating at Christmastime last year and have now succeeded in erecting most of the walls for the first floor.

It will be unlike anything you have seen, Edgar. The carpenters, I should add, are Spanish-speaking people—Californios—and are building a structure that would look appropriate in Mexico City. The builders use a material they call adobe, which is a sort of stuccolike cement lathered over stone. The house will have thick walls and log beams for posts and pillars. I have been in such dwellings and find them cool in the summer and warm in the winter.

It will be a grand home—far larger than any dwelling in Monterey and perhaps in San Francisco as well. It will be so unlike our home in New York—no dark wood, no heavy fabrics, no fancy carvings. It will have wide windows and open porches that overlook the sea.

Again, thank you for your letter. If you ever notice that my father returns to lucidity—even if for a brief moment—would you tell him that I think of him all the day—and that without his teaching and example I would never have become the success that I am today. It is my greatest regret that I did not tell him such things more often when I could. Our lives are so brief—and our time with our loved ones so fleeting. Perhaps the greatest thing I have learned since Harvard is that I must take each day as a gift and treat it as if I will never see such wonders again.

Walton appears to be doing very well—at least according to what I read in the Post. I saw Mother's name mentioned as well. I assume that the pair of them are evenly matched—and I trust you will not mention my bitterness to either of them.

Thank you for forwarding the letter from the Boston Female Medical School. The letter indeed was from Hannah Collins. She is enrolled there and will be a licensed physician in short order, thanks to her Harvard training, which from the very beginning puts her at the top of the first graduating class of the institution.

I will close now. Carty Todd, my associate, has appeared unexpectedly. I assume he has pressing business to attend to.

Always regards,

G. D.

<hr />

November 1850

Gage often smiled when he thought of Carty Todd. He proved over and over to Gage the importance of basing some decisions on visceral, internal impulses, rather than rational, logical facts and figures. Had any sensible businessman seen Carty's condition or his past, no offer of employment would ever have been extended. Still, Gage knew that he had been right to follow his instincts in hiring Carty.

Much of Gage's success, at least early on, was due to Carty's skill at getting ships to stop in Monterey. Ships soon clamored to find GD Enterprises. Gage paid well and promptly and was honest to a fault—a rarity in the rough-and-tumble business of the frontier.

Another serendipity was the arrival of Charles Thornton in Monterey.

Gage had no reason to seek out participation in the theatrical arts. No logical business plan could have been drafted that included funding an untried vaudeville troupe. Charles and his group of actors amused Gage greatly. And Gage knew of the popularity of such shows all across the country. If such minor entertainment was seen as enjoyable, Gage realized that the rest of the new arrivals in the territory would be just as desperate for pleasant diversions as he was.

Gage sent the troupe first to San Francisco. It was a more populous town. Once the troupe arrived in San Francisco, the city embraced them. Their first theater was an open lot, with borrowed benches and chairs. The troupe acted out scenes from Shakespeare with great gusto and charm, even if they lacked a certain professional polish.

Audiences were starved for diversion. No matter that only portions of plays were performed; no matter that their lead singer, Marla Barrie, a very plain girl with slightly crossed eyes from Rhode Island, could scarce hold a tune; no matter that their juggler had trouble with even three objects at a time; no matter that their jokes and patter were older than the union—the crowds simply loved them.

In a matter of three or so months, they found more permanent quarters in a large tent, lit with gas lamps. A few months later, they moved into a real building. They added a stage and footlights and tore off a rear wall to expand and make room for scenery and props.

Charles Thornton had a definite flair for the dramatic. He sent his actors, in full costume, out to the docks to meet ships as they arrived, passing out handbills, improvising scenes, promising audiences a thrill beyond expectations.

And for this, patrons would pay one dollar for a two-hour show. Charles told Gage that men would sit through four shows in a row, lost in a dreamy state, laughing at ancient and tired routines, in tears as Marla sang sweet songs from their youth, shouting in excitement as actors would duel upon the stage, acting out scenes from *Hamlet* or *Julius Caesar*.

Almost every seat was sold for nearly every performance. Three hundred seats times up to six shows a day times six days a week times a dollar a ticket equaled a profit of over half a million dollars each year.

Even with wages and rent and taxes, and a percentage to Charles Thornton, Gage's profit from the operation was astounding.

Gage had never yet seen a show, so infrequently did he leave

Monterey. Charles harangued and cajoled him, sending letters and notes, threatening to drop him as a partner if Gage refused to attend at least one performance.

Finally Gage relented. He left his best assistant, Thomas Lee, in charge. He rented a horse and followed the well-marked trail along the ocean. Gage was amazed at the number of settlements along the shore. It was his first time away from business since arriving in California. He was surprised at how much he enjoyed the solitude and the sound of nothing but the sea. There were no customers, no clerks, no problems, no frustrations.

On the last day of his trip, in a small inn with only four rooms overlooking a rocky promontory, Gage took out his tattered journal. He scooted a chair close to the window. Placing the lantern on the table behind him, he turned up the wick. Then he stretched out, propping his feet against the open windowsill. He closed his eyes and breathed in deeply. His senses swarmed with the smell of pine from the inn's freshly cut logs, the crackling sound of fish being cooked over an open flame, and the sharp taste of salt in the air as the breeze shifted.

He also identified the faint odor of mildew from his journal, now so seldom opened. Opening his eyes, he turned the pages slowly, reliving each moment. It was the same journal he had carried that first day to Harvard. Gently he touched the self-portrait he drew on that first train ride into Boston. He knew his face had become more drawn and lined. He knew there was now a frosting of gray at his temples.

Such a thing only happens to old men, he reflected, laughing to himself.

His thoughts went back to the golden hours spent with his three friends around the tables of the Destiny Café in Cambridge. The faces of his three dear friends floated before him, the sounds of their young voices echoing in the silence of his room as he gazed out the window, then down at the pages before him.

His smile was bittersweet as he read of his youthful ambitions and his views on wealth and the world.

301

So a boy grows into a man.

Gage took out a pencil from his pocket and began to write.

FROM THE JOURNAL OF GAGE DAVIS
NOVEMBER 1850

I have come so far.

I am now a wealthy man again. I have taken stock of my accounts recently, and if I liquidated all my holdings, even accounting for a greatly inflated market, I would have enough to retire today and live nearly an expansive, if not truly indolent life. California can be a land of quick success if one is willing to risk everything.

I will not retire, of course. I learned at my father's side that to be lazy is to be worthless.

Business has grown beyond my wildest expectations. I have found that my training at Harvard has served me well. I recall from business classes that in all times of expansion, there will follow a most natural contraction. This gold fever will eventually subside. The first gold is easy to find, but it will not be so easy tomorrow—or the next day, or the day after that. Prospecting is like an Easter egg hunt—the first eggs are found quickly. Then it is only the dedicated child who finds the stubborn eggs still hidden.

With that always in mind, I have not invested too heavily in inventory or buildings. Yet not all these men who have come to California will return home. It is as easy (or hard) to farm here as it is in Iowa or Ohio.

Some of these young men on their way to the gold fields will get rich and return home as conquering heroes. Some will die here. Some will fail and stay—unwilling to face disapproving fathers or gossiping townsfolk.

The ones who remain will be my customers. Even if business contracts, I will have taken advantage of the expansion.

I must close for this evening. Our host just shouted up the stairs that dinner is done. There are no waiters in tuxedos here, ringing elegant silver bells.

I admit no desire to return to that world. The sea air and the ride along the beautiful forests are more than sufficient to offset what I have left behind.

I look forward to San Francisco and Charles Thornton in the morning.

⚜

Thornton's Vaudeville and Legitimate Theatrical Emporium,
San Francisco
November 1850

"Ah . . . Gage, my dear friend, my benefactor, my muse, how glorious the moment doth thou make the day by your appearance."

Gage pumped Charles Thornton's hand. The two men had met outside the "Theatrical Emporium." On one side of the small entrance was a canvas poster, painted in a most lurid style. A beautiful young woman in a very revealing tunic reclined on a marble bed. Her hand was at her bosom, clutching a delicate vial. Her eyes were closed. Underneath the painting were the words: JULIET'S TRAGIC DEATH SCENE FROM WM. SHAKESPEARE. As Gage eyed the poster, he knew it would be a good draw for every man who passed by.

"Charles, do you always talk like a character from Shakespeare? Doesn't it make you weary by the end of the day?"

"Forsooth, it does not, my prosperous confrere. One finds it such a natural descent that the slide is seldom noticed." Charles spun around the lobby of the theater as he spoke, his arms raised as if he were saluting an audience. "But I do so wish to please that I will endeavor to reclaim the speech of my youth. . . ."

He bowed deeply, then stood up. "And I realize how aggravating my speech might become to a man not involved in the theater day after day. I think we thespians play with words like some men might whittle at a piece of wood. It passes the time and it amuses us."

Charles wore an elegant, frilled coat with burgundy trim and bits of lace at the collar and sleeves.

"Yes, I know, Gage," Charles said before Gage had a chance to comment, "this suit is a tad pretentious. But when one is in the public eye, the public expects a certain level of eccentricity. I am simply obliging my public."

Gage laughed. "Your public, Charles? You have a public? Does that mean I have to put on a costume to have dinner with you?"

Charles stood back, held his hand to his chin, then narrowed his eyes. "Well, Gage, I think not. Perchance my public will think you are simply dressed so plainly for a role in an upcoming farce."

Gage laughed again. "You know, Charles, I may have to reconsider my participation in this venture. A farce indeed. I would think I would be well suited for a romantic lead, perhaps a tragic young man in one of Shakespeare's plays."

Charles wrapped his arm about Gage's shoulder. "If playing such a role would continue your support, then by all means, Gage, I think you should. But . . ."

"But what?"

"I think the time is past for either of us to assume the young romantic lead."

"You think I am too old? Charles! I am not yet thirty."

"But just barely, I am sure, Gage. The plum roles go to men much younger than either you or I."

"Well, then, you must commiserate with me over dinner. And since dinner is on me tonight, select the city's finest."

Less than twenty minutes later, they were both seated in a quiet booth at McGuires', a new, very expensive restaurant specializing in thick steaks.

"You should leave that backwater town of Monterey and move up here, Gage," Charles said as he stabbed a large piece of meat. He missed and stabbed again, then gestured in the air with his fork. "I am serious. Monterey will never be the town that San Francisco is. There is too much going on here. I hear that another theater and a third casino are being built just east of the fisherman's wharves. When that happens, the entire area will explode. You should be here."

Gage listened politely, nodding where appropriate.

"But, Charles, I like Monterey. It may be more quiet–but I like it that way."

"Nonsense. A man of your ilk and reputation—you need to be here. This is the New York of California."

"Well . . . I'll consider it."

Both men ate in silence for a moment.

"So tell me, Charles, what else is happening here? I read the newspapers, but nothing compares to an actual observer."

Charles took a last bite of steak, chewed thoughtfully, then swallowed and rubbed his chin. "Let me see . . . you know that the theater is almost filled at every performance. People thirst for good entertainment. And we provide that deep well of cool water. But what else? Let's see. Well, the city bought two fire engines, and the firemen drove them up and down the streets with dogs and horses and a great deal of hoopla. And we passed that new two-story building on the hill. They installed some sort of device . . . the telegraph I think it's called."

"Truly? A telegraph? Out here?" Gage asked.

"So they say," Charles replied. "But I am not in favor of such inventions. I am not a Luddite, mind you, but such devices have no soul. Mark my words. People will rue the day such contraptions have come about. Men's souls will suffer."

Gage nodded, though he did not agree with Charles.

"Then there is this group of minstrels from Philadelphia that opened a show on Washington Street."

"Are they competition for you? Did they affect our business?"

Charles shook his head no. "We do more serious theater than they." His words were frosty.

Surprised, Gage said, "But you have a juggler and singer and only do snippets of Shakespeare."

"Gage . . . sweet treachery . . . you wound me. It may be true that we do but 'snippets,' but those pathetic minstrels . . . well, it is only song and dance with them. Not serious thespians, I hasten to add. They are not like us." Charles glared with mock anger, then laughed. "My charade is uncovered—yet we are all serious thespians compared to Rowe's Olympic Circus and Ethiopian Singers that opened on Kearney Street. That group has an elephant." Charles leaned in close. "And you know what is even more shocking than an elephant in a theater?"

Gage shrugged.

"They are charging three dollars for a single ticket."

"Three dollars! Then we are giving our performances away," Gage replied.

"They do have an elephant. Perhaps you might purchase us one of those. Then we could raise our ticket prices."

"No, I think we can do without an elephant for now," Gage said, smiling.

Charles laughed as well. "I agree that an elephant is a bit over the top, but we do need to stay current."

"I read recently of a man named P. T. Barnum," said Gage. "A master promoter and showman. He imported some Swedish soprano singer, and she now commands hundreds of dollars a show. I read that in New York, thirty thousand people clamored about her hotel, hoping to get a glimpse of this 'Swedish Nightingale.' Barnum is making a fortune off of her."

Charles smiled slyly.

"What are you smiling at?" asked Gage.

"This Barnum story confirms my belief that there is much more profit to be made in the entertainment business."

"I'll think of something to invest your profits in. After all, we do need to attract the attention of all the new arrivals. Someone counted the ships landing here and quit at a thousand. And fully a third were from foreign lands."

"Truly? A third?"

"That is what I hear. And a great many of them are from China."

"And they are staying in the city, or do they just move inland?"

"Some stay here. They already have their own neighborhood and restaurants. I saw a whole boatload take the steamer up to Sacramento City, though—headed to the gold fields, I imagine."

Gage signaled for coffee, and the waiter brought a silver service complete with cream and white sugar. A fan of delicate cookies dipped in chocolate was brought to the table on a gold tray.

"I am at home in such luxury," Charles said as he sipped the coffee and nibbled on the cookies. He still had the sly smile on his face. "I believe I was destined to be a rich man."

Gage looked at him without replying. He knew Charles had no idea of what pain being rich could entail. He stared out the window to the harbor below and thought of all that he once had and all he had lost because of greed and jealousy.

Gage snapped out of his reverie when Charles spoke up. "You should build a hotel here, Gage."

"A hotel? Why?"

"There aren't any proper hotels here. There are a dozen seedy hotels where even I would not sleep a single night. Then there are a few that charge exorbitant rates for simply a decent room. And a decent room means that the bugs are kept to a minimum and there are no fisticuffs—at least during the week. Yet this town simply has no good hotel."

Puzzled, Gage asked, "What brings that subject up?"

"What subject?"

"Hotels. I'm curious—why bring up a hotel now? Doesn't your troupe sleep in rooms above the theater?"

"Most of them. It saves a great deal of money—both for them and me. I pay them less, and they spend less. But recently—ah—I had to actually rent an apartment in town for one of my new performers. It was the only decent thing to do, and I would not have her stay in a filthy hotel with characters of dubious reputation."

"Her? A new performer? In a rented apartment? That seems most extravagant."

"Oh, not for this talent. She is special. And she'll pay off. With her on the bill, we can legitimately start charging three or four dollars a ticket. Not as much as for the 'Swedish Nightingale,' but more in line with those presumptuous circus people."

"And who is this person I am paying for a private apartment for?"

Charles leaned close. "I have heard she was once the talk of New York. But then there was this scandal, and she ran afoul of the law.

So she had to head west to escape. It was a most delicious oppro-brium—and it will be great for ticket sales, I assure you."

"And who is she?" Gage asked, impatient.

"A beauty, I tell you. A real beauty. Even some of my lads in the theater who don't bother being bothered were bothered by this one. She is that much a looker."

"Then she must be special. Now tell me—what's her name?"

Charles took a wrinkled handbill from his jacket, smoothed it out, then spun it around to face Gage.

Gage's heart nearly stopped.

"Her name is Nora Wilkes."

And from the wrinkled handbill, a perfect image of Nora's beauti-ful face stared back at him.

And the world around him fell silent and dark.

"Gage! Are you all right? Gage!"

Gage blinked his eyes and tried to focus.

"Yes . . . I'm fine." His words were halting and soft.

"You dropped your coffee cup and then stared off into space. I thought you were having a spell or something. Are you sure you're fine?" Charles's face had gone white.

"Yes," Gage said, his senses returning. "It's just that I think I may have . . . I mean, I may have heard this woman. . . . I mean, I think she was at a party I was at . . . you know . . . back in New York."

Charles squinted at Gage.

"A party?"

"I think I heard her play. She was quite striking, as I recall."

"If you saw her before, you would remember," Charles said. "Obvi-ously, it was a different woman."

Gage took a deep breath. "Well, perhaps you're right. Perhaps I was mistaken."

He shook his head to clear a flood of images from his thoughts and signaled to the waiter for their check.

"And when does she begin at the theater?" Gage asked, attempting to keep his words calm. A band of sweat formed at his brow, and he tried to wipe it off without drawing attention to it.

"She will play twice tonight," Charles replied. "At the eight and ten o'clock performances."

Gage took out a bill and placed it on the waiter's tray. "Well, then. Perhaps I will . . . take in tonight's performance."

The men stood. "Shall I reserve a seat in front for you, Gage?"

"No. . . no. I will watch from the back," he replied almost too quickly. "I mean, I would not want to displace a paying customer, after all."

❖ ～≈✦⋙⋘✦≈～ ❖

Nora Wilkes sat alone at a solid black grand piano. She wore an elegant black gown with white lace that gathered like a flower at her throat and then flowed down over her shoulders. As she walked out onto the stage, Gage could feel the entire audience, virtually all male, gasp.

At first she did not speak, just simply looked out across the audience as if she were seeking eye contact with every man in the building. After a heartbreaking silence, she sighed and returned to face the keys of the piano.

Gage had actually turned his face as he felt her eyes pry into the back of the room. He stood, half behind a pillar, and then hid behind it as her gaze swept past his location. His heart pounded fast and loud in his chest.

She began to play a piece by Beethoven, slow and elegant. Each note built a hint of sadness on the next until, at the end, men were actually in tears from the depth and force of her playing.

She waited, head bowed, until, like an exploding volcano, the audience erupted in a roar of applause and cheers.

But Nora did not acknowledge them. She only sat, hands folded in her lap, eyes averted. When at last the applause diminished, she pushed the piano bench back and stood. Then, facing the audience, she walked slowly forward, as if she would step right off the stage, so purposeful were her strides. At the last instant she stopped, almost teetering at the edge.

Her hands fluttered to her side. She waited for silence, obviously expecting it. She closed her eyes and began to sing, simply, without accompaniment. It was an Irish song Gage had once heard in a tavern on the docks of New York. The song told the story, from a woman's point of view, of her lover, who had gone to America seeking his fortune. A decade had passed, and she had no word of his life in America. Then finally a small envelope came addressed to her. The envelope was too thin to contain money or a ticket—just a single sheet of paper.

The final refrain told of how the woman, now old, continued to hold that envelope and never opened it.

It was a moving song in New York, but in California, in a hall of displaced and homesick men, the story took on vastly more powerful meaning. At the end of the song, Nora's last words floated over a stunned and silent audience. Gage heard a collective sob, then, at last, a cacophony of applause and calls, as if a great release had been triggered. Men stood on their chairs and screamed Nora's name, crying and applauding at the same time.

Nora stood in the light, not smiling, simply staring out into the darkness, and as the applause and cheers reached a crescendo, she turned and, like a wisp, disappeared into the darkness.

The crowd broke into a near frenzy of applause and cheers.

One piano piece. One song.

And after five minutes had passed, the crowd was spent, slumped in their seats.

Gage waited in the shadows until the last performance. He sent a lad back to Charles with a note. Charles found Gage in the near darkness of the lobby.

"Charles," he said softly, "how much do you pay Miss Wilkes?"

"Uh . . . I am not sure. I can find out, if you would like."

"It is no matter," Gage said quickly. "But whatever the figure is, you shall pay her five times that amount."

"Five times? But that would be almost more than I am . . ."

"It is not your concern. This will come from my share."

"Well, you do own the majority of . . ."

"And one more thing."

"Yes, Gage."

"Miss Wilkes must never know that I am associated with this theater. Or that I saw this performance. Or that I was responsible for this raise."

Charles glanced around, as if checking to see if Gage were being held hostage as to explain these odd demands. "But, Gage . . ."

"I am serious about this, Charles. If you tell her of me, you will have to leave this town more rapidly than you did New York. Do you understand?"

Gage had never once spoken like this in California. His words were cold, final, and as hard as New England granite.

Charles swallowed, then nodded. "I understand."

Chapter Twenty

Monterey, California
August 1851

After seeing Nora that evening, Gage fled home to Monterey. It had taken him four days to leisurely cover the distance north after only a day and a half heading south. It was as if he had been pursued. His heart raced the entire journey, and his breath caught in his throat at every step.

Once back home along the gentle arc of the bay, Gage began to relax, although there was now a tension in his chest that had not existed until that day. He threw himself again into his work and spent little time alone. He tried not to allow the image of Nora to haunt him—although it did.

And he told no one of the incident. He allowed himself only a moment or two each day to dwell upon that night. The memory both hurt and tantalized him.

How in all the world could she have found her way to be in his employ? How could the fates destine her to be no more than a hundred miles from where he now called home?

He had no answers. As he rode home, he thought again of

Joshua's words—that all things are part of God's intricate plan—and that if we give ourselves to God, then those plans become clearer.

If he had been able to, Gage would have gone to God with his questions. But he did not. He told himself that he had ignored God for too long for God to reveal his plans now.

In business, matters were much clearer, much more understandable. And that is where Gage spent his heart.

Success begat success, and GD Enterprises continued to grow larger and more profitable than Gage had imagined even a year prior. He added stores in several mining towns—Angels Camp, Placerville, Diamond Spring, and others. Gage's process of adding a new location in the gold fields was disarmingly simple. All it took were two large wagons, two teams of sturdy horses, and three men. One wagon held a huge tent, complete with poles, stacks, signs, a stove, and a floor that fit into place like a puzzle. The other wagon held the store's first month's worth of provisions and stock, right down to the paper and string. The three men could erect the tent in a day and by the second day, be open and ready for business. In a week, one man would return to the city with the larger wagon, take on fresh supplies, then return to the store. By the time he returned, the next fellow would be ready to make the journey back to the city for another load of supplies.

To Gage, it was easy to ascertain the optimum assortment of materials and products. Gage sat in the store at Monterey and watched customers. Men would quickly buy what they had to have—picks, shovels, pans, flour, lard, cornmeal. Then they would return to the store and gently handle the merchandise that they wished they could afford—cots, stoves, thick blankets, telescopes, heavy boots, rifles. From his observations and his customers' behavior, Gage concluded that each wagon would be loaded with 75 percent of the essential items and 25 percent of the expensive, luxury items.

If a miner hit a heavy vein of gold, then the luxury items soon became his necessities.

Gage used his rapidly accumulating wealth to purchase land, ranches, cattle, partial ownership in a steamship venture, a newspaper, a cannery, and an assortment of other ventures. There was a number of rich men in the territory, but many squandered their newfound wealth on the standard three vices: wine, women, and song. Few of the newly rich thought to invest their money where they lived. For Gage, it was such an obvious strategy. One fact that he quickly observed—the weather in California was extremely temperate, but rainfall was not particularly abundant. So he bought up huge tracks of land in the higher elevations where snowfall and river water were plentiful.

He imagined that, at some point, having access to a source of clean water might be valuable.

His home on the bay was completed, all save landscaping. The structure was massive, Gage admitted to himself with a hidden smile, yet it looked as if it belonged to the hill. At night, when the moon was hidden in the heavens, Gage could look out from his store and see the radiant shine from the windows of his new adobe abode.

The house had a spacious entry from which radiated the social spaces. The main room was dominated by a two-story fireplace and was large enough to entertain a huge party. The glazed terra-cotta tile floors gleamed. The dining room was furnished with a long wooden table around which stood twenty-four high-back chairs upholstered in soft leather, all of which were hand carved in the Spanish manner. Most of the furniture in the house mimicked this style. From the highly polished exposed beams on the ceiling hung three massive chandeliers, from which glowed countless candles. There were ten bedrooms on the second floor, all accessed by two wide, curving staircases, both in the front and back. Gage could accommodate a score of visitors in comfort. The servants' quarters were in a separate structure just behind the main house but connected to it by a system of bells that were used to let them know when they were needed. Gage was beginning to collect accessories, such as paintings and carpets, and found great pleasure when he came across an interesting piece to display in one of the many rooms.

The first few nights in his new residence, he found it difficult to sleep. He missed the comforting creaks and groans of his small apartment above the store. But that space was now occupied by six clerks and delivery boys in his employ.

He had hired three Mexican women to tend to his house. He tried to find a proper manservant, but such a creature did not yet inhabit California society. The women–petite, round, and innately cheerful–scurried about the large kitchen, chattering away in Spanish. He attempted to learn as much of the language as he could, and within a few months was fluent enough to ask for specific meals and carry on an elementary conversation with them upon his return each day.

Gage had been true to his word. He wrote a letter in the summer of that year to his old valet and manservant, Edgar. He asked him first not to consider his offer if he thought his leaving would imperil the life of Gage's father–diminished as it might be. And he asked that Edgar not consider his offer if Walton would in some manner attempt to extract revenge on Edgar's family, or Gage's father. His handsome offer had been tempered with oddly phrased admonitions, warnings, and caveats.

And it would be months until Gage heard a reply.

That's why we need a telegraph out here, Gage said to himself as he posted the letter. *I would truly like to know if Edgar is considering this situation at all.*

<hr/>

Fall 1851

Besides his new home, his business, and his new ventures, Gage had become, in spite of his initial reservations, involved in the political life of Monterey. In many respects, it was a decision he could not avoid. A small town can have only so many powerful men. By the nature and scope of Gage's business, he had become the town's most powerful man–although he had never once attempted to use or leverage that power.

He truly had no need. True, the town had a mayor but had only a few laws on the books. By comparison to the legal strangulation that gripped New York City, Monterey was a lawless place. Of course, there were the standard statutes against killing, stealing, and assault—laws that were common to every state in the Americas. But included with those laws were a handful of fairly specific laws tailored at some very specific wrongs. The town fathers of Monterey passed a law that fined the owners of runaway pigs five dollars for every loose animal. Gage smiled because he knew the mayor's garden had been rooted up a dozen times by loose pigs.

Gage knew that political power and influence did not always depend on votes and ballots and elections. The townsfolk held Gage in awe—as much for his wealth as for his good nature and easy common sense. Many people stopped in to ask his advice over all sorts of matters—from farming to shipping to mining. Gage was glad to help as he could, but what he began to notice is that the citizens treated his opinions as law.

"Mr. Davis said building on that hill would be wrong—the soil is too shallow to hold a house."

"Mr. Davis said that the customs duty on that anvil should be figured by units, not gross weight."

"Mr. Davis said that any new house has to have a privy dug at least forty feet deep and a good ways from any stream or house."

And what surprised Gage is that many of these casual observations would indeed be assumed to have the force of law.

When he found his own opinions being quoted back to him as the law of the land, he knew it was time. He knew he must find a way to accommodate his dislike of political machinations with the need to have an orderly government look after the public's welfare in Monterey.

In the fall elections, Gage was elected mayor in a nearly unanimous vote of approval. In reality, he had only two opposing votes. One was his own, since he cast his vote for his opponent in a gesture of goodwill. And the other vote was his opponent's—who quite obviously did not share his magnanimous nature.

Yet in all his busyness, in all his frantic activity, Gage felt haunted.

And it was because of Nora.

The day he arrived back in Monterey from San Francisco he had fought the urge to turn around and head back to see her again. Every day he awoke, he fought the same urge.

And he was not altogether positive why he resisted.

But he did.

The urge to see her was powerful, coming upon him at unexpected moments. When it did, he would lose focus for a moment, perhaps stare off into space, then immediately double and redouble his efforts at whatever task was at hand. He was troubled by visions of her face and her voice, but he remained eminently productive.

And every week or so, another letter, bearing the flamboyant signature of Charles Thornton, would be delivered to his home. Charles's last letter, written at the beginning of summer, was not much different from the first.

❧❧❧

San Francisco, California
October 1, 1851

Gage, my dear, silent, and invisible benefactor,

Things go splendidly here. I have entered into negotiations as you requested for another property. I did as you directed and imagined myself as Shylock from The Merchant of Venice. Never did this city see such a hard and devious negotiator as I had become in that role.

I purchased the building for thousands less than you said would be your top offer. Renovations have already begun, and we will soon transform this building into a proper theater. You are correct–a talent like Miss Wilkes, who remains a most aloof star, needs to be showcased in an appropriate setting. With her on the bill, we could sell out a theater three times the size. Our contractor assures me that the theater will be completed well within our schedule.

Miss Wilkes's appearances continue to attract new audiences and wild adulation. She has the ability to cast a spell over men–it is as if she is a bewitcher, a temptress. Yet she is extremely quiet and most proper when alone. And should you ask–and I know you will–the answer is no. She has no idea of your involvement in this enterprise. If she were to learn of it, it would not be from my lips. I took your ominous threat most to heart–your coldness had me chilled to the marrow of my bones. I would do nothing to risk my current position. In New York I groveled and begged to be allowed on stage and I was tossed crumbs for roles. Here I am the star of the legitimate stage. I say this without haughtiness, for it is true.

(I have enclosed a clipping from a recent California Star. *They agree with my assessment of myself and I thought you should know, as it were.)*

Please, Gage, will you not reconsider another trip here? I do enjoy your company. Harvard men should stick together. And I am afraid that most of my troupe of thespians are lacking in matters involving coherent thought and civil, polite discourse. They are actors and not much above rutting animals. Clever words, pretty faces, empty heads.

Such are actors.

Such am I.

Wishing your next visit is soon,

C. T.

P.S. Your idea of a second troupe of thespians traveling to the hinterlands and mining camps was a capital idea. I have sent out a handful of youngsters who are long on drive and ambition, yet short of skill. I provided a tent, costumes, signs, and handbills–just as you suggested. I have received word that they draw hundreds of patrons every night–regardless of their play or how well it is delivered. A few hundred dollars–as you said–will reap thousands upon thousands in return.

FROM THE JOURNAL OF GAGE DAVIS
OCTOBER 14, 1851

I am busy–busier than I ever could have imagined. I have somehow become the mayor of Monterey. Had that been a suggestion a few years ago, I would have thought it daft beyond belief. While the position pays nothing and offers only frustration and headache, it is a role that I find invigorating. I have never imagined that men could be as quarrelsome and disagreeable as they are, especially when truly insignificant issues are on the table. When it came to voting for statehood, the issue passed on a unanimous vote with three minutes of discussion. When it came to the distance a privy must be from a rear door, the arguments lasted for three weeks and resulted in at least three fistfights that I know of—one occurring right in the chamber hall.

We resolved this particularly weighty issue with a compromise. One faction argued for fifty feet, another for twenty-five. We settled on forty-three feet. I am not sure how that number was selected, but the entire village council went home that night without fisticuffs.

Such is the life of a small town mayor.

And yet . . . small towns become stepping-stones, they tell me. Several men have stopped by my home, men of breeding and intelligence. These thoughtful men urged me to consider running for the position of governor of the new State of California—a state as of September of last year.

I am polite and listen to their entreaties, but I am not certain that a life in politics would suit me. I am used to making all the decisions in business—but in political matters, one must build compromises and bridges to other factions. Do I have that sort of temperament? Yet it is most flattering to be considered. How proud my father would be if he knew.

And how I wish he would still be lucid, though I know the man I once knew and looked up to is gone. I hurt when I consider my loss.

And this week, I have not thought of the journey to San Francisco more than a score of times. My heart must be healing.

November 1851

"Sir, how long have I worked for you?" Thomas Lee asked Gage one morning. Lee was a tall young man from upstate New York, with a thatch of red hair that resisted his best efforts to tame it.

Gage looked at the young man, then returned his attention to the ledger he was attempting to balance.

"I think for nearly three years," Gage said, scribbling in numbers. "You came here a month or two after I arrived. Good grief—have I been here that long?"

"You have been, sir."

Gage nodded and returned to the ledger. "Time does pass quickly when you are busy."

Thomas appeared nervous, as if he were most unsure of how exactly to phrase his next thought. "Sir, in that time . . . I have done an adequate job, have I not?"

Gage turned back to his clerk, thinking this was his first step in asking for another raise. "You have done well, Thomas. Very well."

Thomas stared at the floor. "Have I ever given you pause to think I was acting on my own interests rather than considering yours?"

"No," Gage said quickly. "I would say you have been a most loyal fellow in that regard."

"And I have never once attempted to play a part in your personal affairs, have I?"

Gage laid his pencil down, almost perturbed. "Mr. Lee, what are you trying to tell me? I feel as if I am in a parlor guessing game—and I do not suffer parlor games with any enthusiasm."

Thomas blanched and stepped back, then, as if he had found the necessary gumption, took a step forward again. "Sir, I know it is not my place to interfere. And if it means you fire me, then so be it. But I do care for you, sir. You have always been most generous and kind. And I cannot let another day pass."

"Mr. Lee," Gage called out, now with an exasperated smile, "get on with it. Please."

"I want you to go back to San Francisco."

Startled, Gage replied, "What?"

"You need to go to San Francisco."

"Excuse me?"

"You need to . . ."

Gage interrupted him. "I heard what you said. But I want to know why you said it."

"Because . . ."

"I'm waiting," Gage said, picking up the pencil and tapping it on the table.

Thomas gulped and continued. "Because of that woman."

Gage narrowed his eyes. "A woman?"

"Mr. Davis, you have to forgive my impudence, but ever since you came back from visiting Mr. Thornton in San Francisco, you were . . . well, different."

"Different? And how so?"

"Ever since then you've been . . . *driven* is the word that comes to mind. It's like you saw something or someone up there and you've been working like a man possessed to forget it. And a man only acts this way if a woman is involved. I am sure of it."

Gage leaned back in his chair. "So I have been a man possessed?"

"You have, Mr. Davis, and if you have to fire me for this, so be it. But I don't want you to make the same mistake that I did."

"You are possessed by the memory of a woman?"

"I am, Mr. Davis, and I regret it every day that has passed. Her name was Sandra Altman. I told her I was going to come back with bags of gold and buy a mansion for her. But I'm not rich, and I don't think I ever will be. I can't go back. And now I see that same look in your eyes, Mr. Davis. I do. If it ain't so, then you tell me, and I'll never mention this again. But I don't want anyone else to suffer like I have suffered."

"You can't ever go back, Mr. Lee?" Gage asked. "Are you sure?"

"Not without a bag of gold, sir. Not without success."

"Then why not go into the gold fields? Perhaps you will not get rich employed as my clerk—but would you not have a chance at finding gold?"

Thomas focused on his hands, then the floor.

"I don't rightly know, sir. Maybe I'm just a coward. Maybe I promised too much. I don't know . . . but I see in your eyes what I feel in my heart. It isn't right. You're a rich man, Mr. Davis. There should be nothing that you can't have. Nothing at all."

"Mr. Lee, thank you for thinking of me," Gage said thoughtfully.

"I am not going to say if you're right or wrong . . . but I will think about what you said."

Thomas nodded. "Then I'm not fired, am I?"

"No, you're not fired, Mr. Lee. Not at all."

And as his clerk returned to stocking the shelves, Gage stared at the ledger book in front of him, then out the window.

Is my heart that obvious? Is there such pain in my eyes?

He closed the ledger book and rubbed the bridge of his nose.

Perhaps I should listen to Mr. Lee. Perhaps it is time to stop running.

San Francisco, California

The curtain had just been lowered. Gage stood in the back of the packed theater, again half hidden by a pillar. He had taken the same position for the past several performances. Each time Nora took to the stage, Gage's heart broke a little more.

He had not found the nerve to announce himself to Nora. In fact, Charles was not even aware of his presence. He watched as Nora performed each night, and as the applause thundered, he slipped out into the streets. He walked and walked, not caring where his steps took him.

This evening, he slipped out as usual, and with the full moon guiding his steps, he found himself at the promontory by the narrow entrance to the Bay of San Francisco. He could see a scattering of lights on the far shore. From the west came the first wisps of fog and within the span of minutes, the fog rolled in from the ocean and grasped the land in a white fist.

He no longer saw the water, but he heard the waves, crashing against the rocks below. He took a seat in the hollow of a boulder, closed his eyes, and let his thoughts go where they may.

Why am I so affected by her? After what she has done to me, and after I have sworn off all thoughts of her, I should be immune to her charms.

But a single glance and I am back to where I have begun.

Is my pain because I still love her? Have I ever loved her?

He ran his hand through his hair and opened his eyes. The moon lit the fog like a thousand tiny candles, as if the night air itself had taken on cold flame.

I do love her.

I have never stopped loving her.

And I don't know if I can ever forgive her for what she has done.

He stood, hesitated a moment, then turned and began to walk back toward town.

But I have taken Mr. Lee's advice to heart. I cannot ignore the pain, nor can I will it away. I thought I could, but I am wrong.

Dear God, can I love her again?

❧

He hoped his pocketwatch was accurate. If so, he had no more than ten minutes before Nora's last show. He hurried through the streets, shrouded in fog, walking faster and faster, then breaking into a run. Sweat gathered at his brow, and his breath came in fast gasps.

A block from the theater the sound of applause washed out into the street. He sprinted the last fifty yards. He rounded the corner and ran to the stage door. The watchman recognized him and stammered a "Good evening, sir," allowing Gage to pass into the darkened staging area and dressing rooms.

Charles Thornton was in the midst of a heated argument with a group of actors. Gage glanced one direction, then another.

"Miss Wilkes?" he asked a man holding a thick rope in his hands.

The man nodded forward, and Gage stepped toward a long series of doors. At the very end, there stood a door with the name N. WILKES painted on it.

He had allowed himself no time to consider and reconsider his next move. If he had thought about it for more than a moment, he would have turned and run the entire way back to Monterey. But an image of his father flashed before his mind. Something inside of him shouted that life is short, and no one has the luxury of waiting till fate smiles a second time. Gage stopped thinking and being analytical and rational. He simply made a fist and tapped at the door. In the heartbeat of silence that followed, he swallowed and, for the first time in his life, uttered a prayer that had not been written by another man.

He simply mouthed the words, *If it be your will, Lord.*

And then the doorknob turned.

Gage would never be sure just how long the two of them stared at each other without talking. It might have been a heartbeat. It might have been an hour. What finally broke the silence was Nora opening the door further, inviting him in.

Her dressing room was not much bigger than Gage's closet at home. It held a tiny table and lamp, a rack of several identical black gowns, and a small sofa with one mismatched cushion.

"Please, Gage, come in," she said, her voice trembling a little at the edges. "It is wonderful to see you again."

He recalled being amazed at her composure. It was clear that he had not yet regained the power of speech. He entered and sat at the far edge of the sofa.

"I can't say I have ever been more surprised," Nora said, her voice as rich and lilting as Gage recalled. "Of all the people I never expected to see again—especially in California—it would be you. Are you visiting here?"

There was a hopeful note in her words.

Somehow Gage managed an answer. Being in her presence again cast his thoughts into a maelstrom. "No . . . I mean, yes. I am visiting the city. I live in Monterey—a hundred miles or so south on the coast."

Nora smiled. "How wonderful. . . . Did you see the show?"

He nodded. "I've seen quite a few of them."

Nora appeared as if upset. "And you haven't been to see me before this?"

Gage could formulate no coherent answer, so he shrugged, as might a callow lad. It was clear that both of them were knocked from their pinnings and were simply floundering, trying to find a comfortable spot from which to talk. It was also apparent neither of them could find that spot.

What they talked about for the next ten minutes would remain a mystery to Gage, for he could not recall a single word of it. He imagined that he told her of his business and that she told him of her journey out west–but he would have no proof that either occurred.

In a moment of silence, he gazed into her eyes and realized she must be thinking he could never forget what she had done. The insight surprised him, for he had never been intuitive in such matters before.

Then as she talked of some theater goings-on, he had, for perhaps the first time in his life, an epiphany that rocked his heart.

Forgive her.

The words echoed in his thoughts like a cannon shot.

Forgive her.

He stared down at his hands, hoping the impulse would fade. He had no intention of offering her forgiveness for her betrayal. It was not in his power to do so.

Forgive her.

He looked up and stared again into her eyes.

Forgive her.

"Uh . . . the real reason I stopped, Nora, was to . . ."

Her mouth was set in a forced smile. "Was to what, Gage?"

"Well, it is true that I never expected to see you again. So many things have happened and so many things . . ."

She lowered her eyes.

"I just came," he said.

I don't want to do this.

"I stopped here . . . to tell you . . ."

That I still love you.

"To tell you that I forgive you for everything. I hold no grudges."

Her face was blank and expressionless.

He waited for a long, silent minute. Then he stood, smoothed his trouser legs with his hands, and reached for the door.

"Gage," she said, her lips trembling, "Gage, I . . ."

He turned the knob and opened the door, then paused.

"Everything happens for a reason, someone told me once," he

said. "I just wanted to say I have no hard feelings. I bear you no ill will. I forgive you."

She can never love me again—I am sure of that. I see it in her eyes.

Finding no more words, he slipped out into the staging area and closed the door behind him.

Before he stepped away, he heard a rustle, as if she ran to the door. He saw the knob turn, but the door remained closed. Then he heard a sob.

And he walked back into the fog and did not stop traveling until he reached his home above the bay.

Monterey, California

The fog followed him home, and for the next week he found it difficult to concentrate on what to eat for breakfast, let alone matters of business—or the heart.

Thomas Lee hovered about when he returned, yet he did not ask anything about the trip or what transpired there.

And as if that confusion had not been enough, a new surprise entered his life. Midweek, Gage received a letter from Alliston Sinclair, the president of the bank Gage had founded a year earlier.

The note read:

Dear Mr. Davis,

I trust this finds you well. I have heard that you stopped in our fair city and did not visit us. Is there a problem, or were you simply pressed for time? I trust it was the latter.

I would like to discuss several matters with you. There is one that you might offer your personal efforts in order to resolve. Up until recently, one of our largest depositors was a prospector from Angels Camp who has kept a substantial sum in our vaults. Then, in the span of a few months, all was withdrawn. The fellow in question has not left the area—my associates tell me he still resides in Angels Camp. I bring this up to you because I have found out that he, too, is a Harvard alumni—who graduated in the same class as yourself. Perhaps you know the fellow and might write him a note to reconsider using the facilities of our bank. We would love to have his money again. His name is Joshua Quittner.

Regards,
Sinclair

Gage gazed at the note with perplexed amazement.

How intricate life can be, he thought to himself as he reread the letter. *Joshua Quittner–a rich man? How can such things be? And so has he found his way to the gold fields? He was serving God in Ohio. I will have to write him.*

He had received greater shocks and surprises in his life, to be sure, but this short note swirled his thoughts so. He sought a quiet time and place to gather his thoughts. It was his custom, after lunch, to take a longer walk and to ponder. His path often took him past the docks. He enjoyed seeing what ships had sailed into harbor. He could often gauge the sales of the day following by the number of new immigrants embarking.

If he had known what he would encounter, he may have avoided this day's walk. He stopped in midstep, his eyes almost refusing to believe what he saw.

On the dock, struggling with a huge trunk and three smaller valises, was a familiar-looking man. Gage stared for a full moment.

It could not be. It simply could not be.

He found himself calling out, "Pastor Kenyon!"

The man dropped his grip, spun about, and nearly fell into the water.

Well, I'll be . . . , Gage thought, startled.

"Gage Davis!" he shouted back. "It is a miracle!"

The two men heartily embraced.

In the span of an hour, Gage had his friend's luggage delivered to his home and a full meal laid out on the massive dining-room table.

Gage watched with pleasure as Pastor Kenyon devoured a huge plate of huevos rancheros–a specialty of his cook.

"Forgive me for being famished," Pastor Kenyon said between

mouthfuls. "But what they served on board was barely edible, and I was so often unable to hold even the barest amount down. All this seems like a gift from heaven."

Gage bid him to eat.

After the pastor finally pushed his plate away, Gage leaned on the table with his elbows.

"So . . . Reverend Kenyon . . ."

"John, please."

"John, then . . . do you mind if I ask you a question?"

"Of course not. You are my host. I am sure I can answer a simple question."

Gage smiled, then replied, "Why in heaven's name are you in California?"

John answered as if he had been rehearsing the answer for weeks. "I left—like half the people in New York—because I was infected with gold fever. That's why we all came. Yes, I can see your face—a pastor leaving his church—how sinful is that? Sinful enough, I tell you, and a common sin to at least twenty other pastors I know. Men are leaving their families to starve to death, so leaving a church isn't that bad in comparison. Gold fever is a terrible illness. My family has probably disowned me by now—I have been such a disappointment."

Gage nodded in sympathy.

"And I wanted to be rich too. Like you, Gage. I desired all the things that gold could buy, especially if the gold was free. But halfway here, I got as sick as a man can get without waking up dead. When I recovered, I realized that God was calling me. From that point on, I knew that God used the gold fever for a reason—to get me here."

"And now that you're here?"

"I think I'm supposed to build a church."

CHAPTER TWENTY-ONE

Monterey, California
December 1851

A church? Here?"

Pastor Kenyon nodded. "Why not here? Has anyone built a church in Monterey?"

Gage stroked his chin. "There's the Spanish mission north of us in Santa Cruz. And I suspect the priests have been through the area on occasion. But no, there isn't a church in the village."

"Then there should be," Pastor Kenyon replied. "And if no one else is building a house for God, then I should."

Gage poured them both another cup of coffee laced with chicory and goat's milk. "And when you build this church for God—will he provide the resources for you? Does he have an account with the bank?"

The pastor shook his head at Gage's flippant remark. "Gage, God will build what he wants to build. Some people may mock that faith—but I must tell you, God is not fond of being mocked."

"I'm not mocking it," Gage said as he walked out on the wide veranda and set his coffee cup on the waist-high wall. "It's just that business out here is no different than business in New York. People expect to get paid for their talents, and materials cost money. I don't know any way to avoid that reality."

The pastor joined him at the wall, and both stared out over the tranquil bay. Numerous ships lay at anchor, lolling in the waves, their night lanterns glimmering over the water. Their bells chimed faintly in the dark as the swells rocked the vessels as a mother would rock a child.

"It is most beautiful here, Gage. I can understand why you selected this spot and this village to live in."

Gage nodded. "I can't say if I actually chose the spot. More like fate conspired to get me here."

"Fate or God?"

"There's a difference?"

Pastor Kenyon's mouth looked like he had just eaten a lemon. "Gage," he said with a warning tone.

"Well, it must have been the fates—because I don't recall hearing God issuing any orders to run the business and which location would be best."

Pastor Kenyon sipped his coffee. "Then you haven't found your faith, have you, Gage?"

He smiled. "I hadn't thought I lost anything—anything that needed to be found, that is."

"You may joke about this, Gage," Pastor Kenyon responded, "but it truly is not a matter to be ignored."

Gage averted his eyes and once again focused on the harbor and the black edge of the sea that was the horizon. Since he had left New York, he had scarcely thought of God or matters that he and Nora had discussed. Pastor Kenyon's letters and advice seldom warranted more than a fleeting image.

Until that night before he faced Nora again, he had seldom found the word *God* on his lips. And Gage found no joy or reason to rejoice over that evening, or to thank God for the outcome.

"I'm not ignoring it, John. All that God talk might be a consideration for the future. I suspect I will know when it's time to address matters of religion. It isn't time now."

"Gage," Pastor Kenyon said softly, "you may think you have all the time in the world. But you don't. Men's lives can end in a heart-beat, and their last breaths come too swiftly for them even to voice God's name. How different a world it might be if we all had the lux-ury of a slow, painless death. We could recant our sins at the end, God would forgive us, then we would smile, live out our last hours, and enter heaven."

"That seems a most convenient method to me," Gage agreed.

"If we could arrange it to be just that way, yes, it would be," Pastor Kenyon said. "But on my voyage here, twenty men died. Half of them found death in an instant as they washed overboard at the tip of the world in the Strait of Magellan. An icy wave . . . a 'rogue wave' they called it . . . the huge wall of water fell upon the ship and, in the blink of an eye, the poor men were swept into the frigid waters. We never even saw them as they disappeared into the sea. Did they have time to repent? Did they have time to wait?"

"Apparently not," Gage replied, "so I shall endeavor to stay away from turbulent southern waters."

"Gage," Pastor Kenyon cautioned. "It is not a jesting matter."

"But I am not jesting. I have heard your cautions. I will think about what you have said."

Gage's guest drained the last of his coffee. "I did not sail halfway around the world to lecture you," he said in a light tone. "But I do want one thing from you."

Gage hesitated, unsure if he could give what Pastor Kenyon desired.

"And that is?" he asked with some trepidation.

"Another cup of this wonderful coffee. It has been months since I have had a decent cup. The coffee on our ship was not to New York standards, I must say."

Laughing, Gage poured another for both of them. "Not much in California is up to New York standards either, John. You'll soon learn that what tastes you loved in New York will never be dupli-cated out here."

"Never?"

"Never."

Gage smiled as he watched Pastor Kenyon's face fall in disappointment.

⚬～≈⊱⊰≈～⚬

Pastor Kenyon's enthusiasm and faith amazed Gage. He busied himself his first few weeks in California by introducing himself to everyone in town. During the course of those conversations he always brought up his dream of building a church in town. Before the year of 1851 had ended, he had been given a small plot of land a half-mile from the ocean and the promise of a great deal of volunteer labor.

Every day someone from town would stop to visit Gage. They would smile and remark how wonderful it was that Pastor Kenyon had taken it upon himself to build a church. Unlike virtually every other matter that concerned the town—from privies to sidewalks—the idea of a church drew unanimous support from everyone.

Gage could not imagine an odder scenario—a young pastor from the East uniting an entire village of misfits and malcontents. At least that is the way Gage viewed them. Most had escaped their own threatening situations at home and headed west to breathe free and do exactly as they chose to do. It was difficult to get them to agree on anything.

But yet all agreed on this matter of the church.

After Gage assessed the support for Kenyon's project, he decided it was time to offer his support as well. He withdrew twenty-five hundred dollars in currency from his bank, securely placed it in a sturdy envelope, gave it to Thomas Lee, and told him to give it to the town's treasurer. He was instructed to say the money came from a wealthy prospector who was simply passing through—and never tell a soul of the actual origin of the money.

If God is pleased with my gift, so much the better on my accounts with him, Gage told himself.

And by the end of January 1852, the foundation was laid for the First Church of Monterey.

February 1852

All but the last rafter had been snugged into place. The crew had been gone for half an hour, and the sun had fully disappeared. Pastor Kenyon walked into the shell of the church and looked up. The rafters, like ribs, cut across the gold glow of the moon. He paced up to where the center aisle would be.

A handsome space, indeed. Almost as big as the church I left in New York.

He winced as he thought of that group of people, so stunned as he told them of his departure. Their surprise turned to anger when he told them of his destination.

It was gold fever–nothing else I can blame it on.

He had found another pastor to take his place before he left. That in itself was no small feat, owing to the number of other men of God who had departed from their congregations as well. Most of his church hardly offered a civil good-bye as he walked away, satchel in hand, his trunks following on a rented livery wagon.

He expected nothing more. He knew he had disappointed them, but he could not ignore the raging blood in his veins that called out for riches and free gold.

But the fever had broken midtrip, and now he knew he had regained his senses and his calling.

He was inside a church, doing God's work. No matter that he had but a few dollars to his name. God would provide. He always had. John was certain God would continue to do so.

From behind him came a faint swishing sound, then a crackling, and then a thump, the crash of lumber, and a loud curse.

"Who's there?" John called out, hoping it was not some wild animal bent on dinner. John did not like wild animals. "What do you want?" His voice wavered.

"It's your friend, Gage, who nearly died falling on some debris. Why didn't I bring a torch with me?"

John hurried to his side. "Are you hurt? Truly?"

Gage snorted. "Yes. I think I sliced open my shin when I fell on that pile of timbers."

"It is most tricky walking here, even in the daylight," John said as he pulled a handkerchief out and offered it to Gage. "Tradesmen are not the neatest people I have ever seen."

Gage took the cloth and held it firmly to his shin. "I imagine they want to clean up but once, rather than every day."

John nodded. "I suppose. I should have been home an hour ago as well. But I like watching the progress. . . . Can you walk? Should I return to town for a carriage?"

Gage stood and inhaled sharply as he put his weight on his right leg. "It hurts, but you'll be hours finding a carriage tonight. Easier and faster if you just lend me a shoulder to lean on. You can take me by Molly's. She's not far from here."

"Molly?"

"Molly Tannte. She's a seamstress. Lives alone in that shanty at the crest of Wilson's Hill. Handy with a needle and thread. She's the best in town at stitching up cuts."

John winced aloud, as if feeling the needle slipping into his own flesh, and grasped Gage about the waist for support.

The two men hobbled and shuffled along the darkened path. Clouds skimmed along the sky and hid the moon for long periods. Then the two would stop, unwilling to risk further injury.

After a half-mile, Gage called out, "Let's stop for a moment. The leg is throbbing a bit and may be bleeding again."

John lowered him to the ground. "I should get help," he said.

"No . . . stay. It's all right. Just let me rest for a minute."

"Gage," John asked, puzzled, "what were you doing out there in the dark?"

Gage laughed. "I'm not sure . . . taking a walk. Looking at the progress of the town's first church. I am the mayor."

John didn't answer. As a pastor he often let silence nudge a fuller answer.

"And I wanted someone to talk to."

"You can always talk to me, Gage. You don't need to break your leg in the dark for an excuse."

"And did you specialize in sympathy in seminary?"

John laughed. "I didn't mean it that way."

"I know."

From the distance a wolf called out, baying at the moon. Its plaintive cry echoed among the cypress trees.

"What was that?" John nearly shouted. It was clear that the shrill howl had frightened him.

"Just a wolf. You don't hear them much anymore. Most have been hunted off. And that one was a far piece away."

"How far is a far piece when it comes to a wolf? Did you bring a gun?"

"No. I didn't bring a gun. And besides, John, what are you worried about? Won't God protect you?" From the tone of Gage's voice it was hard to tell if he was joking or being serious.

"I guess I shouldn't be afraid," John finally said, his voice calm, almost cheerful.

"Because of God's protection?"

"No, because if the wolf attacks, all I have to do is run faster than you. I think tonight I have the race pretty well won."

Gage swung his arm playfully in John's direction. "You'll never be a great pastor. It's the sympathy issue again."

After a long silence, Gage coughed once, then spoke. His voice was a velvet whisper. "I saw her."

"Saw who?"

"Nora."

"What?" John shouted. "Nora Wilkes?"

"Yes." Gage did not raise his voice.

"Saw her where?"

"In San Francisco."

"San Francisco? Good heavens. What was she doing there? I didn't mention her name to you because . . . well, because her family thought she was dead. I didn't know how you would take that news. Her poor mother—she will be so relieved."

"Dead? They thought she was dead? Why?"

John cleared his throat. "Well . . . it's a long story."

"I think we have time now," Gage said. "But it's only a short walk to Molly's. Help me up, and you can tell me the story as we limp in that direction."

And as the two hobbled along the trail, John told him what he knew of the tale.

Within several weeks of Gage leaving New York, most everyone surmised what had happened—that he had been forced out of the family business because of some impropriety. No one believed that Gage would have stepped aside on his own accord. Hints and guesses filled the newspapers.

Most knew nothing of Nora's role in the affair, but John had heard rumors of her involvement during a trip back home to Portland. He went to see Nora directly. She admitted nothing, but John saw the pain on her face.

Then three months later, she simply disappeared. There was no note, no hints—just an empty room.

And less than a month after that, a more hurtful rumor began, having to do with Nora's father and slaving and men and children starving to death in a port in Hispaniola.

"The scandal was all over Portland," John said. "Nora's parents suffered immensely. Her mother still will not show her face in public. The pain of the scandal was doubled by her daughter's disappearance."

Gage interrupted John's account. "Was my brother, Walton, involved in this story at all? Could he be behind it?"

"Your brother? How?"

"I don't know how . . . but he did make a trip to Hispaniola. Could he have found out about the incident and used that knowledge to force Nora to betray me?"

John stopped walking. "I suppose that's possible. But, Gage—wasn't what you did wrong? I mean, wasn't it illegal?"

At first Gage did not answer. Then he said, hesitating, "Yes . . . but . . ."

"Then whether Nora went before a judge or Walton or no one, you were still guilty of what your brother accused you."

"Well, yes . . . but . . ."

"So what Nora said or didn't say would have had little impact on the truth and what ultimately happened."

Gage finally nodded. "That is true, I guess."

The two started off again. Well off in the distance, they could see the flickering light of a small cabin.

"That's Molly's over there. I think I'm bleeding again. We should hurry."

<hr />

With deft strokes and a firm tug on the thread, Molly neatly sewed the gash in Gage's leg.

"Now this will hurt," she said, as she poured a full cup of warm rum over his injury. Gage writhed in his chair and held a scream behind closed lips. His head quivered as he held back the pain from exploding.

"But soon the pain will stop. The rum gets rid of the poison," Molly said cheerfully. "Or at least gets it too drunk to cause any mischief. Now you sit and rest, and I'll get us some stew. You in the mood for some stew, Pastor?"

John nodded eagerly. "But only if it's no trouble."

"No trouble at all serving a man of God like yourself. You should take lessons from him, Mr. Davis. On how to serve and all."

Gage shot a withering look in John's direction, and the pastor simply smiled in return.

After dinner, Molly insisted on a wagon to get Gage home. John offered to make the dark trip to town.

"I'll not hear of it, Pastor, though I am touched by your offer. You're a stranger here. You'd get lost or bust your leg open like Mr. Davis. And I'll have none of that. You two just cool your heels till I get back with the wagon."

Wincing, Gage maneuvered himself into a more comfortable position on the chair.

"Does it hurt?"

"No," said Gage through gritted teeth. "I always do this when I feel good."

The fire crackled and hissed.

"So you think she was forced into it?"

"Nora?" John asked.

"Yes. Do you think my brother forced her into betraying me?"

"Gage, I don't know for certain, but she would have tried to move heaven and earth in order not to hurt her parents. Especially her mother. They doted on each other."

"Then it makes sense. It all makes sense," Gage said softly.

Neither man spoke. A log rolled and then resettled in the fireplace. John used a poker to edge it back in place.

"I forgave her, John," Gage said.

"What?"

"Nora," Gage said. "I went to see her. We spoke for a few moments. I said I forgave her for what she did. I told her I hold no grudge, and not to feel guilty."

"You did?"

Gage's voice became a whisper. "It was the first time in all my life that I spoke to God. I said, 'If it be your will.' And I then I got the most urgent feeling that I had to forgive her."

"And what did she say?"

"She didn't say anything. I left. I knew she couldn't love me anymore."

"But you prayed about it?"

"If you call those few words a prayer."

"Gage, anytime a man calls out to God, it is a prayer."

"Then it was a prayer."

"But Nora didn't answer you?"

Gage looked away. "I didn't wait for an answer. I could see it in her eyes. She didn't want me to be there."

John shook his head. "Gage, I know so little about women, but I don't think she would have turned you away."

"Truly?" Gage asked, wondering.

"Truly, Gage."

"I forgave her. She destroyed everything I had and I forgave her. Why couldn't she accept it?"

John thought awhile, then answered, "To truly forgive one must be first forgiven. That's not easy, Gage. I believe that only children of God can truly understand what it is to forgive others—because they themselves are forgiven."

"Then I didn't do it right? I told her I forgave her. What more do I need to do?"

John shrugged. "Gage, only God can show you that. . . . But you need to see her again. You need to let her tell you what she feels."

Gage held back a tear and nodded.

That winter brought waves of cold rain that kept most people indoors for days at a time. The month of February proved to be crueler yet. The sun remained hidden by the gray scud of clouds, and the damp air chilled to the bone. Only five or so ships had sailed into the bay during these months, and no more than a hundred men had disembarked from the ships on their way inland in all of February.

Business was slow, and Gage paced about the store in nervous agitation. It was not that the sparse sales were truly problematic, since his other locations were exceeding the sales from the previous year. Gage could have blamed his unsettled behavior on the shrinking sales, but in his heart, he knew it was caused by Nora.

After his talk with Pastor Kenyon, thoughts of Nora tempted him daily. At dawn, he would resolve to travel north, joyfully constructing a new scene in which Nora accepted his forgiveness. Then by sunset, he would have dismantled the plans in anger, imagining that Nora truly desired never to see him again.

He attempted to write in his journal, to make some sense of his feelings, but the blank page mocked him, and he sat staring at the white expanse, unable to add a single word.

Pacing about his house, he unnerved his servants, who jumped every time he unexpectedly entered a room. He would stare for a second, then turn and exit without speaking.

He heard them mutter in Spanish as he walked away. They called him *fantasma*–"ghost."

Pastor Kenyon told him that he had written to Nora's parents. "They have a right to know their daughter is alive."

Gage agreed, though he cautioned him, "Best not to tell them too much–I'm sure Nora had a reason for her disappearance."

❧

March 1852

At the beginning of March, the sun appeared for the first time in weeks. Gage took it as a sign. For the first time in months, a ray of hope and warmth entered his soul. He realized he could not hide from the truth for the rest of his life. Nora was less than a hundred miles away. That was true. Gage was miserable with anxiety. That was true. And he knew that his misery would not diminish unless he took efforts to change the situation. He acted decisively in all his business matters, so why could he not exhibit the same traits in his personal life?

In the span of an hour on a Tuesday morning, he packed a large bag with clothes and supplies, rented a horse at the livery, bid his house servants and store clerks good-bye, and headed to San Francisco.

❧

San Francisco, California

The weather remained mild during his journey. Gage let his horse slow to a walk and wiped his forehead with his sleeve. The closer to San Francisco they came, the more nervous he became. And they had only one more hill to climb. The horse turned his head back to Gage, as if to ask for directions. Gage nicked him with the reins, and in a moment, the theater came into view.

Charles was a born promoter. On the second story, running the full width of the theater, was a huge painting. Virtually all of the canvas was coal black, save a lone female figure, outlined in white as if lit from behind by the sun.

It was Nora, her image standing nearly a full story tall. Underneath that image was her name painted in scarlet letters.

Gage gasped when he saw it. The horse stopped in front of the marquee and whinnied. Gage looked up at the image, turned his head, and dug his heels into the horse's sides. The animal whinnied again, this time in protest, and took off at a gallop down the street. Gage would not let him stop running until they reached the waterfront.

Then he pivoted in the saddle, glancing over his shoulder. He tried to take a deep breath.

I can't see her today. I simply can't. I want to, but I can't.

His heart thudded frantically.

I know whom I can talk to, Gage told himself. *That is, if he's still there.*

He finally managed a full breath. Pulling the reins to the right, he nudged the horse, this time in a more gentle fashion, to the east.

Angels Camp, California

"I have surprised you again, haven't I? I'm a full month early," Gage said as the door swung open. Then he stared in at the smiling Oriental face that peered out of the dim interior. Gage stepped back, confused.

This is not Joshua for certain . . . but they said in town this was his land. Has he moved?

"Sir," the woman said, "you seeking?"

"Uh . . . I am looking for . . . I mean . . . Joshua Quittner . . . I am looking for Joshua Quittner. I'm an old friend, Gage Davis. We knew . . . I mean we . . . we were both at Harvard together."

The young woman with the beautiful almond eyes and inviting

smile nodded. "You have found his home, Gage Davis. A friend must enter, please."

Gage ducked through the doorway and blinked, adjusting to the light. Two lanterns glowed at the far end of the cabin. The walls had been covered with white plaster. The exterior of the cabin gave no hint of the spacious feeling of the interior. A loft at one end held the sleeping quarters, and a small section at the other end held a cast-iron stove and a hand pump and sink. The floor was a puzzle of smooth, tight-fitting stones. And a series of thick cushions lay on a rug in a ring about the fireplace.

He lowered himself to a cushion.

This looks like an engraving I saw of a Chinese temple, Gage thought.

The young woman bowed before him. "Tea?" she asked.

Unsure of what to do, he answered, "Yes, if it's not a bother."

The woman hurried off to the kitchen and in a moment bowed again before him, this time presenting a wooden tray with a single cup and a pot of steaming water.

"Thank you. . . ."

She smiled, almost blushed, and said in a petal-soft voice, "I am called Quen-li."

She set the tray before him and bowed again.

Gage sat, confused.

If this is where Joshua lives . . . is this woman a servant? Or perhaps something more . . . No, Joshua would not have changed so much as to take on a concubine . . . or would he?

Gage struggled to remain calm as he sipped his tea. The liquid was pale green and soothing to the taste.

Quen-li sat in the far corner, averting her eyes, smiling. Just then, from the loft above them, came a gurgling cry. Quen-li rose immediately and hurried up the ladder to the loft. She cooed at the sound, but the cries increased.

She hurried down the ladder and knelt a few feet from Gage. "Sir, the baby cry. I not disturb honored guest. Shall I go outside?"

Outside? It's chilled out there.

"No . . . Quen-li, attend to the child. You may bring him down here if you would like. . . . It's not my home. . . ."

She hurried up the ladder and returned with a tiny bundle in her arms. She carefully undraped a blanket from the infant's face and kissed and soothed.

"Little one not cry," she sang, then added a long plaintive song in a foreign tongue. Gage felt dislocated as he listened to the odd phrasing and strange sounds.

Quen-li finished the song and shifted the newborn in her arms. The blanket fell away from its face, and the light shone on its features.

Gage drew in a deep breath and found it stuck in his chest.

The baby, save the almond slant of its eyes, was an exact duplicate of Joshua Quittner.

⚶

The door banged open, and Joshua bounded into the room. He saw his wife and child in one corner, and Gage holding a teacup in the other corner. He smiled.

"Gage! They told me in town that a strange man in an expensive coat was looking for me. I know only one man with an expensive coat. How are you?"

He held his arms wide and embraced Gage, who struggled to return the hug and not spill any tea.

"I am fine, old friend. I am fine indeed," Gage replied. "You are one person I never thought I would see again after I left New York."

Joshua leaned back. "I heard, Gage, and I'm sorry. A day after your letter arrived here, I received a most cryptic letter from Jamison. Odd, isn't it—he can write a million words for the *New York World,* but when it comes to personal correspondence, it is as if he is paying for every word."

Gage smiled in reply. "Then you know about Walton and all."

"Some. Bits and pieces. Mostly from what Jamison wrote. Some I read in the New York papers. They get here—late—but they do get here. Even that recent one, the *Daily Times.*"

Gage shrugged as if attempting to describe it all would lead to defeat.

Joshua offered a sad smile in reply. "Gage, I don't claim to understand the human heart anymore—especially after what led me here to California. It's hard to understand why a brother might do what he did."

Gage peered over Joshua's shoulder. He turned and stared at Joshua with a questioning look.

"I see you met Quen-li," Joshua said.

"I have."

"And the little one—Joshua Yat-sen Quittner?"

"I heard him first. Good lungs."

Joshua laughed. "He takes after me in that regard. Quen-li seldom raises her voice."

Confusion apparent, Gage glanced at the young woman, then back at Joshua.

"She's my wife, Gage. We're married," Joshua explained.

Gage stepped back and took his hand. "Congratulations, Joshua. I mean that. For both the marriage and the child. I wondered . . . I mean, California changes people . . . people do things that I wouldn't have thought possible."

Joshua nodded. "I understand. It happens a lot—Quen-li being a Chinese woman and all. People ask."

"I didn't mean . . . I mean . . . I was just surprised. . . ."

Joshua clapped his hand over Gage's shoulder. "We are used to the stares, my friend. It is of no matter now—and I cannot get angry over something that I know I would just as easily do."

"Well, it's not like I have any right to say anything about it," Gage said.

"And some of it hasn't been easy, but I have never been happier. Come, we should leave Quen-li alone to feed the child. I'll show you around."

Joshua and Gage walked around the acreage. Joshua showed him the barn and the cows he had just bought, and the plow, and talked about the ox that he hoped to buy. At the end of the tour, as the two rested against the fence by the cabin, Gage addressed his friend. "I am not sure how to ask this question, Joshua."

"Harvard's most obvious man suddenly getting shy? California has changed you, hasn't it, Gage?" Joshua said with a grin.

"I suspect it has."

"And what's your question? Why the hesitation?"

"You were rich, Joshua. Very rich."

"And how do you know that? Do I look different?" Joshua asked.

"No, nothing that obvious. But you kept your money in a bank I own. What you have built here is wonderful—but this isn't the farm of a rich man. What happened? Have you buried your money behind the barn?"

For the next hour Joshua told Gage of his journey out west, of his abandonment of his church, of his partnership with Giles Barthlemon, of his ever-increasing gold finds, of Giles's death, of his loneliness, of his romantic relationship with Quen-li, and ultimately of his "purchase" of Quen-li's freedom.

"So you paid twenty thousand dollars? But wasn't slavery illegal in the territory?"

Joshua laughed harshly. "How many judges did you pass between San Francisco and Angels Camp? And police? Any county sheriffs? ... But the money does not matter, Gage. It truly does not. I could not imagine myself any happier and more satisfied than I am today. My only regret is that if I were wealthy, I could afford a new organ or Bibles for the church. But I have enough. We have enough. Our house is warm in the winter. We have plenty of food. Quen-li is a wonderful wife. The church is growing. God is blessing me, Gage. He really is. When I had all the money of Midas, I was miserable. Now that I have just enough, he has filled my heart with joy and my house with love and the laughter of a baby. How much more could I ask for?"

Gage shrugged.

"Are you hungry? Quen-li is busy preparing a huge repast for you."

"But you did not ask ... I mean ... she did not tell you. ..."

347

"I don't need to ask. It is what I know she will do. Have you ever eaten food prepared in the Chinese style?"

Gage shook his head no. "There was a restaurant in New York that offered it, but I don't think I will be in the neighborhood anytime soon."

"No matter, old friend. Quen-li is a master. You will be delighted. And as a favor to you, I will not make you eat with chopsticks."

⌘

The fire had dwindled to embers. Gage stared at the glow. He rubbed at the scar on his leg. Joshua stood up, walked outside, and returned with arms full of wood. He tossed on a fresh log and tumbled the rest into the wood box at the side of the hearth.

From the loft came the mewing sounds of a baby. Joshua smiled.

"I am not one who is comfortable with infants," Gage admitted, "but the young Joshua is quite handsome. More so than his father."

"And if I had not returned to the pulpit, I would be forced to make you take that back."

"Even if the observation is true?"

"All the more reason," Joshua said with a laugh.

The wood took flame and crackled.

"You have a wonderful life here," Gage said.

"I know. It is a gift from God—and testimony that God does not hold grudges over his children who for a time have turned from him."

Gage hesitated. "If you say so."

"I do."

"And I thought as much."

"And just as I knew you would respond with doubts," Joshua said, smiling. "Doesn't this remind you of our late-night talks back at Harvard? We would argue the night away."

"I miss those days," Gage said.

Joshua nodded, then seemed to be considering his next words carefully. "Have you heard from Hannah?"

Gage had anticipated the question. *A first love dies hard, if ever,* he thought to himself. "I have not heard much."

"Has she married?"

"Joshua, I have not heard for certain. I have not asked, and Jamison has not mentioned that fact in his few letters to me. And there is no one back in New York whom I hear from with any regularity. I could ask, but I haven't."

Joshua nodded. "Has she become a doctor?"

Gage shrugged. "The last I heard she was attending a medical college–where women are actually allowed to enroll. The Boston Female Medical School, it is called. Opened in '48."

"Then perhaps she has realized her dream."

Gage nodded. "I do miss the days when all of us gathered at the Destiny. So many wonderful memories."

"I miss them as well, Gage. I suspect that if I were unhappy today, I would be plagued with more regrets. I imagine that the longer one lives, the more decisions one makes, and the more what-might-have-beens come to mind."

Gage nodded.

"Yet I take great comfort in the fact that even if somehow things could have been different–and Hannah and I would be together–then I never would have met Quen-li and never have had a son. I cannot imagine my life without them. I never imagined such a fierce love as I have for them both."

"And back in the pulpit as well," Gage said. "I believe you are renting a building that I own."

"I did recently find out about our landlord. And had I known earlier, I would have petitioned for a reduced rent. However, we may not be renting much longer. There is such a hunger for God's Word here. People have to stand during two Sunday services. We simply don't have enough chairs or space. Now the elders are talking about building a church of our own. We have land, but money is always tight in a church."

"So you've returned to the life you left in Ohio?"

"It took me this long to realize what gave my soul joy. I was born to serve God this way. And I was a fool to think otherwise."

"So God forgives you for being a fool?"

"He does."

Gage stood and winced as he placed his weight on his right leg.

"Are you hurt?"

"Old church injury," Gage replied and told him the story. And as he talked, he began to feel emotionally limber. He told Joshua of Nora, and her role in his journey to California, how he had visited her at the theater and offered her forgiveness, yet still returned home with an ache in his heart.

Gage talked for nearly an hour. At the end, his voice wavered, and his words tumbled past a hitch in his throat.

Joshua said quietly, "To understand forgiveness, Gage, and to truly be able to forgive totally—a person needs to know what it is to have been forgiven."

Gage nodded. "I heard the exact same advice from another pastor."

"Then my theology has been verified," Joshua said. "But it is true. A man might say 'I forgive you,' but unless he knows how it feels to be forgiven, unless he has let God forgive him for his sins, unless he takes God's gift of forgiveness and salvation, then I believe his forgiveness is hollow."

Gage stared into the darkness with liquid eyes. "But I said all the right words. I know I did. What more could I offer her?"

"What did you want her to do? How did you imagine her response?"

Gage sighed. "I wanted her to say that she accepted my forgiveness."

"And ..."

"I wanted her to say she still loved me."

"And ..."

Gage closed his eyes tight. "And then I was going to walk away from her like she walked away from me." He inhaled deeply, then began to sob. "I wanted to hurt her like she hurt me. I never thought I would say this—but it's true. I wanted to break her heart."

Joshua placed his arm around his friend. "Sometimes we get a glimpse into our souls, and the view frightens us. I don't claim to understand evil, but I understand that even in my soul such blackness exists. All men are broken, Gage. All men have blackness in their hearts."

"I didn't think I did, Joshua. I truly thought I didn't."

"Come, let me talk to you."

Both men sat on thick cushions by the fire.

"We are born into a broken world, Gage. We may mask our sin and pain and pettiness, but it's all there inside of us."

Gage's face showed the faint tracing of tears. "But I was a good man. I still am."

"None of us is good enough for a holy God. He is perfect. Nothing we do can make us perfect. And that's why he sent his Son to assume our sins, die on the cross—so we don't have to—and then come back to life. He took our place."

"Joshua, you have told me this before. And I say anything free is not worth having."

"But if it wasn't free, no man would be able to pay the price. What price would you put on eternal life?"

He opened his hands as if in surrender.

"Gage, if you accept God's gift, then you can be forgiven. You can have the peace and contentment that only God can provide. Your money hasn't given you true happiness, has it?"

"No." Gage's voice was but a whisper.

"If you want the peace of God, then you have to accept the gift."

Gage bowed his head, yet remained silent.

"Gage, it's time. I know you are tired of being empty. Accept it. Take God's gift."

The only sound was the crackling of the fire. Then came the gentle mewing of the baby.

"Gage, reach out for it. You don't have to fight anymore. Give him your heart."

In the smallest of voices, Gage said, "I can't. I just can't."

And then he stood, limped toward the door, and slipped out into the darkness.

Gage stayed with Joshua and Quen-li for only another full day. Neither man mentioned their talk until Joshua reached up as Gage sat on his horse and offered him his hand in farewell.

"What you have is so pleasing to see, Joshua. I will be back. I promise you that."

Joshua smiled. "It was nice to see you again. I'm glad you are close. I am glad you met Quen-li and our son."

Gage let go of his hand and tugged at the reins.

"Don't let too much time pass, Gage. Not to decide is to decide. You may not have as much time as you think."

Gage waved and spurred the horse down the narrow lane and onto the wider trail that followed the stream into town.

The sound of the rushing water grew louder and louder with each step the horse took. Gage followed the trail along the river, well worn now by thousands of others who trekked back and forth along the banks. Deep ruts grooved into the dirt where wagon wheels cut into the earth. Gage edged the horse closer to the water to avoid them. Branches switched at his shoulders and face, and he often burrowed close to the horse's neck to avoid getting a pine branch across his forehead.

The horse began to whinny and pull, so Gage dismounted and led him to the river. The animal bent down and drank, then backed off and began to munch on the fresh grass.

Gage took the reins and tied them to a fallen tree. He stretched in the warm air and walked downriver, toward a thick grove of pine and laurel. He suddenly saw the source of the noise. A small cataract of water gushed over a narrow shale precipice. The drop was no more than a man's height. Froth and mist swirled about the water.

He walked to within an arm's length of the falls. The cool air felt good. He took his hat and coat and tossed them to the side, then peered up and down the trail. He was alone.

He stripped down to his shorts and stepped under the chilled water. He gasped in response as his chest immediately tightened. The water beat on his shoulders like a thousand tiny fingers. He closed his eyes and rolled his head, feeling the muscles loosen.

And in that moment, he again heard Joshua's voice . . . "*Not to decide is to decide. You may not have as much time as you think.*"

Gage's shoulders slumped.

I am so very tired.

He slowly sank to his knees, the water cascading in torrents about him. After a minute, he could hear no sound, save his own thoughts.

Lord . . . I am lost. I thought I would always be in control. A wealthy man must be in control. But my heart hurts so much. I feel as if I am wounded beyond my body's ability to heal. I close my eyes and I see her, Lord. I open my eyes, and my thoughts are about her.

He bowed his head.

I had to do this on my own. Please Lord, hear my prayer . . . and accept the life of this foolish man. I am done fighting. I am done resisting. Take my life. I accept the gift. I want your forgiveness.

And the salt of his tears mingled with the clear water of the river, carrying his pain to the waiting arms of the sea.

San Francisco, California

"Gage, I am overjoyed that you have finally found peace with God. I have prayed so often for such news. I truly am overwhelmed."

"It was because of you," Gage replied. "What you did brought me here . . . to God."

Nora looked away. Her eyes darkened with the painful memory.

"I didn't mean to bring that up. Such things are history—and never to be thought of again."

Nora nodded and offered a weak smile. "Thank you, Gage."

"And what I told you before . . . about forgiving you for all of it . . . I truly meant it. At least I thought I did at the time. But I realize now that I wasn't being honest with you—not honest in the least."

"It doesn't matter, Gage. Not now."

"But it does, Nora. I had two people—both men of God, by the way—tell me that unless I was forgiven, I could not forgive. And they were right. I can now see how wrong I was. I hadn't given up the anger. I hadn't given up the bitterness. I hadn't given up the hurt."

"And now . . . ?"

"And now I have. My heart is new, Nora. It's as if I was not alive until now. As if I saw only in dim light. But all that has changed. I have changed."

Nora closed her eyes, and tears streaked down her cheeks.

"What's wrong, Nora? Did I say something wrong? I thought you would be happy for me. Isn't that what you wanted? For me to acknowledge God?"

She looked up, pain obvious on her face. "I am happy for you, Gage," she said, sniffing. "I truly am. I mean that. But . . ."

"What? I have come back to offer you forgiveness . . . and to tell you that . . ."

Gage took a deep breath. "And to tell you that I love you. I have never stopped loving you."

Nora gently sobbed in response.

"What is it, Nora? What's wrong? I know there isn't another man. Charles says you hardly ever leave your apartment except to come to the theater. What is it then? Why are you crying?"

He knelt beside her and took her hand. She allowed him to hold it for an instant, then spun away from him.

"Don't," she called out.

"Don't what?" Gage implored.

"You cannot be here. You can't. You can't touch me—ever again."

"But I love you. I may not have said it often enough before, but I do. The past is past. We need not think of it again."

She pivoted back around. Her eyes were red and swollen."I am not the person you loved. I destroyed your family. I have destroyed my family. I know my mother sits in her lonely room, never leaving, never showing her face. My father is a broken man. My family is as good as dead. None of that would have happened if it had not been for me."

Gage took her arms again and turned her to face him. "It was not you—it was Walton. His was the evil that caused all this. It was him, not you."

"No, that's not true. It was me. It was my fault. It was my fault for falling in love with a man who didn't know God. My parents begged me never to look outside my faith for a man. I disobeyed them—and God. I caused it. This has been my punishment."

Gage stood back, not knowing what to say, not knowing any argument that might be effective.

"And even if it wasn't my fault," she continued, sobbing, "then it would be the sins of my father visited on me. Evil will have evil done, Gage. There is no escape for me."

"But I love you," he finally whispered.

"It's not enough to save me." Nora choked out her reply. "You can't see me again. I won't let you."

"But, Nora . . . I love you."

"And if you try to see me," she said, wiping her tears with the palm of her hand, "I will leave and you will never find me. I mean this, Gage. You must leave now and never return. I have received what I deserve. No man can want me after the evil I have caused. No man alive. Now go."

And with that she forced him from her dressing room. From the darkened hall, Gage heard the sound of the lock being turned in the door, and Nora's soft, full sobs from within.

CHAPTER TWENTY-TWO

San Francisco, California
March 1852

The road back to Monterey was long and lonely. A chilled wind blew in off the ocean and Gage trembled at times, the cold clattering against his bones. As the horse plodded south, Gage turned up the collar of his coat. He stared only at the few yards of road in front of the horse.

He had wanted to break down the door to Nora's dressing room. He had wanted to shake her, then hold her in his arms until her pain left. He had wanted to scream at the decisions that brought them both to places of sorrow.

But in his heart, God was molding and moving, and Gage was very unsure of what might be appropriate and what might not.

Do I force the truth of my feelings on her? Is that enough? Is that something God would have me do? his thoughts cried out.

He had stood outside the darkened theater for hours, his thoughts in a dull throb, not even knowing what needed to be decided. In the end, he had turned away and headed home.

If she says she will leave, then do I not believe her? If she says that we

*can never be together again, am I not bound by the honor of a gentleman
. . . and now a Christian, to honor her words?*

The joy in his soul over his newfound faith was offset by the pain
and hurt in his heart over Nora's decision.

❦

Monterey, California

Gage arrived at his home near midnight. Rain sleeted down on the
stones of the front walk. The stones on the broad front walk glistened.

He tossed his wet coat over a chair and stood by the fire, holding
his hands to the flame.

"Mr. Davis, you are home."

He turned and smiled at Rosala. She was an enthusiastic woman
who bustled about the house with an organized, cheerful demeanor.

"I am. Thank you for the fire. It has been a wet ride back."

"Sí. Spring here can be colder than winter. A fire is a good thing."

He attempted a smile.

"You are sad, Mr. Davis?" the woman asked softly.

"Tired, Rosala."

She peered at him closely. "No, you are sad. Tired and home
brings smile. Sad brings dark cloud in eyes." She rubbed her hands
together as if worried. "Is it that woman?"

Does everyone know of my personal life? Gage asked himself.

"And what has Pastor Kenyon told you?" he asked her.

"He say nothing. Rosala can see it in your face. Only woman
cause the pain here and here," she said pointing at her heart first,
then her head. "No pain like it."

Gage was too tired to argue. He offered a weary smile and nodded. "Rosala, I know it's late, but is there anything in the kitchen?"

"Ah, food. Rosala knows that food will help your discomfort.
Come, I will make you a meal. You will forget pain for a little bit."

Gage ate for an hour and listened as Rosala chattered on, half in
English and half in Spanish. Without trying, Gage began to

understand most of what she said, regardless of her choice of words. She told him of her journey here from Mexico and the loss of her husband. She spoke of her son who remained in Mexico.

"Have you heard from him recently? What is he doing?"

She crossed herself. "Not for two years. He is a fisherman."

"Two years? You must miss him."

She nodded. "But he is always in my heart. I go to mission in Santa Cruz, and I light candles for him. He is never far from my heart. Love is that. No matter the miles or the years. He is always in my heart."

Gage picked up a slice of roast beef and slowly chewed.

◦⟿⟾◦

"Honestly, Gage, I have never mentioned Nora to another soul in California. If Rosala said she saw it in your eyes, then you can believe that."

Gage narrowed his stare.

"I am telling you the truth," Pastor Kenyon pleaded. "I would not be much value to God if I repeated confidences, now would I?"

Gage shrugged. "It just seemed too great a coincidence, that's all."

"I can't say that I understand why Nora behaved the way she did. I would have thought your coming to God would have caused great celebration. I know my soul is lighter today because of it."

Gage held his palms up. "She said she was happy for me—but that it didn't change things. I have to believe there is no future for us—regardless of what I might say or do."

Pastor Kenyon put his hand to his chin thoughtfully. "Gage, I am at a loss on how to counsel you. I do believe that we are to honor other people's requests. You always said you were not ready to make a choice for God—and I felt as if I had to honor that. Would you have responded if I tried to force you to make the decision?"

"No. I would have pushed you away. I would have stopped visiting."

"Then is Nora's choice any more difficult to understand?"

Gage gazed out over his store, watching as a trio of prospectors carefully examined a gold sluice.

"No, John, I guess it isn't."

He turned to the pastor. "But what would God want me to do? I thought when I made this step of faith that God would clear up these sorts of matters. I thought if I gave my soul to God, then he would tell me what to do."

Pastor Kenyon shrugged. "He does sometimes, but . . ."

"But what?"

"But other times, he doesn't."

Frustrated, Gage threw his hands in the air.

"Gage, I know what you face is difficult. But you have to wait on God. He is not like the gypsies who tell your 'fate' for a dollar on demand. Pray to him. Ponder these things in your heart. He will nudge you in the right direction."

Gage sank back to his stool behind the counter.

"I don't want a nudge, John. I want an answer—an answer that I can see."

⁕

That evening, Gage sat alone on the open veranda of his home. Rosala had been right. Some days spring in Monterey felt colder than the coldest New England winter with the damp chewing at the very marrow of a man. Other days, like this one, were as balmy as the gentlest summer evening on Boston's Back Bay.

Gage sipped a glass of sweet lemonade. It pleased him that lemon trees grew on the hillside behind his house, and that he could simply stroll out and pick some of the fruit. As the sun settled, a quartet of boats slipped away from the piers, heading out to fish in the golden twilight. He heard the echo of a shout.

Is that Portuguese?

A group of Portuguese fishermen had arrived in town several months ago.

Monterey is becoming a most cosmopolitan village, he thought with a smile.

He took a long sip, then opened a gray ledger. He turned several pages. The ledger was his master record, a combination of all his varied interests. Month by month he charted his savings and holdings in gold and currency. He ran his finger down the first column, halted at the last entry, and smiled.

Not counting the actual assets of his investments—the land and buildings and inventory—but just the actual cash on reserve in his bank, Gage would be considered an extremely wealthy man. He was not near the level of his father's wealth, for certain, but then, not many were. If compared to everyone else in the state of California, Gage would no doubt be in the top twenty wealthiest men, if not a member of the top ten.

As he stared at the number, his smile began to fade. True, the money brought him all manner of privilege and luxury and freedom from want, but it had not brought peace to his soul or heart.

He looked back into his home. Lanterns were lit, and the fire in the main hall issued a warming glow. While he enjoyed it, Gage also realized that he had been just as happy, if not more so, when he had lived above the store in those three small rooms.

He studied the number again. Then he lifted the ledger and removed two slips of paper. They were blank bank drafts. Drawing the pen and ink close, he began to write.

Gage enjoyed the faint scratching sounds the nib made on the heavy paper. The first draft was made out to Pastor John Kenyon. The second draft was made out to Joshua Quittner. Both were for very large sums of money. The amount would see to it that proper churches could be built, with hymnals and organs and stoves and even a stained-glass window or two, with more than enough left over to fund a pastor's salary for a decade.

He blew on his signature, snugged the bank drafts into envelopes, and addressed them. He did not include a note, but simply wrote on the corner of the checks, "For God's work."

He placed both envelopes on the table in the front hall. He would give them to a messenger in the morning.

I suspect I shouldn't feel smug or proud . . . but I do a little. Nevertheless, I do hope God will be pleased and the money will be used well.

An hour after Gage sent his two letters off, a messenger tapped at the front door to his home. He handed Gage two letters. One bore the scrawled writing of Jamison Pike. The postmark indicated it had been mailed from Morocco, a country that Gage thought was in Africa. He eagerly tore it open.

> *Casablanca, Morocco*
> *January 4, 1852*

Dear Gage,

Greetings from the land of the Sallee pirates.

I have officially been asked to leave Marrakesh. It seems I have offended some sultan by not paying the proper respect. These Berbers have absolutely no sense of humor. I left under cover of darkness and wrapped head to foot in tunics and turbans.

It is a most amazing land and people.

I am now in Casablanca, an exotic, romantic, and quite dangerous port. Every man carries a dagger at his waist and none seems the least bit hesitant to use it.

The World *has been kind enough to continue to pay me while I explore the world, turning in the odd story or two every so often. To be paid for having adventures seems much like a college prank–but so far no one has quite caught on to my ploy.*

Perhaps you have heard that my first book–a retelling of my journey to California–has been published and is selling quite well. The folks in New York love tales of the frontier with savage Indians and buffaloes and daring exploits. In truth, every person I have met in Europe is just as enthralled with the North American red men. So I oblige them and tell my tales. A man could earn a very handsome living by having just one great story–and telling it over and over again.

But it remains the task of the poor reader or listener to determine what is fact and what is fiction.

I have heard from Hannah. She is full of surprises. She has persevered and done what we all thought impossible. I have written her that she and I will celebrate upon my return to civilization.

Just one more word on Hannah–I do not consider that all is lost.

Have you heard from Joshua? How is he faring in California? All I truly know is that he left Ohio lured by the treasure of gold! Has he found it? Is he a rich man?

And how are you, my friend? Please write to me in care of the World. *I so miss our days at the Destiny. I suspect we all do. And in a curious way I miss the cynical young man that I used to be. I am still most cynical– except in my letters–but I am no longer a callow youth.*

All my regards,
J. Pike

Gage read the letter twice and then a third time.

What does he mean about Hannah? Is she a doctor? Has she married? Does Jamison carry a torch for her as well? Joshua was right–the man writes the most infuriatingly cryptic letters I have ever read.

He looked at the second letter. It was from Edgar.

New York City
February 5, 1852

Dear Sir,

It is with great regret that I must decline your most generous offer of employment. It was not an easy decision, but I do not think I would fare well on a journey west–even if I were to believe only a trifling of Mr. Pike's book. I am not well suited to such arduous activities such as fighting off a band of buffaloes and savages. And I must consider my sister in Albany as well. She depends on me for support, and I would not feel right abandoning her.

And staying in New York allows me to maintain daily contact with your father. Walton has not been miserly in his care. There are doctors and nurses and full-time servants about him at all times. Yet, he has become even more unresponsive. I mention your name, and occasionally I see a spark of something in his eyes. Then it so quickly vanishes.

Walton continues to manage Davis Enterprises with skill and has

363

continued to turn profits. I cannot abide with his tactics, but that is not my concern.

Your mother is quite busy with a great many social obligations.

Sir, I hesitate to write of things of a personal nature, but I have greatly missed being in your employ. Our relationship did expand past what might be considered proper.

Perhaps . . . in the future, we may see each other again. I would like that.

Again, my deepest regrets over having to respond in a negative manner. I am afraid that I am not a true pioneer. But then, God did not call us all to be pioneers.

In your debt,
Edgar Hethold

Gage wandered about his house that morning without purpose to his steps. By midmorning he found himself on the upper veranda again, simply staring out at the blue water. From below him came the sound of knocking. He leaned over the edge to look.

"Carty!" he called out. "I didn't expect you back until the end of the month."

Carty waved up at Gage. "I got restless. Didn't see any new ships in San Diego, so I had to leave. Keep moving, you know."

"Come in—let's talk."

Rosala shouted from the first floor, "Mr. Davis, Mr. Carty is here!"

Gage smiled. *Such an announcement style would never be acceptable in New York.*

In the span of a few minutes, Rosala had laid out a full lunch for both men. Carty leaned over the tray of food and breathed in deeply. "Rosala, this smells delicious. I am honored by your work."

She almost blushed. Gage knew she considered Carty a personal success story since his added pounds and fuller face were silent testimony to her skill at cooking.

"I just got back from talking with Pastor Kenyon," Carty explained, "and while he's a good man, he didn't offer anything as tempting as this."

Rosala giggled. "You eat, Mr. Carty. You, too, Mr. Davis. You finish and I bring more."

Carty never had to be offered a meal a second time. He sat in a chair and began to heap rice and beans and meat onto his plate.

"I hear that you finally stopped fooling God, Mr. Davis. That's very good news. Pastor Kenyon didn't say so, but I think he's telling God that it was pretty much all his own doing."

Gage laughed at Carty's observation. "I thought he might."

"But don't you tell him I said that. He's a good man."

Gage nodded. Virtually everyone in town, when mentioning Pastor Kenyon's name, invariably added "and he's a good man."

"I won't say a word, Carty."

Gage only nibbled at the food. After finishing off his third plate, Carty sat back and sighed. "You have a wonderful cook in Rosala, Gage. Ain't nothing I tasted anywhere else on the coast comes close to her touch. Wish I could stay here longer each time."

Gage eyed his friend and partner. "You can, Carty. You don't have to worry about intercepting ships anymore. I would say nearly every ship's captain knows to make Monterey a regular stop. Plus, we have our own vessels. You don't have to keep moving."

"Oh, I know I don't have to travel anymore, Mr. Davis. I knew that a long time ago."

"Then why don't you stop? You have enough money to build a nice place here. Watch the ships come in. Go fishing. Relax."

"But I can't, Mr. Davis. I stop, and I get afraid my old demons will catch up."

Gage folded his hands. "But didn't you say God was all-powerful? Seems he could handle it."

Carty brightened. "Oh, God can handle it, Mr. Davis. But I'm not sure I can. Every day I don't touch liquor is sort of a miracle to me. Every day I ask God to keep me from finding a bottle. And he has done it. But I ain't a strong man on my own. I still hear that bottle. It's faint, but I hear it. I stop for a few days, and the voices get stronger. And I don't want to be tempting God with my weakness. He can do anything he wants, I know that, but I know I can't. So I made a bargain with God. I keep moving, he helps me keep away from the drink, and since I'm traveling, I talk to a lot of people about God. I feel like the apostle Paul from the Bible at times—always in a strange room, always telling strangers about God."

"And you'll never stop?" Gage asked.

"Maybe when I get real old. Maybe. But I like my life now. I like it a lot."

Gage stood and began to pace.

"And you, Mr. Davis—I know you have God's peace now. But what about your life? I asked Pastor Kenyon about that woman in San Francisco, but he wouldn't tell me a thing. I got a feeling things aren't settled."

"Does everyone know about Nora?" Gage asked, perturbed.

"Nora? That her name? Truth be told, Mr. Davis, I don't think anyone knows much of her. You don't do a lot of sharing. I think we all figured it out—you being moody like this every so often. That only happens 'cause of a woman."

"But, Carty, how would you know that? Have you ever been in love?"

He shook his head. "Not really. But it don't take being stung by a bee to know that it hurts. People around you can tell. And I know that women been confusing men for a number of years now. Or is that the other way around?" Carty grinned. "I'm not the one to be wagering my money on that, Mr. Davis. But you got to do what your heart tells you to do."

"And you're sure of that?"

"Yep. Look at me. Maybe the Bible says that I can stop drinking just by faith alone. Maybe I don't have all the faith I need—'cause in my heart, I know I got to keep moving. So if that woman has a hold of your heart, you need to get matters straight between her and you. Sounds like you left things undone. If your heart is saying that you love that woman, you got to tell her again. You got to."

Gage tilted his head. "And you got all that from how I look? Pastor Kenyon didn't say one word to you?"

Carty offered a sly smile in reply. "I'm not saying more than I said, Mr. Davis."

Gage laughed.

"But you got to know the truth when you hear the truth," Carty added. "Go and get it settled. Neither of us is getting younger."

"I'll think about it, Carty. I promise." Gage clapped him on the shoulder. "And thanks for being a friend."

❦

San Francisco, California

Gage took another shaky breath. For the past half-hour he had stared, thinking, at the nameplate on the door: N. WILKES.

She cannot tell me whom I can love and whom I can't. She is not at fault. Her father sinned and his sin would be found out regardless of what Nora had done or did not do. And I am sure God would not punish her entire family because she and I had a relationship. Didn't what she do help open my eyes to God? Without her, I never would have made that decision.

He breathed in again.

So I have to do this. I have to see her again. She has to listen to me.

He lifted his hand, held it at the door, then dropped it again. He shut his eyes tight, then at last, tapped on the door. His knuckles on the wood sounded so very loud.

He held his breath and waited. From behind the door, he heard a faint rustling. He stared at the doorknob. It slowly turned. The door opened and there stood Nora.

From behind, the sun streamed in and lit her dark hair like an auburn halo about her face and shoulders. Her eyes widened.

"Gage . . . ," she whispered.

"I know you said we should never meet again. I know that. But I had to see you again, Nora. I have to talk with you."

He had rehearsed that speech a thousand times on his journey north and had tried out a thousand variations.

Her eyes looked to the door first, then to her hand, still on the doorknob, then they found Gage's eyes. He thought he saw a softness there, a softness he had not seen before.

"Gage . . . I . . ."

"Please let me come in. I must talk with you."

With some hesitation, she backed up and Gage stepped in.

He could see the entire apartment from where he stood. The door opened onto a sitting room, with a red velvet couch facing away from the floor-to-ceiling windows. The windows overlooked the bay. He could see a thin sliver of water between two larger buildings down the block.

A few books and a Bible lay on the table by the sofa. On either side were small tables and kerosene lamps with crystal teardrops encircling their shades.

To the right was a room of similar minuscule size, separated by a thick, red velvet curtain. He could see a single four-poster bed covered in a simple cotton counterpane. Except for that, the room was devoid of personality, as if the occupant wanted to leave no record of being or existing. The walls were bare plaster. There were no pictures or flowers, nor any item of a feminine nature.

"Please . . . sit down."

Nora's words resounded of defeat and resignation.

"I could offer you something to drink," she said with a slight rise in her voice. "There is a small stand around the corner that sells all manner of food and drink. Would you like something?"

Gage sat and shook his head no. "I don't think I could eat or drink anything," he offered cheerfully. "I have been too nervous all day."

Nora perched on the far end of the sofa, as far away from him as she could get without finding another location.

She folded her hands in her lap, studied him for a minute, then lowered her eyes. Gage sat staring at her profile for several silent seconds.

How wondrously beautiful she is, he thought. *It is not that I am recalling past happiness through distorted eyes. She is truly breathtakingly beautiful.*

His eyes, as if thirsting for such beauty, traced the elegant rise of her throat, her skin like ivory, her full lips, her deep, expressive eyes, the wonderful cascade of her hair.

"Nora," he whispered. "Nora, I have not thought of much else since I came to you with news of my salvation. It is true that I expected such news to be met with an entirely different outcome than what occurred. Yet I hold no animosity or anger—just confusion."

Nora did not raise her head or speak.

Relieved he had practiced this speech well, Gage continued. "I offered you forgiveness. I know that when I did at first, it was done with the wrong intentions. And you were right to refuse me. You were."

"But, Gage . . . ," she said, her voice barely audible, "I . . ."

"No, I must finish, or I will lose my nerve. . . . I have thought of little else these past days. I have sought out wise counsel from men of God. I have prayed about this matter, which is a most foreign activity for me. And as best as I can offer, this is from my heart, without taint of anger or pride or any motive not of God's own acceptance."

Nora glanced up, a tear in her eye.

"I love you, Nora. I have from the first day I met you. You have my heart totally and completely. Yes, I was hurt when all the unpleasantness transpired. But the past is past. There is nothing that either of us can do to change it. We both must make a clean start. That is what California has offered us. That is what God has offered us. Who else could author such a serendipitous reunion? Nora, I love you. Let us forget everything until this moment. Please, Nora. This is my life that you hold in your hands."

Gage searched her eyes. His speech had not gone exactly as he anticipated. He spoke longer than he had rehearsed. He was unsure if he had said too much or too little.

"Gage, I am so moved . . . ," she said. Her words were like velvet covered in snow.

She sniffed, turned to him, opened her arms, and threw herself into his waiting embrace. He drew her close and for a long moment, neither spoke nor moved. He could feel her beating heart, as he was sure she could feel his.

In that wonderful moment, the world at last seemed right and perfect and sound again. And in her gentle arms, Gage allowed his heart to relax.

After what seemed a lifetime had passed, he leaned back and gazed tenderly into her eyes, then slowly, ever so slowly, bent forward to taste the sweet wine of her lips.

Gage whistled as he bounded up the stairs. He carried a bouquet of the most expensive flowers he could find. He was at last a happy man again.

He had left Nora, late that previous day. Neither had spoken a great deal. They simply held each other and looked for hours into each other's eyes. As he heard the tower bell toll ten, Gage rose and said he would let her retire for the night.

"But on the morrow, I will return, and we shall take up where we left off. I promise you, Nora Wilkes. I have lost you once—and I shall never lose you again."

She smiled, kissed him one last time good night, and closed the door. He had waited until it latched and locked, then he had skipped out into the darkness and the fog.

Now as he climbed the stairs, he saw shadows washing the wall before him. He heard angry voices. He bounded up the last steps two at a time. The door to Nora's apartment stood open. Framed in the sunlight pouring through was a tall figure with a cane.

"There you are!" shouted Charles Thornton. He waved a flapping piece of paper in his hand. "What have you done? Do you want to kill me? If so, take a bullet and end my days, but do not torment me! You are a torturer, Gage Davis, and if you were not my partner, I would hire someone to thrash you within an inch of your pitiful existence! Traitor! Scalawag!"

Charles spun about on the narrow landing, gesturing and flailing about.

"What happened?" Gage shouted. "What's the matter? Where is Nora?"

"As if you didn't know—you evil Lothario!"

"I don't know! Tell me—is there foul play? Where is she? What happened? Tell me now!"

"You know all too well, I am sure," Charles shouted, then thrust the paper he held in his right hand at Gage. "Read this. It explains it all."

Gage took it as Charles moaned, "I am ruined. It will be the death of me."

The note was written by Nora. Gage could tell from the graceful strokes.

March 21, 1852

Dear Gage,

I was wrong. I do not wish to hurt you, but I do not deserve your love. I deserve no man's love—only pity and scorn. I cannot allow you to waste your heart on a wicked, terrible woman as myself. God seeks to punish wrongdoers. He must punish me.

I have left San Francisco at dawn. Do not attempt to find me. I will only cause you more pain.

I do not deserve you, Gage. I am happy for your newfound faith. I will have no part in the destruction of one of God's children.

Forgive me for all I have done.

Nora

Gage lowered the note, his face marked with pain.

"I suspect you were only thinking of yourself." Charles taunted. "You caused her to run off!"

Gage jumped at Charles, grabbed him by the lapels, and jerked him forward. Charles dropped his cane and blanched white.

"I knew nothing of this, you fool. I did not intend this outcome."

Charles squirmed free. "Then there is no need to resort to violence."

Gage turned and thundered down the hall to the steps. "When was high tide?" he shouted.

"High tide? Why on earth did you ask that?"

Gage shouted back, "Do you know?"

Charles shrugged. "Do I look like a sailor?"

Gage ran towards the docks.

❧ ❧ ❧ ❧

High tide had been at early dawn. Gage knew Nora would not run off overland. That would make her much too easy to find. A fast horse, a few riders, and anyone could be stopped. So she must have found a ship sailing that morning. But no matter the conveyance, the result was the same: Nora Wilkes had slipped out of his life again.

But this time, I shall fight for the woman I love. She is done punishing herself. God has forgiven her as I have. She will have to understand that.

On the log sheet posted at the harbormaster's office, Gage slid his finger down until he found the date. He winced. The *Kathryne Hawkes* sailed from the cold waters of the bay at dawn, headed west to the Sandwich Islands.

❧ ❧ ❧ ❧

By nightfall of that same day, Gage had bought a full ship, complete with cargo.

"You don't even want to know what we got in the holds?" the captain asked.

"Will the material spoil or explode?" Gage asked as he wrote out the bank draft.

The captain scratched his head. "No, I reckon it won't."

"Then I don't care," Gage replied. "Just tell me we will be ready to sail west at dawn."

The captain looked at the size of the draft. "We'll be ready, sir. We will all be ready."

Chapter Twenty-Three

Pacific Ocean
March 22, 1852

Gage stood in the bow of the ship and braced himself from the swells with a firm grip on either gunwale. A strong, warm wind filled the sails. The ship pitched into the waves, a salty spray exploding as the vessel made its way west. The winds were strong indeed. The captain claimed that if the breezes held, they might make landfall in less than three weeks' time.

He breathed in deeply, trying to clear all the troubling thoughts from his mind.

***

March 28, 1852

During the voyage Gage paced about the ship as best he could in the rolling seas, holding to rope and rail. Now he bravely managed a weak smile, thinking that his anxiety had held any sea-caused illness at bay. Every morning at dawn, and at four-hour intervals during the day, he borrowed the captain's telescope and scanned the horizon for any sighting of a sail.

"You'll not find any hint of canvas out there," the captain had warned. "The sea is a sight bigger than any man might imagine—and there are a thousand paths a ship might take to reach these islands. Take patience, Mr. Davis. We'll get there fine. You'll find her all right. There ain't many places for a woman to hide—especially one so beautiful as Miss Wilkes."

It seemed that every sailor who stopped at San Francisco knew of Miss Wilkes and had attended at least one of her performances.

Every day Gage had returned the telescope to the captain, frustrated and more impatient.

"Can we throw the cargo overboard?" Gage asked after one day of only modest winds. "Wouldn't that improve our speed?"

The captain looked aghast at the suggestion. "It might, Mr. Davis, by a day or two, but to throw good items overboard seems an affront to all that's right and proper. I know you might have money, sir, but no one should squander it like that."

But when he scrutinized Gage, the captain's tough visage softened. "This woman truly has your heart, doesn't she?"

"She does. I cannot bear the thought of missing her by a single day. What occurs if she simply makes a short stop and continues west?"

The captain offered his reassurances. "She won't. A long voyage like this and even them tough old salts need a day or two on firm ground. And there ain't that many ships in and out of where we're going. Most just head back and forth between San Francisco and there."

"But don't a lot of ships head farther west? Don't they sail to the Orient from there?"

"Some do. Not many. Ain't a good season to be sailing that way. Weather ain't good until fall. Now over on the island they call *Maui* is a whaling port—there's always a lot of ships in and out of there. But most of them ships come from Nantucket and won't be heading home till after whaling season. So I suggest you relax a bit, Mr. Davis. You got at least a fortnight or so till she could even book passage on another ship."

Gage visibly relaxed. The captain scratched his chin. "I know it ain't proper to be asking an owner this question. . . ."

Gage had heard the question in his mind a thousand times. "You want to know why she's running, right?" he asked. "You want to know why I'm obsessed with seeing her again? You want to know why she has run from me like a rabbit runs from a fox?"

"The questions do come to mind, Mr. Davis. I mean, the crew has asked me—on the side, of course—and never meaning no disrespect, sir. You know that some of these old-timers have seen a lot of odd things in their day—but they ain't seen nothing like this. A man buying a boat with hard cash on the barrelhead—just to chase down a woman."

"Have they seen her? You said a lot of them had. Have you?"

The captain considered the question, then rubbed his chin harder. "Well . . . that does explain a lot, I grant you. I ain't never seen a woman quite as fetching as Miss Wilkes, that be sure. But the fact that she's running so far has got some of us perplexed. I mean . . . you ain't done nothing immoral or illegal? I mean, is the woman scared of you and just trying to get away? I suspect I should have asked you this before we pulled anchor, but I plumb didn't give it any thought till a few days ago. I may be a good thinker, but I don't think all that fast."

Gage tried not to smile.

"It's nothing like that, Captain. I assure you of that. The men don't have to worry about being involved in something that God would look askance upon. And God could be my witness on that. But this is a long, personal story. Miss Wilkes and I were in love. And that was the truth. But she did something to me that caused me a great deal of pain. Now she thinks I can't forgive her for it. But I can. I have," Gage said firmly, the pain of losing her evident in his eyes.

"I pride myself on being a good judge of men, Mr. Davis. But you had me tossed about like a longboat in a hurricane. Now my heart says to trust you. You say all is well—then I suspect I believe you. And that's good enough for me, Mr. Davis. I mean, even if you were doing something that the good Lord might think wrong—well, we're a bit of a ways into this voyage. And I suspect that if God wants you to find Miss Wilkes, then you will. If he's against it, then I guess no power on earth will help you."

❦

Having no official duties on board, Gage spent his time composing voluminous letters to Carty Todd, Charles Thornton, and Thomas Lee, his clerk in Monterey. Before the ship sailed, he penned each man a short letter, stating that since he might be gone for several months, they would now be officially in charge. Carty would handle all purchasing and shipping. Charles would handle all items related to the theater and touring troupes. Thomas would handle all matters related to the retail operations.

Gage had no doubt that each man was honorable and skilled, but as the miles slipped under the heel, he grew more anxious. Once reaching the islands, Gage expected to quickly find a ship headed back to San Francisco. He began to draft pages and pages of advice, instructions, counsel, and coaching to the three men.

As he finished one aspect of business, another would come to mind, and he would begin again. When the pages began to number in the hundreds, Gage considered using the material to craft an instructional book on business matters. He hoped that the port of Honolulu would include a printing firm.

"The port was not much more than a few shanties, taverns, and brothels," the captain advised, "but I haven't been back in nearly five years. A lot could have changed."

❦

April 6, 1852

The winds had been weak all day. As dusk approached, the breeze had nearly died. Gage turned towards the west. He listened. There was no longer the hiss of wind cutting across the waves—just a gentle lap of water to the bow.

"Not a good sign, Mr. Davis," the captain said. "If the winds don't pick up by sunset, we may be in for a touch of the doldrums."

"Is such weather to be expected?"

The captain shrugged. "Haven't been this way in a while. And when I made the route, it was a different season. If the winds die off at dark, then I think we'll be floating awhile."

Gage sat in the bow of the ship, his face turned to the west and his destination. The sun was an hour above the horizon. Golds and reds glinted off the calm waters.

Dear Lord, he prayed, *I am still so unsure of how to go about this matter of praying. It seems so wrong to simply talk to you. But I am not a man who can sprinkle my thoughts with* thees *and* thous, *although I am afraid that I should.*

I am perplexed by all that is happening and has happened. I have taken Carty's advice and followed my heart. I am not sure I have ever truly done that before. I followed in my father's footsteps, for that path was ordained for me. Gold flowed into my hands, and I felt that was my destiny. I was to be rich—and powerful. And then, as I stood astride the world like a golden Colossus, my wealth and status were torn from my hands. I fell from the heights like Icarus foolishly seeking the heavens.

And my pursuit only brought pain.

Was that you, God? Did you allow such events to occur to teach me? If so, it was a lesson I failed to grasp.

I followed the path to California and then, in spite of things, I once again find my pockets filled with gold. I once again have Nora in my arms, and she disappears like a wisp. Has she once again fled because I am rich? What must I do to reclaim my heart?

If there is a lesson, Lord, help me learn it. If it means that my fortune is to be given away, then so be it. I know I have learned that riches offer no guarantee of happiness.

Lord, I am but a babe. Help me find the way. Help me reach the islands in time. Help me assure Nora that she is indeed forgiven.

And as Gage silently moved his lips, he felt a freshness in the air and a gust of cooler wind. From behind the slap of canvas filled with a breeze, rope and wood groaned. Then the ship, almost imperceptibly at first, began to angle, and within minutes, began to race the wind.

Thank you, Lord. Thank you.

Hawaii
April 16, 1852

"There it is!" the captain shouted. "That's the island of Oahu."

From various spots on the ship, men ran to the gunwales. They offered a cheer. After weeks at sea, finding landfall was always a heartening experience, even to the most seasoned sailor.

"The winds have been most kind to us, Mr. Davis," he said. "Almost as if the heavens wanted us to make the crossing in good time."

Gage heard little of the captain's words. His eyes were fixed on the green slip of land off in the distance. As soon as it came into view, his heartbeat quickened and his face flushed.

"We'll see Makapuu Point first," the captain said. "They talked of placing a lighthouse there, but I wager no one has built it yet. Then we round that to the south and set a course to Diamond Head. Then it's a short slip to the harbor and the East Loch. We should be tied up in a few hours."

Gage could not wait until the ropes were secured. He jumped from the deck onto the pier and began to run down the wooden walkways. A jumble of ships lay by piers and on anchor. The *Kathryne Hawkes* had not come into view, and Gage began to grow exceedingly worried.

Suppose they changed plans? Suppose they headed to Vancouver first . . . or back east? It has been known to happen. What if they continued sailing and simply didn't stop?

He grabbed the first sailor he saw.

"The harbormaster—where is he?"

The sailor responded with a grunt, pointing down the lane to a small frame building nearly hidden by palms. He took off at a run. He scarcely looked left or right.

"The *Kathryne Hawkes*. Did she put in? Where is she?" Gage shouted even before he yanked the door open to the harbormaster's office.

"Kathryne who? This ain't the brothel, sailor. That's down at the other end of the docks. You can't miss it. This is the office of the harbormaster."

Gage stood at the man's desk, his hands flat against the wood. "I'm not looking for a woman . . . I'm looking for the *Kathryne Hawkes*."

The harbormaster, a short man, had a schoolteacher's air about him. "Like I said—the brothel's that way," he replied in a loud voice, pointing over Gage's shoulder.

"No, you fool. Listen very carefully to me," Gage shouted. "I am looking for a ship. The ship is called the *Kathryne Hawkes*. She sailed out of San Francisco about three weeks ago."

"Well, why didn't you say you were looking for a ship? You go on and on about women first, and you got me and everything else flummoxed."

He bent to a large ledger, placed a finger at the top end of a narrow column, and slowly slid his finger down the page. As he did, he repeated every ship's name on the list.

"Let's see . . . there's the *Ashland Princess, Isle of Wright, Nantucket Fog, Queen's Fancy, Rose and Arms, Denizen's, Lord of the Sea, Royal, Baltimore Pride, Scarlet's Rose* . . . well, I don't see any *Kathryne Hawkes*."

I have come all this way for naught. Gage's world began to collapse about him. He closed his eyes. His heart sank. It was all he could do to maintain breath to his lungs.

"Oh, now that's a fool for you," the harbormaster muttered. Then he brightened. "I was looking at the wrong page. Sorry."

Gage snapped to attention.

"Yes, there she is–the *Kathryne Hawkes*–out of San Francisco. A hold full of nails and flour, she says. Good cargo, I should say. It'll fetch a pretty penny here, with all the building going on."

Thank you, Lord.

"Where is she? What pier?"

The little man looked up, peering over his nose. "Why she ain't here. She sailed yesterday."

Gage had never felt such an odd mixture of emotions. He wanted to collapse on the floor, exhausted and broken. He wanted to tighten his fist and smash the harbormaster's nose. He wanted to run from the building, screaming in anger and frustration. But instead, he said, holding his voice calm, "How long ago did she sail?"

The harbormaster consulted the ledger again. "Just yesterday morning, I have written down here."

"How long was she here?"

"Just a day. Took on water and left."

Gage leaned closer. "What? That's all? Just water?"

The harbormaster scratched his head, then closed his ledger.

"Well, the ship was just headed for Lahaina. That's the whaling port over on Maui. Then they turn around and head back to California. At least that's what the captain told me. And to get to Maui is only a few days' sail, if that. No need to take on more than water, I reckon."

Before the harbormaster was halfway through his explanation, the door had slammed shut.

<hr />

"You'll get me to Lahaina by sunrise?" Gage queried anxiously.

The dark skinned man nodded. He was naked to the waist and dressed in a garment that looked, for all intent and purpose, like a dress. The entire crew of twelve was outfitted in the same manner.

"Moon rise soon. We sail. By sunrise we at Lahaina."

Gage examined the long, wooden, canoelike boat. Attached to one side were two long poles and at their end was a float.

Gage's ship captain shrugged. "I couldn't get you there that quickly, Mr. Davis. I couldn't be sailing these waters by moonlight, that be a certainty. This fellow says he can do it, and I have no reason to doubt him. Besides, only a fool would risk his life for a few gold coins, don't you think?"

"All I know is that I have to get there–by tomorrow," Gage insisted.

"Then Godspeed. We'll wait here for the word. And don't worry about the cargo none. We'll handle all that for you."

"Thanks so much, Captain. I'm much obliged."

<hr />

April 17, 1852

Gage had been accustomed to being on the open seas in a large vessel with three masts of sails above him and a thick wall of oak between him and the deep, dark liquid that surrounded them. But this was so very different. Gage sat in the middle of the long canoe-shaped vessel. The twelve men sat in two rows about him. Each carried a paddle about five feet long, decorated with a series of intricate, carved designs.

The captain of the craft, or the chief, or whatever title he was, called out a cadence to the crew. The vessel leapt over the line of breakers, nosing through the water like some great sea beast. Gage had never heard the language before–a lyrical, musical sound, composed of soft beats and no rough utterances. It was as if the language imitated the sound of the sea and the gurgling of tidal pools.

The moon was an hour in the sky when the dark mass of land behind them disappeared into the darkness. The chief called out an order, the men shouldered their oars, and like dominoes, shifted from one side to the other, then resumed paddling, without allowing the vessel to slow even a breath.

The night was cloudless, and the moon a giant gold disk of ghostly light. Gage saw it reflected in the calm waters. From ahead, a fish broke the waters. One of the crew called to it, laughing. The rest hooted while their strokes continued. The speed of the craft was disarming. It was faster than any scull Gage had watched on the Back Bay.

The Harvard rowing team could take a lesson or two from these fellows, he thought with a smile. The wind rippled through his hair in a salty rush.

Again the chief called out, and each call was met with all dozen paddles as if a single unit.

Gage gazed up into the dark sky and the million stars and prayed. *Lord, let me not be a fool. Let me find Nora, and let me say all the proper words. Prepare her heart. Prepare mine.*

He closed his eyes and bowed his head.

If it be your will, Lord. If it be your will.

Amen.

❦

Gage felt the sunrise before he saw it. The water took on a new color, a color pushed up from the black depths. He stared down at the currents and eddies about the boat and no longer saw an inky color but a subtler shade of darkness, a gunmetal gray hint to the liquid.

He looked ahead of them. There at the far eastern horizon was the palest sliver of gold. The chief saw Gage's gesture and smiled. Then he pointed forward. "There. Maui. We see land as sun rises."

Gage strained to look. There was a slight rise to the horizon, a darker slip. It was land. His heart quickened.

They rounded the far western edge of the island as the sun brightened.

"We be there soon."

And within the hour the canoe slipped into the harbor crowded with the stench of whaling ships, and oily with a coating of melted blubber and ambergris. Gage pointed to an empty section of pier.

"There. That's good. I'll go ashore there."

Gage stood, steadied himself against a piling, then reached into his pocket. To do what these men had done was a feat he would have said was impossible a day earlier. They had paddled without stopping, all through the night, and made their destination as promised. Gage opened his palm. He held a dozen gold coins. It was a substantial amount of money. The crew all stood, and their eyes widened. One man moved to take a coin from Gage's hand. But the chief barked out a warning, and the man's hand snapped away as if burnt.

Then the chief smiled and took seven of the coins. He bowed and closed Gage's hand over the remaining coins.

"Not be greedy. Bible tells us. We not greedy. These coins enough."

And as Gage walked to the end of the dock, he watched as the crew turned the canoe around and began to paddle back out to sea.

The harbor was filled with the stench of decaying flesh and acrid barrels of oil squeezed from animal flesh. Gage wondered how any man could endure this hellish odor for more than a few days, knowing that whalers spent up to three years at sea, hunting the giant creatures.

As he made his way past the docks, the breezes began to carry the smells from him. He found the harbormaster sitting under a canopy of palm trees, hunched over a desk that had warped into a gentle curve.

"*Kathryne Hawkes?* That's her out in the harbor at far anchor. She's waiting to clear our customs and pay tariff before unloading."

"Did she set off any passengers?"

The man, not wearing a shirt, and burnished as a lobster, hulked down trying to recall the details. "There were a few. . . ." Then he brightened. "And one woman who looked as beautiful as a princess."

I have found her! Thank you, God.

"Where is she? Do you know where she went?"

The man scratched his stomach. "There ain't many places to stay here. There's Randolph's—down by the water. They got rooms, but . . . a woman like that. Well, she ain't one to stay at Randolph's. And then there is the Bull and Finch—but that place been booked solid since them Argentine fellows set up shop."

Gage danced nervously from foot to foot, waiting for the harbormaster to finish his musing and grace him with an answer.

"And then there's the Sprekle Inn. That might be the only place I wouldn't be afraid of falling asleep in. They say it's right respectable."

"Where is that? How do I get there?" Gage asked, his words impatient.

The man turned and pointed. "You head up that trail. About three miles. The place sets out by the sea. A big porch out front. You can't miss it. The road ends there, so you'll know when you get there for certain."

Gage nodded and was on his way, his steps hurrying into a fast trot.

In all the days that had passed since he sailed from California, throughout all the restless nights, Gage had pondered and considered and revised just what he might say to Nora if he were to see her again. He had devised a thousand greetings and imagined a thousand replies, and yet as his steps brought him closer to the inn, the words vanished from his thoughts.

The inn was as described. It was a rambling building with a massive porch wrapped around three sides and cantilevered over the surf and rocks below. The trail ended at the front steps. Gage leapt up the stairs and found the manager. Nora's room was the only one on the third floor. Soon Gage was once again standing, silent, in front of Nora's door.

He offered a short prayer, asking that God's will be accomplished. He bowed his head, let his heart calm, then tapped at the door.

From beyond there came a faint rustling. He heard her voice, but the words were muffled. She was saying something about the rent and being able to wait for another few days.

He tapped again.

There was silence.

Once more, a gentle tap, and then he heard the door being unlatched and saw the doorknob slowly turn. The latch undone, the door slipped open a crack. Gage stepped back.

Then the door swung open, not eagerly, but with hesitation. Nora had been staring at the floor as if in supplication. She looked up and saw Gage before her. Her eyes were as the moon on a summer night. Her right hand fluttered to her heart. Her left hand found her mouth and covered her shocked expression.

Gage stared into her eyes. For a minute he was afraid she might bolt as a wild mustang and charge off again, but while she wavered, she did not move.

From behind, Gage heard the tumble of seawater against the shore rocks.

Neither of them spoke.

A bird called off in the distance. A clatter of palm leaves lifted and shook in the breeze. There was a hint of sweetness in the air.

And neither of them spoke. Their eyes were focused on each other.

In the dining room, a waiter lifted a tray of china, its chiming clear like a porcelain bell.

Gage saw her eyes grow liquid with tears. Her lower lip, red and full, began to quiver, like the tremble of a newborn fawn.

Nora blinked her eyes. A single tear coursed down her cheek, on a damp journey over her white and flawless skin.

Gage, almost involuntarily, reached up and wiped away the tear.

The silence became deafening.

And then Nora closed her eyes and collapsed into Gage's open and welcoming arms.

"You . . . you . . . you have followed me," Nora said, when she could finally speak.

"I had no choice," he said. "To go on living, I had to follow you. I had to find you."

Gage had carried her, in a faint, to the bed in her cozy room. A gauze of curtains danced with the breeze. Gage knelt at the side of the bed and took her hand, stroked the softest skin he had ever touched.

"How did . . . how did you know?" she asked.

"It is a long story. But I believe God directed me here. Without him, I would never have found you."

"You followed me. You found me," she whispered, then swooned again, her head falling to the pillow, her face surrounded by a halo of her dark, cascading hair.

He stood and rushed to the kitchen, and in short order, demanded a pot of tea and a plate of sweets or sandwiches be brought to Miss Wilkes's room immediately.

He was back at her side before she regained her senses. She turned her head, and her eyes found Gage's. She offered him the smile of a saint. Gage smiled back, relief washing away the desperation in his eyes.

"I love you, Nora," he said as he took her hand.

She began to reply. Gage placed his finger upon her lips. "Do not speak. It is I who must speak first."

She was about to offer an objection, then she lowered her eyes and nodded.

"Nora, I have thought of nothing else on my journey here save you. I prepared a thousand arguments that I would use—and I believed that the sheer artistry of my logic would win your heart again."

He looked at her delicate hand in his.

"But now, kneeling at your side, I find all my well-rehearsed words to be filled with sound and fury and signifying nothing. I shall not offer you a speech but simply tell you of my heart."

He took a deep breath. "I forgive you, Nora. Your offense was minor. It was not you who caused my downfall—it was me. I was the one who sinned. I was the one who committed the transgressions. You have blamed yourself for a sin that I alone was responsible for. And if Walton drove you to be a witness—you were a witness to the truth."

Nora watched him as he spoke. And while Gage stared into her eyes, he could not divine her thoughts from her expression.

"Whatever the sins of your father or of me—they are not of consequence to you."

Nora sat up in bed and placed her hand on Gage's forearm. "But, Gage," she said timidly, "what of all the pain I have caused? What of all the suffering that was caused by what I did? No man can forgive all that."

"Jesus did," Gage replied. "And he expects us to forgive as he did."

"But some sins are just too . . ."

Gage interrupted. "There is no sin that God will not forgive. And now that he has forgiven me, then shall I not forgive others? Nora, this is no longer a question that we need to debate. The past is over. The past is gone. Whatever sins your father committed, whatever sins Walton committed, whatever sins I committed are no longer in the present."

He took her hand again in his. "I look in your eyes, and my soul is at peace. I hold your hand in mine, and my heart yearns for you. You are the only treasure my heart desires. So much has transpired to keep us apart. But can't you see? So much has transpired to place us together again. When you left my side in New York, could you have imagined us one day being reunited? And now, God helped direct me here to you. I am sure of it. If it was not ordained, then my ship could have sunk or you could have traveled on or a thousand other things could have transpired to keep us apart. None of that occurred. Nora, we are meant to be together."

She closed her eyes.

"We do not know the number of our days. We are not to be foolish and squander them in bitterness or sadness. Let us not abandon our treasure because of our pride. It is time for you to give up on the pain of your past."

He took her hand and placed it on his chest. "Do you feel that? Do you feel my heart?" he asked.

She nodded.

"It beats for you, Nora. My life is yours. I love you, and I want to be with you forever."

Having fought back tears for too long, Nora blinked twice, and her eyes swam with tears. She sat up and embraced Gage, her arms tight around him. "You won't disappear, will you?" she said, sobbing into his ear.

"I will always be at your side, Nora. Always."

As she leaned back, he tenderly wiped away the tears on her cheeks.

"Gage, I never stopped loving you–I simply stopped being worthy of your love."

"Never."

"But it was how I felt."

"And now?"

"From the bottom of your heart–the truth. Am I forgiven?"

"You are."

"And will the past forever stay in the past?"

"It will."

She embraced him again. "Then love me again, Gage. Let me into your heart–for in truth, you have never left mine."

"You will be my wife?"

"Yes, Gage, oh yes. I will."

From off in the distance, from the dense greening about the inn, came a glorious song from a strange bird that Gage had never heard before. He imagined it was singing only for them.

⁂

"Gage . . ."

"Yes, my love?"

Nora stopped walking, yet held on to Gage's hand. It was dusk, and the two strolled along the expanse of white sand that edged the shore just below the inn. The waves were calm and the water warm as soup.

"It is not my affair, I know, but I must ask."

"You may ask anything. Are not a husband and wife to share all things?"

"It's just that I . . . in our home . . . my father was most silent about his business. Perhaps, looking back, it is understandable . . . but . . ."

Gage took both her hands in his and turned to face her. The water lapped at their bare feet. "Nora, ask any question."

She looked down, then spoke. "Are you a wealthy man?"

He smiled. "I am. Again."

She did not look up. "I ask, not to pry, but because money was the apparent cause of so much pain in our past."

Gage nodded. "It was. And I struggle with this as well. I have had much time to ponder on this subject. We all have certain gifts. Mine appears to be making money. It is not a gift I sought, but it is simply in my bones. And you, Nora, you have a gift. It's music—and I think it is in your bones as well. But as I considered these things, I have concluded that all gifts are best when given away. Your gift of music is best expressed when given away. I think that I can do the same. Too much wealth can be dangerous. I have enough for twenty life-times. Perhaps I can use my surplus to help God's work. Perhaps that is why God has gifted me so."

Nora smiled. "Perhaps."

She reached up and kissed him lightly on the cheek. "You are such a wise man, Gage."

May 1, 1852

From a distance, it might have seemed odd that a small gathering of people assembled at the edge of the vast ocean. No boat was nearby, no one carried poles for fishing nor buckets for clamming. A thin veil of clouds held the glare of the sun in check. The breezes stirred occasionally, the palm leaves clicked their green fingers in a soft chorus. Gulls hung in the air like kites, cawing and diving. There were other deserted beaches, of course, but none perfumed with so many subtle scents of flowers and spice.

This day, on this deserted beach, five people gathered about in a circle—three men, two women.

One woman wore white.

Nora was dressed in the finest dress of exotic silks that could be found on the islands on such short notice. Once she had said yes to Gage's proposal, he desired that they waste no time. Traveling back home to California was simply too long to wait. His urgency was as if he had a premonition that for the two of them to wait would be foolish.

Nora found a ready-made dress, in white silk, at a tiny shop in Honolulu. A few alterations, a long length of lace for a veil, and the simple white dress became a most elegant wedding gown. A garland of flowers encircled her neck in the tradition of the island.

Gage had found a black morning coat that nearly fit his frame. Several touches from a local tailor, and it fit perfectly. His starched white shirt was open at the collar, owing to the warmth of the day, and he, too, sported a necklace of tropical flowers—although he was much less comfortable with it than Nora.

They found two witnesses. One was Captain LeClarc, the captain of Gage's sailing ship, and the other, a small, mouse-quiet woman, was the wife of the officiating minister.

Finding a minister proved to be the most daunting task. There were dozens of missionaries on the islands—some with established churches and impressive buildings as well. But none would offer to perform a wedding ceremony unless the bride and groom were first members of the congregation. Gage had balked at this requirement, claiming they may not be staying on the island for any length of time.

"Then I suggest you look elsewhere," was the commonly sniffed reply.

Finally, after ten negative responses, Gage had located a missionary, an ordained minister, who had just arrived on the island a few weeks prior. His church back home wished him Godspeed and supplied him with a monthly stipend, but after that he was on his own. So he and his wife lived in a canvas tent and held their meetings in the open air near the shore just outside Lahaina. Gage thought the enterprise a bit odd, but he was willing to overlook much in order to be married.

Since no church was available, they would be married by the sea.

And now, the minister, holding the Bible in both hands because of the riffling breeze, addressed Gage and Nora. "I now pronounce you man and wife."

The three stared at each other in awkward silence until the

minister's wife nudged her husband in the side. "Oh, yes . . . you may now kiss the bride."

And Gage did so with a gentle enthusiasm and passion.

The minister and his wife looked on with bemused, uncomfortable smiles while Captain LeClarc beamed and began to applaud.

Gage leaned away from his wife of but a moment, grinning and a little embarrassed. Nora simply had the smile of indescribable joy upon her face.

"Will you join us for lunch then, all of you, at Randolph's?" Gage asked.

The minister shook his head. "There's no public place that serves food that refrains from the use of alcohol. I'm afraid we could not be seen at such an establishment. What would such activity indicate to the heathen? One must avoid the appearance of evil, you know. Our church back home would never tolerate that sort of behavior."

Gage turned to the captain. "Captain LeClarc, will you join us?"

"Well, I would love to, but since you've decided to stay here awhile, I must leave right away. The tide will be slipping away soon, and I promised the crew we would set sail tomorrow. Some of the men get most restless when they spend more than a few days on land. And others get anxious 'cause they have families back in California. I promised them we would be sailing, and I need to keep my promise. If I don't leave this island now, then I miss the tides. And that cargo of ambergris and sugar will fetch a pretty penny back in San Francisco. You'll have quite a share waiting for you."

The men shook hands, and the captain gave Nora a quick, awkward embrace.

"Shall I drive you to the docks? I have the carriage rented for several days," Gage offered.

"No, thank you. I love the sea, but my legs want firm ground for as long as they can. The walk will be a good memory."

"Then good fortune, Captain. I trust we will soon see each other. You have my contacts in California."

The captain waved and began his walk to the village and the docks to the south. Suddenly Nora and Gage found themselves alone, dressed in great finery, only inches from the hush of the sea on white sand.

Gage took her hand and squeezed. Nora shyly looked away. He could see a faint blush come to her cheeks.

"Then, shall we have lunch? I know Randolph's offers a fine meal."

Nora smiled. "If you are hungry, then by all means we should go to Randolph's."

"It has been a busy day—even though we did not have quite the wedding either of us imagined. Are you not hungry, dear?"

She averted her eyes, but he thought he saw a little smile on her face.

"No. But if you are . . ."

And she squeezed his hand.

He peered closer. This time he was certain he saw a blush color her cheeks.

"Well, then . . . I imagine . . . well, I am certain we can catch a light meal later back at the inn. There always seems to be someone in the kitchen. Yes, perhaps that would be the better plan."

Nora only smiled in return. He lifted her into the carriage and marveled at how light she was and how beautiful she looked. He slid in beside her and took the reins in his hands. He snapped them, and the horses took off at a fast run. Nora slipped her arm through his and laid her head on his shoulder, snuggling close to him.

Gage was set to pull back on the horses, slowing them to a walk, since the inn was several miles away. But then Nora slipped her other hand to his shoulder and caressed him, moving even closer. His chest tightened, and his breath grew rapid and shallow. Instead of slowing the horses, he slapped the reins again and let them run.

Nora squeezed his arm tightly against her.

Their small room at the inn was strewn with a thousand flowers, the scent and color an explosion for the senses.

"They said it was a native tradition on the island," the American innkeeper said. "They wanted to give you a proper send-off. They said that if a man and woman spend their first night on a bed of flowers, then the gods will grace them all their life together. I don't claim that they're right—but it is something special we can do for you. You're our first freshly marrieds."

The innkeeper then nudged at Gage and winked. "And the champagne is my tradition."

Gage awoke, and the silver light from the moon poured over him. He looked over at Nora and again marveled at her beauty and his good fortune. God had smiled on Gage, blessing him with such bounty.

He slipped out of bed, gently draping a sheet over Nora's bare shoulder. He carefully made his way through the forest of flowers and spice leaves and sandalwood. Sitting on the windowsill, he focused on the sea.

The moonlight glistened off every wave, exploding into a glittering mist on the rocks and the sand below. The distant horizon was as black as the darkest night. To the south Gage saw a cluster of lights from the village. He turned to the north and saw a single point of light reflected on the sea. He strained to see farther, thinking it might be the square shape of a building, hidden in the dense greenings. A breeze came up, and the fingers of the palms knitted and nicked together.

I wonder where that light is? A fisherman's camp? A house?

"Gage, where are you?" Nora asked, her voice thick with sleep.

"Right here by the window, my love," he said. "Just enjoying the view."

"I woke, and you were gone from my arms. I am already accustomed to the touch of your skin. I felt sad without you."

"Then let me return to you, my sweet Nora," he said, walking around to his side of the bed. "For I will never do anything that will make you sad."

"Never?"

"Never."

And he leaned over and placed his lips on hers as she wrapped her arms about him and held him tightly, as if her very life depended on having him in her arms.

❦

"The light you saw was from the old Cumminses' place," the innkeeper said as he poured Gage's coffee. Nora sat at his side, nibbling on a small brown roll, dusted with chopped native nuts. She averted her eyes, but the smile never left her face.

"The old Cumminses' place? Is it a home or a factory or what? How old is it?"

"The Cumminses were settlers here, from what stories I hear. Came here fifteen or so years ago. The wife took ill and passed away a year back. The husband didn't want to be alone, so he sailed back to New York. They left a native fellow in charge of the property. Trying to sell it is what I hear."

Gage thought for a moment. "Who would I see about looking into the property?"

❦

May 5, 1852

"As you can see, the home is in fine shape, and there's no sign of rot or insect infestation at all. Mr. Cummins was a good builder and spared no expense. You noticed the large kitchen—with a pump inside the house?"

Gage nodded. Nora excitedly hurried from room to room.

The house was, in essence, a much smaller version of the Davis summer home in Southampton. It was shuttered, shingled, gray with white trim, and had a porch that wrapped all the way around the first floor. It sat on a bluff some twenty yards above a cove with fine white sand and was framed by several braces of palms on either side. Frangipani bushes adorned the structure with brilliant color. There was a smaller guesthouse well behind the main house, which was the residence of the native man who had cared for the property in the Cumminses' absence.

Gage stood at the front door, overlooking the tidy lawn and the sea beyond. Nora ran through the doors and embraced her husband with a great hug.

"It's perfect, Gage. Just perfect. It is the house I always dreamt of."

"But we are so very far from everyone we know," he replied. "We are so far from the rest of America."

She squeezed him tight to her. That alone would have been enough to win the day. "But I don't care about going home. We can make this our home, can't we? Aren't there business things here on the islands that you could do?"

He looked into her deep eyes. She smiled up at him.

"Do you want to live here?" he asked.

"Yes, Gage, if I can live here with you."

Gage turned to the man from the bank in Honolulu. "We'll take it."

June 5, 1852

Gage had never seen more boxes and cartons and packages in his life. They had sailed back to Honolulu to sign the deed and arrange for bank drafts. Once the banker had learned of Gage's obvious wealth, he was most deferential.

Nora had visited every shop on the island and procured most of what she would need to set up housekeeping. It was fortunate that the Cumminses had left their furniture, since little was offered for sale owing to the long trip from America to the islands.

Nora busied herself unpacking and cleaning and arranging help to run the house. She found two local women who would clean and cook for them. Gage made arrangements with the fellow in the Cumminses' employ to continue his duties.

June 21, 1852

Within a fortnight, the house was snug with their new possessions. Floors and walls had been scrubbed clean again, and the glass windows sparkled in the tropical sunshine.

Gage had spent more than a few days investigating their new surroundings. He bought a small carriage and three horses and rode up the coast as far as the trails allowed. The coastline grew rugged and impassable only ten miles to the north of them, with angry, sharp cliffs fingering the space from mountains to the sea. Birds in vast profusion populated the area, flying about in a wild tangle of colors and calls. The winds were most favorable along the shore, and the natives claimed the weather was always temperate and warm. Gage noted that vast fields of sugarcane were planted in some locations, while others were still under dense jungle vegetation.

Nora asked if he might start a farm for cane, but Gage said he would not.

"Too much labor and too many headaches," he explained. "It would be much easier to operate as a supplier and importer of required supplies and an exporter of sugar. That way, my only expense in capital is a few ships. No sense buying land when others are willing to take that risk."

Nora found herself surrounded by a coterie of women from the States who had followed their husbands to the islands. All were searching for a place to belong, and soon the Cumminses' place was called "the Davis house" and had a daily stream of visitors and guests.

They lacked little. News was slow from the States, and Gage fumed about that on occasion, but soon newspapers began to arrive on a regular basis, though a few weeks late.

After they had settled into a comfortable routine, Gage spent one long evening penning a series of letters. He wrote to the townspeople of Monterey, resigning his mayoral duties. He penned long missives to Carty Todd, Thomas Lee, and Charles Thornton, asking for reviews of their business activities, and providing what guidance he could from so far away. He had already received some correspondence from each, all with positive reports on their current activities and prospects for the future. But the letters he wrote this time were of a different nature. Each was specific to the person, but all contained much the same information. He wrote to Joshua, Pastor

Kenyon, and Hannah, asking each of them if additional money might add to their work. He wrote that he had acknowledged his gift, and God had led him to share the fruits of that gift with others. He ended each letter with a simple request: "Tell me of your dreams, tell me of your goals, tell me of your needs—and I will share what treasure I can with you. In this way God's work will be amplified by my gifts. I would like to offer what help I may to see your dreams come to fruition."

He passed those letters to Nora, who read them by the light of a warming fire. She looked up at last and offered her husband a gracious and sweet smile.

"I think God's work will be aided greatly by your generosity. I think this is a fine use of your treasure."

April 1853

And in the spring of the following year, after Gage and Nora had been husband and wife for almost a year, Nora came to Gage.

It was a clear morning, with a hint of rain in the clouds above them. Nora found her husband sitting on the porch, reading a New York newspaper three weeks old. She placed her hands on his shoulders and gave him a tender squeeze. When he turned his head up toward her, she smiled and came around to sit on his lap, oblivious to his paper.

"You're about to ruin my news," he said cheerfully, extracting the crumpled paper from his lap. She giggled and offered him a brief kiss.

"I think my news is more important."

"The Crystal Palace for the World's Fair is nearly completed in New York," Gage read from the now-wrinkled paper. "It has the largest cast-iron and glass dome ever built in the United States. They're calling it 'Aladdin's Palace.' "

"My news is even more astounding than that."

He looked into her eyes, a sight that never ceased to intrigue and fascinate him.

"And what might that be? A party planned for the weekend? A new native dish to try? Was there a new bird sighted?"

She playfully pushed his shoulder. "You think I am but a flighty woman, don't you?"

He laughed. "I do not. But news here is of a smaller nature than back in New York."

Her smile vanished and was replaced by a deeper expression. "This news is not smaller."

Gage placed his hand over hers, now resting on his chest. "And what might that be, my beautiful bride?"

She took his hand, brought it to her lips, and kissed his open palm with the barest of kisses. Then she slowly lowered his hand and placed it firm against her belly. Leaning toward him, she whispered, "You will be a father, Gage Davis. There is a baby inside of me."

And with those simple words, his heart was swept into a hurricane of joy and delight. He stood, carrying Nora in his arms, and held her, their tears mixing in the gold of the morning light.

CHAPTER TWENTY-FOUR

Island of Maui
August 1853

Nora reveled in her growing belly. She would sit on the porch and watch the sunsets, cradling the life growing within her, smiling, laughing, chatting with friends as they came to call. The small group of women came from a wide group of settlers and adventurers. Included in Nora's group of new friends were the wife of the owner of a sugar mill, the wife of a whaling ship captain, the wife of a builder, the wife of a shipwright, and the wife of a surveyor—all new to the islands within the last two years. Nora had attempted to befriend several of the missionary wives on the island but was cooly and summarily rebuffed.

"We must be of heaven and not of the world," said one. "And I must be doing God's business only." Nora did not agree with nor understand their logic, but she smiled and wished the women a pleasant day.

Her friends brought all manner of comment and advice.

"It will be the first white baby born here since . . . since I don't know when," claimed one visitor.

"You are going to take the child back to civilization, aren't you?" said another.

"Best keep the natives away. Who knows what mischief they might do," warned an acquaintance.

But most commented on her wonderfully joyous look, her cheerful air, and her radiant beauty. Even Gage was nonplussed in a most pleasant way. He would have sworn, before she grew large with child, that Nora could not become more beautiful than she was. But as he watched her each day, there was a radiance about her that magnified her features and brought her loveliness into sharper focus.

And Gage doted on her. He brought her drinks and pillows and food and behaved as if she were an exquisite yet fragile jewel. She allowed him to do so, yet never indulged in frivolous demands. She knew that if she did, he would turn the islands upside down to satisfy her desires.

One evening, near the middle of her time, Gage returned home near dark. He had been on the other side of the island, negotiating an arrangement to provide shipping, while returning with supplies for a group of men who owned tracts of land. The meeting had gone well, and Gage had their assurances that he would be their shipper of choice. It would mean a tidy sum at the end of the year. In addition, he pledged financing for new equipment that they required. Both the shipping and the loans helped ensure the completion of all elements of the contracts.

"Gage," Nora called, "I am still out on the porch. It was a most wonderful sunset."

He came out holding a small tin.

"What's that?" she asked.

"A surprise."

She smiled up at him and his knees weakened.

"What sort of surprise?"

"And what do I get if I tell you?"

She winked. "A kiss, perhaps. If I like the surprise, that is."

"Well, the terms seem sufficient, but I am not sure of the quality. I think I may have to sample some merchandise before I agree."

Laughing, she reached up for his hand and pulled him down and met his lips with hers. They lingered for a moment.

"Sufficient?" she asked.

He held out the tin and hoped she did not notice the tremble in his hands. "More than sufficient."

With childlike glee, she pried the lid off and then squealed. "Chocolate! Where ever did you find chocolate on this island? Gage, you are such a dear husband. And I despaired over ever tasting this treasure again."

Gage sat at her feet on a hassock.

"A ship arrived from San Francisco. Brought crates of it with them."

She sat upright as she chewed the first piece. "And you only brought one tin? Gage! I will have to go back and buy more!"

He laughed. "Don't despair, Nora, a full crate is on its way. I couldn't bring it on horseback. I knew a single tin would be but a tease."

Relaxing, she took another square of the dark candy and popped it into her mouth.

Gage began to massage her feet. She moaned in pleasure.

"You will spoil me, Gage. I will not be fit to be a wife or mother after I am so extravagantly indulged by you."

Grinning, Gage continued. "It provides me as much pleasure as it does you. I see your smile, I watch your belly grow, and I realize that there is not a happier, more contented man in the entire world. Why God has blessed me so abundantly, I will never understand, but I will be eternally grateful."

She touched his cheek. "You are a dear man, Gage. You have been my salvation. Truly, you have."

"No, Nora, it is you who have saved me. Without you, I would never have found my faith in God, and I would be as lost as a bird in a storm on a dark night."

"Then we have saved each other," she concluded.

She looked out to the darkness over the water, then asked in a small voice, "What time did you say the rest of the chocolates will arrive?"

Gage laughed until his sides hurt.

⬥⬥⬥⬥⬥

A sudden wind chilled the air, and Gage immediately wrapped a shawl about Nora, insisting that she retire for the evening. He helped her climb the stairs, offering a steadying arm.

Gage sat with Nora till her breath became slow and steady. He pulled the sheet up over her shoulder and quietly slipped out of the bedroom and padded down to his office overlooking the dark seas.

He turned up the wick on the lantern and from his case, he extracted a thick sheaf of letters. He separated the pile into three smaller stacks. One pile represented contracts and agreements with growers and exporters for their shipping requirements. One stack represented invoices, bills of lading, and ship manifests. The third pile, and the smallest, was made up of personal letters and notes. He had read them all once but would read them again now, at a more leisurely pace, and begin to fashion his responses.

The reports from Carty, Thomas, and Charles were all positive. He imagined that if there had been unsettling news, they may not have included it in their letters. He made a note to himself to insist that he be apprised of the entirety of the business situation, not simply the positive elements. He was sure they would comply.

He spent longer reading the letters from his old friends. Joshua wrote a long expansive letter, detailing every element in what he hoped to accomplish in Angels Camp. He envisioned a large church structure, a fund for helping the desperate citizens in the area, perhaps even a school. He worried about the fate of the myriad of children in town—none of whom had the advantage of receiving instruction. And after he listed all his current activities and goals, he politely asked, as if expecting to be turned down, for a sum of a hundred dollars to start a fund that would be set aside for wood for the new church.

Gage took out a fresh sheet of paper and began to write to his old friend. Before he sealed the letter, he slipped in a bank draft for five thousand dollars and instructed Joshua to spend it wisely—but to spend it all.

"You must spend it all on the work of the church, Joshua," Gage wrote, "for if I find that you have not, I will personally come to Angels Camp and take the remainder from you."

He hoped that his false bravado would be apparent in his words.

The letter from Pastor Kenyon was filled with all manner of stories about Monterey. He prefaced nearly every paragraph with "I don't want you to think of this as gossip, but . . ." and then would launch into a long story about the latest machinations of the new mayor and of the battles between him and the council, or stories about the Portuguese fishermen, or any number of other citizens in the area.

By the time Gage reached the sixth page, he said aloud, "The man missed his calling—he should have been a reporter."

At the end of the letter, almost as an afterthought, he asked if Gage would like to contribute a small sum toward an organ and Bibles. He included no suggested amount. "If I tell a man what to give," he wrote, "then I take from him the chance to have God speak to his heart. But whatever the amount you provide for this church, I will not let on about it to anyone—for if the average citizen of Monterey hears of any largesse from a wealthy contributor—then they will shirk back from their responsibility to honor their tithes. So you will be named, but no amount shall ever escape my lips. And this letter is an anomaly, for I am usually more close-lipped than this. And, after all, you are in the Sandwich Islands. Who would you see to repeat my stories?"

Gage smiled, for he knew human nature as well as Pastor Kenyon. He included in his reply the same amount as he sent to Joshua. He did not include a suggestion to spend it all, for he knew that Pastor Kenyon would have no problem in doing so.

Hannah had written a most brief note. Her penmanship, once flowing and gentle, appeared to be scratched out in anger or frustration. Hannah included barely a hint of personal details, and for this Gage was worried. A man, or woman, would easily share the pleasant details of their lives, but if troubles blackened their existence, then some would keep all news hidden. He worried that this was the case with Hannah. He made another note to himself to pen a letter to Jamison, giving him the task of finding the truth out of Hannah's situation.

Hannah wrote that she was getting by and that if he wanted to help "the least of them" she had a means to do just that. She made no mention of what she planned, but she wrote that ten thousand dollars would be a proper start to cure the ills that she faced.

Gage did not hesitate. He wrote the bank draft for the full amount she mentioned. Then he added a postscript to his letter.

Island of Maui
August 2, 1853

Hannah,

I am not requiring you to account for this money, but I have faith in your heart and in your judgment. If this money will help solve some ills, then it is money spent well. I wish to help improve conditions however God wants.

But I do have to inquire after you—and your spiritual condition. Perhaps you have heard that I have found the proper relationship with God. I have found faith. I have found joy and happiness. And I want that same joy for every person I know. Do you know Christ? Have you found faith?

I am not one to lay out the tenets of faith—for I barely understand them myself. But I pray that you will find someone to lead you, Hannah. There is no greater joy in life than giving it to the one who created you. Please, Hannah, allow God to do that work in your heart.

Then he signed the letter, sealed the envelope, bowed his head, and prayed.

November 1853

It was the darkest shank of the evening, and Gage awoke with a start. His face was marked with sweat, and he struggled to keep his arms from flailing about in the darkness. The moon slipped in and out from behind clouds, lighting the room in silver, then allowing darkness to wash over the sea. Gage sat up, wiped his face, and felt for the arms of the chair. When the cloud cover cleared again, Gage stood and bounded up the steps to the bedroom. He took a deep breath and opened the door. He could see Nora's form under the sheet. He stepped closer. He could see the rise and fall of her chest. Then he slowly let the breath out of his lungs. He sat on the edge of the bed and tenderly placed his hand upon his wife's arm. She did not stir.

He closed his eyes, hoping the troubling images would fade.

He had fallen asleep at his desk, which happened often enough, but this evening he had been tormented by nightmares. He had dreamt of this very home on the island, now filled with flowers and laughter. In his dream, black shrouds covered the doorways, and the rooms were silent and bare. He dreamt that he entered the house and heard no sound. At the foot of the stairway he stopped, unable to take another step. Petrified, he was certain that Nora was gone. Then he heard the wail, and that snapped his eyes open.

But Nora was still sleeping, and he slipped under the sheet beside her and gently cradled her in his arms until the dawn lit the sea with gold.

December 24, 1853

It appeared to Gage that every woman on the island was now in residence at his home. Nora had awakened three days earlier with sharp pains, and Gage, in a panic, ran from the house, sending servants in several conflicting directions to locate the doctor and the midwife. He then ran back upstairs to find his wife, sitting in bed, with her feet propped on a pillow.

"It's not coming?"

"What's not coming?" Nora asked innocently.

Gage stared back at her, uncomprehending.

"Sweet husband, forgive me. I was attempting a joke."

"Then it's not coming?"

She winced once, then attempted a brave smile.

"No sweet husband, you will soon be a father. That much I am certain."

Then she called out in pain.

His eyes were frantic as he tore down the steps to send the rest of the servants out for the doctor. He literally stumbled over all of them who were still seated at the top of the back steps.

As he rose and dusted himself off, he knew he would never understand the difference between island time and real time.

"The baby is coming," he cried.

Leanua, the eldest of the women servants, smiled and nodded. "Mama have pain, but baby not ready yet. Not now. New mother. No come first-time pain. We all know. Now you know."

Word of Nora's first pains spread quickly, and by the afternoon, five women had gathered in her bedroom, chatting, holding her hand, offering her tea and advice. Gage was not sure if such company was expected or even wanted, but he also knew he was too nervous to ask them to leave. His pacing made Nora nervous. She never said so, but he could see it in her cringing expression every time he spun on his heels and turned back to her.

And the women apparently were taking up residence until the child arrived. The weather had remained quite warm, and Gage had slept the last few nights on a hammock installed on the front porch. The visiting women must have spread out in the upper bedrooms.

On this, the third day of their residency, Gage awoke to the sound of a hushed choir of voices, tighter and more drawn than before. He shook his head and ran up the stairs.

"You stay out," Mrs. Rosen said, meeting him halfway up, placing her hands on his shoulders.

"Is she . . . is the child . . . ?" he replied, his eyes looking past Mrs. Rosen's formidable frame.

"Soon enough," she answered, "and there's no need for you here to clutter things up. You've done enough, thank you."

"But I'm . . . I'm her husband."

"A fact we are all aware of. Now, perhaps you could make yourself useful and locate the midwife and the doctor. Do you think you can do that?"

Gage was set to make a cutting reply, but then heard a sharp cry. It was Nora.

Mrs. Rosen did not move or flinch. She peered down at Gage from the step above.

"She will be fine. There is no place for a man in the middle of things right now. Please, go fetch the doctor and midwife."

Torn, Gage hesitated. Then, at another shriek, he turned and ran down the stairs on his mission.

❦

The doctor held on tightly to Gage as the horse galloped up the palm-lined trail.

"Is the midwife here?" Gage called out as he jumped from the horse, knocking the doctor into the dust. Gage had spent nearly three hours finding the doctor and bringing him back.

Just then a wail burst through the air—a gasping, angry, excited first wail. Then a cry, and what sounded like a collective sob of relief from a dozen mouths. Gage did not wait and raced up the steps. This time he vowed to knock Mrs. Rosen to the ground if she prevented him from seeing his wife.

The door was unlatched. When he entered the room, the women about the bed parted as if directed by the winds and formed a corridor to the side of the bed. Gage came in and knelt down. On Nora's breast was a tightly bundled package.

Nora looked up. Sweat tangled her hair, and her eyes were darkened pools, but she offered Gage a beatific, blissful smile as a greeting. Gage touched her cheek. Then the bundle moved.

Nora turned back the edge of the blanket.

Two dark eyes riveted Gage to the floor. A tiny hand flailed in the air. The child blinked twice, then closed its eyes and rested.

"It's a beautiful girl, sweet Gage," Nora whispered. "A beautiful Christmas girl."

"She has your eyes."

"And your nose."

"And your chin."

Gage could not take his eyes off his wife and daughter.

"How are you, Nora? How do you feel?"

She nodded, closed her eyes for a minute, then smiled. "I am fine."

Gage knew she masked pain when she shut her eyes like that.

"Merry Christmas, darling."

"Merry Christmas."

After a few moments, Gage said, "I brought the doctor. Perhaps he should look in?"

Nora nodded. Gage rose and called out to the doctor.

"She is fine," Dr. Larson said, wiping his hands on a towel. "I didn't see anything out of the ordinary. A little loss of blood, and she's tired, but there appeared to be no complications."

Gage continued to pace. "And you're certain of that?"

"As certain as I can be," he replied. "Just make sure she has enough food and drink. And since you have servants, they can help with the baby—changing the child and all that."

Gage nodded.

The doctor placed his hand on Gage's shoulder. "Mr. Davis, women have been having babies for a long time. God didn't make the process easy, but he did make it natural. Your wife is tired, that's all. Just be gentle with her for a few weeks. Let the servants do all they can and keep her from trying to do too much. She's young. She'll be up and healthy in a matter of days, I am sure."

January 1, 1854

Though Gage did not truly believe the doctor, he was right. By the third day, Nora felt well enough to venture downstairs, and by the end of a full week, on New Year's Day, was taking her meals with

Gage and the baby on the porch. Nearly three weeks passed until Gage felt at ease holding the squirming infant. The first time Nora passed the child to him, he tensed with fear and held her briefly before nervously handing her back.

"She won't break, you know," Nora told Gage.

"I'm not so sure," he replied shakily.

March 24, 1854

They had named her Hope, a name the natives struggled with greatly and usually pronounced with two or three extra syllables. They took to calling her *little ha'a'poa,* which they said meant "child with smiles." Nora had offered to use that name instead of Hope, but Gage politely refused.

"She is an American and will have an American name."

Hope proved to be a good baby, with a most pleasant disposition. And the child appeared to thrive, gaining weight and becoming more and more observant. Even though many of the new arrivals to the island swore that the sea air and the salt water would be detrimental, Gage refused to keep the child indoors as they had suggested.

And now at three months of age, the child began to respond to her father, cooing excitedly when she heard his voice. When Gage reached into her bassinet to pick her up, Hope would grow still, staring intently at her father's features, as if trying to memorize them. He would giggle and sing soft songs to her, and after a moment, she would giggle and Gage would cuddle her close.

Nora sat in her chair, rocking, watching her husband and daughter at play. She let them be together longer than any of those around her advised.

"A father should stay in the background," they said. "Fathers are so clumsy with children. You take care of the baby until she's older."

Nodding, Nora agreed with them until they left, then she would encourage Gage all the more to pick Hope up and carry her about the house and grounds, and even to the edge of the sea itself.

"Won't she be frightened by the sound of the waves?" Gage asked when Nora suggested it.

"Only if you are. She does not know what fear is. She'll learn it from you, and I beg you not to teach her fear."

Gage nodded, then picked Hope up and set off for the sand beach below the house. He turned at the last, saw Nora's face and, for a bare instant, saw something amiss. It was as if a sharp pain had touched her, and she refused to let on—the look was that brief and that subtle. He was near to running to her side, but he knew she would claim it was nothing. So he stared for a moment, and she smiled at him in return. Her cheerful expression was almost enough to convince him that all was well.

The ocean was calm that day, and Gage walked along the edge of the surf, never allowing himself to get wet. He walked for a full ten minutes in one direction, then returned towards home.

Hope, the feathery bundle in his arms, cooed and snuggled as he walked with her.

When he came to the steps that led to the house, he looked toward the porch. But Nora was not there, sitting in her chair, waiting for their return.

That's odd. Every time I have walked out of view Nora waits and paces like a lioness, despite her assurances of my competency.

Gage hurried up the steps. What he saw chilled him to the very marrow of his soul.

Nora lay sprawled at the foot of her chair, her arms spread wide, her eyelids closed. Gage sprinted the last few feet, calling for servants, calling for anyone who could listen, calling out to Nora to rise, calling on God for help.

March 31, 1854

The second doctor came a week later from Honolulu. He was a Harvard graduate, and a fellow that Gage had a nodding acquaintance with back in Cambridge. The local doctor had been baffled and told Gage of the new physician on the islands. It did not take long for Gage to arrange his call.

"I am certain I have seen this before," Dr. Neally said as he wiped his spectacles. His voice offered no cheer or optimism. "There have been five cases back on Oahu—five cases that I have seen personally. There may be more. The symptoms are nearly identical."

Gage felt like he had been pacing for a week, and he probably had. He stopped in front of the doctor. "And what is the illness called?"

Dr. Neally sighed. "I'm not even sure it has a name. It seems to be one of the fevers that occur often in tropical settings such as this."

"And what medication will you prescribe?"

The doctor did not speak for a long time. He merely stared at his hands. Finally, he looked up. His eyes were drawn. "There is no medication."

At first Gage was confused; then he grew angry. "What do you mean—no medication? You learned nothing of how to treat this at Harvard? Come now, there must be a medicine you can use."

Dr. Neally shook his head. "Gage, I'm afraid there is much that modern medicine does not know. And this is one of those times. The five people I saw with this . . . well, I suppose there is no easy way to say this . . . but they all . . . died."

Gage did not speak or move.

"Harvard never taught us how to handle the times when fate ties our hands." The doctor stood face-to-face with Gage. "But I have no power over this illness."

"No, doctor," Gage insisted. "That is not what I intend on hearing. There must be a medicine. She just had a child. She is tired, that's all. She'll recover from this." Gage's voice became more shrill with each word.

The doctor put his hand on Gage's shoulder. "If she does, then it will have been the intervention of God. I can offer no more help."

Gage slapped his hand away. "No more help? I have not brought you here to tell me my wife is dying. You did not go to Harvard to pass a sentence of death on a woman who had a child no more than four months prior. I will not tolerate this. I will not!"

Several servants peeked out around doors, unaccustomed to ever hearing Mr. Davis shout.

"I will not let you let my wife die!"

Gage clutched the doctor's lapels as if intending on thrashing the man. The doctor did not struggle but placed his hands on Gage's forearms, then embraced him. After a minute of silence, first one sob, then another, and one more, wracked Gage's body. He sniffed and stepped away from Dr. Neally.

The doctor shook his head. "I am so sorry, Gage. I am. This is not why I became a doctor, and I hate it. But there is nothing I can do."

Gage nodded. He looked at the floor. "How long then?" He could barely get the words out.

"A week."

Gage gasped.

"Maybe two. No more."

"Does she know?"

"I didn't tell her a thing. But she knows that she is ill . . . very ill."

Gage clenched his eyes shut. "And the child?"

"I saw no symptoms. I think there is no danger. I think that if anyone else were to sicken, it would have already occurred. But do not allow your wife to feed the child anymore. Find a wet nurse. Or use goat's milk."

Tears streamed down Gage's face.

"I can pray about it, can't I? You said God could cure her, didn't you?"

Dr. Neally nodded.

"You can pray."

<hr />

April 6, 1854

A week later Gage startled awake. He had taken up a position in the large chair in their bedroom and seldom left it. He would stare at his wife as she slept and kneel at her side when she was awake, bathing her forehead with cool water, stroking her arm, offering her bits of fruit or bread.

She winced often in pain as the fever coursed through her body and as coughs wracked her lungs.

Gage spent hours in prayer, begging and pleading with God to save Nora. He often wept as he prayed, silent, bitter tears. He offered God his entire treasure, everything that he owned, if the Almighty would only spare his wife. He offered to spend his life witnessing on street corners if that is what God wanted. He pointed out to God that no one could understand why a new mother would be taken. He prayed with every breath and with every bit of his faith and being.

Still Nora lay in her bed, moaning and tossing and sweating.

And now Gage was awake. The lantern offered a soft golden glow. He checked his pocketwatch. It was 2:00 A.M.

"Gage," Nora called. Her voice rattled.

He was at her side an instant later.

"You are a sweet man," she said and tried to smile. Then she winced again and her eyes closed briefly. She opened them and gazed into her husband's face, then touched his cheek. "You have taken such good care of me."

"It is what brings me pleasure."

She coughed once.

"Do we have any of that chocolate left?"

Gage grinned through his pain. "I think we do. Would you like some?"

"No," she said and caressed his cheek again. "Maybe when I'm better."

Gage brightened. "Yes, we will save it until you're better. Then we'll have a wonderful party, and all our friends will be here and Hope will be there and she'll laugh."

"She is a good baby, isn't she?"

"She is the most perfect baby I have ever known," Gage said proudly. "She takes after you, not me. That is a most comforting development."

Nora smiled. "I am glad that she is healthy. Did she eat well tonight?"

Gage nodded. "The scale may not be accurate, but it appears she has gained a full half pound since we weighed her last."

"That is good news," Nora said happily. "She is such a ray of sunshine, isn't she?"

"She is, sweet Nora. She is."

Gage listened to his heart. He got up and embraced his wife most tenderly. Her body relaxed in his arms and he held her, as carefully as he held Hope, for perhaps fifteen minutes.

She coughed once, and he returned to kneeling.

"Gage," she said softly, "I have something to ask you."

"You may ask anything at all."

"You must promise me."

"Promise what?"

"Just promise."

"If it is in my power, then I will promise."

"It is in your power. I know it is. God knows it is as well. So you will promise me?"

Gage nodded. "I will. Tell me what you will have me do."

Nora's dark eyes focused on him. "You must not blame God."

"Blame God?"

"For sickness. For taking me."

Gage was set to interrupt, but she placed her finger on his lips. "I know, Gage. I have known for weeks. God has been preparing my heart. I have been praying that he is preparing yours as well."

"But, Nora, God can work miracles."

She hushed him like a mother will hush a restless child. "He can. And he already has. He has brought you into my life. He has given you life. He has allowed us to produce a wonderful baby. Those are all miracles."

"But, Nora, I meant he can . . ."

She hushed him again. "I know what you meant. He could. But I do not think he will. I don't understand, but I am ready."

Gage could not hold back his tears; a sob grabbed his chest.

"You must promise me you will take care of Hope."

Gage tried to nod through his tears. "I will, Nora. I will."

Nora smiled. "She will have my heart, Gage, and you must do what a father will do. Teach her of God. Teach her of love and beauty. Teach her of joy."

Gage buried his head in Nora's neck. She cradled his head in her arm.

"You must continue to do God's work. He is teaching you, Gage. Learn well this lesson. You must not be sad."

"But you cannot leave, Nora. I will die without you." Gage was sobbing now.

Her words grew angry and harsh. "You will do no such thing, Gage Davis. If you are to be a proper father to our daughter, you must be brave. Shed tears, fine, but then tighten your heart and raise our child well. You must promise me this. You must."

He nodded.

"I want to hear you say it," she ordered.

"I promise," he whispered.

"Be calm now, my darling Gage. I am asking that. Be calm. Let God's grace show through your bravery. You must."

Nora coughed, and her body tightened as she did.

"Tell Hope about me."

Gage could not control his tears. "I will, sweet Nora. I will."

"Then hold me for a little while," Nora said sweetly.

Gage climbed onto the bed and held his wife. They lay together in silence. After a long time, after the moon slipped behind a cloud, Nora spoke softly. "We will always be young in each other's hearts. We will never grow older than we are now. Our love will always be as sweet as it is now. Gage . . . we have been given a rare and beautiful gift."

She coughed once more, and for several minutes, she strained to find purchase to a breath. Gage wanted to run and find help, but in that moment, he realized he must be at her side. Just then God brushed a corner of his heart with his hand and Gage felt a peace wash over him.

Nora opened her eyes, smiled at him, and then whispered his name.

And then she was gone.

Gage could not move.

Then he cradled her in his arms.

"Sweet Jesus," he cried softly, "take her home. Oh, sweet Jesus, take her home."

And as Gage wept, his tears splashing on her face, the wind rattled through the palms.

After a long hour, Gage opened his eyes.

Hope, in the nursery down the hall, began to wail. He rose, offered a prayer, and made his way to the nursery.

CHAPTER TWENTY-FIVE

*The Island of Maui
April 16, 1854*

For perhaps an hour, Gage stared at a spot on the western horizon. He no longer could see the faint tuft of green that marked the mountaintops. When all became blue and green and gray, he turned away, his expression neither somber nor happy, neither sad nor joyous, but a curious mixture of resignation and anticipation.

Nora lay beneath the island soil. Her grave was on a high bluff overlooking the ocean and the home where her daughter was born. Gage spent days there, silent and ashen, taking in the stone, then the sea, then the sky.

If he was on a search to find answers, no new revelations came to him in the days following Nora's passing. That time felt like a dark fog to him now. He recalled everything in exquisite detail up until the moment she breathed her last, then all became muddy and confused. Friends swept in, he was sure, and took care of arrangements and food and all manner of the ordinary details of life.

Gage struggled now, as the ship slipped farther east, to recall the details, even broad brush strokes of the church service and burial and messages, but almost none had been retained in his thoughts and memories.

All save one.

It must have been at the church. Hope was next to him, held by a native nursemaid, who rocked her to the sway of the music and the breeze. Gage sat stoic, forcing his eyes to remain dry. The pastor, or perhaps a friend, made mention of Nora's smile and her joy, and at that instant Hope leaned back in the nursemaid's arms and laughed her sweet, innocent, loud, childish giggle. The tension in the church broke like a wave on the rocks. Gage saw that laugh as a sign that the humor and joy that filled Nora's heart had been passed on to her daughter.

But that was the only detail he recalled. It was as if he had awakened from a dark and disturbing dream. He was at the gravesite. A thick scud of clouds swept in, and a squall of rain thrashed through the foliage. Gage rose and took cover but was soaked to the skin before he got twenty yards.

Then, as often happens in the tropics, the clouds opened for a second, and a ray of sunshine poured out in a tight circle. It snaked along the beach and then fell upon Gage, where it hovered and hesitated. He looked up and saw only clear skies and sunlight while all around him was gray and wet and wind.

That's how it is without God, Gage imagined. *And I cannot let myself stay there.*

Nora's grave remained in the gray.

She is in my heart, not there.

And then he looked up.

She is in heaven, not in the grave.

As the wind moaned and wailed about him, he bid the grave a good-bye and held his tears again. Then he headed toward home and his daughter.

December 1854

On the recommendations of doctors and most friends, he did not consider traveling with Hope until she passed her first birthday. She was a healthy and happy child, and Gage was thankful that because of her young age, she was not aware of her mother's absence—or at least not that Gage could discern.

He was able to lose himself during the days in his business dealings. The islands continued to attract the odd, eccentric, and entrepreneurs. All kinds of farm and plantation and small industry sprung up along the coast and in the lush fertile valleys. A clever man, with good timing and instincts, could easily find ways to become rich. And Gage did so. In the thousands of details to be attended to, he could forget for a time his greatest loss.

Hope began to walk and talk, and every step and word reminded Gage of Nora. His daughter was his joy, though at times, she was a bittersweet treasure.

There was not one single thing that led Gage to decide to return to America. One day he awoke to the sound of Hope's cheerful cooing in the dark hours before dawn. He rose before the nursemaid had a chance to awaken and slipped into the nursery. He picked Hope up from the crib, and she giggled and pawed his face with her delicate hands. As he laughed and kissed her forehead, she wrapped her arms about his neck and burrowed into him, her tiny, sweet face pushed against his rougher skin. He shut his eyes, and tears formed.

When he opened them, all he saw was the image of Nora, hiding behind the door and in the cloudless sky and in the palms outside and in the scent of the flowers that ringed the house and in the twine of the native rug on the floor . . . and then he knew it was time.

It took several months to arrange all his affairs on the island and find capable replacements for himself in a number of positions.

Captain LeClarc had been in the islands, and Gage told him to take one more trip, bringing back with him a few empty crates for their household goods.

They were going home, he said.

***

Monterey, California
February 1855

The captain vacated his compact stateroom on the ship for Gage and his daughter. While the largest, it was still barely big enough for Gage, a crib, and a baby.

Hope's nursemaid, a tiny native woman by the name of Pahala, insisted that she return with Gage. She was widowed and had no man to forbid her to leave.

"This baby mean more than mine," she declared. "I go or die."

Gage allowed her to come, and she brought with her two young daughters and a son. Hope would have no further separations if Gage could help it, so he agreed with a bemused smile at his new employees.

The ship's crew was on their best behavior on the voyage. Gage marveled that he had heard no cursing the entire trip. As Hope was brought out on deck during the day, one could see the hard faces soften as they looked at her rosy cheeks and innocent smiles.

He left the islands without encumbrances to hold his heart. He set up a trust fund with the local doctor as administrator and deeded his house to the town, requesting that it be made into the island's first hospital. The trustees quickly agreed and named the structure the Nora Wilkes Memorial Hospital.

Now as Gage first saw the brown hills of California, his heart quickened. He had not anticipated an emotional return, but he realized that tears were not far from coming.

In defense, he found Hope and lifted her in his arms.

"See there," he said pointing, "that's California. That's going to be your new home."

"New home," Hope repeated. "New home."

Monterey Bay looked the same and so very different. The geography was the same, but a hundred new buildings dotted the shoreline and the hills beyond. One building rose to at least four stories tall.

Gage quickly found the vast green area about his home on the bay. On a street beyond his, several other large homes had been built. He was glad that he had the foresight to have bought all the land between him and the sea, for that would always allow him an unobstructed view of the ocean.

As the ship neared the dock, Gage became puzzled. A crowd of people were gathered at the dock. Even from a distance, Gage estimated the number to be near a hundred. As he looked farther up the streets, he counted scores more making their way to the waterfront.

"Captain," he asked, "what do you suppose that might be? Why would a crowd gather like that in midday?"

The captain smiled. "Mr. Davis, those folks are here to see you. I told 'em all I was bringing were you and your daughter back. They're all your friends. They want to see you, I imagine, and see Hope . . . and you know, express their regrets as well. None of 'em ever had that chance till now, other than writing a letter, and that just ain't the same."

"All those folks have come to meet me? I don't have that many friends."

"You do, Mr. Davis. You have touched a lot of people."

Hope could not understand the reason for her father's tears.

"No, Papa," she called out as she hugged his neck. "No sad."

They were swarmed by well-wishers and friends, all wanting to do exactly as the captain said—to see him again and to share in his sorrow, now almost a year old.

The fact that so many people were ready and willing to divide his sorrow by sharing it brought Gage to the point of tears numerous times as he made his way through the crowd.

Rosala and Pahala traded holding Hope for the rest of the day. At first the two women eyed each other warily. But as soon as both realized they idolized Mr. Davis and would dote on his only daughter, then smiles replaced the wary greetings.

Pahala marveled at the size of the home, especially at the size of the kitchen. Both women wanted to begin cooking immediately and would have done so if Hope had been able to sleep.

Gage stood on the veranda, along with Carty Todd, Thomas Lee, Pastor Kenyon, Charles Thornton, and thirty or so of his closest friends and associates. Hope toddled through the crowd, giggling and speaking in a childish mixture of English and Hawaiian, dancing and singing for her new audience.

At last Pahala snatched the child up, and she and Rosala headed upstairs to the newly painted nursery.

There was a moment of silence in her wake.

Carty stepped up to Gage, cleared his throat, and the rest of the crowd turned to face him. "I know a lot of us have already said this, but we are powerfully glad you're back. I think we didn't know how much we missed your friendship and your laughter and your wise counsel till you up and left us."

Gage offered a bittersweet smile.

"And I know many of us offered our condolences, Mr. Davis, but you got to know that these simple words just don't say enough. I ached when I heard the news. I mean I cried for a week, and I never met Nora. But I knew that if she loved you and you loved her, then she must have been a mighty fine woman. And we are just so terribly sad over what happened. God does things sometimes that I plumb can't figure out. To take a young bride with a child don't make sense. But then, God is busy being God, and in time, we'll all see that his plan was the right plan."

Carty sniffed and wiped his nose with his sleeve.

"But we all be powerfully sad over your loss, Mr. Davis. You been prayed for—prayed for a lot. And now we are all so glad to have you back with us."

Gage sniffed this time. "And I am so glad to back with you as well."

Then he turned, embraced Carty, and both began to weep. Soon they were surrounded by a tight circle of people placing their hands on shoulders and arms.

And in time, the tears were replaced by laughter, small and silver, precious as a jewel.

"I believe the gold has peaked. They're still taking it out, but some of them are using water hoses and dams and half tearing down hillsides to get at it," Thomas said as he and Gage reviewed the books and ledgers.

"So business is down?" Gage asked.

"No, though we did close a store here and there when the towns dried up. But for every mining town that's been deserted, another town's sprung up—though farther down the valleys. Farmland around here is fertile, and crops bring good prices."

"So not everybody went home after they found that gold wasn't in the streams waiting to be picked up?"

"Hardly any of them did. At least not the ones who had a good trade, like farming or farriers or coopers or joinery. They will do fine."

"And who won't?"

"Well, the ne'er-do-wells and the adventurers. The folks who are out on a lark."

Gage nodded.

"I imagine we won't keep doubling and tripling every year, but GD Enterprises has built a powerful reputation. We'll stay in the black and then some."

Gage offered Thomas his hand. "You have done very well. I am proud of you."

The young man who had started as a lowly store clerk beamed.

Angels Camp
February 29, 1855

Dear Gage,
I have heard you are back in Monterey. I hope all goes well. I trust that you have received my other letters. Sending them to the Sandwich Islands

seemed such a risky proposition–halfway across the world. I suspect that I am becoming provincial again, now that I am leading a life in a much smaller circle.

I am sure you have been apprised that the gold, while not all taken, is becoming harder to extract. No longer can a single prospector hope to strike it rich–unless he is incredibly lucky. Now it is a business for companies of men with massive equipment that tear up earth and rivers. It has become a rich man's game now.

As a result, Angels Camp is a third of what it once was. I was wise not to spend all your money–and I never believed for a minute that you would come for it. I am right, am I not? If Angels Camp shrinks further and the population continues to decrease–perhaps down to a few hardy souls–we may look elsewhere. God needs to be preached where the people are. Perhaps we will head to Stockton or Sacramento. After all, that's where the farmers are going . . . and I am just a simple farm boy in truth.

And I will spend all your money there. I promise.

But you must promise to visit, now that you are back on American soil.

All God's blessings. May his peace fill your heart.

Joshua Q.

"I shall not deny that. I am a gossip. It is my failing. But I never do it maliciously nor do I ever repeat something that is not true. And I never repeat something that a person tells me in confidence."

Gage laughed at Pastor Kenyon's defense.

"If you want to know what happened at the town council meeting, you can read the paper or ask me. Which one will provide a more accurate telling?"

"You would," Gage admitted, "and more entertaining."

"I provide color where color is due," Kenyon said, laughing. "But I dare you to find one person in this town who holds a grudge against something I have said of them. What I tell others is what I would tell them to their face."

"John, I do not need convincing. I know this about you."

Pastor Kenyon lowered his fork. The two men dined on Gage's veranda.

"Pahala is even a more marvelous cook than Rosala. This fish is tremendous." He stabbed at another mouthful. "Why is it that you have all the luck with servants who cook? I have employed ten women in the time that you have been gone and have never had a decent meal."

Gage looked down at his friend's stomach.

"Well, perhaps that was an exaggeration. But none were of this quality," the pastor said with a smile.

Gage slid his plate away. "So the church goes well."

Pastor Kenyon brightened. "I am overjoyed. We have grown so much. But what is more exciting is that people are coming to know God. I could preach to a handful, and if they had knowledge of God, then I would be happy. But here, that dozen is multiplied by a dozen more. I am blessed. Monterey is blessed."

"Everyone I have talked to truly appreciates your work, John. They say you preach a most effective sermon."

John beamed. "I do. I do indeed, God be praised."

After a moment, his smile slipped away. "Gage, we have not talked of this, really. Besides sermons, people say I am most sympathetic. I find myself knowing of people's pain and problems before they even admit them to themselves. It is a gift, I suppose. And that is why I need to ask you this question now. It is something I see in your eyes and hear in the sound of your words."

He looked hard at Gage. "Are you lonely?"

FROM THE JOURNAL OF GAGE DAVIS
MARCH 21, 1855

John's question took me by surprise. I must admit I was feeling adrift. Back in Monterey, surrounded by friends and activities, watching my daughter grow and laugh and dance, and in the midst of all that—I am lonely.

The act of considering the question helped liberate me. Once I admitted that fact, I began to feel less lonely. I began to let friends be my friends again. I began to let my roots in California grow deeper. Even though I will always have a great scar on my heart, I am allowing it to heal. I no longer wince every time I think of her name. I can hold her memory in my thoughts without pain. I can see her face in my memory again without wanting to turn away in tears.

I have given God my loneliness, and his peace has begun to fill my heart again. How good of John to see that in my life.

And now . . . where do I go with my life? What path do I now follow?

I look back on the last twelve or so years of my life and ask myself, what have I learned? I have learned that the treasure I thought I wanted as a young man was nothing more than fool's gold. Money is useful to do God's work, but money is never a reason to sell one's soul.

Money comes easily to me—but I now know I must use it to spread God's Word. I am gifted in this way, and I will make use of that gift. Pastor Kenyon may be a gifted preacher, and so I am a gifted businessman.

But that is only a portion of my life.

What happens after sunset, when I have time to think and evaluate my life, is much more me.

I must admit that, in these past months, I am doing well. I am sad and lonely at times, but Nora was right. She is as beautiful as she ever was in my thoughts. Her smile will always thrill me when I recall the joy I had seeing it. I miss her every morning when I wake and every evening when I sleep, but I have the reassurance I will see her again.

I remind myself that I had been blessed to know her—even if it was for such a short time. No other man had such a rare privilege.

And what of other rare treasures?

One would be my daughter, Hope.

To watch a child grow is to rediscover the joy and wonders of this world. Just today I walked with her and she let go of my hand to chase a butterfly. She screamed with laughter as it fluttered just beyond her reach. The joy on her face, the amazed look in her eyes, taught me more of nature and God and joy than any sermon might teach.

I take my time with her, and every morning she and I sit on the veranda, watching the fishing boats return from their night upon the waters. The questions she asks are my joy. As I watch Hope grow, I see more of Nora emerge from this little child every day. She has started singing now, and the purity of her voice brought tears to my eyes—it was that much like her mother's voice.

And what of my soul? What of my faith—the rarest of all treasures?

I found God after following a most curious and convoluted path. But find him I did—or should I say that he found me, hiding in my weakness. It is my faith that has enabled me to endure the pain with a certain kind of joy that God provides. I am not happy that Nora is gone, but I know that she is not truly gone. We will be reunited.

And the final treasure is that God has granted me peace. In both day and night, my soul is at peace. I would not have expected it to follow such loneliness and darkness. But it has. I know God is holding me in his hands. Life may be bittersweet, yet I am secure in God's protection and love.

Gage stopped writing and closed his eyes. He felt the warm sun on his face. He heard the call of the gull and the faint ring of a ship's bell. The gentle hiss of the surf filled in the silent gaps.

He opened his eyes and smiled, gazing out to the west and the vast ocean beyond him. He slid aside his journal and picked up a single sheet of expensive vellum with his initials at the top of the page. He dipped his pen in the ink and began to write.

Monterey, California
March 21, 1855

Dear Hannah,
  I have a most interesting proposition for you.
  But before I outline what I have in mind, let me pose one question.
  What do you think of California?

EPILOGUE

I wish at times I were a painter, not a writer, for the light here is magical, glinting off the ocean in slivers and diamonds of color. I look about me and despair at ever describing my surroundings in an honest way that conveys the true depth of what God has created.

Yet even the greatest master of pigments and colors might find the task impossible. I think even Rembrandt would cry in frustration at man's feeble attempts at capturing the world about him in all its true and undistorted glory.

Now my second tale is done. I look back and know that I have failed at documenting even a sliver of the truth of each action, each event, each emotion. I have tried my best, using the words as I can. But how does one wrap the universe up into mere words? How is a life reduced to black smudges on paper? No, it cannot be done, but I still must tell these tales, since I have vowed to do so.

You, my loyal and noble audience, must bear with me in my humble efforts as I attempt to explain the truth of our lives.

Gage Davis made and lost fortunes. He has known success, and he has known the pain and darkness of failure and loss. To lose money, he told me, is merely an aggravation, but to lose a love is pain—true, heart-searing pain that he would wish on no man.

Yet he knows it is part of our destiny.

And he knows that God provides a balm for that pain.

And that is found through God's love and grace.

It is found in faith in the Almighty.

There is laughter and love in Gage's life again—despite all his sorrow and loss. His daughter is his joy, and through her eyes, Gage is seeing the world afresh.

In the quiet of a moonless evening, when our talk was lit by the glow of a single lantern, Gage admitted that his greatest success has been to know the love of two women—his wife and his daughter. He said quietly that some men travel the world and spend their lives seeking that sort of treasure, and many fail, dying alone and empty.

His smiles still come, perhaps a little less quickly than before, but deeper, and richer, more deserved. When his daughter laughs, his eyes sparkle, and his heart finds its solace.

God's planning is intricate, yet perfect.

And on the morrow, I will take pen again to paper and begin to write again.

I will tell you of Hannah Collins. Hers is a story about promises.

I will ask you this one question, dear reader. Which can be more painful—a promise that does not come true . . . or one that does?

Until the sun greets you on the morrow,

Jamison Pike
Monterey Bay
The State of California
March 1861